W9-BYH-678

The Best
AMERICAN
SHORT
STORIES
2001

GUEST EDITORS OF
THE BEST AMERICAN SHORT STORIES

The Best
AMERICAN
SHORT
STORIES
2001

Selected from
U.S. and Canadian Magazines
by Barbara Kingsolver
with Katrina Kenison

With an Introduction
by Barbara Kingsolver

HOUGHTON MIFFLIN COMPANY
BOSTON · NEW YORK   2001

Visit our Web site: www.houghtonmifflinbooks.com.
ISSN 0067-6233
ISBN 0-395-92689-0
ISBN 0-395-92688-2 (pbk.)

Printed in the United States of America

DOC 10 9 8 7 6 5 4 3 2 1

Contents

Foreword

IN THE 1942 VOLUME of *The Best American Short Stories,* the anthology's new annual editor, Martha Foley, attempted to define the form. "A good short story," she wrote, "is a story which is not too long and which gives the reader the feeling he has undergone a memorable experience."

Over the past eleven years, during my own tenure as annual editor of this eighty-six-year-old series, I've run across numerous other writers' attempts to come up with some sort of standard by which to measure the short story. Few have managed to add much to Ms. Foley's democratic and rather obvious criteria.

At symposiums and writers' conferences, I've learned to duck and weave around the inevitable question "What do you look for in a short story?" I wish I knew! Heart? Soul? Truth? Voice? Integrity of intention and skill in execution? The answer is all of the above, and none of the above. For I don't really "look" for anything; when a story works, I know it in my gut, not in my head, and only then — after laughing, after brushing away a tear, after taking a moment to catch my breath and return to the here and now — do I set about analyzing the successes and failures of a writer's effort. It would certainly be nice to have a checklist, a foolproof grading system, a tally sheet of pluses and minuses. But reading is a subjective activity, even for those of us who are fortunate enough to read for a living. We editors may read more pages than the average American, and we may read faster, but when it comes right down to it, I believe we all read for the same reason: in order to test our own knowledge of life and to enlarge on it.

Out of the three thousand or so short stories I read in any given year, I may file two hundred away. And I always marvel at how precious this stash of chosen fiction seems to me; these are the stories that, for one reason or another, exerted some kind of hold on the priorities of my heart. Even now, I have boxes of old stories, going back a decade and more, stacked up in the basement; I've saved every file card I've filled out since 1990 as well — a treasure trove of stories, a king's ransom of human wisdom caught and held on those hundreds of moldering pages. When it comes to cleaning closets, I'm ruthless. But those stories . . . well, how could I throw them away? Who knows when a particular bit of fiction will prove useful? Someday, I think, someone will need that story about the emotional roller coaster of new motherhood; or this one, which reminds us what sixteen years old really feels like; or that one, which could help a friend prepare for death . . .

Toward year's end, I sift through the current piles and begin to ship batches of tales off to the guest editor, always wondering whether he or she will share my tastes and predilections and curious to know whether the narrative voice that whispered so urgently in my ear will speak with as much power to another. Truth be told, it is an anxious time. Just as, when I was a teenager, I wanted my parents to agree that my boyfriend was indeed Prince Charming, I can't help but hope that the guest editor will share my passion for the year's collection of short story suitors.

I have no clue about Barbara Kingsolver's taste in men, but I discovered right away that she and I could fall in love with the same short stories. And when her introduction to this volume came spooling through my fax machine, I stood there reading it page by page, nodding in agreement with her discoveries and full of gratitude for the pickiness (her word) and devotion she brought to this task of reading, judging, and finally choosing. And then, as the next-to-last page emerged into my waiting hands, I saw it: a new definition for the short story, at last. To Martha Foley's sixty-year-old criteria we can now add Barbara Kingsolver's useful dictum: "A good short story cannot simply be Lit Lite, but the successful execution of large truths delivered in tight spaces." Writers take heed!

In choosing this year's collection of *The Best American Short Stories,* Kingsolver has done writers and readers a great service, for her own love for the form and her exacting standards have resulted in a volume that is as varied in subject matter, style, voice, and intent as even the most eclectic reader could wish for. Collectively, these stories hum with the energy of twenty disparate voices raised under one roof. They are a testament to our contemporary writers' vigorous engagement with the world and to the robust good health of American short fiction.

Some years ago, John Updike revealed, "Writing fiction, as those of us who do it know, is, beneath the anxious travail of it, a bliss, a healing, an elicitation of order from disorder, a praise of what is, a salvaging of otherwise overlookable truths from the ruthless sweep of generalization, a beating of daily dross into something shimmering and absolute." Mr. Updike, who made his first appearance in *The Best American Short Stories* in 1959, returns this year for the twelfth time as a contributor. (He also served as guest editor in 1984 and coedited *The Best American Short Stories of the Century*, published in 1999.) He is the only writer in the history of the series to appear in these pages for six consecutive decades — an achievement that we feel is worth noting. May he continue to beat the daily dross into such shimmering and absolute works as "Personal Archeology," which begins on page 326.

The stories chosen for this anthology were originally published between January 2000 and January 2001. The qualifications for selection are (1) original publication in nationally distributed American or Canadian periodicals; (2) publication in English by writers who are American or Canadian, or who have made the United States or Canada their home; (3) original publication as short stories (excerpts of novels are not knowingly considered). A list of magazines consulted for this volume appears at the back of the book. Editors who wish their short fiction to be considered for next year's edition should send their publications to Katrina Kenison, c/o The Best American Short Stories, Houghton Mifflin Company, 222 Berkeley Street, Boston, MA 02116.

K.K.

Introduction

I HAVE ALWAYS WONDERED why short stories aren't more popular in this country. We Americans are such busy people you'd think we'd jump at the chance to have our literary wisdom served in doses that fit handily between taking the trash to the curb and waiting for the carpool. We should favor the short story and adore the poem. But we don't. Short story collections rarely sell half as well as novels; they are never blockbusters. They are hardly ever even block-denters. From what I gather, most Americans would sooner read a five-hundred-page book about southern France or a boy attending wizard school or how to make home decor from roadside trash or *anything* than pick up a book offering them a dozen tales of the world complete in twenty pages apiece. And I won't even discuss what they will do to avoid reading poetry.

Why on earth should this be? I enjoy the form so much myself that when I was invited to be the guest editor for this collection, forewarned that it would involve reading thousands of pages of short fiction in a tight three-month period, I decided to do it. This trial by fire, I thought, would disclose to me the heart of the form and all its mysteries. Also, it would nicely fill the space that lay ahead of me at the end of the year 2000, just after my planned completion of a novel and before its publication the following spring. The creative dead space between galley proofs and a book's first review is a dreaded time in an author's life, comparable to the tenth month of a pregnancy. (I've had two post-term babies, so I know what I'm talking about.) I look at the prepublication epoch as a Great Sargasso Sea and always try to fill it with satisfying short-term projects. I reexamined the previous editions of this series on my shelf and considered the assignment. Amy Tan, who edited *The Best American Short Stories 1999,* described the organized pleasure of reading one story a day for three months. That sounded like a tidy plan to put on my calendar. Editing a story collection, plus a short family vacation to Mexico and a week-long stint lecturing on a ship in the Caribbean, would fill those months perfectly, providing just enough distraction from my prepublication doldrums.

If you ever want to know what it sounds like when the universe goes "Ha! Ha!" just put a tidy plan on your calendar.

My months of anticipated quiet at the end of 2000 turned out to be the most eventful of my life, in which I was called upon to attend to an astonishing number of unexpected duties, celebrations, and crises. I weathered a tour and publicity storm with the release of my new novel, eight months ahead of schedule. While handling this plus the lectures at sea, I learned of a family member's catastrophic illness, I was invited to have dinner with President and Mrs. Clinton, and I took my eighth-grader to the funeral of her beloved friend — not to mention the normal background noise of family urgencies. These two months of our lives were stitched together by trains, automobiles, the M.S. *Ryndam,* and thirty-two separate airplane flights. (A perverse impulse caused me to save my boarding passes and count them.) Naturally this would be the year when I also experienced a true airplane emergency, and I don't mean the garden-variety altitude plunge. I mean that I finally got to see what those yellow masks look like.

Through it all, as best I could, I read stories. On a cold Iowa afternoon with the white light of snowfall flooding the windows, sitting quietly with a loved one enduring his new regime of chemotherapy, I read about a nineteenth-century explorer losing his grasp on life in the Himalayas. On another day, when I found myself wide-eyed long after midnight on a ship so racked by storms that the books were diving off the shelves of my cabin, I amused myself with a droll fable about two feuding widows in the Pyrenees. I read my way through a long afternoon sitting on the dirty carpet of Gate B-22 at O'Hare, successfully tuning out all the mayhem and canceled-flight refugees around me, except for one young woman who kept shouting into her cell phone, "I'm almost out of minutes!" (This was not the same day my airplane would lose its oxygen; the screenwriter of my life isn't *that* corny.) I read through a Saturday while my four-year-old dozed in my lap with a mysterious fever that plastered her curls to her forehead and burned my skin through her pajamas; I read in the early mornings in Mexico while parrots chattered outside our window. Some days I was able to read no stories at all — when my youngest was *not* asleep on my lap, for instance — and on other days I read many. Eighteen stories got lost in my luggage and took a trip of their very own, but returned to me in time.

My ideas about what I would gain from this experience collapsed as I began to wrestle instead with what I would be able to give to it. How could I read 125 stories amid all this craziness and compare them fairly? In the beginning I marked each one with a ranking of minus, plus, or double-plus. That lasted for exactly three stories. It soon became clear that what looks like double-plus on an ordinary day can be a whole different thing when the oxygen masks are dangling from the overhead compartment. I despaired of my wildly uncontrolled circumstances, thinking constantly, *If this were my story, would I want some editor reading it under these conditions?*

Maybe not. But the problem is, life is like that. Editors, readers, all of us, have to work reading into our busy lives. The best of it can stand up to the challenge — and if anything can do it, it should be the genre of short fiction, with its economy of language and revving plot-driven engine. We catch our reading on the fly, and that is probably the whole point anyway. If we lived in silent white rooms with no emergencies beyond the wilting of the single red rose in the vase, we probably wouldn't need fiction to help us explain the inexplicable things, the storms at sea and deaths of too-young friends. If we lived in a room like that, we would probably just smile and take naps.

What makes writing good? That's easy: the lyrical description, the arresting metaphor, the dialogue that falls so true on the ear it breaks the heart, the plot that winds up exactly where it should. But these stories I was to choose among had been culled from thousands of others, so all were beautifully written. I couldn't favor (or disfavor) the ones by my favorite writers, because their authorship was concealed from me. I knew only that they had been published in magazines in the last year and preselected by the series editor, Katrina Kenison, who had done for me the heroic service of separating distinguished stories from the run-of-the-mill. My task was to choose, among the good, the truly great. How was I supposed to do it?

With a pile of stories on my lap, I sat with this question early on and tried to divine why it is that I love a short story when I do, and the answer came to me quite clearly: I love it for what it tells me about life. If it tells me something I didn't already know, or that I maybe suspected but never framed quite that way, or that never before socked me divinely in the solar plexus, then the story is worth the read.

From that moment my task became simple. I relaxed and read for the pleasure of it, and when I finished each story, I wrote a single sentence on the first page underneath the title, in the space conveniently opened up for me where the author's name had been masked out. Just one sentence of pure truth, if I'd found it, which generally I did. No bumpy air or fevers or chattering parrots could change this one true thing the story had meant to tell me. This is how I began to see the heart of the form. While nearly all the stories were expertly written, and most were pleasant to read, they varied enormously in the weight and value of what they carried — in whether it was sand or gemstones I held in my palm when the words had trickled away. Some beautifully written stories gave me truths so self-evident that when I wrote them down, I was embarrassed. "Young love is mostly selfish," some told me, and others were practically lining up to declare, "Alcoholism ruins lives and devastates children!" In the privacy of my reading, I probably made that special face teenagers make when forced to attend to the obvious. Of all the days of my life, these were the ones in which I was perhaps most acutely aware that time is precious. So please, tell me something I don't already know. Sometimes I couldn't find anything at all to write in that little space under the story's title, but most were clear enough in their intent, and many were interesting enough to give me pause. And then came one that rang like a bell. "An orphaned child needs to find her own peculiar way to her mother's ghost, but then will need an adult to verify it." As soon as I'd jotted that down, I knew this story had given me something I would keep. I slipped it into a pocket of my suitcase, and when I got home I set it on the deep windowsill beside my desk where the sun would fall on it in the morning, and over two months it would grow, I hoped, into a pile of stories. Words that might help me be a better mother, a wiser friend. I felt I'd begun a shrine to new truths, the gifts I was about to receive in a difficult time.

Slowly that pile did grow. Too slowly, I feared at first, for when I'd conquered nearly half my assigned reading, it still seemed very small. I am too picky, I thought. I should relax my standards. But how? You don't lower the bar on enlightenment. I couldn't change my heart, so I didn't count the stories in my shrine, I just let them be what they were. Cautiously, though, I made another pile called "Almost, maybe." If push came to shove, I would reread these later and try to be more moved by them.

If it sounds as if I'm a terribly demanding reader, I am. I make no apologies. Long before I ever heard the words (and I swear this happened; this pilot should go to charm school) "We're going to try an emergency landing at the nearest airport that can read our black box," it had already dawned on me that I'm not going to live forever. This means I may never get through the list of the great books I want to read. Forget about bad ones, or even moderately good ones. With *Middlemarch* and *A Pilgrim at Tinker Creek* in the world, a person should squander her reading time on fashionably ironic books about nothing much? *I'm almost out of minutes!* I'm patient with most corners of my life, but put a book in my hands and suddenly I remind myself of a harrowing dating-game shark, long in the tooth and looking for love *right now,* thank you, get out of my way if you're just going to waste my time and don't really want kids or the long-term commitment. I give a novel thirty pages, and if it's not by that point talking to me of till-death-do-us-part, sorry, buster, this date's over. I've chucked many half-finished books into the donation box. You might be thinking right now that you're glad I was never your writing instructor, and a few former students of mine would agree with you. Once in a workshop after I'd already explained repeatedly that brevity is the soul of everything, writing-wise, and I was still getting fifty-page stories that should have been twenty-page stories, I announced: "Starting tomorrow, I will read twenty-five pages of any story you give me, and then I'll stop. If you think you have the dazzling skill to keep me hanging on for pages twenty-six-plus because my life won't be complete without them, just go ahead and try."

I'm sorry to admit I was such a harpy, but this is a critical lesson for writers. We are nothing if we can't respect our readers. It's audacious enough to send a piece of writing out into the world (which already contains *Middlemarch*), asking readers to sit down, shut up, ignore kids or work or whatever important things they have going, and listen to *me*. Not for just a minute but for hours, days. It had better be important. The stories in this collection earned every minute I gave them, with interest. A few of them are long, but they dazzled me to the end. Most are short — some only three or four pages — and while they weren't chosen for that reason, I admire them for it. Probably the greatest challenge of the form is to get a story launched and landed efficiently with a whole worthwhile journey in between. The launch is apparently easier than the landing, because I've been entranced by many a first paragraph of a tale that ended with such an unfulfilling thud that I scrambled around for a next page that simply wasn't. It may be that most Americans don't read short stories because they don't like this kind of a ride. A good short story cannot simply be Lit Lite; it is the successful execution of large truths delivered in tight spaces. If all short fiction did it perfectly, more readers would surely sign up.

The stories in this book have survived my harpy eye on all accounts: they've told me something remarkable, they are beautifully executed, and they are nested in truth. The last I mean literally. I can't abide fiction that's too lazy to get its facts straight. People learn from what they read, they trust in words, and this is not a responsibility to take lightly. I've stopped reading books in which birds sang on the wrong continents or full moons appeared two weeks apart (it wasn't set on Jupiter). I've tossed aside fiction because of botched Spanish or French phrases uttered by putative native speakers who were not supposed to be toddlers or illiterates. When faced with a mountain of stories to eliminate, my tools were sharp and unforgiving. One fascinating story was headed for my "Yes!" shrine until its physician narrator informed me authoritatively, "The opposable thumb is the only thing that separates us from lemurs and baboons." Hooey — lemurs and baboons have opposable thumbs; that's part of what defines them (and us) as primates. Biological illiteracy is a problem I care about, and I believe fiction should inform as well as enlighten, and first, do no harm.

For a story to make the cut, I asked a lot from it — asked of it, in fact, what I ask of myself when I sit down to write, and that is to get straight down to it and carve something hugely important into a small enough amulet to fit inside a reader's most sacred psychic pocket. I don't care what it's about, as long as it's not trivial. I once heard a writer declare from a lectern, "I write about the mysteries of the human heart, which is the only thing a fiction writer has any business addressing." And I thought to myself, *Excuse me?* I had recently begun thinking of myself as a fiction writer and was laboring under the illusion that I could address any mystery that piqued me, including but not limited to the human heart, human risk factors, human rights, and why some people practically have to scrape flesh from their bones to pay the rent while others have it paid for them all their merry days, and how frequently the former are women raising children by themselves even though that wasn't the original plan. The business of fiction is to probe the tender spots of an imperfect world, which is where I live, write, and read. I want to know about the real price of fast food in China, who's paying it, and why. I want to know what it's like in Chernobyl all these years later. Do you? This book will tell you.

Last week in my own living room I finished the last of the stories Katrina had sent me, including several batches of "*very* last ones." After that final page I took a deep breath and went to my office to count the stories in my pile on the windowsill. There were twenty, exactly. I counted again. Unbelievable. I'd been asked to select twenty plus one extra "just in case," but I couldn't bear to go back through the "maybes" and pick an alternate. When life performs acts of grace for you, you don't mess with the program.

I thank these twenty authors and offer their stories to you as pieces of truth that moved me to a new understanding of the world. When I look back now on the process, I understand that editing this collection was not a chore piled onto an already over-scheduled piece of my life, but rather a kind of life raft through it. While the people around me in Gate B-22 swore irritably into their cell phones, I was learning how a man in an Iranian prison survived isolation by weaving a rug in his mind. The night after my teenager and I returned from her friend's funeral and she asked me how life could be so unfair, I lay down on my bed to read of the pain and healing of a child from Harlem in 1938. These stories were, for me, both a distraction and an anchor. They were my pleasure, my companionship, my salvation. I hope they will be yours.

BARBARA KINGSOLVER

ANDREA BARRETT

Servants of the Map

FROM SALMAGUNDI

1.

HE DOES NOT WRITE to his wife about the body found on a mountain that is numbered but still to be named: not about the bones, the shreds of the tent, the fragile, browning skull. He says nothing about the diary wedged beneath the rock, or about how it felt to turn the rippled pages. Unlike himself, the surveyor thinks, the lost man traveled alone. Not attached to a branch, however small and insignificant, of the Great Trigonometrical Survey of India. On this twig charged to complete the Kashmir Series, he is nothing. A leaf, an apricot, easily replaced; a civil junior sub-assistant in the Himalayan Service.

The surveyor, whose name is Max Vigne, reads through the diary before relinquishing it to his superiors. The handwriting trembled in the final pages, the entries growing shorter and more confused. Hailstorms, lightning storms, the loss of a little shaving mirror meant to send a glinting signal from the summit to the admiring crowds below — after noting these, the lost man wrote:

> I have been fasting. Several weeks — the soul detaches from the flesh. The ills of spirit and body are washed away, and here on the roof of the world, in the abode of snow, one becomes greatly strengthened yet as fresh as a child.

Although Max pauses in wonder over these lines, he still doesn't share them with his wife. Instead he writes:

April 13, 1863

Dear Clara —

I can hardly understand where I am myself; how shall I explain it
to you? Try to imagine the whole chain of the Himalaya, as wide as
England and four times its length. Then imagine our speck of a
surveying party tucked in the northwest corner, where the Great
Himalaya tangles into the Karakoram — or not quite there, but almost there. We are at the edge of the land called Baltistan, or Little
Tibet: Ladakh and Greater Tibet lie to the east. And it is so much
more astonishing than we imagined. The mountains I wrote you
about earlier, which we crossed to enter the Vale of Kashmir — everything I said about them was true, they dwarf the highest peaks I
saw at home. But the land I am headed toward dwarfs in turn the
range that lies behind me. Last Wednesday, after breakfast, the low
clouds lifted and the sun came out. To the north a huge white mass
remained, stretching clear across the horizon. I was worried about
an approaching storm. Then I realized those improbable masses
were mountains, shimmering and seeming to float over the plains
below.

How I wish you could see this for yourself. I have had no mail
from you since Srinagar, but messengers do reach us despite our
frequent moves and I am hopeful. This morning I opened an envelope from the little trunk you sent with me. Have any of my letters
reached you yet? If they have, you will know how much your messages have cheered me. No one but you, my love, would have
thought to do this. On the ship, then during our tedious journey
across the plains to the Pir Panjal, and even more throughout the
weeks of preparation and training in Srinagar, your words have
been my great consolation. I wait like a child on Christmas Eve for
the dates you have marked on each envelope to arrive: I obey you,
you see; I have not cheated. Now that the surveying season has
finally begun and we're on the move, I treasure these even more. I
wish I had thought to leave behind a similar gift for you. The letters
I wrote you from Srinagar — I know the details about my work
could not have been of much interest to you. But I mean to do
better, now that we're entering this astonishing range. If I share
with you what I see, what I feel: will that be a kind of gift?

Yours marked to be opened today, the anniversary of that wonderful walk along the Ouse when I asked you to marry me and,
against a background of spinning windmills and little boys search-

ing for eels, you stood so sleek and beautiful and you said yes — it made me remember the feel of your hand in mine, it was like holding you. I am glad you plan to continue with your German. By now you must have opened the birthday gifts I left for you. Did you like the dictionary? And the necklace?

I should try to catch you up on our journeys of these last few weeks. From Srinagar we labored over the Gurais Pass, still knee-deep in snow: my four fellow plane-tablers, the six Indian chainmen, a crowd of Kashmiri and Balti porters, and Michaels, who has charge of us for the summer. Captain Montgomerie of the Bengal Engineers, head of the entire Kashmir Series, we have not seen since leaving Srinagar. I am told it is his habit to tour the mountains from April until October, inspecting the many small parties of triangulators and plane-tablers, of which we are only one. The complexities of the Survey's organization are beyond explaining: a confusion of military men and civilians, Scots and Irish and English; and then the assistants and porters, all races and castes. All I can tell you is that although we civilians may rise in the ranks of the Survey, even the most senior of us may never have charge of the military officers. And I am the most junior of all.

From the top of the pass I saw the mountain called Nanga Parbat, monstrous and beautiful, forty miles away. Then we were in the village of Gurais, where we gathered more provisions and porters to replace those returning to Srinagar. Over the Burzil Pass and across the Deosai Plateau — it is from here that I write to you, a grassy land populated by chattering rodents called marmots. The air is clear beyond clearness today, and to the north rises that wall of snowy summits I first mistook for a cloud: the Karakoram Range, which we are to map. Even this far away I can see the massive glaciers explored by Godfrey Vigne, to whom I am so tangentially related.

I wonder what he would have thought of me ending up here? Often people ask if I'm related to that famous man, but I deny it; it would be wrong of me, even now that he's dead, to claim such a distant connection. My eccentric, sometimes malicious supervisor, Michaels (an Irishman and former soldier of the Indian Army), persists in calling me "Mr. Vaahn-ya," in an atrocious French accent. This although I have reminded him repeatedly that ours is a good East Anglian family, even if we do have Huguenot ancestors, and that we say the name "Vine."

All the men who've explored these mountains — what a secret, isolated world this is! A kind of archipelago, sparsely populated, visited now and again by passing strangers; each hidden valley an island unto itself, inhabited by small groups of people wildly distinct from each other — it is as if at home, a day's journey in one direction took us to Germany, another's to Africa. As if, in the distance between the fens and the moors, there were twenty separate kingdoms. I have more to tell you, so much more, but it is late and I must sleep.

What doesn't he tell Clara? So much, so much. The constant discomforts of the body, the hardships of the daily climbs, the exhaustion, the loneliness: he won't reveal the things that would worry her. He restrains himself, a constant battle; the battle itself another thing he doesn't write about. He hasn't said a word about the way his fellow surveyors tease him. His youth, his chunky, short-legged frame and terribly white skin; the mop of bright yellow hair on his head and the paucity of it elsewhere: although he keeps up with the best of them, and is often the last to tire, he is ashamed each time they strip their clothes to bathe in a freezing stream or a glacial tarn. His British companions are tall and hairy, browning in the sun, the Indians and Kashmiris and Baltis smoother and slighter but dark; he alone looks like a figure made from snow. The skin peels off his nose until he bleeds. When he extends his hat brim with strips of bark, in an effort to fend off the burning rays, Michaels asks him why he doesn't simply use a parasol.

Michaels himself is thickly pelted, fleshy and sweaty, strong-smelling and apparently impervious to the sun. They have all grown beards; shaving is impossible. Only Max's is blond and sparse. He gets teased for this, for the ease with which he burns, and sometimes, more cruelly, for the golden curls around his genitals. Not since he was fourteen, when he first left school and began his apprenticeship on the railway survey, has he been so mocked. Then he had his older brother, Laurence, to protect him. But here he is on his own.

The men are amused not only by his looks but by his box of books and by the pretty brass-bound trunk that holds Clara's precious gift to him: a long series of letters, some written by her and others begged from their family and friends. The first is dated the week after he left home, the last more than a year hence; all are marked to be opened on certain dates and anniversaries. Who but Clara would have thought of such a gift? Who else would have had the imagination to project herself into the future, sensing what he might feel like a week, a month, a year from leaving home and writing what might comfort him then?

His companions have not been so lucky. Some are single, others married but to wives they seem not to miss or perhaps are even relieved to have left behind. A Yorkshireman named Wyatt stole one of Clara's missives from Max's campstool, where he'd left it while fetching a cup of tea. "Listen to this," Wyatt said — laughing, holding the letter above Max's head, and reading aloud to the entire party. "Max, you must wear your woolly vest, you know how cold you get." Now the men ask tauntingly, every day, what he's read from the trunk. He comforts himself by believing that they're jealous.

A more reliable comfort is his box of books. In it, beyond the mathematical and cartographical texts he needs for his work, are three other gifts. With money she'd saved from the household accounts, Clara bought him a copy of Joseph Hooker's *Himalayan Journals*. This Max cherishes for the thought behind it, never correcting her misapprehension that Sikkim, where Hooker traveled in 1848, is only a stone's throw from where Max is traveling now. At home, with a map, he might have put his left thumb on the Karakoram Range and his right, many inches away to the east, on the lands that Hooker explored: both almost equally far from England, yet still far apart themselves. Clara might have smiled — despite her interest in Max's work, geography sometimes eludes her — but that last evening passed in such a flurry that all he managed to do was to thank her. For his brother Laurence, who gave him a copy of Charles Darwin's *Origin of Species*, he'd had only the same hurried thanks. On the flyleaf, Laurence had written: "New ideas, for your new life. Think of me as you read this; I will be reading my own copy in your absence and we can write to each other about what we learn."

Repeatedly Max has tried to keep up his end of this joint endeavor, only to be frustrated by the book's difficulty. For now he has set it aside in favor of a more unexpectedly useful gift. Clara's brother, far away in the city of New York, works as an assistant librarian and sometimes sends extra copies of the books he receives to catalogue. "Not of much interest to me," he wrote to Max, forwarding Asa Gray's *Lessons in Botany and Vegetable Physiology*. "But I know you and Clara like to garden, and to look at flowers in the woods — and I thought perhaps you would enjoy this."

At first, finding his companions uncongenial, Max read out of boredom and loneliness. Later he fell under the spell of the books themselves. The drawings at the back of Gray's book, the ferns and grasses and seedpods and spore capsules: how lovely these are! As familiar as his mother's eyes; as distant as the fossilized ferns found by a British explorer on the shores of Melville Island. As a boy he'd had a passion for botany, a charmed few years of learning plants and their names before the shock of his mother's death, his father's long decline, the necessity of going out, so young, to earn a living and help care for his family. Now he has a family of his own. Work of his own as well, which he is proud of. But the illustrations draw him back to a time when the differences between a hawkweed and a dandelion could fascinate him for hours.

Charmed by the grasses of the Deosai Plateau, he begins to dip into Dr. Hooker's book as well. Here too he finds much of interest. When he feels lost, when all he's forgotten or never knew about simple botany impedes his understanding, he marks his place with a leaf or a stem and turns back to Gray's manual. At home, he thinks, after he has safely returned, he and Clara can wander the fields as they did in the days of their courtship, this time understanding more clearly what they see and teaching these pleasures to their children. He copies passages into his notebook, meaning to share them with her:

Lesson I. Botany as a Branch of Natural History

The Organic World is the world of organized beings. These consist of *organs;* of parts which go to make up an *individual,* a *being.* And each individual owes its existence to a preceding one like itself, that is, to a parent. It was not merely formed, but *produced.* At first small and imperfect, it grows and develops by powers of its own; it attains maturity, becomes old, and finally dies. It was formed of inorganic or mineral matter, that is, of earth and air, indeed, but only of this matter under the influence of life; and after life departs, sooner or later, it is decomposed into earth and air again.

He reads, and makes notes, and reads some more. The *Himalayan Journals,* he has noticed, are "dedicated to Charles Darwin by his affectionate friend, Joseph Dalton Hooker." What lives those men lead: far-flung, yet always writing to each other and discussing their ideas. Something else he hasn't told Clara is this: before leaving Srinagar, in a shop he entered meaning only to buy a new spirit level, he made an uncharacteristically impulsive purchase: a botanical collecting outfit, charming and neat. He could not resist it, although he wasn't sure, then, what use he'd make of it. But on the Deosai Plateau he found, after a windstorm, an unusual primrose flowering next to a field of snow. He pressed it, mounted it — not very well, he's still getting the hang of this — and drew it; then, in a fit of boldness, wrote about it to Dr. Hooker, care of his publisher in England. "The willows and stonecrops are remarkable," he added. "And I am headed higher still; might the lichens and mosses here be of some interest to you?" He doesn't expect that Dr. Hooker will write him back.

In his tent made from blankets, with a candle casting yellow light on the pages, Max pauses over a drawing of a mallow. About his mother, who died when he was nine, he remembers little. In a coffin she lay, hands folded over her black bombazine dress, face swollen and unrecognizable. When he was five or six, still in petticoats, she guided him through the marshes. Her pale hands, so soon to be stilled, plucked reeds and weeds and flowers. *You must remember these,* she said. *You must learn the names of the wonderful things surrounding us.* Horsetails in her hands, and then in his; the ribbed walls and the satisfying way the segments popped apart at the swollen joints. Pickerel rush and mallow and cattail and reed; then she got sick, and then she died. After that, for so many years, there was never time for anything but work.

2.

May 1, 1863

Dearest Clara —

A great day: as I was coming down an almost vertical cliff, on my way back to camp, a Balti coming up from the river met me and handed me a greasy, dirty packet. Letters from you, Laurence, and Zoe — yours were marked "Packet #12," which I had thought lost after receiving #13 and #14 back in Srinagar. From those earlier letters I knew you had been delivered safely of our beloved Joanna, and that Elizabeth had welcomed her new sister and all three of you were well: but I had no details, and to have missed not only this great event but your account of it made me melancholy. How wonderful then, after five long months, to have your description of the birth. All our family around you, the dawn just breaking as Joanna arrived and Elizabeth toddling in, later, to peer at the infant in your arms: how I wish I had been with you, my love.

And how I wish I knew what that long night and its aftermath had really been like; you spare my feelings, I know. You say not a word about your pains and trials. In #13 you mentioned recovering completely from the milk fever, but in #12 you did not tell me you had it, though you must have been suffering even then. Did we understand, when I took this position, how hard it would be? So many months elapse between one of us speaking, the other hearing; so many more before a response arrives. Our emotions lag so far behind the events. For me, it was as if Joanna had been born today. Yet she is five months old, and I have no idea of what those months have brought. Zoe says Elizabeth is growing like a cabbage, and Laurence says he heard from your brother in New York and that the family is thriving; how fortunate that the wound to his foot, which we once so regretted, has saved him from conscription.

I am well too, though terribly busy. But what I want, even more than sleep, is to talk to you. Everything I am seeing and doing is so new — it is nothing, really, like the work I did in England — so much is rushing into me all at once — I get confused. When I lie down to sleep, everything spins in my brain. I can only make sense of my new life the way I have made sense of everything since we first met: by describing it to you. That great gift you have always had of *listening*, asking such excellent questions — when I tell you enough to let you imagine me clearly, then I can imagine myself.

So, my dearest: imagine this. If this were an army (it almost is; three of Montgomerie's assistants are military officers, while others, like Michaels and his friends, served in the military forces of the East India Company until the Mutiny, then took their discharge rather than accept transfer to the British Army), I'd be a foot soldier, far behind the dashing scouts of the triangulating parties who precede us up the summits. It is they who measure, with the utmost accuracy, the baseline between two vantage points, which becomes the first side of a triangle. They who with their theodolites measure the angles between each end of that line and a third high point in the distance, and they who calculate by trigonometry the two other sides of the triangle, thus fixing the distance to the far point and the point's exact position. One of the sides of that triangle then becomes the base for a new triangle — and so the chain slowly grows, easy enough to see on paper but dearly won in life. In the plains these triangles are small and neat. Out here the sides of a triangle may be a hundred miles or more.

Is this hard to follow? Try to imagine how many peaks must be climbed. And how high they are: 15,000 and 17,000 and 19,000 feet. My companions and I see the results of the triangulators' hard work when we follow them to the level platforms they've exposed by digging through feet of snow, and the supporting pillars they've constructed from rocks. Imagine a cold, weary man on the top of a mountain, bent over his theodolite and waiting for a splash of light. Far from him, on another peak, a signal squad manipulates a helio-trope (which is a circular mirror, my dear, mounted on a staff so it can be turned in any direction). On a clear day it flashes bright with reflected sunlight. At night it beams back the rays of a blue-burning lamp.

The triangulators leap from peak to peak; if they are the grass-hoppers, we plane-tablers are the ants. At their abandoned stations we camp for days, collecting topographical details and filling in their sketchy outline maps. You might imagine us as putting muscle and sinew on the bare bones they have made. Up through the snow we go, a little file of men; and then at the station I draw and draw until I've replicated all I see. I have a new plane-table, handsome and strong. The drawing board swivels on its tripod, the spirit level guides my position; I set the table directly over the point corre-sponding to the plotted site of my rough map. Then I rotate the board with the sheet of paper pinned to it until the other main landscape features I can see — those the triangulators have already plotted — are positioned correctly relative to the map.

As I fill in the blank spaces with the bends and curves of a river valley, the dips and rises of a range, the drawing begins to resemble a map of home. For company I have the handful of porters who've carried the equipment, and one or two of the Indian chainmen who assist us — intelligent men, trained at Dehra Dun in the basics of mapping and observation. Some know almost as much as I do, and have the additional advantage of speaking the local languages as well as some English. When we meet to exchange results with those who work on the nearby peaks and form the rest of our group, the chainmen gather on one side of the fire, sharing food and stories. In their conversations a great idea called "the Survey" looms like a disembodied god to whom they — we — are all devoted. Proudly, they refer to both themselves and us as "Servants of the Map."

I will tell you what your very own Servant of the Map saw a few days ago. On the edge of the Deosai Plateau, overlooking Skardu, I saw two faraway peaks towering above the rest of the Karakoram, the higher gleaming brilliant blue and the lower yellow. These are the mountains which Montgomerie, seven years ago, designated K1 and K2. K2 the triangulators have calculated at over 28,000 feet: imagine, the second highest mountain in the world, and I have seen it! The sky was the deepest blue, indescribable, sparkling with signals the heliotropes of the triangulating parties twinkled at one another. Do you remember our visit to Ely Cathedral? The way the stone rose up so sharply from the flat plain, an explosion of height — it was like our first glimpse of that, magnified beyond reason and lit all about by fireflies.

We have thunderstorms almost every day; they are always terrifying. The one that shook us the afternoon I saw K2 brought hail, and lightning so close that sparks leapt about the rocks at my feet and my hair bristled and crackled. The wind tore my map from the drawing board and sent it spinning over the edge of the plain, a white bird flying into the Indus Valley below. But I do not mean to frighten you. I take care of myself, I am as safe as it is possible to be in such a place, I think of you constantly. Even the things I read remind me of you.

In Asa Gray's book, I read this today, from "Lesson VII: Morphology of Leaves":

> We may call foliage the natural form of leaves, and look upon the other sorts as *special forms,* — as *transformed* leaves . . . the Great Author of Nature, having designed plants upon one simple plan, just adapts this plan to all cases. So, whenever any special purpose is to be accomplished, no new instruments or organs are created for it, but one of the three general organs of the vegetable, *root, stem,* or *leaf,* is made to serve the purpose, and is adapted by taking some peculiar form.

Have I told you I have been working my way through this manual, lesson by lesson? I forget sometimes what I have written to you and what I have not. But I study whenever I can and use what I learn to help make sense both of my surroundings and of what I read in the *Himalayan Journals,* which I treasure, because it's from you. As the book Laurence gave me requires more concentration than I can summon, I've set it aside for now (my guilty secret; don't tell him this): but Dr. Hooker I think even more highly of since my arrival here. The rhododendron that Zoe, my thoughtful sister, gave us as a wedding present — do you remember how, when it first flowered, we marveled at the fragrant, snowy blossoms with their secret gold insides? It was raised in a greenhouse in St. John's Wood, from seeds sent back by Dr. Hooker. I wish I could have been with you this spring to watch it bloom.

I am drifting from my point, I see. Forgive me. The *point,* the reason I copy this passage, is not to teach you about leaves but to say these words brought tears to my eyes; they made me think of our marriage. When we were together our lives were shaped like our neighbors', as simple as the open leaves of the maple. Now we are apart, trying to maintain our connection over this immense distance. Trying to stay in touch without touch; which effort changes us deeply, perhaps even deforms us.

To an outsider we might now look like the thick seed leaves of the almond or the bean, or the scales of buds or bulbs; like spines or tendrils, sepals or petals, which are also altered leaves. Do you know that in certain willows, pistils and stamens can sometimes change into each other? Or that pistils often turn into petals in cultivated flowers? Only now do I begin to grasp the principles of growth and change in the plants I learned to name in the woods, those we have grown at home — there is a science to this. Something that transcends mere identification.

I wander, I know. Try to follow me. The point, dear heart, is that through all these transformations one can still discern the original morphology; the original character is altered yet not lost. In our separation our lives are changing, our bond to each other is changing. Yet still we are essentially the same.

I love you. So much. Do you know this?

It is raining again; we are damp and cold. I miss you. All the time.

Max regards the last page of his letter doubtfully. That business about the alteration of leaves; before he sends it, he scratches out

the line about the effects of his and Clara's separation. *Deform:* such
a frightening word.

His days pass in promiscuous chatter, men eating and drinking
and working and snoring, men sick and wounded and snow-blind
and wheezing; always worries about supplies and medicines and
deadlines. He is never alone. He has never felt lonelier. There are
quarrels everywhere: among the Indian chainmen, between the
chainmen and the porters, the porters and his fellow plane-tablers;
between the plane-tablers and the triangulators; even, within his
own group, among the parties squatting on the separate peaks. Michaels, their leader, appears to enjoy setting one team against another. Michaels takes the youngest of the porters into his tent at
night; Michaels has made advances toward Max and, since Max re-
buffed him, startled and furious, has ceased speaking with him directly and communicates by sarcastic notes.

Wyatt has approached Max as well, and a man from another
party — the only one as young as Max — with a shock of red hair as
obtrusive as a kingfisher's crest. Now all three are aligned against
him. When the whole group meets, he has seen, in the shadows just
beyond the ring of light sent out by the campfire, men kneeling
across from each other, breeches unbuttoned, hands on each other
. . . He closed his eyes and turned his back and blocked his ears
to the roar of laughter following his hasty departure. Yet who is he
to judge them? So starved for love and touch is he that he has, at
different times, found himself attracted to the middle-aged, stiff-
necked wife of an English official in Srinagar, a Kashmiri flower-
seller, a Tibetan herdsman, the herdsman's dog. He has felt such
lust that his teeth throb, and the roots of his hair, the skin of his
whole body itching as if about to explode in a giant sneeze.

In the act of writing to Clara, Max makes for himself the solitude
he so desperately needs. He holds two strands of her life: one the
set of letters she writes to him now — or not *now,* but as close to
now as they can get, four months earlier, five, six — and the other
the set of letters she wrote secretly in the months before he left, trying to imagine what he might need to hear. Occasionally he has allowed himself the strange pleasure of opening one letter from each
set on the same day. A rounded image of Clara appears when he
reads them side by side: she is with him. And this fills him with a desire to offer back to her, in his letters, his truest self. He wants to
give her everything: what he is seeing, thinking, feeling; who he

truly is. Yet these days he scarcely recognizes himself. How can he offer these aberrant knots of his character to Clara?

He tries to imagine himself into the last days of her pregnancy, into the events of Joanna's birth, the fever after that. He tries to imagine his family's daily life, moving on without him. Clara is nursing Joanna, teaching Elizabeth how to talk, tending the garden, watching the flowers unfold; at night, if she is not too weary, she is bending over her dictionary and her German texts, and then . . . He wonders what would happen if he wrote, *Tell me what it feels like to lie in our bed, in the early morning light, naked and without me. Tell me what you do when you think of me. What your hands do, what you imagine me doing.*

He doesn't write that; he doesn't write about what he does to himself on a narrow cot, in a tent made from a blanket strung over a tree limb, the wind whistling as he stifles his groans with a handkerchief. Even then he doesn't feel alone. Close by, so near, his companions stifle noises of their own. His only truly private moments are these: bent over a blank page, dreaming with his pen.

3.

June 11, 1863

Dearest, dearest Clara:

The packet containing this letter will follow a very zigzag course on its way to you; a miracle that my words reach you at all. Or that yours reach me — how long it has been since the last! A ship that sailed from Bordeaux in March is rumored to have arrived at Bombay and will, I hope, have letters from you. Others from England have reached me, yet none from you — which is why I worry so. But already I hear your voice, reminding me that the fate of mail consigned to one ship may differ so from that consigned to another. I know you and the girls are well.

I am well too, although worried about you. I do what I can to keep busy. Did I tell you that I received, in response to some modest botanical observations I had sent to Dr. Hooker, a brief reply? He corrected my amateur mistakes, suggested I gather some specimens for him, and told me his great love of mosses dated from the time he was five or six. His mother claims that when he was very tiny he was found grubbing in a wall, and that when she asked what he was doing, he cried that he had found *Bryam argenteum* (not true, he notes now), a pretty moss he'd admired in his father's collection. At any age, he says — even mine — the passion for botany may manifest itself.

I found this touching and thought you would too. And I'm honored that he would answer me at all. In the hope of being of further use to him, I plan to continue my observations. Where I am now — deep in the heart of the Karakoram — nothing grows but the tiny lichens and mosses that are Dr. Hooker's greatest love. I can do little with them yet; they're extremely difficult. Except for them the landscape is barren. No one lives here — how would they live? Yet people do pass through from the neighboring valleys, the glaciers serving as highways through the mountains: I have met Hunzakuts, Baltis, Ladakhis and Nagiris and Turkis. But so far no travelers from home, although I hear rumors of solitary wanderers, English and German and French. One elderly adventurer has apparently haunted these mountains for decades, staying at times in Askole and Skardu, traveling even on the Baltoro Glacier and its branches — can this be true? If he exists, no one will tell me his name.

Around me is a confused mass of rock and glacier and mist, peaks appearing, then disappearing beyond the curtains of clouds. The glaciers, covered with rocks and striated like frozen rivers, you would never mistake for snowfields or for anything else; the porters fear them and have their own names for them, while the chainmen claim that deep within them are the bodies of men who died in the mountains and are now being slowly carried down the stream of ice. Some decades from now, at the foot of the glacier, a glove or a couple of bones may be spit out.

I have seen wild sheep the size of ponies. I have slept ten nights at a stretch above 15,000 feet; I have woken buried in snow, lost in clouds; days have passed when I could make no sightings and sketch no maps, when we have nothing to eat and huddle together forlornly, watching avalanches peel down the side of the peaks. The weather here is beastly. At the snout of the Baltoro we were nearly swept away by a river leaping from an ice cave. There are no vistas when one travels the glaciers, more a sense of walking along a deep corridor, framed by perpendicular walls. I have a headache nearly all the time, and my neck aches from always gazing upward. The mornings are quiet, everything frozen in place by the frosts of the night. By afternoon the landscape has come alive, moving and shifting as rocks fall, walls of mud slide down, hidden streams dammed by the ice break free with a shout. No place for men.

I travel now in a party of six. Me in charge, the sole Englishman (the others lead similar parties, on other glaciers, on their way to other peaks); two Indian assistants who aid me with the measurements and mapping; three porters. We are on the Baltoro itself as I write. So frequent are the crevasses, and so deceitfully covered with snow, that we tie ourselves together with ropes and move like a single long caterpillar. Yesterday we stopped by the edge of a huge open fissure, and while the other men rested, I tied all our ropes together and sounded the depth; 170 feet of rope failed to reach bottom. Framing us, on both sides of the glacier, are some of the world's highest peaks.

My task has been to map where Montgomerie's K2 lies in relation to the Karakoram watershed. And this I have done, though there is no clear sight of it from the glacier itself. With my men I climbed the flank of an enormous mountain called Masherbrum. My men — I ought to try and tell you what it's like to live in such enforced companionship. They . . . I will save this for another letter. You know how awkward I have always been. With my own family, with you, I can be myself, but here, with strangers — it is terrible, the old shyness seizes me. Without you by my side, to start the conversation and set everyone at ease, I am so clumsy. I do try, but it does no good. Especially with the porters and the chainmen, I am at a loss. The barriers of language and our very different circumstances and habits and religions — I ought to be able to break through these, given the bonds of our shared work. Somewhere they too have wives and children, families and homes, but I can't imagine them, I can't see these men in any other setting, and I think they can't see me any more clearly. For them, I am simply the person who gives orders. In my early days surveying seemed like a perfect career for such a solitary creature as myself. I didn't understand that out here I would be accompanied ceaselessly by strangers.

Yet one does not need to talk all the time. And some things are beyond conversation — several thousand feet up the flank of Masherbrum, as we were perched on a sharp bleak shoulder, there it suddenly rose: K2, sixteen or seventeen miles away, separating one system of glaciers from another. We believe the reason it has no local name is that it isn't visible from any inhabited place; the nearest village is six days' march away, and the peak is hidden by others almost as large. I cannot tell you how it felt to see it clearly. I have spent two days here, mapping all the visible peaks and their relationships to each other and the glaciers.

I will entrust this to the herdsman I met, who is on his way to Skardu; may it find its way to you. One of our porters speaks a language somewhat familiar to this herdsman. The pair had a discussion involving much pointing at Masherbrum, an insistent tone on the part of the porter, violent head-shakings from the herdsman. Later I asked the porter what they'd been talking about. The herdsman had asked where we'd been; the porter had shown him the shoulder from which we saw K2. "You have never been there," the herdsman apparently said. "No one can go there. It is not for men."

He does not write to Clara about his glacial misadventures. Walking along on a hazy day with his party strung out behind him, he had seen what resembled a small round rock perched on the ice in the distance. Fresh snow had fallen the night before, and the glare was terrible; over his eyes he'd drawn a piece of white muslin, like a beekeeper's veil, which cut the worst of the blinding light but dimmed the outlines of everything. One of his companions had bound a sheet of slit paper over his eyes, while others had woven shades from the hair of yaks' tails or had unbound their own hair and combed it forward until it screened their eyes. Max was nearly upon the round rock before he recognized it as a head.

A narrow crevasse, its opening covered by drifted snow; a wedge-shaped crack the width of a man at the top, tapering swiftly to a crease: inspecting it, with his veil raised, Max could imagine what had happened. The testing step forward, the confident placement of the second foot; and then one last second of everyday life before the deceitful bridge crumbled and the man plunged down, leaving his head and neck above the surface. The slit would have fit as intimately as a shroud, trapping the man's feet with his toes pointed down. No room to flex his knees or elbows and gain some purchase — but his head was free, he was breathing, he wasn't that cold and surely — surely? — he could pull himself out.

The man had a name, although it would take a while to determine it: Bancroft, whom Max had met only once, a member of one of the triangulating parties, disappeared three days before Max arrived. The ice inside the crevasse, warmed by the heat it stole from Bancroft's body, would have melted and pulled him inch by inch farther down, chilling him and slowing his blood, stealing his breath as fluid pooled in his feet and legs and his heart struggled to push it back up. By nightfall, with the cold pouring down from the stars, the cold wind pouring down from the peaks, the slit that had parted and shaped itself to Bancroft's body would have frozen solid around him. After hours of fruitless work, Max and his companions had reluctantly left Bancroft in a grave that would move until someone, a lifetime away, would puzzle over the boots and bones deposited in a moraine.

Max had not told Clara any of this: it would have frightened her. It frightened him. And yet despite that he went walking alone, ten days later. The sun was out, the sky was clear; the men had stopped in the middle of the afternoon, refused to go farther without a rest, and set up camp against his wishes. Irritated, he'd refused to waste the day. He'd mapped this section already but wanted more detail for his sketches: how the ice curved and cracked as it ground past the embracing wall of the mountain. In Wales, when he was being trained, he and Laurence had seen erratic boulders and mountains with deeply scored flanks which were caused, said the bookish young man who led them, by a glacial period that covered all Europe with ice. Now it was as if he'd walked backward into that earlier time.

He fell into a fissure, forty feet deep. A leaf of ice, like the recalcitrant piece of heartwood bridging two halves of a split log, stretched between the uphill and downhill walls of the crevasse and broke his fall. He landed face down, embracing a narrow slab, calling himself back to life and aware of his arms and legs dangling into space. Above him was a ceiling of snow, with a narrow slit of blue sky where his body had broken through. He could move his feet, his hands, his shoulders; apparently nothing was broken. Slowly, hugging the ice with his thighs, he sat upright. Before him the uphill wall of the crevasse glimmered smooth in the blue shadows. Slim ribs of ice, bulges and swellings reminiscent of Clara's back and belly. Behind him the downhill wall was jagged and white and torn. To his right the crevasse stretched without end, parallel faces disappearing into darkness. But to his left the walls appeared to taper together.

He might make of himself a bridge, he thought. A bridge of flesh, like the bridge of ice. With his back pressed against the wet uphill wall, his legs extended, and his boots pressed into the crunching, jagged downhill wall, he suspended himself. He moved his right foot a few inches, then his left; sent all his strength into the soles of his feet and then slid his back a few inches, ignoring the icy stream that chattered so far below. Again and again, right foot, left foot, heave. Time stopped, thinking stopped, everything stopped but these small painful motions. The walls drew closer together and he folded with them, his legs bending at the knees, then doubled, until finally he was hung in a sideways crouch.

He reached the corner without knowing what he'd do when he got there. The crevasse was shaped like a smile; where the two lips met, the bottom also curved up. He released his right leg and let it slide down, touching some rubble on which he might balance. He stood, he straightened partway. Soaked, scared, exhausted, and so cold. Above him was not the sky but a roof of snow. Like a mole he scratched at the bottom surface. He tore his fingernails and ripped his hands. When he realized what was happening he stopped digging with his right hand and dug only with his left.

He dug himself out. He hauled himself up. How many hours did this take? His left hand was bloody and blue, his right torn but still working; how lucky he had been. On the surface of the glacier, under the setting sun, he closed his eyes and fixed in his mind the dim, shadowed, silent grave he'd known for a few hours. Among the things he would not write to Clara — he would never write a word of this — was how seductive he'd found the cold and quiet. How easy he would have found it to sleep on the leaf of ice, his head pillowed on his arm while snow drifted over the broken roof, sealing him in silent darkness. Nothing would have been left of him but his books and maps, and the trunk with Clara's letters. So many still unopened, dated months in the future, a year in the future. It was the thought of not getting to read them that made him wake up.

4.

July 21, 1863

Dear heart —

This week I received your Packet #15, from March; you cannot know what a relief it is to hear from you. But why do I say that when I know you suffer the same torments? It is very upsetting to hear that none of my letters have reached you, and that you have as yet no news of my travels across the country to Kashmir, never mind news of my journeys in the mountains. Although perhaps by now you do: it was still *March,* I remind myself, when you hadn't heard from me. It may be September or December before you receive this, and you will be in possession of all my other letters by then, smiling to see me worry in this.

We heard that a ship leaving Calcutta was burnt down to the waterline just after it embarked; all the passengers were saved but everything else on board was lost and I wonder if some of my letters were on it, now bits of ash on the sea. When I think about the hands through which these must pass to find their way to you: a passing herdsman to another party of the Survey, to another messenger, to some official in Srinagar; perhaps to Calcutta, perhaps to Bombay; through a merchant's hands, or a branch of the military — hand to hand to hand, to a ship, or several ships; and the hazards of weather and human carelessness every inch of the way . . . My dear, you must keep these accidents in mind when you worry about me. It grieves me to think of your suffering. Remember the promise we made to each other, to consider not just the accidents that might happen to us but to our correspondence. Remember how tough I am. How prudent.

Thank you for the story about Elizabeth and the garden. I love to think about the three of you, bundled up and watching the birds as they flick within the branches on the hedgerow. Joanna in your arms, Elizabeth darting along the hawthorns, pursuing the sparrows: these glimpses of your life together keep me going. If you knew how much I miss you . . . but I have promised myself I will write *sensibly.* I want you to think of me as I am, as you have always known me, and not as a stranger perpetually complaining. I'm glad Mrs. Moore's nephew — Gideon? — has been so helpful during his stay with his aunt and has been able to solve the problem with the drains. When next you see him, please tell him I am grateful. Do you see him often?

I received with the letters from you and our family two more letters from Dr. Hooker. He *has* received mail from me, from as late as April; how is it my letters are reaching him but not you? When I get home I will let you read what he writes; you will find it fascinating. He is in touch with botanists and collectors all over the world; involved with so many projects and yet still he takes the time to en-

courage an amateur such as myself. On his own journey, he said, as
he climbed from the terai to the snowline he traversed virtually
the entire spectrum of the world's flora, from the leech-infested,
dripping jungle to the tiny lichens of the Tibetan plateau. I have a
similar opportunity, he says. If I am wise enough to take it. I copy
for you here a little paragraph, which he included with questions
about what is growing where and requests for a series of measurements of temperature and altitude.

"When still a child," he writes,

> my father used to take me on excursions in the Highlands, where I
> fished a good deal, but also botanized; and well I remember on one oc-
> casion, that, after returning home, I built up by a heap of stones a repre-
> sentation of one of the mountains I had ascended, and stuck upon it
> specimens of the mosses I had collected, at heights relative to those at
> which I had gathered them. This was the dawn of my love for geograph-
> ical botany. It pleases me greatly that, though you have started your
> botanizing as a grown man, you may come to share a similar passion.

Is that not a lovely tale? The mountain was a little one, by our
standards here, less than 4,000 feet. He has been very encouraging
of my efforts, and with his help I have set myself a study plan, as if
I'm at university. I would like to make myself *worthy;* worthy to write
to such a man as Dr. Hooker and receive a response. Worthy of
seeking an answer to the question that now occupies everyone:
how the different forms of life have reached their present habitats.
When else will I have a chance like this?

What draws me to these men and their writings is not simply
their ideas but the way they defend each other so vigorously and
are so firmly bound. Hooker, standing up for Darwin at Oxford
and defending his dear friend passionately. Gray, in America,
championing Darwin in a series of public debates and converting
the world of American science one resistant mind at a time. Our
group here is very different. Although the work gets done — the
work always gets done, the maps accumulate — I have found little
but division and quarrels and bad behavior.

You may find my handwriting difficult to decipher; I have suffered much from snow blindness. And a kind of generalized mountain sickness as well. We are so high, almost all the time; the smallest effort brings on fatigue and nausea and the most piercing of

headaches. I sleep only with difficulty; it is cold at night, and damp. Our fires will not stay lit. But every day brings new additions to our map, and new sketches of the topography: you will be proud of me, I am becoming quite the draftsman. And I manage to continue with my other work as well. I keep in mind Hooker's travails in Nepal and Sikkim: how, in the most difficult of circumstances, he made excellent and detailed observations of his surroundings. I keep in mind Godfrey Vigne and all he managed to note. Also a man I did not tell you about before, whose diary passed through my hands: how clearly he described his travels, despite his difficulties! By this discipline, and by my work, I hold myself together.

This week my party climbed a peak some 21,000 feet high. We were not the first ones here: awaiting us was the station the strongest and most brilliant of the triangulators built last season. I have not met him; he remains an almost mythical creature. But I occupied his heap of stones with pride. He triangulated all the high peaks visible from here, and the map I have made from this outline, the curves of the glaciers and the jagged valleys, the passes and the glacial lakes — Clara, how I wish you could see it! It is the best thing I have ever done, and the pains of my body are nothing.

I have learned something these past few months. Something important. On the descent from such a peak, I have learned, I can see almost nothing: by then I am so worn and battered that my eyes and mind no longer work correctly; often I have a fever, I can maintain no useful train of thought, I might as well be blind.

On my first ascents, before I grasped this, I would make some notes on the way up but often I would skip things, thinking I would observe more closely on the way down. Now I note *everything* on the way up. As we climbed this giant peak I kept a notebook and pencil tied to my jacket pocket and most of the time had them right in my hand: I made note of every geological feature, every bit of vegetation or sign of a passing animal; I noted the weather as it changed over the climb, the depth of the snow, the movements of the clouds. This record — these records; I do this now with every ascent — will I think be invaluable to subsequent travelers. When I return I plan to share them with Dr. Hooker and whoever else is interested.

It's an odd thing, though, that there is not much pleasure in the actual recording. Although I am aware, distantly, that I often move through scenes of great beauty, I can't *feel* that as I climb; all is lost in giddiness and headache and the pain of moving my limbs and drawing breath. But a few days after I descend to a lower altitude, when my body has begun to repair itself — then I look at the notes I made during my hours of misery and find great pleasure in *them*. It is odd, isn't it? That all one's pleasures here are retrospective; in the moment itself, there is only the moment, and the pain.

I must go. A messenger from Michaels came by the camp this morning with new instructions and leaves soon to contact three other parties; if I put this into his hands it will find its way down the glacier, out of the mountains, over the passes. To you.

After relinquishing the letter to Michaels's messenger, he thinks: What use was that? For all those words about his work, he has said little of what he really meant. How will Clara know who he is these days if he hides both his worries and his guilty pleasures? He still hasn't told her about the gift he bought for himself. A collecting box, like a candle box, only flatter, in which to place fresh specimens. A botanical press, with a heap of soft drying paper, to prepare the best of his specimens for a herbarium, and a portfolio in which to lay them out, twenty inches by twelve, closed with a sturdy leather strap and filled with sheets of thin, smooth, unsized paper. Always he has been a man of endless small economies, saving every penny of his pay, after the barest necessities, for Clara in England. He has denied himself warm clothes, extra blankets, the little treats of food and drink on which the other surveyors squandered their money in Srinagar and before. But this one extravagance he couldn't resist: not a dancing girl, not a drunken evening's carouse, but still he is ashamed.

A different kind of shame has kept him from writing about the doubts that plague his sleepless nights. He knows so little, really — why does he think his observations might be useful? He ought to be content with the knowledge that the work he does each day is solid, practical, strong; these maps will stand for years. In Dehra Dun, and in Calcutta and back in England, copyists and engravers will render from his soiled rough maps clean and permanent versions. In a year the Series will be complete: Jammu and Kashmir, Khagan, Ladakh and Baltistan, caught in a net of lines; a topographical triumph. Still he longs to make some contribution more purely his.

He dreams of a different kind of map, in shades of misty green.

Where the heads of the Survey see the boundaries of states and tribes, here the watershed between India and China, there a plausible boundary for Kashmir, he sees plants, each kind in a range bounded by soil and rainfall and altitude and temperature. And it is this — the careful delineation of the boundaries of those ranges, the subtle links between them — that has begun to interest him more than anything else. *Geographical botany,* Dr. Hooker said. What grows where. Primulas up to this level, no higher; deodar here, stonecrops and rock jasmines giving way to lichens . . . Why do rhododendrons grow in Sikkim and not here? He might spend his life in the search for an answer.

Part of the reason he has formed no close ties to either the men with whom he daily climbs and maps or those who lead the other small parties is that when they gather at night, they argue about the ebb and flow not of plant life but of politics. The Sikh wars and the annexation of the Punjab, the administration of Lord Dalhousie, the transfer of power from the East India Company to the Crown, the decisions of the regional revenue officers — it is embarrassing how little all this interests him. Among the surveyors are military men who have served in the Burmese war or in Peshawar; who survived the Mutiny or, in various mountains, that stormy year when supplies to the Survey were interrupted and bands of rebels entered Kashmir. He ought to find their stories fascinating. Germans and Russians and Turks and Chinese, empires clashing; Dogras and Sikhs, spies and informants — currents no one understands, secrets it might take a lifetime to unravel. Yet of all this, two stories only have stayed with him.

The first he heard on a snow bench carved in a drift on a ridge, from an Indian chainman who'd served for a while in the Bengal Army and who worked as Max's assistant for two weeks and then disappeared. They were resting. The chainman was brewing tea. At Lahore, he said, his regiment had been on the verge of mutiny. On a June night in 1857, one of the spies the suspicious British officers had planted within the regiment reported to the brigadier that the sepoys planned an uprising the following day. That night, when the officers ordered a regimental inspection, they found two sepoys with loaded muskets.

There was a court-martial, the chainman said. He told the story quietly, as if he'd played no part in it; he had been loyal, he said. He had been simply an observer. Indian officers had convicted the two sepoys and sentenced them to death. "There was a parade," the chainman said. His English was very good, the light lilting accent at odds with the tale he told. "A formal parade. We stood lined up on three sides of a square. On the fourth side were two cannon. The sepoys —"

"Did you know them?" Max had asked.

"I knew both of them — I had tried to talk them out of their plan. They were . . . the officers lashed those two men over the muzzles of the cannons. Then they fired."

Below them the mountains shone jagged and white, clean and untenanted. Nearby were other Englishmen and other Indians, working in apparent harmony in this landscape belonging to neither. Yet all this had happened only six years ago.

"There was nothing left of them," the chainman said. He rose and kicked snow into the fire; the kettle he emptied and packed tidily away. "Parts of them came down like rain, bits of bone and flesh, shreds of uniforms. Some of us were sprinkled with their blood."

"I . . . ," Max had murmured. What could he say? "A terrible thing," he said. The chainman returned to work, leaving Max haunted and uneasy.

The other story was this, which Michaels encouraged a triangulator to tell one night when three different surveying teams gathered in a valley to plan their tasks for the next few weeks. An Indian atrocity to match the British one: Cawnpore, a month after the incident reported by the chainman. Of course Max had heard of the massacre of women and children there. No one in England had escaped that news, nor the public frenzy that followed. But Michaels's gruff, hard-drinking companion, who in 1857 had been with a unit of the Highlanders, told with relish certain details the newspaper hadn't printed.

"If you had seen the huts," said Michaels's friend; Archdale, Max thought his name was. Or maybe Archvale. "A hundred and twenty women and children escaped the first massacre on the riverboats — the mutineers rounded them up and kept them in huts. We arrived not long after they were butchered. I saw those huts — they looked like cages where a pack of wild animals had been set loose among their prey."

"Tell about the shoes," Michaels had called from the other side of the fire. All the men were drinking; Michaels had had a case of brandy carried in from Srinagar. His face was dark red, sweating, fierce. That night, as always, he ignored Max almost completely.

"The shoes," Archdale said. He emptied his glass and leaned forward, face shining in the firelight. "Picture this," he said. "I go into one hut and the walls are dripping with blood, the floor smeared, the smell unthinkable. Flies buzzing so loudly I thought I'd go mad. Against one wall is a row of women's shoes, running with blood, draped with bits of clothing." The Indian chainmen and the Balti porters were gathered around their separate fires, not far away: could they hear Archdale? Max wondered. Was it possible Archdale would say these things within earshot of them? "Against the other wall, a row of children's shoes, so small, just like those our children wear at home. And" — he leaned further forward here — "do you know what was in them?"

No one answered. Was Joanna wearing shoes yet? Max wondered. "What?" he'd said, unable to stop himself.

"Feet!" Archdale roared. "*Feet!* Those filthy animals, those swine, they had lopped off the children's feet. We found the bodies in the well."

That terrible story had set off others. The night had been like a night in hell; Max had fled the campfire soon after Archdale's tirade and rolled himself in a blanket in a hollow, far from everyone, carved into the rocky cliffs. When he woke he'd been surprised not to find the campground littered with bodies.

Since hearing those tales he has wondered how there could be so much violence on both sides; and how, after that, Englishmen and Indians could be up in these mountains, working so calmly together. How can he make sense of an empire founded on such things? *Nothing,* he thought after hearing those stories. And still thinks. I *understand nothing.*

Dr. Hooker wrote at great length, in a letter Max didn't mention to Clara, about the problems of packing botanical collections for the journey home: the weight, the costs; the necessity of using Ward's cases; the crating of tree ferns and the boats to be hired. How kind he was, to take such trouble in writing Max and to warn him of these potential hazards! And yet how little Dr. Hooker understands Max's own situation. There is no possibility of paying for such things without depriving Clara and his daughters. His collections are limited to the scraps he can dry and preserve in his small press — bad enough he spent money on that; the herbarium sheets he can carry; the sketches and observations in his notebook. He can offer Dr. Hooker only these, but they are not nothing, and he hopes his gifts will be received without disappointment.

The lost man whose skull he found when he first entered these mountains: at least that solitary explorer left behind a record of the movements of his soul. What is he doing, himself? Supporting his family, advancing his career; when he returns to England, he'll have no trouble finding a good position. But he would like also to feel that he has *broadened* himself. Hunched over his plane-table, his temples pounding as he draws the lateral moraines of the glacier below him, he hears his mother's voice.

Look. Remember this. The ribbon of ice below him turns into a snow-covered path that curves through the reeds along the river and vanishes at the horizon; across it a rabbit is moving, and his mother stands, her hand in his, quietly keeping him company. They watch, and watch, until the path seems to be moving not away from them but toward them, the stillness of the afternoon pouring into their clasped hands. *There is something special in you,* she said, *in the way you see.*

A few days ago, on his twenty-eighth birthday, he opened the birthday greeting Clara had tucked in his trunk. She had written about the earlier birthdays they'd shared. And about this one, as she imagined it: *Your companions, I know, will have made you a special birthday meal. Perhaps you'll all share a bottle of brandy, or whatever you drink there. I am thinking of you, and of the birthdays in the future we will once more spend together.*

Reading this, he'd felt for the first time that Clara's project might fail. He is no longer the person she wrote to, almost a year ago now. She may have turned into someone else as well. That Gideon she mentions, that nice young man who prunes the trees and brings her wood and does the tasks Max ought to be doing himself: what other parts of Max's life is he usurping? Max conjures up someone broad-shouldered, very tall — Max and Clara are almost the same height — unbuttoning his shirt and reaching out for Clara . . . Impossible, it makes him want to howl. Surely she wouldn't have mentioned him if their friendship were anything but innocent. Yet even if it is, it will have changed her.

He himself has changed so much, he grows further daily from her picture of him. There was no birthday celebration; he told no one of this occasion. If he had, there would have been no response.

It is his mother, dead so many years, who seems to speak most truly to the new person he is becoming. As if the years between her death and now were only a detour, his childhood self emerging from a long, uneasy sleep. Beyond his work, beyond the mapping and recording, he is *seeing;* and this — it is terrifying — is becoming more important to him than anything.

5.

October 1, 1863

Dearest Clara —

Forgive me for not writing in so long. Until I received your Packets #17, 18, and 19, all in a wonderful clump last week (#16, though, has gone astray), I had almost given up hope of us being in touch before winter. I should have realized your letters couldn't find me while we were among the glaciers. We are in the valley of the Shighar now, and from here will make our way back to Srinagar. I don't yet know what my winter assignment will be. The triangulating parties will winter at the headquarters in Dehra Dun, recalibrating the instruments and checking their calculations and training new assistants. There is talk of leaving a small group of plane-tablers in Srinagar, to complete topographical maps of the city and the outlying areas and lakes. I will let you know my orders as soon as I get them.

At least you know I am alive now. Though how can you make sense of my life here on the evidence of one letter from when I first arrived in Kashmir and one from deep in the mountains? The others — I must have faith they will find their way to you. Your description of your journey to London, trudging through those government offices as you tried to get some word of me — this filled me with sadness, and with shame. You are generous to say it is not my fault that you went so long without word of me, that you blame a careless ship's captain, clumsy clerks, and accidents: but it is my fault, still. I am the one who left home. And that I have not written these last weeks — can you forgive me? I console myself with the thought that since my earlier letters were so delayed, perhaps a trickle of them will continue to reach you during the gap between then and now. But really my only excuse is the hardships of these last weeks. I am so weary; the cold and the altitude make it hard to sleep. And when I do catch a few brief hours, I am plagued by nightmares. The men I work with tell me stories, things I would never repeat to you; and though I try not to think about them, they haunt me at night.

The season in the mountains is already over; we stayed too long. We crossed one high pass after another during our retreat. And Clara, you can't imagine the weather. I couldn't work on my maps, or keep up my notes, or even — my most cherished task — write to you; when I heated the inkpot, the ink still froze on its short journey to the paper. My hands were frozen, my beard a mass of icicles. I wore everything you packed for me, all at once, and still couldn't stay warm. Lamb's wool vest and drawers, heavy flannel shirt and lined chamois vest, wool trousers and shirt, three pairs of stockings and my fur-lined boots, thick woolen hat, flannel-lined kidskin jacket, over that my big sheepskin coat and then a Kashmir shawl wrapped twice about me, binding the whole mass together — I sweated under the weight of all this, yet grew chilled the instant we stopped moving. Nights were the worst; there is no firewood in the mountains, and we had already used up all we'd carried. Food was short as well.

I shouldn't tell you these things; never mind. Now that we are down in the valleys, things are easier. And I am fine. Soon enough we'll reach Srinagar, and whether I stay there or move on to Dehra Dun, I am looking forward to the winter. Long quiet months of cleaning up my sketch maps, improving my drawings, fitting together the sections into the larger picture of the Himalayan system. From either place I may write to you often, knowing the chances of your getting my letters in just a few months are good; and I may look forward to receiving yours with some regularity. Still I have some of the letters in your trunk to look forward to as well: I ration these now; I open one only every few weeks, sometimes ignoring the dates with which you marked them. Forgive me — I save them for when I most need them. This evening, before I began to write to you, I opened one intended for Elizabeth's birthday. How lovely to be reminded of that happy time when you leaned on my arm, plump and happy as we walked in the garden and waited for her birth. The lock of Elizabeth's hair you enclosed I have sewn into a pouch, which I wear under my vest.

What else do I have to tell you? So much has happened these last weeks that I don't know how to describe it all; and perhaps it wouldn't interest you, it is just my daily work. Yesterday I had a strange encounter, though. Camped by the edge of a river, trying to restore some order to my papers while my companions were off in search of fuel, I looked up to see a stranger approaching; clearly a European, although he wore clothes of Kashmiri cut. When I invited him to take tea with me, he made himself comfortable and told me about himself. A doctor and an explorer, elderly; he calls himself Dr. Chouteau and says he is of French birth, though his English is indistinguishable from mine. This he explains by claiming to have left home as a boy of fourteen; claiming also to have been exploring in these mountains for over forty years. We did not meet in Srinagar, he told me, because he lives in a native quarter there. I think he may be the solitary traveler of whom I heard such odd rumors earlier in the season, though when I asked him this he shrugged and said, "There are a few of us."

We passed together the most interesting afternoon I've had in weeks. My own companions and I have grown weary of each other; we seldom speak at all. But Dr. Chouteau talked without stopping for several hours. A great liar, I would have to say. Even within those hours he began to contradict himself. But how intriguing he was. He is very tall, thin, and hawk-nosed, with a skin burnt dark brown by years in the sun and deeply lined. His ragtag outfit he tops with a large turban, from which sprout the plumes of some unidentifiable bird. He showed me his scars: a round one like a coin on the back of one hand, and another to match on the front — here a bullet passed through, he said, when he was fighting in Afghanistan. A hollow in his right calf, where, in Kabul, a bandit hacked at him with a sword as he escaped by horse. For some time he lived among a Kafir tribe, with a beautiful black-eyed mistress; the seam running from eyebrow to cheekbone to chin he earned, he says, in a fight to win her. He has been in Jalalabad and the Kabul River basin, in the Pamirs among the Kirghiz nomads, in Yarkand and Leh, Chitral and Gilgit.

Or so he says. Myself, I cannot quite credit this; he is elusive regarding his travel routes, and about dates and seasons and companions. But perhaps he truly did all these things, at one time or another, and erases the details and connections out of necessity: I think perhaps he has been a spy. For whom?

I try to forget what you have said about the way you gather with our families and friends and pass these letters around, or read them out loud; if I thought of that I would grow too self-conscious to write to you at all. But I will tell you one peculiar thing about Dr. Chouteau if you promise to keep this to yourself. He has lived to such a robust old age, he swears, by the most meticulous attention to personal hygiene. And how has he avoided the gastric complaints that afflict almost all of us when we eat the local foods? A daily clyster, he says. The cleansing enema he administers to himself, with a special syringe. I have seen this object with my own eyes; he carries it with him and showed it to me. It looked rather like a hookah. Far better this, he said, looking at my bewildered countenance, than the calomel and other purgatives on which less wise travelers rely.

Some of the other things he told me I can't repeat, even to you: they have to do with princes and dancing girls, seraglios and suchlike: when I am home again I will share these with you, in the privacy of our own bed.

Clara, I am so confused. Meeting this stranger made me realize with more than usual sharpness how lonely I am, how cut off I feel from all that is important to me. My past life seems to be disappearing; my memories grow jumbled. Who was the Max Vigne who went here or there, did this or that? It's as if I am dissolving and re-forming; I am turning into someone I don't recognize. If I believed in the doctrine of the transmigration of souls, I might suspect that the wind is blowing someone else's soul in through my nostrils, while my old soul flies out my ears. In the mountains I lay awake in the cold, frozen despite my blankets, and my life in England — my boyhood, even my life with you — passed by my eyes as if it had been lived by someone else. Forgive these wanderings. The household details of which you wrote, the problems with the roof, the chimney, the apple trees — I know I should offer some answers in response to your questions, but it feels pointless. You will have long since had to resolve these things before you receive my advice. I trust your judgment completely.

Good night; the wind is blowing hard. What a fine thing a house is. In my tent I think of you and the girls, snug inside the walls.

After that, he does not write to Clara for a while.

The river valleys, the high plains, the dirt and crowds and smells and noise of Srinagar, where the surveying parties are reshuffled and he finds himself, with three other plane-tablers, left behind in makeshift quarters, with preliminary maps of the city and the valley and vague instructions to fill in the details while everyone else (Michaels too; at least he is finally free of Michaels!) moves on to Dehra Dun, not to return until spring: and still, he does not write Clara. He does not write to anyone, he does not keep up his botanical notes, he makes no sketches other than those required for the maps. He does his work, because he must. But he does no more. He cannot remember ever feeling like this.

6.

If he could make himself write, he might say this:

Dearest Clara —

Who am I? Who am I meant to be? I imagine a different life for myself, but how can I know, how can anyone know, if this is a foolish dream or a sensible goal? Have I any scientific talent at all? Dr. Hooker says I do; he has been most encouraging. If he is right, then my separation from you means something, and the isolation I've imposed on myself, and the long hours of extra work. But if I have no real gift, if I am only deluding myself . . . then I am wasting everything.

There is something noble, surely, in following the path of one's gifts; don't we have a duty to use our talents to the utmost? Isn't any sacrifice in the pursuit of that worthwhile? In these past months I have often felt that the current which is most truly me, laid aside when I was still a boy and had to face the responsibilities of family life, has all this time continued to flow, the way water moves unseen beneath the glaciers. When I am alone, with my notes and plants and the correlations of weather and geology and flora springing clear before me, I feel: This is who I am. This is what I was born to do. *But if in fact I have no real capacity for this work, if it is only my vanity leading me down this path — what then?*

He has grown morose, he knows. Worse than morose. Maudlin, self-pitying. And self-deluding: not just about his possible talents, but in the very language with which he now contemplates writing to Clara. Nobility, duty, sacrifice — whose words are those? Not his. He is using them to screen himself from the knowledge of whatever is shifting in him.

On the journey back to Srinagar, among the triangulators and plane-tablers led by Michaels and eventually joined by Captain

Montgomerie himself, he was silent, sullen, distant. If he could, he would have talked to no one. In Srinagar, once the crowd of officers and triangulators left for Dehra Dun, he felt still worse. Investigating the streets and alleys, the outlying villages and the limestone springs, he was charmed by what he saw and wished it would stay the same. But meanwhile he couldn't help hearing talk of his government annexing Kashmir and turning the valley into another Simla: a retreat for soldiers and government officials, people he would prefer to avoid.

When he returns at night to the room he shares with three other plane-tablers, he flops on his cot and can't understand why he feels so trapped. The walls that shelter him from the cold and the wind — didn't he miss these? Perhaps it isn't the dark planks and the stingy windows that make him grind his teeth, but his companions' self-important chatter about measurements and calculations, possibilities for promotion. He shuts his ears to them and imagines instead talking with the vainglorious old explorer whose tales left him feeling lost, and full of questions.

The stories he wrote to Clara were the least of what happened that afternoon. Dr. Chouteau had been everywhere, Max learned. Without a map; maps meant nothing to him. Max's work he'd regarded with detached interest, almost amusement. Looking down at the sheets of paper, the carefully drawn cliffs and rivers and glaciers, Dr. Chouteau had said, *I have been here. And here. Here. And so many other places.* He spoke of the gravestone, seen in Kabul, that marked the resting place of an Englishman who had passed through there a century and a half ago. Of wandering Russians, Austrians, Chinese, Turks, the twists and turns of the Great Game, the nasty little wars. Godfrey Vigne, he'd said — *Isn't it odd, that you share that last name?* — had been no simple traveler but a British spy. Those forays into Baltistan a way of gathering information, and his attempts to reach Central Asia a way of determining that the only routes by which the Russians might enter India lay west of the Karakoram. *I knew him,* Dr. Chouteau said. *We were in Afghanistan together. He was the one who determined that Baltistan has no strategic importance to the British plans for India.*

More than anyone else, Dr. Chouteau made Max understand the purpose of his work. *I never make maps,* Dr. Chouteau said. *Or not maps anyone else could read. They might fall into the wrong hands.* Max's maps, he pointed out, would be printed, distributed to governments, passed on to armies and merchants and travelers. Someone, someday, would study them as they planned an invasion, or planned to stop one. What can Max's insignificant hardships matter when compared to the adventures of such solitary travelers as Dr. Chouteau, or the lost man he saw when he first arrived in the mountains; of Godfrey Vigne or of Dr. Hooker? In Srinagar, Max understands that his journeys have been only the palest imitations of theirs.

He hasn't heard from Dr. Hooker in months. And although he knows he ought to understand, from Clara's trials, that accident may have been at work, he interprets this as pure rejection. The observations he sent weren't worthy; Hooker has ceased to reply because Max's work is of no interest. All he will leave behind is maps, which will be merged with all the other maps, on which he will be nameless: small contributions to the great *Atlas of India,* which has been growing for almost forty years. In London a faceless man collates the results of the triangulations into huge unwieldy sheets, engraved on copper or lithographed: two miles to an inch, four miles to an inch — what will become of them? He knows, or thinks he knows, though his imagination is colored by despair: they will burn, or be eaten by rats and cockroaches, or obliterated by fungus. Frayed and dust-stained, uncatalogued, they'll be sold as waste paper, or burned. Those that survive will be shared with allies, or hidden from enemies.

Max might write to Dr. Hooker about this; in Sikkim, he knows, Dr. Hooker and a companion had been seized while botanizing and held as political hostages. That event had served as excuse for an invasion by the British army and the annexation of southern Sikkim. Although Dr. Hooker refused to accompany the troops, he gave the general in charge of the invasion the topographical map he'd drawn. That map was copied at the surveyor general's office; another map, of the Khasia hills, made its way into the *Atlas of India,* complimented by all for its geological, botanical, and meteorological notes. Max has seen this one himself, though its import escaped him at the time. Dr. Hooker did it in his spare time, tossing off what cost Max so much labor.

But what is the point of tormenting himself? In the increasing cold he reads over Dr. Hooker's letters to him, looking for the first signs of disfavor. The letters are imperturbably kind; he can find no hint of where he failed. For comfort he turns not to the remaining

letters in Clara's trunk — those forward-casting, hopeful exercises
make him feel too sad — but instead to the first of her letters to
reach him. From those, still brave and cheerful, he works his way
into the later ones. A line about Joanna's colic, and how it lingered; a line about the bugs in the rhubarb: unsaid, all the difficulties that must have surrounded each event. *The roof is leaking,
the sink is broken, Elizabeth has chickenpox,* Clara wrote. *Zoe is bearing
bravely her broken engagement, but we are all worried about her.* What
she means is *Where are you, where are you? Why have you left me to face
this all alone?*

Her packet #16, which failed to reach him in October with the
rest of that batch, has finally arrived, along with other, more recent
letters. In early April she described the gardens, the plague of
slugs, the foundling sparrow Elizabeth had adopted and Joanna's
avid, crawling explorations, the death of a neighbor and the funeral, which she attended with Gideon. Gideon again. Then something broke through and she wrote what she'd never permitted
herself before:

> Terrible scenes rise up before my eyes and they are as real as the rest of
> my life. I look out the window and I see a carriage pull up to the door, a
> man steps out, he is bearing a black-bordered envelope; I know what is
> in it, I know. He walks up to the door and I am already crying. He looks
> down at his shoes. I take the letter from him, I open it; it is come from
> the government offices in London and I skip over the sentences which
> attempt to prepare me for the news. I skip to the part in which it says you
> have died. In the mountains, of an accident. In the plains, of some terri-
> ble fever. On a ship which has sunk — I read the sentences again and
> again — they confirm my worst fears and I grow faint — hope expires
> in me and yet I will not believe. In the envelope, too, another sheet:
> the words of someone I have never met, who witnessed your last days.
> *Though I am a stranger to you, it is my sad duty to inform you of a most terrible
> event.* And then a description of whatever befell you; and one more
> sheet, which is your last letter to me.
>
>   You see how I torment myself. I imagine all the things you might write.
> I imagine on some days that you tell me the truth; on others that you lie,
> to spare my feelings. I imagine you writing, *Do not grieve too long, dearest
> Clara. The cruelest thing, when we think of our loved ones dying in distant
> lands, is the thought of them dying alone and abandoned, uncared for — but
> throughout my illness I have had the attentions of kind men.* I imagine, I imag-
> ine . . . how can I imagine you alive and well, when I have not heard from
> you for so long?

I am ashamed of myself for writing this. All over Britain other women wait patiently for soldiers and sailors and explorers and merchants — why can't I? I will try to be stronger. When you read this page, know that it was written by Clara who loves you, in a moment of weakness and despair.

At least that is past now, for her; from her other letters he knows she was finally reassured. But that she suffered like this; that he is only hearing about it now . . . To whom is she turning for consolation?

Winter drags on. Meetings and work; official appearances and work; squabbles and work. Work. He does what he can, what he must. Part of him wants to rush home to Clara. To give up this job, this place, these ambitions; to sail home at the earliest opportunity and never to travel again. It has all been too much: the complexities and politics, the secrets underlying everything. Until he left England, he thinks now, he had lived in a state of remarkable innocence. Never, not even as a boy, had he been able to fit himself into the world. But he had thought, until recently, that he might turn his back on what he didn't understand and make his own solitary path. Have his own heroes, pursue his own goals. But if his heroes are spies, if his work is in service of men whose goals led to blood-stained rooms and raining flesh, nothing is left of the world as he once envisioned it.

He wanders the city and its outskirts, keeping an eye out, as he walks, for Dr. Chouteau. He must be here; where else would he spend the winter? Stories of that irascible old man, or of someone like him, surface now and then; often Max has a sense that Dr. Chouteau hides down the next alley, across the next bridge. He hears tales of other travelers as well — Jacquemont and Moorcroft, the Schlagintweit brothers, Thomas Thomson and the Baron von Hugel. The tales contradict each other, as do those about Dr. Chouteau. In one story he is said to be an Irish mercenary, in another an American businessman. Through these distorted lenses Max sees himself as if for the first time, and something happens to him.

That lost man, whose skull he found when he first arrived in the mountains — is this what befell him? As an experiment, Max stops eating. He fasts for three days and confirms what the lost man wrote in his diary: his spirit soars free; everything looks different.

His mother is with him often during that airy, delirious time. Dr. Chouteau strolls through his imagination as well. In a brief break in the flow of Dr. Chouteau's endless self-regarding narrative, Max had offered an account of his own experiences up on the glacier. His cold entombment, his lucky escape; he'd been humiliated when Dr. Chouteau laughed and patted his shoulder. *A few hours,* he said. *You barely tasted the truth. I was caught for a week on the Siachen Glacier, in a giant blizzard. There is no harsher place on this earth; it belongs to no one. Which won't keep people from squabbling over it someday. The men I traveled with died.*

When Max hallucinates Dr. Chouteau's voice emerging from the mouth of a boatwoman arguing with her neighbor, he starts eating again, moving again. The old maps he's been asked to revise are astonishingly inaccurate. He wanders through narrow lanes overhung by balconies, in and out of a maze of courtyards. The air smells of stale cooking oil, burning charcoal, human excrement. He makes his way back and forth across the seven bridges of Srinagar so often he might be weaving a web. Temples, mosques, the churches of the missionaries; women carrying earthenware pots on their heads; barges and bakeshops and markets piled with rock salt and lentils, bottles of ghee — his wanderings he justifies as being in service to the map, although he also understands that part of what drives him into the biting air is a search for Dr. Chouteau. If Max could find him, if he could ask him some questions, perhaps this unease that has settled over him might lift.

As winter turns into early spring, as he does what he can with his map of the valley and, in response to letters from Dehra Dun, begins preparations for another season up in the mountains, his life spirals within him like the tendril of a climbing plant. One day he sits down, finally, with Laurence's gift to him and begins working slowly through the lines of Mr. Darwin's argument. The ideas aren't unfamiliar to him; as with the news of Cawnpore and the Mutiny, he has heard them summarized, read accounts in the newspapers, discussed the outlines of the theory of descent with modification with Laurence and others. But when he confronts the details and grasps all the strands of the theory, it hits him like the knowledge of the use made of Dr. Hooker's maps, or the uses that will be made of his own. He scribbles all over the margins. At first he writes Laurence simply to say, *I am reading it. Have you read it? It is marvelous. The world is other than we thought.* But a different, more complicated letter begins to unfurl in his mind.

A mountain, he reads, *is an island on the land. The identity of many plants and animals, on mountain-summits, separated from each other by hundreds of miles of lowlands, where the alpine species could not possibly exist, is one of the most striking cases known of the same species living at distant points, without the apparent possibility of their having migrated from one to another . . . The glacial period affords a simple explanation of these facts.*

He closes his eyes and sees the cold sweeping south and covering the land with snow and ice, arctic plants and animals migrating into the temperate regions. Then, centuries later, the warmth returning and the arctic forms retreating northward with the glaciers, leaving isolated representatives stranded on the icy summits. *Along the Himalaya,* Mr. Darwin writes, *at points 900 miles apart, glaciers have left the marks of their former low descent; and in Sikkim, Dr. Hooker saw maize growing on gigantic ancient moraines.* The point of Dr. Hooker's work, Max sees, is not just to map the geographical distribution of plants but to use that map in service of a broader theory. Not just *The same genus of lichen appears in Baltistan and in Sikkim,* but *The lichens of the far ends of the Himalaya are related, descending from a common ancestor.*

It is while his head is spinning with these notions that, on the far side of the great lake called the Dal, near a place where, if it were summer, the lotus flowers would be nodding their heads above their enormous circular leaves, by a chenar tree in which herons have nested for generations, he meets at last not Dr. Chouteau but a woman. Dark-haired, dark-eyed: Dima. At first he speaks to her simply to be polite, and to conceal his surprise that she'd address him without being introduced. Then he notices, in her capable hands, a sheaf of reeds someone else might not consider handsome but which she praises for the symmetry of their softly drooping heads. Although she wears no wedding ring, she is here by the lake without a chaperone.

The afternoon passes swiftly as they examine other reeds, the withered remains of ferns, lichens clustered on the rocks. Her education has come, Max learns, from a series of tutors and travelers and missionaries; botanizing is her favorite diversion. He eyes her dress, which is well cut although not elaborate; her boots, which are sturdy and look expensive. From what is she seeking diversion? She speaks of plants and trees and gardens, a stream of conversation that feels intimate yet reveals nothing personal. In return he tells her a bit about his work. When they part and she invites him to call on her a few days later, he accepts. Such a long time since he has spoken with anyone congenial.

Within the week, she lets him know that he'd be welcome in her bed; and, gently, that he'd be a fool to refuse her. Max doesn't hide from her the fact that he's married, nor that he must leave this place soon. But the relief he finds with her — not just her body, the comforts of her bed, but her intelligence, her hands on his neck, the sympathy with which she listens to his hopes and longings — the relief is so great that sometimes, after she falls asleep, he weeps.

"I have been lonely," she tells him. "I have been without company for a while." She strokes his thighs and his sturdy smooth chest and slips down the sheets until their hipbones are aligned. Compactly built, she is several inches shorter than he but points out that their legs are the same length; his extra height is in his torso. Swiftly he pushes away a memory of his wedding night with long-waisted Clara. The silvery filaments etched across Dima's stomach he tries not to recognize as being like those that appeared on Clara after Elizabeth's birth.

He doesn't insult her by paying her for their time together; she isn't a prostitute, simply a woman grown used, of necessity, to being kept by men. Each time he arrives at her bungalow he brings gifts: little carved boxes and bangles and lengths of cloth; for her daughter, who is nearly Elizabeth's age, toy elephants and camels. Otherwise he tries to ignore the little girl. Who is her father, what is her name? He can't think about that, he can't look at her. Dima, seeming somehow to understand, sends her daughter off to play with the children of her servants when he arrives. Through the open window over her bed he sometimes hears them laughing.

Dima has lived with her father in Leh and Gilgit and here, in a quarter of Srinagar seldom visited by Europeans; she claims to be the daughter of a Russian explorer and a woman, now dead, from Skardu. For some years she was the mistress of a Scotsman who fled his job with the East India Company, explored in Ladakh, and ended up in Kashmir; later she lived with a German geologist. Or so she says. In bed she tells Max tales of her lovers, their friends, her father's friends — a secret band of wanderers, each with a story as complicated as Dr. Chouteau's. Which one taught her botany? In those stories, and the way that she appears to omit at least as much as she reveals, she resembles Dr. Chouteau himself, whom she claims to know. A friend of her father's, she says. A cartographer (but didn't he tell Max he never made maps?) and adviser to obscure princes; a spendthrift and an amateur geologist. Bad with his servants but excellent with animals; once he kept falcons. She knows a good deal about him but not, she claims, where he is now.

One night, walking back from her bungalow, a shadowy figure resembling Dr. Chouteau appears on the street before Max and then disappears into an alley. Although the night is dark, Max follows. The men crouched around charcoal braziers and leaning in doorways regard him quietly. Not just Kashmiris: Tibetans and Ladakhis, Yarkandis, Gujars, Dards — are those Dards? — and Baltis and fair-haired men who might be Kafirs. During this last year, he has learned to recognize such men by their size and coloring and the shape of their eyes, their dress and weapons and bearing. As they have no doubt learned to recognize Englishmen. If Dr. Chouteau is among them, he hides himself. For a moment, as Max backs away with his hands held open and empty before him, he realizes that anything might happen to him. He is no one here. No one knows where he is. In the Yasin Valley, Dr. Chouteau said, he once stumbled across a pile of stones crowned by a pair of hands. The hands were white, desiccated, bound together at the wrists. Below the stones was the remainder of the body.

When he leaves the alley, all Max can see for a while are the stars and the looming blackness of the mountains. How clear the sky is! His mind feels equally clear, washed out by that moment of darkness.

During his next weeks with Dima, Clara recedes — a voice in his ear, words on paper; mysterious, as she was when he first knew her. Only when Dima catches a cold and he has to tend her, bringing basins and handkerchiefs and cups of tea, does he recollect what living with Clara was really like. Not the ardent, long-distance exchange of words, on which they've survived for more than a year, but the grit and weariness of everyday life. Household chores and worries over money, a crying child, a smoking stove; relatives coming and going, all needing things, and both of them stretched so thin; none of it Clara's fault, it is only life. Now it is Dima who is sick and who can no longer maintain her enchanting deceits. The carefully placed candles, the painted screen behind which she undoes her ribbons and laces to emerge in a state of artful undress, the daughter disposed of so she may listen with utmost attention to him, concentrate on him completely — all that breaks down. One day there is a problem with her well, which he must tend to. On another her daughter — her name is Kate — comes into Dima's bedroom in tears, her dress torn by some children who've been teasing her. He has to take Kate's hand. He has to find the other children and scold them and convince them all to play nicely together, then report back to Dima how this has been settled. He is falling, he thinks. Headfirst, into another crevasse.

During Dima's illness it is with some relief — he knows it is shameful — that he returns at night to his spartan quarters. Through the gossip that flies so swiftly among the British community, the three other surveyors have heard about Dima. Twice Max was spotted with her, and this was all it took; shunned alike by Hindus and Moslems, Christians and Sikhs, she has a reputation. That it is Max she's taken up with, Max she's chosen: to Max's amazement and chagrin, his companions find this glamorous. They themselves have found solace in the brothels; Srinagar is filled with women, and they no longer turn to each other for physical relief. But to them, unaware of Dima's illness and her precarious household, Max's situation seems exotic. The knowledge that he shares their weaknesses, despite the way he has kept to himself — this, finally, is what makes Max's companions accept him.

They stop teasing him. They ask him to drink with them, to dine with them, which on occasion he does. They ask for details, which he refuses. But despite his reticence, his connection to Dima has made his own reputation. When the rest of the surveyors return from Dehra Dun and they all head back to the mountains, Max knows he will occupy a different position among them. Because of her, everything will be different, and easier, than during the last season. It is this knowledge that breaks the last piece of his heart.

April arrives; the deep snow mantling the Pir Panjal begins to shrink back from the black rock. Max writes long letters to Laurence, saying nothing about Dima but musing about what he reads. Into Srinagar march triangulators in fresh tidy clothes, newly trained Indian assistants, new crowds of porters bearing glittering instruments, and the officers, Michaels among them. But Michaels can no longer do Max any harm. Max and his three companions present their revised map of Srinagar and are praised. Then it is time to leave. Still Max has no answers. Dr. Chouteau has continued to elude him; Dima, fully recovered now, thanks him for all his help, gives him some warm socks, and wishes him well with his work.

Which work? Even to her he has not admitted what he is thinking about doing these next months. He holds her right hand in both of his and nods numbly when she says she will write him, often, and hopes that he'll write her. Hopes that they'll see each other again when the surveying party returns to Srinagar.

More letters. Another person waiting for him. "Don't write," he says, aware the instant he does so of his cruelty. The look on her face — but she has had other lovers (how many lovers?), and she doesn't make a scene. Perhaps this is why he chose her. When they part, he knows he will become simply a story she tells to the next stranger she welcomes into her life.

And still he does not write to Clara. Other letters from her have arrived, which he hasn't answered: six months, what is he thinking? Not about her, the life she is leading in his absence, the way her days unfold; not what she and their children are doing, their dreams and daily duties and aspirations and disappointments. Neither is he thinking about Dima; it is not as if his feelings for her have driven out those he has for Clara. He isn't thinking about either of them. This is his story, his life unfolding. The women will tell the tale of these months another way.

7.

April 21, 1864

My dearest, my beloved Clara —

Forgive me for not writing in so long. I have been sick — nothing serious, nothing you need worry about, although it did linger. But I am fully recovered now, in time to join the rest of the party on our march back into the mountains. This season, I expect, will be much like the last. Different mountains, similar work; in October I

will be done with the services I contracted for and the Survey will
be completed. From my letters of last season you will have a good
idea of what I'll be doing. But Clara —

Max pauses, then crosses out the last two words. What he should say
is what he knows she wants to hear: that when October comes he'll
be on his way back to her, as they agreed. But he doesn't want to lie
to her. Not yet.

His party is camped by a frozen stream. The porters are butcher-
ing a goat. Michaels, in a nearby tent, has just explained to the men
their assignments for the coming week; soon it will be time to eat;
Max has half an hour to finish this letter and no way to say what he
really means: that after the season is finished, he wants to stay on.

Everything has changed for me, he wants to say. *I am changed, I know
now who I am and what I want, and I can only hope you accept this and
continue to wait for me. I want to stay a year longer. When the Survey ends,
in October, I want to wait out the winter in Srinagar, writing up all I have
learned and seen so far; and then I want to spend next spring and summer
traveling by myself. If I had this time to explore, to test myself, discover the secrets of these mountains — it would be enough, I could be happy with this,
it would last me the rest of my life. When I come home, I mean to try to estab-
lish myself as a botanist. I have no hope of doing so without taking this time
and working solely on my studies.*

But he can't write any of that. Behind him men are laughing, a
fire is burning, he can smell the first fragrance of roasting meat. He
is off again, to the cold bare brilliance of a place like the moon, and
what he can't explain, yet, to Clara is that he needs other time, during the growing season, to study the plants in the space between
the timberline and the line of permanent snow. How do the species
that have arisen here differ from those in other places? How do
they make a life for themselves in such difficult circumstances?

But how could Clara possibly understand this? He will break it to
her gently, he thinks. A hint at first, a few more suggestions in letters over the coming months; in September he'll raise the subject.
Perhaps by then he'll have more encouragement from Dr. Hooker,
which he can offer to Clara as evidence that his work is worthwhile.
Perhaps by then he'll understand how he might justify his plans to
her. For now — what else can he say in this letter? He has kept too
much from her these last months. If his letters were meant to be a

map of his mind, a way for her to follow his trail, then he has failed her. Somehow, as summer comes to these peaks and he does his job for the last time, he must find a way to let her share in his journey. But for now all he can do is triangulate the first few points.

— I have so much to tell you, Clara. And no more time today; what will you think, after all these months, when you receive such a brief letter? Know that I am thinking of you and the girls, no matter what I do. I promise we'll do whatever you want when I return: I know how much you miss your brother; perhaps we will join him in New York. I would like that, I think. I would like to start over, all of us, someplace new. Somewhere I can be my new self, live my new life, in your company.

Next to my heart, in an oilskin pouch, I keep the lock of Elizabeth's hair and your last unopened letter to me, with your solemn instruction on the envelope: *To Be Opened If You Know You Will Not Return to Me.* If the time comes, I will open it. But the time won't come; I will make it back, I will be with you again.

This comes to you with all my love, from your dearest

Max

RICK BASS

The Fireman

FROM THE KENYON REVIEW

THEY BOTH STAND on the other side of the miracle. Their marriage was bad, perhaps even rotting, but then it got better. He — the fireman, Kirby — knows what the reason is: that every time they have an argument, the dispatcher's call sounds, and he must run and disappear into the flames — he is the captain — and while he is gone, his wife, Mary Ann, reorders her priorities, thinks of the children, and worries for him. Her blood cools, as does his. It seems that the dispatcher's call is always saving them. Their marriage settles in and strengthens, afterward, like some healthy, living, supple thing.

She meets him at the door when he returns, kisses him. He is grimy — black, salt-stained, and smoky-smelling. They can't even remember what the argument was about. It's almost like a joke — the fact that they were upset about such a small thing, any small thing. He sheds his bunker gear in the utility room and goes straight to the shower. Later, they sit in the den by the fireplace and he drinks a few beers and tells her about the fire. Sometimes he'll talk about it till dawn. He knows he is lucky — he knows they are both lucky. As long as the city keeps burning, they can avoid becoming weary and numb. Always, he leaves, is drawn away, and then returns, to a second chance.

The children — a girl, four, and a boy, two — sleep soundly. It is not so much a city that they live in but a town — the suburbs on the perimeter of the city — and it could be nameless, so similar is it to so many other places: a city in the center of the southern half of the country, a place where it is warm more often than it is cold, so that the residents are not overly familiar with fires — the way a fire spreads from room to room, the way it takes only one small errant thing in a house to invalidate and erase the whole structure, to bring it all down to ashes and send the building's former occupants — the homeowners, or renters, or leasers — out wandering lost and adrift into the night, poorly dressed and without direction. They talk until dawn. She is his second wife; he is her first husband. Because they are in the suburbs, unincorporated, his is a volunteer department. Kirby's crew has a station with new equipment — all they could ask for — but there are no salaries, and he likes it that way; it keeps things purer. He has a day job as a computer programmer for an engineering firm that designs steel girders and columns used in industrial construction: warehouses, mills, and factories. The job means nothing to him: he slips along through the long hours of it with neither excitement nor despair, his pulse never rising, and when it is over each day he says goodbye to his coworkers and leaves the office without even the faintest echo of his work lingering in his blood. He leaves it all the way behind, or lets it pass through him like some harmless silver laxative.

But after a fire — holding a can of cold beer and sitting there next to the hearth, scrubbed clean, talking to Mary Ann, telling her what it had been like — what the cause had been, and who among his men had performed well, and who had not — his eyes water with pleasure at his knowing how lucky he is to be getting a second chance, with every fire.

He would never say anything bad about his first wife, Rhonda — and indeed, perhaps there is nothing bad to say, no fault or failing in which they were not both complicit. It almost doesn't matter; it's almost water under the bridge.

The two children asleep in their rooms; the swing set and jungle gym out in the back yard. The security of love and constancy — the *safety*. Mary Ann teaches the children's choir in church, and is as respected for her work with the children as Kirby is for his work with the fires.

It would seem like a fairy-tale story; a happy marriage, one that turned its deadly familiar course around early into the marriage, that day he signed up to be a volunteer for the fire department six years ago. One of those rare marriages, as rare as a jewel or a forest, that was saved by a combination of inner strength and the grace and luck of fortuitous external circumstances — *the world afire.* Who, given the chance, would not choose to leap across that chasm between a marriage that is heading toward numbness and tiredness and one that is instead strengthened, made more secure daily for its journey into the future?

And yet — even on the other side of the miracle, even on the other side of luck — a thing has been left behind. It's almost a perfect, happy story; it's just this side of it. The one thing behind them — the only thing — is his oldest daughter, his only child from his first marriage, Jenna. She's ten, almost eleven.

There is always excitement and mystery on a fire call. It's as if these things are held in solution, just beneath the skin of the earth, and are then released by the flames; as if the surface of the world, and the way things are, is some errant, artificial crust — almost like a scab — and that there are rivers of blood below, and rivers of fire, rivers of the way things used to be and might someday be again — true but mysterious, and full of power, rather than stale and crusty.

It does funny things to people — a fire, and that burning away of the thin crust. Kirby tells Mary Ann about two young men in their thirties — lovers, he thinks — who, bewildered and bereft as their house burned, went out into the front yard and began cooking hamburgers for the firefighters as the building burned down.

He tells her about the man with a house full of antiques that could not be salvaged. The attack crew was fighting the fire hard, deep in the building's interior — the building "fully involved," as they say to one another when the wood becomes flame, air becomes flame, world becomes flame. It is the thing the younger firemen live for — not a smoke alarm, lost kitten, or piddly grass fire but the real thing, a fully involved structure fire — and even the older firemen's hearts are lifted by the sight of one. Even those who have been thinking of retiring (at thirty-seven, Kirby is far and away the oldest man on the force) are made new again by the sight of it, and by the radiant heat, which curls and browns and sometimes even ignites the oak leaves of trees across the street from the fire. The paint of cars that are parked too close to the fire sometimes begins to blaze spontaneously, making it look as if the cars are traveling very fast . . .

Bats, which have been out hunting, begin to return in swarms, dancing above the flames, and begin flying in dark agitated funnels back down into the chimney of the house that's on fire, if it is not a winter fire — if the chimney has been dormant — trying to rescue their flightless young, which are roosting in the chimney, or sometimes the attic, or beneath the eaves. The bats all return to the house as it burns down, but no one ever sees any of them come back out. People stand around on the street, their faces orange in the firelight, and marvel, hypnotized at the sight of it, not understanding what is going on with the bats, or any of it; and drawn too like somnambulists to the scent of those blood rivers, those vapors of new birth that are beginning already to leak back into the world as that skin, that crust, is burned away.

The fires almost always happen at night.

This fire that Kirby is telling Mary Ann about, the one in which the house full of antiques was being lost, was one of the great fires of the year. The men work in teams, as partners, always within sight or one arm's length contact of one another, so that one can help the other if trouble is encountered — if the foundation gives way or a burning beam crashes across the back of one of the two partners, who are not always men; more and more women are volunteering, though none have yet joined Kirby's crew. He welcomes them, since from what he's seen from the multiple-alarm fires he's fought with crews in which there are women firefighters, the women tend to try to outthink rather than outmuscle the fire, which is almost always the best approach.

Kirby's partner now is a young man, Grady, just out of college. Kirby likes to use his intelligence when he fights a fire rather than just hurl himself at it and risk getting sucked too quickly into its born-again maw and becoming trapped — not just perishing in that manner, but possibly causing harm or death to those members of his crew who might then try to save him — and for this reason he likes to pair himself with the youngest, rawest, most adrenaline-rich trainees entrusted to his care, to act as an anchor of caution upon them, to counsel prudence and moderation, even as the world burns down around them.

The fire in the house of antiques — Kirby and Grady had just come out to rest, and to change oxygen tanks. The homeowner had at first been beside himself, shouting and trying to get back into his house, so that the fire marshal had had to restrain him —

he had the homeowner bound to a tree with a canvas strap — but now the homeowner was watching the flames almost as if hypnotized. Kirby and Grady were so touched by his change in demeanor, by his coming to his senses — the man wasn't struggling any longer, was instead only leaning slightly away from the tree, like the masthead on a ship's prow, and sagging slightly — that they cut him loose so that he could watch the spectacle of it in freedom, unencumbered.

He made no more moves to rejoin his burning house, only stood there with watery eyes — whether tears of anguish or irritation from the smoke, they could not tell — and, taking pity, Kirby and Grady put on new oxygen tanks, gulped down some water, and though they were supposed to rest, they went back into the burning building and began carrying out those pieces of furniture that had not yet ignited, and sometimes even those that had — burning breakfronts, flaming rolltop desks — and dropped them into the man's back-yard swimming pool for safekeeping, as the tall trees in the back yard crackled and flamed like giant candles, and floating embers drifted down, scorching whatever they touched; and the neighbors all around them climbed up onto their cedar-shingled roofs in their pajamas and with garden hoses began wetting down their own roofs, trying to keep the conflagration, the spectacle — the phenomenon — from spreading . . .

The business of it has made Kirby neat and precise. He and Grady crouched and lowered the dining room set carefully into the deep end (even as some of the pieces of furniture were still flickering with flame), releasing them to sink slowly, carefully to the bottom, settling in roughly the same manner and arrangement in which they had been positioned back in the burning house.

There is no longer any space or room for excess, unpredictability, or recklessness; these extravagances can no longer be borne, and Kirby wants Grady to see and understand this, and the sooner the better. The fire hoses must always be coiled in the same pattern, so that when unrolled, they can be counted upon; the female nozzle must always be nearest the truck, and the male farthest. The backup generators must always have fresh oil and gas in them and be kept in working order; the spanner wrenches must always hang in the same place.

The days go by in long stretches, twenty-three and a half hours at a time, but in that last half-hour, in the moment of fire, when all the

old rules melt down and the new world becomes flame, the importance of a moment, of a second, is magnified ten thousandfold —
is magnified to almost an eternity, and there is no room for even a
single mistake. Time inflates to a density greater than iron. You've
got to be able to go through the last half-hour, that wall of flame,
on instinct alone, or by force of habit, by rote, by feel.

An interesting phenomenon happens when time catches on fire
like this. It happens to even the veteran firefighters. A form of tunnel vision develops — the heart pounding two hundred times a
minute, and the pupils contracting so tightly that vision almost vanishes. The field of view becomes reduced to an area about the size
of another man's helmet, or face: his partner, either in front of or
behind him. If the men ever become separated by sight or sound,
they are supposed to freeze instantly and then begin swinging their
pikestaff or a free arm in all directions; and if their partner does
the same and is within one or even two arm's lengths, their arms
will bump one another, and they can continue — they can rejoin
the fight, as the walls flame vertical and the ceiling and floors melt
and fall away. The firefighters carry motion sensors on their hips,
which send out piercing electronic shrieks if the men stop moving
for more than thirty seconds. If one of those goes off, it means that
a firefighter is down — that he has fallen and injured himself or
has passed out from smoke inhalation — and all the firefighters
stop what they are doing and turn and converge on the sound, if
possible, centering back to it like the bats pouring back down into
the chimney.

A person's breathing accelerates inside a burning house — the
pulse leaps to over two hundred beats a minute — and the blood
heats, as if in a purge. The mind fills with a strange music. Sense of
feel and the memory of how things *ought* to be become everything;
it seems that even through the ponderous, fire-resistant gloves, the
firefighters could read Braille if they had to. As if the essence of all
objects exudes a certain clarity, just before igniting.

Everything in its place; the threads, the grain of the canvas weave
of the fire hoses, is canted such that it tapers back toward the male
nipples; if lost in a house fire, you can crouch on the floor and
with your bare hand — or perhaps even through the thickness of
your glove, in that hypertactile state — follow the hose back to its
source, back outside, to the beginning.

The ears — the lobes of the ear, specifically — are the most tem-

perature-sensitive part of the body. Many times the heat is so intense that the firefighters' suits begin smoking and their helmets
begin melting, while deep within, the firefighters are still insulated
and protected, but they are taught that if the lobes of their ears begin to feel hot, they are to get out of the building immediately —
that they themselves may be about to ignite.

It's intoxicating; it's addictive as hell.

The fire does strange things to people. Kirby tells Mary Ann that
it's usually the men who melt down first — who seem to lose their
reason sooner than the women. That particular fire in which they
sank all the man's prize antiques in the swimming pool in order
to save them — that man becalmed himself after he was released
from the tree (the top of which was flaming, dropping ember-
leaves into the yard, and even onto his shoulders, like fiery moths),
and he walked around into the back yard and stood next to his
pool, with his back turned toward the burning house, and began
busying himself with his long-handled dip net, laboriously skim-
ming — or endeavoring to skim — the ashes from the pool's surface.

Another time — a fire in broad daylight — a man walked out of
his burning house and went straight out to his greenhouse, which
he kept filled with flowering plants and where he held captive
twenty or more hummingbirds of various species. He was afraid
that the fire would spread to the greenhouse and burn up the
birds, so he closed himself in there and began spraying the little
birds down with the hose as they flitted and whirled from him, and
he kept spraying them, trying to keep their brightly colored wings
wet so they would not catch fire.

Kirby tells Mary Ann all of these stories — a new one each time he
returns — and they lie together on the couch until dawn. The
youngest baby, the boy, has just given up nursing; Kirby and Mary
Ann are just beginning to earn back moments of time together —
little five- and ten-minute wedges of time — and Mary Ann naps
with her head on his freshly showered shoulder, though in close
like that, at the skin level, she can still smell the charcoal, can taste
it. Kirby has scars across his neck and back, pockmarks where embers have landed and burned through his suit, and she, like the
children, likes to touch these; the small, slick feel of them is like

smooth stones from a river. Kirby earns several each year, and he says that before it is over, he will look like a Dalmatian. She does not ask him what he means by "when it is all over," and she holds back, reins back like a wild horse to keep from asking the question "When will you stop?" Everyone has fire stories. Mary Ann's is that when she was a child at her grandmother's house, she went into the bathroom and took off her robe, laid it over the plug-in portable electric heater, and sat on the commode; but as she did so, the robe quickly leapt into flame. The peeling old wallpaper caught on fire too — so much flame that she could not get past — and she remembers even now, twenty-five years later, how her father had to come in and lift her up and carry her back out, and how that fire was quickly, easily extinguished.

But that was a long time ago and she has her own life, needs no one to carry her in or out of anywhere. All that has gone away and vanished; her views of fire are not a child's but an adult's. Mary Ann's fire story is tame, it seems, compared to the rest of the world's.

She counts the slick, small oval scars on his back: twenty-two of them, like a pox. She knows he is needed. He seems to thrive on it. She remembers both the terror and the euphoria after her father whisked her out of the bathroom, as she looked back at it — at the dancing flames she had birthed. Is there greater power in lighting a fire or in putting one out?

He sleeps contentedly, there on the couch. She will not ask him — not yet. She will hold it in for as long as she can, and watch — some part of her desirous of his stopping, but another part not.

She feels as she imagines the street-side spectators must, or even the victims of the fires themselves, the homeowners and renters: a little hypnotized, a little transfixed; and there is a confusion, as if she could not tell you, or her children — could not be sure — whether she was watching him burn down to the ground or was watching him being born and built up, standing among the flames, like iron being cast from the earth.

She sleeps, her fingers light across his back. She dreams the twenty-two scars are a constellation in the night. She dreams that the more fires he fights, the safer and stronger their lives become.

She wants him to stop. She wants him to go on.

They awaken on the couch at dawn to the baby's murmurings from the other room, and soft sleep-breathings of their daughter, the four-year-old. The sun, orange already, rising above the city. Kirby gets up and dresses for work. He could do it in his sleep. It means nothing to him. It is its own form of sleep, and these moments on the couch and in the shells of the flaming buildings are their own form of wakefulness.

Some nights he goes over to Jenna's house — to the house of his ex-wife. No one knows he does this: not Mary Ann, and not his ex-wife, Rhonda, and certainly not Jenna — not unless she knows it in her sleep and in her dreams, which he hopes she does.

He wants to breathe her air; he wants her to breathe his. It is a biological need. He climbs up on the roof and leans over the chimney and listens — *silence* — and inhales, and exhales.

The fires usually come about once a week. The time spent between them is peaceful at first but then increasingly restless, until finally the dispatcher's radio sounds in the night, and Kirby is released. He leaps out of bed — he lives four blocks from the station — kisses Mary Ann, kisses his daughter and son sleeping in their beds, and then is out into the night, hurrying but not running across the lawn. He will be the first one there, or among the first, other than the young firemen who may already be hanging out at the station, watching movies and playing cards, just waiting.

Kirby gets in his car — the chief's car — and cruises the neighborhood slowly, savoring his approach. There's no need to rush and get to the station five or ten seconds sooner, when he'll have to wait another minute or two anyway for the other firemen to arrive.

It takes him only five seconds to slip on his bunker gear, ten seconds to start the truck and get it out of the driveway. There used to be such anxiety, getting to a fire: the tunnel vision beginning to constrict from the very moment he heard the dispatcher's voice. But now he knows how to save it, how to hold it at bay — that powerhousing of the heart, which now does not kick into life, does not come into being, until the moment Kirby comes around the corner and first sees the flames.

In her bed — in their bed — Mary Ann hears and feels the rumble of the big trucks leaving the station; hears and feels in her bones the belch of the air horns, and then the going-away sirens. She listens to the dispatcher's radio — hopefully it will remain silent after the first call, will not crackle again, calling more and more stations to the blaze. Hopefully it will be a small one, and containable.

She lies there, warm and in love with her life — with the blessing of her two children asleep there in her own house, in the other room, safe and asleep — and she tries to imagine the future: tries to picture being sixty years old, seventy, and then eighty. How long — and of that space or distance ahead, what lies within it?

Kirby gets her — Jenna — on Wednesday nights, and on every other weekend. On the weekends, if the weather is good, he sometimes takes her camping and lets the assistant chief cover for him. Kirby and Jenna cook over an open fire; they roast marshmallows. They sleep in sleeping bags in a meadow beneath stars. When he was a child, Kirby used to camp in this meadow with his father and grandfather, and there would be lightning bugs at night, but those are gone now.

On Wednesday nights — Kirby has to have her back at Rhonda's by ten — they cook hamburgers, Jenna's favorite food, on the grill in the back yard. This one constancy — this one thing, small, even tiny, like a sacrament. The diminishment of their lives shames him, especially for her, she for whom the whole world should be widening and opening rather than constricting already.

She plays with the other children, the little children, afterward, all of them keeping one eye on the clock. She is quiet, inordinately so — thrilled just to be in the presence of her father, beneath his huge shadow; she smiles shyly whenever she notices that he is watching her. And how can she not be wondering why it is, when it's time to leave, that the other two children get to stay?

He drives her home cheerfully, steadfastly, refusing to let her see or even sense his despair. He walks her up the sidewalk to Rhonda's like a guest. He does not go inside.

By Saturday — if it is the off-weekend on which he does not have her — he is up on the roof again, trying to catch the scent of her from the chimney; and sometimes he falls asleep up there, in a brief catnap, as if watching over her and standing guard.

A million times he plays it over in his mind. Could I have saved the marriage? Did I give it absolutely every last ounce of effort? Could I have saved it?

No. Maybe. *No.*

*

It takes a long time to get used to the fires; it takes the young firemen, the beginners, a long time to understand what is required: that they must suit up and walk right on into a burning house.

They make mistakes. They panic, breathe too fast, and use up their oxygen. It takes a long time. It takes a long time before they calm down and meet the fires on their own terms, and the fire's.

In the beginning, they all want to be heroes. Even before they enter their first fire, they will have secretly placed their helmets in the ovens at home to soften them up a bit — to dull and char and melt them slightly, so anxious are they for combat and its validations, its contract with their spirit. Kirby remembers the first house fire he entered. His initial reaction was "You mean I'm going in *that?*" But enter it he did, fighting it from the inside out with huge volumes of water, the water sometimes doing as much damage as the fire, his new shiny suit yellow and clean among the work-darkened suits of the veterans . . .

Kirby tells Mary Ann that after that fire he drove out into the country and set a little grass fire, a little pissant one that was in no danger of spreading, then put on his bunker gear and spent all afternoon walking around in it, dirtying his suit to just the right color of anonymity.

You always make mistakes, in the beginning. You can only hope that they are small or insignificant enough to carry little, if any, price — that they harm no one. Kirby tells Mary Ann that on one of his earliest house fires, he was riding in one of the back seats of the fire engine so that he was facing backward. He was already packed up — bunker gear, air mask, and scuba tank — so that he couldn't hear or see well, and was nervous as hell; and when they got to the house that was on fire — a fully involved, "working" fire — the truck screeched to a stop across the street from it. The captain leapt out and yelled to Kirby that the house across the street was on fire.

Kirby could see the flames coming out of the first house, but he took the captain's orders to mean that it was the house across the street from the house on fire that he wanted Kirby to attack — that it too must be burning — and so while the main crew thrust itself into the first burning house, laying out attack lines and hoses and running up the hook-and-ladder, Kirby fastened his own hose to the other side of the truck and went storming across the yard and into the house across the street.

He assumed there was no one in it, but as he turned the knob on the front door and shoved his weight against it, the two women who lived inside opened it so that he fell inside, knocking one of them over and landing on her.

Kirby tells Mary Ann that it was the worst he ever got the tunnel vision; that it was like running along a tightrope; that it was almost like being blind. They are on the couch again, in the hours before dawn; she's laughing. Kirby couldn't see flames anywhere, he tells her — his vision reduced to a space about the size of a pinhead — so he assumed the fire was up in the attic. He was confused as to why his partner was not yet there to help him haul his hose up the stairs. Kirby says that the women were protesting, asking why he was bringing the hose into their house. He did not want to have to take the time to explain to them that the most efficient way to fight a fire is from the inside out. He told them to just be quiet and help him pull. This made them so angry that they pulled extra hard — so hard that Kirby, straining at the top of the stairs now, was bowled over again.

When he opened the attic door, he saw that there were no flames. There was a dusty window in the attic, and out it he could see the flames of the house across the street, really rocking now, going under. Kirby says that he stared at it a moment and then asked the ladies if there was a fire anywhere in their house. They replied angrily that there was not.

He had to roll the hose back up — he left sooty hose- and footprints all over the carpet — and by this time the house across the street was so engulfed, and in so great a hurry was Kirby to reach it, that he began to hyperventilate and blacked out there in the living room of the nonburning house.

He got better, of course — learned his craft, his calling better, learned it well in time. No one was hurt. But there is still a clumsiness in his heart, in all of their hearts — the echo and memory of it — that is not that distant. They're all just fuckups, like anyone else, even in their uniforms, even in their fire-resistant gear. You can bet that any of them who come to rescue you or your home have problems that are at least as large as yours. You can count on that. There are no real rescuers.

Kirby tells her about what he thinks was his best moment of grace — his moment of utter, breathtaking, thanks-giving luck. It happened when he was still a lieutenant, leading his men into an apartment fire. Apartments were the worst, because of the confusion; there was always a greater risk of losing an occupant in an apartment fire, simply because there were so many of them. The awe and mystery of making a rescue — the holiness of it, like a birth — is in no way balanced by the despair of finding an occupant who's already died, a smoke or burn victim, and if that victim is a child, the firefighter is never the same and almost always has to retire after that; his or her marriage goes bad, and life is never the same, never has deep joy and wonder to it again . . . The men and women spend all their time and energy fighting the enemy, *fire* — fighting the way it consumes structures, consumes air, consumes darkness — but then when it takes a life, it is as if some threshold has been crossed — it is for the firemen who discover that victim a feeling like falling down an elevator shaft, and there is sometimes guilt too, that the thing they were so passionate about, fighting fire — a thing that could be said to bring them relief, if not pleasure — should have this as one of its costs . . .

They curse stupidity, curse mankind, when they find a victim, and are almost forever after brittle rather than supple . . .

This fire, the apartment fire, had no loss of occupants, no casualties. It was fully involved by the time Kirby got his men into the structure, Christmas Eve, and they were doing room-to-room searches. No one ever knows how many people live in an apartment complex: how many men, women, and children, coming and going. It can never be accounted for. They had to check every room.

Smoke detectors — thank God! — were squawling everywhere, though that only confused the men further — the sound slightly less piercing than but similar to the motion sensors on their hip belts, so that they were constantly looking around in the smoke and heat to be sure that they were all still together, partner with partner.

Part of the crew fought the blazes while the others made searches: horrible searches, for many of the rooms were burning so intensely that if they did still house an occupant, no rescue could be made, and indeed, the casualties would already have occurred . . .

You can jab a hole in the fire hose at your feet if you get trapped by the flames. You can activate your ceased-motion sensor. The water will spew up from the hose, spraying out of the knife hole like an umbrella of steam and moisture — a water shield, which will buy you ten or fifteen more seconds. You crouch low, sucking on your scuba gear, and wait, if you can't get out. They'll come get you if they can.

This fire — the one with no casualties, the one with grace — had all the men stumbling with tunnel vision. There was something different about this fire — they would talk about it afterward — that they could sense as no one else could: that it was almost as if the fire wanted them, had laid a trap for them.

They were all stumbling and clumsy, but still they checked the rooms. Loose electrical wires dangled from the burning walls and from crumbling, flaming ceilings. The power had been shut off, but it was every firefighter's fear that some passerby, well-meaning, would see the breakers thrown and would flip them back on, unthinking.

The hanging, sagging wires trailed over the backs of the men like tentacles as they passed beneath them. The men blew out walls with their pickaxes, ventilated the ceilings with savage maulings from their lances. Trying to sense, *to feel*, amid the confusion, where someone might be — a survivor — if anyone was left.

Kirby and his partner went into the downstairs apartment of a trophy big-game hunter. It was a large apartment — a suite — and on the walls were the stuffed heads of various animals from all over the world. Some of the heads were already ablaze — flaming rhinos, burning gazelles — and as Kirby and his partner entered, boxes of ammunition began to go off: shotgun shells and rifle bullets, whole caseloads of them. Shots were flying in all directions, and Kirby made the decision right then to pull his men from the fire.

In thirty seconds he had them out — still the fusillade continued — and thirty seconds after that the whole second floor collapsed: an inch-and-a-half-thick flooring of solid concrete dropped like a fallen cake down to the first floor, crushing the space where the men had been half a minute earlier, and the building folded in on itself after that and was swallowed by itself, by its fire.

There was a grand piano in the lobby, and somehow it was not entirely obliterated when the ceiling fell, so that a few crooked, clanging tunes issued forth as the rubble shifted, settled, and burned; and still the shots kept firing.

No casualties. They all went home to their families that night.

Grace. One year Rhonda tells Kirby that she is going to Paris with her new fiancé for two weeks and asks if Kirby can keep Jenna for that time. His eyes sting with happiness — with the unexpected grace and blessing of it. Two weeks of clean air, a gift from out of nowhere. A thing that was his and taken away, now brought back. This must be what it feels like to be rescued, he thinks.

Mary Ann thinks often of how hard it is for him — she thinks of it almost every time she sees him with Jenna, reading to her or helping her with something — and they discuss it often, but even at that, even in Mary Ann's great lovingness, she underestimates it. She thinks she wants to know the full weight of it, but she has no true idea. It transcends words, spills over into his actions, and still she, Mary Ann, cannot know the bottom of it.

Kirby dreams ahead to when Jenna is eighteen; he dreams of re-uniting. He continues to take catnaps on the roof by her chimney. The separation from her betrays and belies his training; it is greater than an arm's length distance.

The counselors tell him never to let Jenna see this franticness — this gutted, hollow, gasping feeling. To treat it as casual.

As if wearing blinders, unsure of whether the counselors are right or not, he does as they suggest. He thinks that they are probably right. He knows the horrible dangers of panic.

And in the meantime, the new marriage strengthens, becomes more supple and resilient than ever. Arguments cease to be even arguments anymore, merely pulsings of blood, lung-breaths, differences of opinion, like the sun moving in its arc across the sky, or the stars wheeling into place — the earth spinning, rather, and allowing these things to be scribed into place. It becomes a marriage as strong as a galloping horse, reinforced by the innumerable fires and by the weave of his comings and goings, and by the passion of it. His frantic attempts to keep drawing clean air are good for the body of the marriage.

Kirby and Mary Ann are both sometimes amazed by how fast time is going by. She worries about the fifteen or twenty years she's heard get cut off the back end of all firefighters' lives: all those years of sucking in chemicals — burning rags, burning asbestos, burning formaldehyde — but still she does not ask him to stop.

The cinders continue to fall across his back like meteors: twenty-four scars, twenty-five, twenty-six. She knows she could lose him. But she knows he will be lost for sure without the fires.

She prays in church for his safety. Sometimes she forgets to listen to the service and instead gets lost in her prayers. Her eyes blur upon the votive candles. It's as if she's being led out of a burning building herself: as if she's remaining calm and gentle, as someone — her rescuer, perhaps — has instructed her to do.

She forgets to listen to the service. She finds herself instead holding in her heart the secrets he has told her, the things she knows about fires that no one else around her knows.

The way light bulbs melt and lean or point toward a fire's origin — the gases in incandescent bulbs seeking, sensing that heat, so that you can often use them to tell where a fire started, the direction in which the light bulbs first began to lean.

A baby is getting baptized up at the altar, but Mary Ann is still in some other zone — she's still praying for Kirby's safety, his survival. The water being sprinkled on the baby's head reminds her of the men's water shields, of the umbrella mist of spray that buys them extra time, time on earth.

As he travels through town to and from his day job, he begins to define the space around him by the fires that have visited it and that he has engaged and battled. The individual buildings — some charred husks, others intact — begin to link together in his mind. *I rescued that one, there, and that one,* he thinks. *That one.* The city becomes a tapestry, a weave of that which he has saved and that which he has not, with the rest of the city becoming simply all that which is between points, waiting to burn.

He glides through his work at the office. If he were hollow inside, the work would take a thing from him, would suck something out of him, but he is not hollow, is only asleep, like some cast-iron statue from the century before. Whole days pass without his being able to account for them. Sometimes at night, lying there with Mary Ann, both of them listening for the dispatcher, he cannot recall whether he even went into the office that day or not.

He wonders what she is doing, what she is dreaming of. He rises and goes in to check on his other children — simply to look at them.

*

When you rescue people from a burning building, the strength of their terror and panic is unimaginable: enough to bend iron bars. The smallest, weakest persons can strangle and overwhelm the burliest. They will always defeat you. There is a drill that the firemen go through on their hook-and-ladder trucks — mock-rescuing someone from a window ledge or the top of a burning building. Kirby picks the strongest fireman to go up on the ladder and then demonstrates how easily he can make the fireman — vulnerable up on that ladder — lose his balance. It's always staged, of course — the fireman is roped to the ladder for safety — but it makes a somber impression on the young recruits watching from below: the big man being pushed backward by one foot, or one hand, and falling backward and dangling, the rescuer suddenly in need of rescuing.

You can see it in their eyes, Kirby tells them, speaking of those who panic. You can see them getting all wall-eyed. The victims-to-be look almost normal, but then their eyes start to cross just a little. It's as if they're generating such strength within, such *torque,* that it's causing their eyes to act weird. So much torque that it seems they'll snap in half — or snap you in half, if you get too close to them.

Kirby counsels distance to the younger firemen. Let the victims climb onto the ladder by themselves when they're like that. Don't let them touch you. They'll break you in half. You can see the torque in their eyes.

Mary Ann knows all this. She knows it will always be this way for him — but she does not draw back. Twenty-seven scars, twenty-eight. He does not snap; he becomes stronger. She'll never know what it's like, and for that, she's glad.

Many nights he runs a fever, for no apparent reason. Some nights it is his radiant heat that awakens her. She wonders what it will be like when he is too old to go out on the fires. She wonders if she and he can survive that: the not going.

There are days when he does not work at his computer. He turns the screen on but then goes over to the window for hours at a time and turns his back on the computer. He's up on the twentieth floor. He watches the flat horizon for smoke. The wind gives a slight sway, a slight tremor to the building.

Sometimes — if he has not been to a fire recently enough —

Kirby imagines that the soles of his feet are getting hot. He allows himself to consider this sensation — he does not tune it out.

He stands motionless — still watching the horizon, looking and hoping for smoke — and feels himself igniting, but makes no movement to still or stop the flames. He simply burns, and keeps breathing in, detached, as if it is some structure other than his own that is aflame and vanishing; as if he can keep the two separate — his good life, and the one he left behind.

PETER HO DAVIES

Think of England

FROM PLOUGHSHARES

ON THE EVENING OF D-DAY, the pub is packed. It's a close June night in the Welsh hills, with the threat of thunder. The radios of the village cough with static. The Quarryman's Arms, with the tallest aerial for miles around, is a scrum of bodies, all waiting to hear the prime minister's broadcast.

There's a flurry of shouted orders leading up to the news at six. Sarah, behind the lounge bar, pulls pint after pint, leaning back against the pumps so that the beer froths in the glass. She sets the shaker out for those who want to sprinkle salt on their drinks to melt the foam. Behind her, down the short connecting passage to the right, her boss, Jack Jones, has his hands full with the regulars in the public bar. At five to six by the battered grandfather clock in the corner, he calls back to the lounge for Sarah to "warm 'er up." She tops off the pint she's pouring, steps back from the counter and up onto the old pop crate beneath the till. She has to stretch for the Bakelite knob on the wireless, one foot lifting off the crate. Behind her, over the calls for service, she hears a few low whistles. The machine clicks into life, first a low hum, then a whistle of its own, finally, as if from afar, the signature tune of the show. The dial lights up like a distant sunset. The noise around her subsides at once, and it's as if she has stilled it. She turns round and for a second looks down into the crowd of faces staring up at the glowing radio.

The men, soldiers mostly in the lounge, sip their beers slowly during the broadcast, making them last. She looks from face to face, but they're all gazing off, concentrating on Churchill's shuffling growl. The only ones to catch her eyes are Harry Hitch, who's mouthing something over and over — "my usual," she finally understands — and Colin, who winks broadly from across the room. Colin's one of the sappers who've been working on the new base they're building near the old holiday camp in the valley. They've been bringing some much-needed business to the Arms for the last month, and for the last week Sarah and Colin have been sweethearts. Tonight she's agreed to slip off with him after work, a date made before D-Day, which somehow feels destined now. She hears the English word in her mind, "sweethearts," likes the way it sounds. She listens to Churchill, the voice of England, imagines him saying it gravely — "Sweetheart" — swallows a smile. She concentrates on the speech, thinks of the men on the beaches, and feels herself fill with emotion for her soldier, like a slow glass of Guinness. There's a thickening in her throat, a brimming pressure behind her eyes. It's gratitude, she feels, mixed with pride and hope, and she wonders if together this blend amounts to love.

The broadcast ends, and the noise builds again in the pub. It's not quite a cheer — Churchill's speech has been sternly cautious — but there's a sense of excitement, kept just in check, and a kind of relief. The talk has been about an invasion all spring, and finally it's here, the beginning of the end. Everyone is smiling at the soldiers, even the locals clustered behind the public bar, and calling congratulations. Sarah steps up on the crate and turns the dial until it picks up faint dance music from the Savoy in London. There's a sound like applause, and looking round, she sees with delight that it's literally a clapping of backs. There's a rush for the bar again. People want to buy the men drinks. They're only sappers — road menders, ditch diggers, brickies — but they're in uniform, and who knows when they could be going "over there." Suddenly, and without doing a thing, they're heroes, indistinguishable in their uniforms from all the other fighting men. And they believe it too. Sarah can see it in Colin's face, the glow of it. She stares at him, and it's as if she's seeing him for the first time; he's so glossily handsome, like the lobby card of a film star.

The crowd in the lounge is three deep and thirsty, and she pulls pints until her arm aches, but when she turns to ring up the orders she sees that the public bar is emptying out. She wonders if it's the sense of its being someone else's party that's sending the farmers home or just that they have to be up early tomorrow. She glimpses her father, Arthur, shouldering his way to the door, shrugging his mac on over the frayed dark suit (Sunday best before she was born) and collarless shirt he wears when out with the flock. He jams his cap on his head, fitting it to the dull red line across his brow, and gives her a nod as he goes, but no more.

She's been working here for almost a year now, since she turned sixteen, but in all that time she has never once served him on his occasional visits. He sticks to the public bar, where most of the local regulars are served by Jack. It's become the Welsh-speaking half of the pub, while she, with her good schoolroom English, serves soldiers and the motley assortment of new arrivals in the lounge. She would stand him a pint or two if he let her (Jack wouldn't mind), although it occurs to her that this is why her father steers clear. They could do with saving even the few pennies he spends on beer — money is why she's working here at all — but of course that's why he barely acknowledges her. It's not that he's ungrateful, she knows. She's been in charge of the housekeeping money in the old biscuit tin ever since her mother died three years ago, but only since she started working has he shown her the books, the bank account, the mortgage deeds. It's a mark of respect, his only way of offering thanks. Of course, she had her own ideas of how bad things were all along, but guessing and knowing are different and now she knows: the war is holding them up — the national subsidy and the demand for woolen uniforms. Her father is a proud man — prouder in hard times than good, she thinks — and she's grateful that poverty in wartime is a virtue, something to be proud of. It reminds her of the epic tales he tells of the great strike, though he was only a boy then. But she wonders sometimes, also, what it'll be like when the war is over.

It crosses her mind that the same thought has sent him out into the night early. Still, she's not sorry to see him go, not with Colin here too. She doesn't want to face any awkward questions, and she doesn't want to tell the truth: that she's stepping out with an Englishman. She catches sight of Colin through the crowd, dipping his shoulders to throw a dart. Beneath the national betrayal is an obscurer one to do with her pride at taking her mother's place beside her father; a sense of being unfaithful somehow.

Pretty soon the pub is down to just soldiers and diehards. She can hear the Welsh voices behind her, wafting over with the smell of pipe tobacco. They're quieter tonight, slower, sluggish like a summer stream. The talk for once isn't politics. This is a nationalist village, passionately so. It's what holds the place together. Like a cracked and glued china teapot, Sarah thinks. The strike, all of forty-five years ago, almost broke the town, and it's taken something shared to stick back together the families of men who returned to work and those who stayed out. The Quarryman's Arms is the old strikers' pub; the hooks for their tankards are still in the ceiling over the bar — a bitter little irony, since most of its regulars, the sons of strikers, are sheep farmers now. Their fathers weren't taken back at the quarry after the strike, blacklisted from the industry. For a generation the families of strikers and scabs didn't talk, didn't marry, didn't pray together. Even today the sons of scabs are scarce in the Arms, only venturing up the High Street from *their* local, the Prince of Wales, for fiercely competitive darts and snooker matches (games the soldiers have monopolized since they arrived).

To Sarah it seems like so much tosh, especially now that the quarry is cutting back and barely one in five local men work there. But the old people all seem to agree that the village would have died if not for the resurgence of nationalism in the twenties and thirties, reminding them of what they had in common, reminding them of their common enemy: the English. Dragoons were stationed here to keep order during the strike, and in the public bar the sappers are still called "occupiers." It's half joking, Sarah knows, but only half. The nationalist view of the war is that it's an English war, imperialist, capitalist, like the Great War that Jack fought in and from which he still carries a limp. But tonight the success of the invasion has stilled such talk. Even the laughter of the locals — raucous, intended to be heard in the lounge by the English, to make them understand that they are the butt of jokes even if the language of the jokes themselves is beyond them — is muted. The Welsh nurse their beer, suck their pipes, and steal glances down the passage to where Sarah is serving.

It thrills her, oddly, to stand between the two groups of men, listening to their talk about each other. For she knows the soldiers, clustered around the small round tables, crammed shoulder to shoulder into the narrow wooden settles, talk about the Welsh too: complain about the weather, joke about the language, whisper about the girls. Tonight they lounge around, legs splayed, collars open, like so many conquerors.

Sarah wonders if the locals are as filled with excitement as she is, just too proud to admit it. She yearns to be British tonight of all nights. She's proud of her Welshness, of course, in the same half-conscious way she's shyly proud of her looks, but she's impatient with all the talk of past glories. Her father is a staunch nationalist. He's never forgiven Churchill for Tonypandy. But she's bored by all the history. Some part of her knows that nationalism is part and parcel of provincialism. This corner of North Wales feels a long way from the center of life, from London or Liverpool or, heavens, America. And nationalism is a way of putting it back in the center, of saying that what's here is important enough. It's a redrawing of the boundaries of what's worthwhile. And this really is what Sarah wants, what she dimly suspects they all want. To be important, to be the center of attention, not isolated. Which is why she's so excited, as she moves through the crowd collecting empties, stacking them up, glass on glass in teetering piles, by the presence of the soldiers, by the relocation of the BBC Light Program a few years ago, by the museum treasures that are stored in the old quarry workings, even by the school-age evacuees. They're all refugees from the Blitz, but she doesn't care. It's as if the world is coming to her.

And she knows others feel this. The sappers are a case in point. No one quite knows who the base they're building is for, but speculation is rife. The village boys, who haunt the camp, watching the sappers from the tree line and sneaking down to explore the building at dusk, are praying for the glamour of commandos. There's talk of Free French, Poles, even alpine troops training in the mountains for the invasion of Norway. Jack is hoping for Yanks and their ready cash. American fliers, waiting to move on to their bases in East Anglia, do occasionally drop in for a drink. But they're always faintly disappointing. Each time they're spotted sauntering around Caernarvon, getting their photos taken under the Eagle Tower, rumors start that it's James Stewart or Tyrone Power, one of those gallant film stars. But it never is. For the most part the Yanks are gangly, freckle-faced farm boys, insufferably polite (in the opinion of the local lads) with their suck-up "sirs" and "ma'ams." Once, one of them, a tail-gunner from "Kentuck," pressed a clumsily wrapped parcel of brown paper and string on Sarah, and when she opened it she saw it was a torn parachute. There was enough silk for a petti-coat and two slips. He'd been drinking shyly in a corner for hours, summoning up his courage. She was worried he'd get into trouble, tried to give the bundle back, but he spread his hands, backed away. "Miss," he told her, and he said it with such drunken earnest-ness, she pulled the parcel back, held it to her chest. He seemed to be hunting for the words. "You . . . ," he began. "Why, you're what we're fighting for!" She's dreamed of him since, getting shot down, bailing out, hanging in the night sky, sliding silently toward the earth, under a canopy of petticoats.

She wonders if Colin will give her a gift before he leaves. She watches him lean against one of his fellows, cocking his head as the other whispers something in his ear. Colin shakes his head, grins beneath his mustache like Clark Gable, taps the side of his nose. She could get him to tell her who the camp is for, she thinks, but she won't. Somehow it would be unpatriotic to ask the sappers themselves what they're building: disloyal to Britain (they all know the slogans — walls have ears, loose lips, etc.), but also, more ob-scurely, disloyal to Wales. It wouldn't do to give the English an ex-cuse to call the Welsh unpatriotic. Only the Welsh, it occurs to her, are allowed to declare themselves that. But whatever the purpose of the new camp, with its long, low barracks and staunch wire fences, there's been a sense in the village over the last month of being part of something, of the preparations for the invasion (although it's odd, she thinks, that here's the invasion itself, and the camp not oc-cupied). Colin, though, has told her, during one of their hurried trysts behind the pub, that the work's nearly over. "Just waiting for our marching orders, and then we're off out of it."

She looks at him now leaning against one of the stained wood beams, chatting with his mates; the dark, cropped hair at the nape of his neck, where it shows almost velvety below his cap. He laughs at something and throws a glance over his shoulder to see if she's heard, and they grin at each other. She sees other heads turn to-ward her, and she looks away quickly. She is wearing one of her parachute-silk slips tonight, beneath her long wool skirt; she likes the feel of it against her legs, the way it slides when she stretches for a glass, while the soldiers are watching her.

The moment is interrupted by Harry Hitch. "Girlie?" he croons. "Another round, eh? There's a good girl." He's trying to wind her up, and she ignores him as she pours. Harry's with the BBC. He's a star, if you can believe it, a comic with the Light Program. "Auntie," as she's learned to call the corporation from Harry and the others, has a transmitter tower on the hillside above the quarry; the radio technicians discovered the Arms when they were building the tower, and they've been coming up of an evening with their "chums" ever since, six or eight of them squeezed into a battered, muddy Humber.

She sets a scotch before him and then a pint, what Harry calls a "little and large." The glasses sit side by side like a double act.

"Nice atmosphere tonight," Harry is saying. "Lovely ambulance." It's a joke of some kind, Sarah knows, but when no one laughs, Harry chuckles to himself. "I kill meself," he says. He's already half gone, she sees, must have had a skinful even before he arrived. Sarah has listened to Harry on the radio, laughed at his skits, but in the flesh he's a disappointment, a miserable, moody drunk, skinny and pinched-looking, not the broad, avuncular bloke she imagined from his voice.

"Ta," he tells her, raising his glass. "See your lot are celebrating tonight too."

"My lot?" she asks absently, distracted by a wink from Colin.

"The Welsh," he says, with a slight slur. "The Taffs, the Taffys, the boyos!" He gets louder with each word, not shouting, just projecting, and as soon as he has an audience he's off, as if on cue. "Here, you know we English have trouble with your spelling. All them *l*'s and *y*'s. But did you hear the one about Taffy who joined the RAF? He meant to join the NAAFI, but his spelling let him down." Sarah only smiles, but there's a smattering of laughter at the bar. Harry half turns on his stool, rocking slightly, to take in the soldiers, their shining faces. "You like that one, eh? On his first day the quartermaster hands him his parachute and Taff wants to know what happens if it don't open, and the quartermaster, he tells him, 'That's what's called jumping to a conclusion.'"

More laughter, not much but enough, Sarah sees with a sinking feeling, for a few more heads to turn. She catches the eye of Mary Munro, the actress. "Here we go," Mary mouths, rolling her eyes. Mary's thing is accents; she can do dozens of them. Once she even did Sarah's just for a laugh, and listening at home, Sarah blushed to the tips of her ears, more flattered than embarrassed.

"Oh, but they're brave," Harry is going. "The Taffs. Oh yes. Did you hear about that Welsh kamikaze, though? Got the VC for twenty successful missions. But he's worried, you know. His luck can't hold. Sure he'll cop it one day, so he goes to the chaplain and tells him what he wants on his headstone." He drops into a thick Welsh accent. "'Here lies an honest man and a Welshman.' And the chaplain says he doesn't know what it's like in Wales, but in England it's one bloke to a hole."

The men are all laughing now, stopping their conversations to listen. The snooker players straighten up from the table, lean on their cues, like shepherds on crooks. "Come on, Harry," Mary calls. "It's supposed to be our night off." But she's booed down by the soldiers, and Harry rolls on, unfazed.

"Reminds me of the tomb of the Welsh Unknown Soldier. Didn't know there was a Welsh Unknown Soldier, did you?" He winks at Sarah. "Nice inscription on that one an' all: 'Here lies Taff So-and-So, well known as a drunk, unknown as a soldier.'"

"Takes one to know one," someone heckles from the public bar behind Sarah, but the delivery is halting, the accent broad and blunt. It's water off a duck's back to Harry.

"'Well-known drunk, unknown soldier,'" Harry repeats happily. "That reminds me," he cries, and gestures for Sarah to refill him.

"Haven't you had enough?" She's aware of the silence in the bar behind her, the listening locals.

"As the sheep said to the Welshman?"

"Very funny," she tells him.

"Oh, you Welsh girls," he says, wagging his finger. "You know what they say about Welsh girls, dontcha, girlie?"

"No," she says, suddenly abashed.

"Give over, Harry." It's Mary again, her voice lower this time, warning.

"'Sonly a bit of fun. And she wants to know, don't she? You want to know?"

Sarah is silent.

"Well, what they say is, you can't kiss a Welsh girl unexpectedly." He pauses for a second to drink. When he looks up his lips are wet. "Only sooner than she thought!" There's a stillness in the bar. Harry shoots his cuffs, studies his watch theatrically. "I can wait," he says.

He turns back, and Sarah throws his scotch in his face.

There's a second of shock, and then Harry licks his lips with his big pink tongue, and the laughter goes off like a gun. There's a cheer from the public bar, and she's conscious of Jack standing in the passage behind her.

"Steady on," Colin is shouting over the din. He's shouldered his way to the bar. "You all right?" he asks Sarah, and she nods.

"No hard feelings," Harry is telling her. He holds out his hand for a shake, but when she reaches for it, he raises his empty glass and tells her, "Ta very much. I'd love one."

"Come on, mate," Colin says. "Leave it now." He lays a big hand on the dented brass bar rail in front of Sarah.

Harry looks at his hand for a long moment and then says flatly, "Did you hear this one, *mate?* Do you know it? About the Welsh girl? Her boyfriend gave her a watchcase? Tell me if you've heard it before, won't you?"

Colin sighs. "I haven't. And I don't want to."

"Really? You might learn something. She was right chuffed with that present, she was. I asked her why. A watchcase? Know what she told me? 'He's promised me the works tonight.'"

Colin shakes his head, puts down his pint. Sarah sees that his mustache is flecked with froth.

"Colin," she says softly.

"The works, sunshine. D'you get it? Penny dropped, 'as it? Tickety-tock. I can wait. All night, I promise you."

"You're asking for it, you are."

"All we're doing is telling a few jokes. Asking for it? I don't think I know that one, though. Is there a *punch*line to it? Is there?"

Jack is there (limp or no limp, he's quick down the length of a bar), his huge arms reaching over to clamp round Colin before he can swing, but somehow Harry still ends up on the threadbare carpet. He leans back on the stool, trying to anticipate the blow, and he's gone, spilling backward. It's a pratfall, and after a second the bar dissolves in laughter again. Jack squeezes Colin once, hard enough to drive the breath out of him. Sarah hears him say, "Not here, lad, *nargois,*" and then he releases him quickly. Colin shrugs, takes a gulp of air, glances at Sarah, and joins in the general laughter.

Harry is helped up by Mary and Tony, one of the sound engineers. "Up you come," Mary tells him. "And they say you can't do slapstick. You're wasted on radio, you are."

"Always told you scotch was my favorite topple," Harry mutters.

Mary leans across to Sarah and says loudly, "Never mind, luv. All you need to know about Englishmen, Welshmen, or Germans, for that matter, is they're all men. And you know what they say about men: one thing on their minds . . . and one hand on their things." There's a round of whistles from the crowd. "Always leave 'em laughing, eh." She grins at Sarah. She turns Harry toward the exit, but at the door he wheels round and lunges over, almost taking her and Tony down in a drunken bow.

"Ladies and gentlement. I thank you." There's a smattering of sarcastic applause, and when it dies out only Colin is clapping, slowly.

"Piss off," he calls. Sarah wishes he'd drop it now. In his own clumsy way, he's trying to be gallant, she knows, but there's an edge of bullying to it.

Harry tries to shake himself loose, but Mary and Tony cling on. "I did see a bloke in here once," he says, "with a terrible black eye."

"Looking in the mirror, was you?" Colin shouts.

"Actually, no. He was a soldier, this fellow. Told me he'd been fighting for his girlfriend's honor. Know what I said to him?"

"Bloody hell!"

"I said," Harry bawls over him, "it looked like she wanted to keep it."

He's red-faced and suddenly exhausted, and Mary and Tony take their chance to frog-march him out.

Over Mary's shoulder he gives the room a limp victory V-sign as he's carried out, and over Tony's arm flashes a quick two fingers at Colin.

And then he's gone, dragged out into the darkness.

"Sorry about that," Colin says, and Sarah tells him quickly it's fine. She needs the job. She doesn't need customers fighting over her. Her English is supposed to be good enough to talk her way out of situations.

"You shouldn't have to put up with it," he goes on, but she shrugs. She's conscious of Jack still keeping an eye out behind her. It's a small village. She doesn't want talk.

"Anyhow," she says, "thank you, sir."

"Don't mention it, miss," he tells her, getting it finally, but still a little peeved.

She wipes down the bar, drops Harry's dirty glasses in the sink. She finds herself feeling a little sorry for the old soak after all. Mary has told her that his wife was killed in the Blitz. An incendiary. "You wouldn't think to look at him, but it was true love." It makes Sarah wonder. She's heard Harry telling jokes about his wife on the show: the missus; her-in-doors; his trouble and strife. "Show*biz!*" Mary told her with a grim, exaggerated brightness. "The show must go on and all that."

The clock strikes ten-thirty. *"Amser, gwr bonheddig. Amser boddio,"* Jack cries, clanging the bell behind her, and Sarah chimes in: "Time, gents. Last orders, please."

She rinses glasses while Jack locks up, pouring the dregs away, twisting each glass once around the bristly scrub brush. They come out of the water with a little belch, and she sets them on the rack. Normally she'd stay to dry and polish them, but Jack says it's enough. "Only gonna get dirty again tomorrow," he tells her. "Gerroff with you." He reaches over her and switches off the radio, and she realizes, with a little flush, that she's been swaying to the muted band music.

"It's all right," she says. "I'll see to these." But he takes the towel from her and nods at the door. She wonders if he knows.

"Long night," he says, handing on her coat. "Get you home."

Colin is waiting for her round the corner.

"Eh up!" he calls softly, appearing from the shadows of the hedge and pulling her to him. He'd been waiting for her here one night last week, when they'd kissed for the first time. His mustache smelled damp, muddy even, but she'd liked it, and she's met him here every night for a week now. Tonight, she's promised to go somewhere more private with him.

She's been kissed before, of course. Only sixteen, but she feels she's acquitted herself well with Colin, surprised him a little. She was wary of his questions about her age, tried to be mysterious and mock-offended — "You can't ask a girl that!" — but the way he'd laughed had made her feel small, childish. "I pull your pints, don't I?" she told him. "There's laws, you know. Can't have kids serving in a pub." But she could see he wasn't convinced, and so she kissed him back. She's practiced with the local boys, but the ones her age are all off now, joined up or in factories. The only one she's kissed lately is David, their evacuee — just goodnight kisses, and one longer one to make him blush on his birthday — but it doesn't count, because he's younger than her, if a bit moony.

Colin clambers onto the bike he's brought and wrestles it around for her to perch herself on the handlebars. She'd been hoping for a jeep, but he is only a corporal. She feels self-conscious raising her bum onto the crossbar, aware of him watching, but then they're off. Colin pedals firmly. She can feel the bike vibrating with his effort as they near the brow of the hill behind the pub, and then her stomach turns over as they start to coast down the far side. Pretty soon they're flying, laughing in the darkness. The wind presses her skirt to her legs and then catches it, flipping the hem up against her waist. Her slip billows in the breeze, as if it remembers its past life as a parachute, and her knees and then one thigh flash in the moonlight. She wants to lean down, to fix it, but Colin has her hands pressed under his on the handlebars, and when she wriggles he tells her, "Hold still, love. I've got you."

She has never been to Camp Sunshine, the old holiday camp, but as a child, before the war, she remembers seeing posters showing all the fun to be had there; pictures of cheerful tots and bathing beauties by the pool. On hot summer days, gathering the flock for shearing from the hillside above, running to keep up with her father's long, loose stride, she would steal glances at the faceted blue gem of the pool below her and imagine its coolness. Of course, these places aren't for locals. Even in better days the most her father could afford was the odd day trip on a growling charabanc to Rhyl or Llandudno. Besides, as he used to tell her, "Who needs a pool when there's the ocean for free?" But she hates the sea, the sharp salt taste, the clammy clumps of seaweed. She's only ever seen swimming pools at the pictures, but she thinks Esther Williams is the most beautiful woman in the world. So as soon as Colin coasts through the back gates of the old camp, she asks him to show her the pool. He looks a little surprised — he has one of the empty, mildewed chalets in mind — but something in her voice, her eagerness, convinces him. He props the bike in the shadows behind a dark hut and leads her through the kids' playground. She clambers up the slide and swishes down on her backside, arms outstretched. He watches her from the roundabout, circling slowly. When she bats at the swings, he calls softly, "Want a push?" and she tells him, "Yeah."

She settles herself, and he puts his hands in the small of her back and shoves firmly to set her off, and then as she swings back he touches her lightly, his fingers spread across her hips, each time she passes. When she finally comes to a stop, the strands of hair that have flown loose fall back and cover her face. She tucks them away, all but one, which sticks to her cheek and throat, an inky curve.

"I saw the pool from up there," she tells him, breathlessly, and she pulls him toward it. She can see the water, the surface, choppy, and she wants, just once, to recline beside it and run her hand through it like a movie star. But when she gets close and bends down, she sees that what she has taken for the surface of the water is an old tarpaulin stretched over the mouth of the pool. She strikes at it bad-temperedly.

"For leaves and that," Colin says, catching up. "So it doesn't get all mucky."

"But what about the water?"

"Well, they drained it, you see."

He can see her disappointment, but he isn't discouraged.

"Come 'ere," he says, taking her hand and pulling her along to the metal steps that drop into the pool.

He climbs down and unfastens the cloth where it's tied to the edge by guy ropes. "Follow me." He slides down, his feet, his legs, his torso, until she can see only the top of his head. She notices a tiny, sunburned bald spot, just as he looks up and she realizes he can see up her skirt. She jumps back, snapping her heels together, and he grins and vanishes.

"Colin," she calls softly, suddenly alone.

There's no answer.

She crouches closer to the flapping gap, like a diver about to plunge forward. "Colin?" she hisses.

Nothing.

Then she sees a ridge in the cloth, like the fin of a shark moving away from her, circling, coming back. "What's that?" she says, and as if from a long way off comes the cry, "Me manhood."

Despite herself she laughs, and in that moment grabs the railing of the steps and ducks below the cover.

It's surprisingly light in the empty pool. The tarpaulin is a thin blue oilcloth, and the moonlight seeps through it unevenly, as if through a cloudy sky. The pool is bathed in a pale, blotchy light, and the illusion of being underwater is accentuated by the design of shells printed on the tiles of the bottom. Overhead the breeze snaps the tarpaulin like a sail. She can just make out Colin, like a murky beast at the far end of the pool, the deep end. She takes a step toward him and finds the world sloping away beneath her suddenly, almost falls, stumbles down toward him.

When she gets closer, she finds him walking around in circles, with exaggerated slowness, making giant O shapes with his mouth.

"What are you doing?" she wants to know.

"I'm a fish," he says. "Glub, glub, get it?" And she joins him, giggling, snaking her arms ahead of her in a languid breaststroke.

He weaves back and forth around her. "Glub, glub, glub!"

"Now what are you doing?" she asks as he steps sideways and bumps her. "Hey!"

"I'm a crab," he says, sidling off, scuttling back, bumping her again.

She feels his hand on her arse.

"Ow!"

"Sorry!" He shrugs, holds up his hands. "Sharp pincers."

"That hurt," she says, pulling away. She starts to backpedal toward the shallow end, windmilling her arms. "Backstroke!" But he catches her, wraps her in a hug.

"Mr. Octopus," he whispers, "has got you."

For a moment she relaxes, kisses him, but he kisses back with force, this soldier she's only known for a week. She feels him turning her in his arms, as if dancing, and she tries to move her feet with him, but he's holding her too tight, simply swinging her around. She feels dizzy. Her shoes scuff the tiles, and she thinks, *I just polished them.* The pressure of his arms makes it hard to breathe. She moans softly, her mouth under his mouth. When they finally stop spinning, she finds herself pressed against the cold tile wall of the pool. Up close it smells sharply of dank, chlorine, and rotten leaves.

"I'll be leaving soon," he whispers. "We're almost done here. Will you miss me?"

She nods in his arms, pressing her head against his chest, away from the hard wall.

"I'll miss you," he tells her, his lips to her ear. "We could be at the front this time next month. I wish I had something to remember you by then. Something to keep up me fighting spirits."

She feels him picking at her blouse, the buttons. She feels a hand on her knee, fluttering with her hem and then under her skirt — "Mermaid," he croons — sliding against the silk of her slip, against her thigh.

"Nice," he breathes. "Who says you Welsh girls don't know your duty. Proper patriot, you are. Thinking of England." Her head is still bent toward him, but now she is straining her neck against his weight. Between them she can feel the bony crook of his elbow, pressing against her side, and across her belly the tense muscles of his forearm, twitching.

"Nargois," she tells him, but he doesn't understand. *"Nargois!"*

She feels pressure and then pain. Colin grunts into her hair, short, hot puffs of breath. She wonders if she dares scream, who would hear her, who might come, wonders if she's more afraid of being caught than of what he's doing to her.

She begins to turn her head against the coarse wool on his chest, trying to shake it, and he says, "Almost, almost," but at this she lifts her head sharply, catches him under the chin with a crack, and he cries out.

He steps back, clutching his jaw.

"Are you all right?" She starts to reach for him.

"Cunt!" he says, snatching at her wrist. She doesn't know the word, it's not in her schoolbooks, but she knows the tone, pulls away, curses him back in Welsh.

"Speak English, will you?" he tells her, turning her loose.

She leaves him there, struggling up the slope toward the steps. She thinks of a flirty argument they had over the bar one night last week. He'd wanted her to teach him some Welsh, but then she'd laughed at his pronunciation, and he'd gotten mock-mad. "Ah, what's the point?" he said. "Why don't you just give it up and speak English, like the rest of us?" She'd turned a little stern then, mouthed the nationalist arguments about saving the language, preserving the tongue.

"Oh, come on," he hisses after her now. "Play the game. I didn't mean it. Come back, eh? We'll do it proper. Comfy, like. Get a mattress from a chalet, have a lie-down."

But she keeps going, slipping a little on the tiles, tugging her skirt down, shoving her blouse back in, and she hears him start to laugh. There's a shout from the deep. "Who are you saving it for, eh? Who you saving it for, you Welsh bitch?"

She expects him to come after her then, feels her back tense against his touch, won't run for fear he'll chase. But before she reaches the opening, she hears shouts, a harsh scrape of feet on the concrete above. It's as if she's willed her own rescue into being, and yet she cowers from it. Torch lights dance over the cover of the pool. Despite herself, she turns to Colin with a beseeching look — *to be found like this!* — but he's already past her, his head in the shelter of the tarpaulin, peering out. Frantically she tries to button her blouse, her fingers fumbling. "Shite," Colin breathes, but the lights and the footsteps are already receding, and she leans against the wall, her heart hammering. The thought of being discovered, the near miss, makes her stomach clench. Her throat feels raw. She looks back at Colin, wanting to share their escape, but he is already scrambling up the ladder and, a second later, gone.

A clean pair of heels, she thinks, the English phrase so suddenly vivid she feels blinded by it.

Her body seems heavy, waterlogged, her arms shaky, too weak to pull her up the metal ladder, and she clings to the cold rail as if she might drown. It's a few moments before she can climb out of the pool. There are shouts at the other side of the camp, where the barracks have been built — the local boys must have broken in again — but she hurries the other way, back over the playground. The seesaw and roundabout are still, the swings rocking gently in the breeze. She finds the bike where he left it, propped up behind a chalet, and climbs on, noticing as she hitches up her skirt that the stitching of her slip is torn. It will take her five minutes to mend with a needle and thread, but she suddenly feels like weeping.

She pushes off, pedaling hard, although she finds it makes her wince to ride. She doesn't care that she's stealing his bike. She'll throw it into the hedge outside the village. She knows he'll never ask about it, and if he does, she decides, staring at her pale knuckles on the handlebars where his fingers have curled, she'll pretend she's forgotten her English.

CLAIRE DAVIS

Labors of the Heart

FROM PLOUGHSHARES

THE REMARKABLE THING IN DREAMS: people say what he never hears in waking. Fat. They say it to his face, not behind his back, or clear of earshot. The word is succulent in their mouths — "faaat" — stretching out like the waist on his Sansabelt pants. Nothing derogatory about it, only an unabashed honesty. On these mornings, for a few moments, he wakes feeling curiously relieved.

Clarence John Softitch, Pinky to his friends, at five foot eight and 482 pounds on a good day, *is* fat, not large, big, or big-boned. Not hefty, husky, generous, or oversized. Nor robust, portly, or pleasingly plump. He is fat. Enormous. Corpulent. And no delicate euphemisms or polite evasions can relieve him of this knowledge when every movement, whether tying a shoe or climbing a short flight of stairs, becomes a labor of the heart.

Not that he has much to do with people in general. He lives in Clarkston, Washington, a scrappy town of twenty-odd thousand on the eastern edge of the state where the paltry rainfall encourages prickly pear in lawns and 12 percent of the population is on welfare. He works as night janitor at Loyola High School, and when most of the town's folk are gathered in families for dinner, or socially at Hogan's Bar, Pinky's company is the clatter of scrub bucket, mop, and brush. For solace he has his voice — a fine, clear tenor to fill the empty rooms. He sings, "When the moon hits your eye like a big-a pizza pie, that's *amore*."

Not that he knows anything about that. *Amore,* that is.

For he is virginal, a moderate embarrassment at his age, having come to terms, he believes, with the reality that no one loves a fat man. And so he has given up on love, the daydreams, the hope, the mooning about, the unsightly chase and precipitous rejections. Until this Monday, that is, on one of his twice-weekly food shopping trips, when he sees *her* in the produce aisle of the northside A & B grocery, a rutabaga under her nose, a peckish look about her mouth. She's little. A narrow, neatly planed body. There is about her the solidity, the starkness of a lightning rod.

He finds this fascinating; more than that, it stirs him in a way he's never imagined, his feet locked like a stammer, his breast tightening unlike the usual angina. But what is it about this woman? Her shoulders pinned at attention — the fierce way she sniffs out the proper rutabaga, so that he feels intimidated. Dwarfed, really. For although Pinky *knows* himself to be large — talcums each pant leg to keep his thighs from chafing, avoids chairs with arms — he's always *believed* himself small, just a tiny voice chirping on the horizon, flotsam in an ocean of flesh. He's amazed at how his vessel sloshes and wags, jiggles and rolls. The *real him* adrift inside like a buoy at high tide. He cannot imagine being of consequence in the larger world beyond bumped tables and broken chairs, the numerous bruises and insulted flesh so common that he has ceased to wonder at the many ways the world is rigged against the fat.

But standing in the grocery aisle, he knows for the first time in his forty-odd years what it means to be *struck* by love.

She passes on the rutabagas, and even as she's whisking out of produce, he's slipping the vegetable under his nose and then into his cart, perhaps as a keepsake, as he's never actually eaten one, doesn't know what to do with the thing bowling down the cart's length, tippling stacked frozen dinners — breaded fish sticks; Hungry Man slabs of Salisbury steak, mashed potatoes, and gravy; lasagna; chicken Kiev — and the comfort foods: doughnut holes, potato chips, a baker's dozen Hostess Ho-Hos, chocolate cheesecake as a chaser. A front wheel turned sideways thumps, ba bump, ba bump, ba bump, calling everyone's attention, he thinks, as he trails her to the checkout lane before he's actually ready.

He tries not to stare, but admires the efficiency of her moves. She retrieves each item with a lean elegance, and he hangs on to the cart handle, dizzy with love, half hopes she notices the rutabaga. When she leaves the store, she's burdened by six plastic sacks hanging plumb from her fists. She staggers out and pauses in the sunlight, the door frozen open at her back so that the heat wafts in, and he imagines her body, that small dark column, immune to the glare of sun on concrete, her clothes dry, armpits forever fresh.

By the time he's checked out, she's gone, and as he pulls onto the street he sees her struggling down the block. He closes his teeth against the knocking of his heart and idles behind her, the wide-body Chevy wallowing like a whale in the shallows as he leans across the seat to roll down the window.

"Can I give you a lift?" he asks.

She angles a suspicious look at him — the friendly stranger — but then she stiffens her back along with her upper lip and marches on.

"Just a ride. I'm safe," he says and has to steer around a parked car.

She glances over her shoulder. "Do I look like I need help?" she says. She crooks her elbows and flexes tidy biceps, causing the plastic bags to twist in slow revolutions, and from the cottonwoods white duff spindles down into curbside drifts, a goldfinch flits overhead — a stab of yellow and gone — and still she holds the bags high, until Pinky begins to feel *he* is that assortment of odd bulges and bumps bundled in an unsightly sack turning this way, then that.

Of course she doesn't need help, certainly not from him, and he ducks his head in apology, cheeks flushing with an old but familiar heat. What is left him is this small dignity — he touches a finger to his forehead, as if to tip a cap, and accelerates down the street as though his heart were still intact.

It's a full week before he sees her again, which is odd, because it turns out she's his new neighbor, rents the old Grieger house kitty-corner. Though given his daytime schedule of sleep and hermitage he hasn't noticed the lights on, the mail delivery, the mowed lawn, before this moment. Curious also is how he recognizes her, half concealed as she is beneath the draped branches of a weeping birch, her back to him, head tilted so that the short nap of hair twists into something like a question mark against her neck. No more clue than the spine's rigidity, the belligerence in her stance, and still Pinky's heart begins to toll. He wishes he were driving, but these last three nights he's begun an exercise program — walking the three blocks to work and back. *Morbidly obese,* he's been categorized. Morbidly. As in deadly, not sadly, which is the way he's preferred to construe it. Midway second block, he'll be winded, and by the time he reaches the school door the back of his shirt will be sweated in the early evening cool. He'd walk by her house without stopping, but she's noticed him, turns, and by the look on her face he can tell she can't place him. He tries not to waddle, wishes he were wearing something other than Carhartt coveralls. He tips his finger to his forehead and gives it away.

"The man in the car," she says.

He nods, pleased in spite of himself. He toes up to the lawn to extend a hand. Her own hand disappears in his, but her grip shakes him. "I live in the yellow house." He points over his shoulder. He tells her his name, says, "Call me Pinky," and he wants to say, *All my friends do,* but thinks, *What friends?* and feels a surge of despair. What folly. What gall. What enormous odds. It's overwhelming, this business of love.

"Pinky." Her voice rises. "Rose. I'm Rose Spencer." She doesn't release his fingertips, instead stalks up the lawn with Pinky in tow. "Tell me, what this is?" Rose disengages her hand to point at a branch. In the upper reaches there is a cocoon, a tented web, with freckled bits splotted here and there. In yet another branch, he sees the start of another, and how is it that he hasn't noticed them before? He sights down the row of cottonwoods streetside, the upper reaches. He sighs.

"Tent caterpillars," he says. He hopes she doesn't register the way his flesh quivers as he thinks of the frantic shivering of worms overhead. A phobia, like some folks have for snakes, spiders.

"Are they bad? For the tree?" she asks.

He knows they'll eat their way down a branch, mature, and drop like fruit. He backs up a pace. No more than a couple tents. Not so bad. "We'll keep an eye on them." And suddenly he's using "we," and such audacity stuns him. But she lets him get away with it, nodding her head and escorting him off her lawn.

"If you need anything," he says. "I have a car," he says, "for groceries, anything." She's watching, and he has the sense she's backing away, though her feet are still rooted to the edge of the lawn. "I'm safe," he says, ducks his head.

"How's that?" she asks.

He flushes. Can't believe he's saying this. "Well, you can probably run faster than I can." He laughs as he's always had to.

Rose arches an eyebrow at him. "I don't know what you expect from me." She crosses her arms, cups an elbow in each palm. "But I'm tapped out when it comes to men. Pity, love, anger, compassion — you name it, and I've exhausted it."

"I'm sorry," Pinky says, and he means it. He wonders what could have hurt her so deeply, briefly envies her pain, the experience of being close enough to wound or be wounded. And then, of course, he realizes that's nonsense. Believes he has the perfect vantage for sympathy, from behind this great bulwark of flesh. He's thinking of himself now — the lifetime alone, avoiding pain. He runs a hand down his chest, down the globe of his belly, a gesture he's developed over the years, familiarizing himself with the expanding boundaries of his body. "We're neighbors," he says, and she seems puzzled, but there's something in his face, or his tone, that puts her at ease.

She relaxes the grip on her arms, and says, "Neighbors. I can handle that."

It's his turn to be confused now. He checks his watch, then looks west, to the sunset, as though that might be more accurate. "I have to get on to work — over at the school? I'm the maintenance technician." A smile sweeps across his face. "Night janitor." He avoids her eyes, looks over her shoulder, and the hills rising above the town turn amber, then the color of autumn rushes, and where the light catches the grasses, the bunched sage, it is a luminous fire. It occurs to him just how long it's been since he's *seen* the hills, wonders how it is that he could have moved through these days, these months without noticing how the crowns levitate with light above the rim rock, the dimming crevasses. He backs up a step, and as she turns her attention once again on the yard, he starts away, first one foot and then the other until he finds himself three blocks gone and on the steps of school. He unlocks the door with a jangle of keys, lets them loose to the satisfying snatch and click of the take-up reel, then enters the building. He clamps the door shut, and, flipping on hall lights, he breaks into his best Johnny Mathis voice, *"Chances are . . ."*

They shop together now. One day a week. Separate carts. He's taken it upon himself to keep Rose advised on lawn maintenance.

"It's the first yard I've ever taken care of," she confides, and so he understands she's always had a man, and no, he won't infringe because it's obvious she takes delight in adding oil to the lawn mower gasoline and pruning the boxwood hedges, regards each task as an indication of competence in the larger world. "I believe a person could fix anything," she says in the house utensils aisle, "given proper instruction and duct tape." Then she adds, "Except trust." And this is the first hint she's given of what keeps her so clearly focused on staying "neighborly."

Not that he's done much more than buddy his grocery cart up to hers, and although it's true, the contents have more and more begun to resemble hers, still he keeps a cautious distance. He's at a standstill, and all the month of long hours mulling over the mop handle at work, dreaming up ways to woo and win her, have yielded nothing more than any neighbor could claim.

Until today, when she lets slip the tidbit about trust. And then the store manager, Ray Tipp, an old classmate — a starved-looking man who keeps himself anxious with coffee — checks out Pinky's groceries, says, "Got a sale on Hostess Ho-Hos." He lifts a head of broccoli and Roman Meal bread. "You on a diet?"

Pinky can't even run. He feels Rose, next in line, caught up in his embarrassment. He shuffles between the checkout stands, the backside of his trousers snag on a magazine rack, and he endures Ray's curiosity while he frees himself without spilling *Vogue* and *Look* into the aisle. He pays Ray, lifts his bagged groceries from the grinning stock boy. He knows that this too Rose must see, how the young boy's eyes widen and the whites shine like twin moons, roll in their sockets.

Stupid. Stupid to have invited her along. To see this. Still stupid — after all these years — to aim yourself at inevitable hurt. But the damage is done. Rose, after all, is guilty by association, and so he pivots on his heel, the great slowing mass of him, to face this small woman and take her disgust in stride.

She's handing money to Ray. Two twenties, a ten. She fishes out a single and another. Some change. She takes her bags from the boy and waits for Pinky to lead the way, which he does with all the grace he can muster. When he breaks out into the sunshine, his heart is cluttering his chest, so huge, so full it's become. He puffs crossing the parking lot, the bags swinging at his sides, and he sets them on the ground to open the car door for her.

Two blocks from the store, she says, "Why don't you pull into the park? I've bought a melon. We can have a bite."

Just like that.

And why not? he thinks. A picnic, something he hasn't done since his mother passed on, and for a brief moment he can almost hear her, see the woman she was, all comfort — bosomy and dimpled elbows — pressing food onto him, the sound of other children chasing and laughing. He is hiccuping tears. "Eat," she says. "Like a good boy. Never mind those others. They're jealous you gotta momma can cook." She chucks a finger under his chin. "Your daddy was a *big* man." By this he understands that he too would be . . . large . . . and in her eyes that was good.

Rose directs him onto River Street and down to the small riverside park. He used to come here as a younger man, walked the levee at night to imagine himself with a woman, strolling the paths or swooning on a bench in the grip of passion and the moony night, like any one of a number of couples whispering from behind the willows' curtains or lolling in the tall blue grasses riverside.

He follows Rose's lead, carrying the plastic-sacked melon in both hands like a gift, an offering of the magi, and she brings them to the base of a cottonwood. He is breaking a sweat, and the air is brilliant with light on water so that he squints the moisture from his eyes, releases a great round sigh, "Aaah," and he's just so damned grateful for these simple pleasures — river, melon, woman — that he's unlikely to recover his voice anytime soon, so he sighs again.

Rose has seated herself in the grass. He wishes she were wearing a flowing skirt, a frilly blouse, a wide-brimmed straw hat, instead of the baggy jeans and T-shirt that slouch on her tiny frame, and then he feels an ingrate. Clothes. What do they signify? Certainly not the moment. She takes the melon from him, plops it in her lap like a placid child, then pats the grass beside her, and he faces the task of lowering himself. Pinky thinks to remain standing, strike a noble pose, but she's already gazing off across the wide blue river to the hills opposite. He braces one hand against the tree, crooks a knee, stretches the other leg behind, and bends cautiously forward and down and down some more. It's a struggle against mass, gravity. His joints pop in series. He tries not to gasp or puff, and that's nearly as much effort as kneeling. His crotch feels like a wishbone, ready to snap, and then he's down without having fallen. His face is red; he can tell. He filches a handkerchief out of his rear pocket and towels off his forehead, neck, the skinny V of flesh in the unbuttoned top of his button-up shirt.

"Do you have a knife?" she asks.

And he does, though he must lean back, lift his stomach, and squeeze his hand into the narrow flap of cloth, cutting the blood to his fingers as he feels for the knife. Finally he frees it, a pocket Buck knife with all the appointments — even a corkscrew. But she lifts the knife away, slaps the screw back into its steel nest, and locks open the large blade. She stabs into the melon's meat, saws a chunk free, and scrapes the seeds back into the exposed heart of the fruit. She hands the wedge to him, and he waits for her to join him.

"People on the whole are an unlikable bunch," she says, sinks the knife to the hilt into the melon's rind. "Take my advice. Never fall in love with them."

Pinky laughs, but it's a squeezed little thing, his chest constricting.

"You think you know cruelty, I know you do." She saws into the melon. "But the cruelty of strangers, or friends, is nothing" — she wags a finger in his face — "compared to what love can do." She is tight-lipped. Her brows beetle, and the air about her seems charged with a static energy. She bites into the melon, tells him about her first husband, his one-night stands, moves on to her second husband and his affairs. Tells it all in four short sentences, as if she can't bite off the ends of words hard enough, spit it out fast enough.

"What did I learn from it, you want to know . . ."

She dabbles at the corner of her mouth with a fingertip, where some melon juice drips down, and Pinky thinks he has never seen anything more delectable. He'd like to take her finger into his mouth and suck it dry.

She stretches her legs out, leans against the tree, and tells him of her third and last husband's affairs. How she then called the woman, wanted to see her. "Couldn't help myself. Called a complete stranger — though it seemed I had the right, we'd shared so much. I don't know what I expected. She came to my house. Not the first time, I could tell that right off — the way she found her way to his chair."

Rose rubbed the back of her head against the tree's bark, a leisurely scratching. "She was a short, stumpy-legged little thing, not cute, no, not even handsome. But interesting. Perky. She says, 'I didn't mean to ruin your life.' She was being sincere, but of course she was flattering herself. After all, my life wasn't ruined. Merely changed. I told her that."

She looked over at Pinky. "Don't you wonder at how I could be so collected? So smug?"

"I can't imagine," Pinky says.

"No." She leans over, pats his hand. "Of course you can't. And of course I was full of crap." She sighed. "If my life wasn't ruined, it was the next thing to it. Rubble. That's what I was left with. Rubble."

She squeezes her left breast, and Pinky knows it is her heart she means, but all he can picture is the tender flesh crumpled in her fist, and he wants to loosen her fingers, cradle her breast and heart in the palm of his hand, which he discovers is sweating, so he swipes it down his pant leg. And then, wonder of all wonders, he reaches over with his newly dried hand and takes the melon from her, lifts the knife away, slices another piece, skins and offers it to her.

Which she declines.

"Three strikes, you're out. Isn't that right?" she asks.

"In baseball," Pinky says, and he wants to sound decisive but hears how his voice trails off. He's stuck with the melon wedge, dripping through his fingers onto his pant leg.

"Yes," she agrees. "In baseball *and in men.*"

And what can Pinky say? He eats the melon slice, wipes his hand on the grass. On the river, a pair of Canada geese paddle upstream, six goslings drifting in their wake. Sunlight crooks across the water's surface, and shadows swim the face of the hills opposite. Pinky blinks, feels moisture budding behind his eyes, and blinks again. He begins to comprehend the scale of his task — wooing this woman — even if he weren't hobbled by his own body. He's still holding the knife, and he looks down at his belly, wishes he could slice away the flesh, pare down to some more supple version of himself that would be capable of the acrobatics — walking, sitting, bending over — that normal, everyday people perform in everyday courtship. He wants to be handsome for her.

A pair of young girls roller-blade down the sidewalk, the wheels buzzing with the sound of enormous hummingbirds. They wind down the path, skinny legs and arms knotted in protective pads. Their laughter is a shouting, and Pinky admires the honesty of it. He wonders what Rose sounds like when she laughs. He wonders if she laughs.

Rubble, she'd said, and he questions the state her heart's in now. "I'm not like those men," he says.

"Why?" she asks. "Because you're fat?" And it's just a statement. "Because you think other women wouldn't find you attractive?"

Truth is he hadn't thought of it that way, but he begins to see this could work for him. He nods.

"Another way that you're safe?" she asks.

He nods again, though he feels like he's stepping into something unseen, something with teeth.

She stares across the river. "Do you think that little of yourself, or me?"

It's worse than he'd feared, certain now that she despises him for his clumsiness, his transparent eagerness. He blames himself and his lack of experience; he blames the hour of the day and the bristling grass that torments his ankles. He tells her he's a fool and that he respects her and her friendship. Those are the words he uses, *respect* and *friendship*, and she continues to stare out across the river. He asks her to understand, he's not used to . . . to . . . picnics.

Her brows furrow, and she says, as if she hasn't heard him, "My last husband was different. Where the others'd been tall, he was short. A bookish man with a sense of humor. He couldn't change the oil in the car, but he was mad for opera. I believed he was different, as day is to night." She wags her head. "But finally he was only a different kind of night. And this is much too lovely a day" — she leans back on her elbows — "to quibble. I'm done with men." Rose rolls onto her side, facing Pinky. "Except as friends. Take it or leave it."

Pinky nods and heaves a sigh, but even as she pats his hand and closes her eyes to rest, he is studying the logistics of getting back on his feet.

Late at night, in the gym, Pinky plots strategy. He turns on the overheads, and the constellation of bulbs shine from the floor's mirror finish. He has cleaning down to an art, dry-mopping the area in under an hour, starting at the foot of the bleachers, left to right, and threading his way in overlapping lanes down and back until he's dusted his way into the boys' locker room, where the real work begins. Though, as it is summer, this chore is reduced to a twice-weekly touchup instead of the nightly tour during the school year. He switches to a wet mop, fills the big steel bucket on casters with hot water, a splash of disinfectant Sparkle, and bleach. He works backward, kicking the bucket ahead of him like a troublesome dog. The mop bangs against lockers, and Pinky loves the rat-a-tat-tat off the empty doors. Sings "Frankie and Johnny" to their machine-gun accompaniment. Sees himself as Johnny, but can't imagine doing her wrong, can't conceive of such discontent. He rolls the bucket into the boys' bathroom. Lifts his voice to the tiled walls. *At least that's the way the story goes. Frankie bought everything for Johnny, from his sports car to his Ivy League clothes.* He buffs the floor, glances in the mirror.

His face seems different, and maybe it's just love has transformed him. Or has he lost weight? He lifts the putty knife from the cart, scrapes at a wad of paper toweling glommed to the underside of a sink. When he straightens up, he fidgets a finger into his waistband, snugs in two. Yes. Oh yes. He's lost weight. *Friend came running to Frankie, said, You know I wouldn't tell you no lie. I saw your man driving that sports car with a chick named Nellie Bly —*

And this is the tough part. He enters a stall. How can he convince Rose of his own true heart? And damn it. He slaps the brush in the toilet bowl, squirts in blue disinfectant, swabs, and flushes. He deserves one good shot at it, doesn't he? He slaps the cover up, scrubs — cover down — scrubs — backs out of the stall, then moves on to the next and the next. Patience, he tells himself, and though he's only known Rose as a friend and neighbor a little over two months, he's got a forty-year backlog of empty nights, and Pinky stops, envisions the calamity of another forty empty years, and finds himself doubled over one of the toilets. When his heart calms in his chest and the angina eases under his left wing bone, he backs out of the stall. The room is bright, as only locker-room bathrooms can be, with the high banks of fluorescent lights buzzing and reflecting off the mirrors and stainless steel doors, the white porcelain sinks and urinals all ablaze, so that when he looks in the mirror this time what he sees is his forehead shining with sweat and the enormous bell of his body overexposed in white overalls, and for a moment he loses himself against the white wall tiles.

He leaves the bucket and mop, the toilet brush and disinfectant, and crosses back through the locker room, turning off lights as he goes, through the gym and out the side door. He stands on the asphalt stoop. In the school parking lot, the arc lamp's cone of light seethes with winged insects — swirling, bumping, a luminous feast that the nighthawks scoop through. Pinky breathes deeply, feels the moist back of his shirt cooling. Crickets pick up where they'd left off. He steps away from the building and walks until the locked school folds into the night. He walks slow and steady, his heart easing, chest lightening. He knows he will have to return to work, but for now he turns up a side street where lamplight streams out onto porches and grass.

He stays to the sidewalk but glances in each house. Where drapes are open, it's the furniture he notices — which place has a piano, or a lamp centered in the window like a beacon. Then there are all the dining rooms with tables bunkered by chairs. So many chairs. Seascapes over the sofa, mounted deer, or the grouping of family pictures like a lineup in the post office. Once in a while he glimpses the people. Sometimes he believes he can smell their dinner: chicken, hamburger, barbecued ribs. Or, more vaguely, Italian cuisine, Oriental, Middle Eastern. He feels a stirring of hunger, but he tucks his two fingers into his waistband again and thinks apple instead of apple pie. He journeys down another side street and exchanges greetings with a man smoking a pipe on his front porch. He passes a young couple and the woman titters, but they don't notice Pinky, so wrapped up in they are, and he finds that utterly disarming. He meets more people strolling under the streetlamps. Why, it seems to him that the whole town must be spilling out into the warm night. Or maybe this is the way the world congregates when he's alone, in his school, his home. And there it is. His house. Locked tight and shuttered close. He opens the front door, the drapes, turns on all the lights. Then he steps back out on the sidewalk to see what he can of himself. He's reluctant to look, but discovers he doesn't fare so badly. Tomorrow, first thing, he will dig out the old photos, frame the one of his mother and father's wedding, the portrait of his grandfather — big-chested, with thighs like a Percheron. It will take so little, he thinks, and he pivots on his

heel to look across the street, to the house of his beloved. The
lights behind the drapes are a wan glow, and he's stricken with how
tidy the place is, how self-contained. He feels . . . what is it? Not exactly love, but a stirring that is equally unfamiliar from his end of
things, and . . . disconcerting — call it pity. He wishes he could step
into her life as easily as into his home, open it wide to this sweet
night. He heaves a sigh and looks up, over the trees and over the
tops of houses to where the distant hills shoulder the dark beneath
the quickening stars.

He means to take her on a date, but he doesn't call it that. He
doesn't dare. He mentions the movie, casually, over groceries. He
tells Rose, "Dutch treat," to allay her suspicion. It's a love story, but
he doesn't mention that either. She offers to buy the popcorn.
"Only fair," she says. "All the gas you've used on grocery trips."
   Pinky accepts. He feels pretty smart. Of course he hasn't thought
about the theater seats, and though his pants are looser now and
sitting upright no longer cuts off his wind, still it's a tight, tight
squeeze, but he manages. He's appreciative for her small kindness
of unbuttered popcorn. She'd noticed his weight loss a couple days
ago. "Hope you're not doing this for me," she'd said, and when he
replied, "No," he could see she was unprepared for the truth, some
small part of her stung by his admission. He felt encouraged.
   It *was* a sappy film. Any other time he would have been the first
to ridicule the sentimentality. Except now it is Rose scoffing, and
that provokes in him a desire to defend it. She curls her lip, and
Pinky lets his heart go soft. Walking back to the car, she recaps
some of the *lowlights*. When she snorts at the dialogue, Pinky taps
her arm with a finger, says, "You could give it a chance."
   "You can't mean it."
   "It had heart," he says.
   She pinches his arm. "It had a lobotomy. Not the same thing."
   "Ouch," he says.
   She goes on. "What you don't know" — she shakes a finger at
him — "is that this kind of willful ignorance about the *realities* of
love wearies me sometimes."
   They drive away from the theater in silence. He wants to talk but
is embarrassed to admit that there's little willful about his igno-
rance. Inexperience, certainly.
   He suggests the 410 Drive-In for a bite, and she agrees. Rose's

hamburger fills her hands, drapes over her fingers, lobs chunks of lettuce and pickle into the napkin covering her lap, while Pinky's grilled chicken breast sandwich is a pale, insignificant thing in comparison. It hardly seems worth the effort. He takes baby bites to stretch it out. She offers him a sip of her malt, and it's so intimate a gesture he's dumbfounded. He accepts the plastic cup from her hands and takes the straw — squeezed between her lips just moments earlier — into his mouth, tongues the tip tenderly. It is a jolt of pure chocolate, cold and clean and sweet. His eyes close.

So this is what it's like — the taste of a woman — and there's a curious quivering at the base of his spine. And of course he *knows* that's not the case, but he enjoys the *idea* of it and has to stop himself from draining her malt.

"You think I'm harsh," she says, "about the movie. But the point is" — she crumples the emptied hamburger wrapping — "romantic love suggests we are incomplete without another, in need of salvation. You're led to believe that you'll be a better person if there's someone around to expect it. But somewhere down the line, you find the cost of these expectations too dear. What? you say. Eat the same cooking? Sleep on the same side of the bed? Give up variety? Implausible, if not impossible. All you will *ask* for is a little kindness, but what you will *want* is more than anybody can give — their undivided attention for the rest of their life — and so you struggle and struggle and hurt each other endlessly.

"Three marriages, over twenty-five years' worth. Imagine — twenty-five years attempting love. Trust me. It's a complication you're better off without."

Rose sighs, pats her lips dry, then sets the soiled napkin and empty malt cup back on the serving tray. "Take me home," she says. She sounds utterly weary.

Pinky takes a deep breath, resettles in the seat. His stomach bumps the steering wheel. He drives the long way, down Bridge Street, over to Riverside, up to Highland, slowly. How painful she makes it sound, *twenty-five years,* but all he can think of is turning over in bed to find someone there, of eating someone else's cooking, and it sounds grand to Pinky, worth the risk, the heartache. He *knows* what it's like to be alone — the long haul of it, not the early phase, when the day winds down because *you've* nothing better to do and stretching across an empty bed still seems a luxury.

It's coming on to seven in the evening, and the sky is yet bright with daylight. He stops at the school, invites her in. He shows her the broom closet, the mops. He shows her classrooms, the new computer lab — shakes his head; feather dusting, he explains. He takes her into the gym, throws on the lights just to show her how the floor shines. He stands center court and lobs a high A at her. He could almost swear she blushes. He proceeds to sing the only song he can think of with her name in the title, "The Yellow Rose of Texas."

On the way out of the building, she says, "A most unlikely but lovely serenade. Thank you." They leave the car there to walk the three blocks home. He knows she slows her pace to match his. It is early evening, and the shortening daylight lapses into a dim gloaming. Dusky-winged ash aphids are swarming — bumbling clouds of blue-bodied mites that rise like yeast from the grass. Late summer, they come down from the Camas and Palouse prairies to swim in the warmer valley air. By full evening, they will web together in gray winding sheets around the south side of the ash tree trunks, where they will shiver into their final, short-lived ecstasy. But now they are a squall, riding the turmoil of heat convections and cooling drafts. They speckle the couple's clothes, dust their hair. Pinky is enthralled with the tiny creatures, the enormous bulb of their bodies and improbable flight. They bobble and fall, rise and fumble. This is not a matter of grace.

Rose waves a hand through the air in front of her. They stop on the far edge of the cloud, and Rose ducks her head, swipes at an eye. Pinky can see a bead of aphids riding her eyelashes.

"Ow," she says, her eye tearing.

"Here," he comforts, nips her chin between thumb and forefinger, lifts her face to what is left of the light. Rose is a woman who has little truck with makeup. There's no attempt to disguise the lines, the thinning skin. He is captivated, as he was the first time he saw her, by the static energy of this woman, her relentless honesty, all her life available in her face, her eyes. And this is the thing he both fears and admires, how she has been pared down to the bone, tried and fired as he never has been. Though his fingers barely grace her chin, he feels her energy, some galvanic current of old doubts running through her, and she sidesteps under his hand. He takes a steadying breath, says, "Hold still." He spits on his free thumb, touches that small drop of moisture to the corner of her eye. The speck of blue floats off the white, onto Pinky's thumb, and he neatly lifts it away.

Up and down the block, house lights come on, and children shoo cats out of front doors. The hills over the town flatten, grow larger with the dark. There's no help for it, but Pinky feels a melancholy he's hard put to explain, and it has to do with the onset of dark and the sudden still. It has to do with the small woman at his side, her mistrust, and his own lifetime of hiding, in his house, his work, and foremost his own flesh. And he sees it has to do with fear — the way we run through our lives in terror of it — and everything to do with despair, and perhaps, he thinks, that is what despair is, finally, a lack of daring. He feels savvy. Overhead, a crow lifts from the treetop, banks toward the river with a hard laugh — ha, ha, ha.

In another block they stop again so that Pinky can catch his breath. He pants in the quiet, shakes his head. He will lose weight — he will because he cannot go on as he always has, he understands this now — but he also knows he will always be big. Not small, or even trim, and he is struck by this. It has been with him so long, this ocean of flesh. Pinky feels he must tell Rose. Warn her. "I will always be fat," he says.

"Yes," she agrees. She lays a hand on his forearm. "As I will always be bitter," she says.

They stand that way in the new dark, and he thinks, should a young husband look out from his living room window, or should the young wife hurrying home from errands come across them standing so, they would think Rose and Pinky some middle-aged couple of long years — the way Rose's hand is anchored on his arm. And he wonders about the couples he has so long envied, how much is illusion — a public face for the private griefs and hurts they harbor? He thinks of the depth of Rose's bitterness, the earnest way in which she confirms it, and he understands it's as deep and abiding as the bones seated in the continent of his flesh. It humbles him, how fiercely she is grounded in her resolve.

And he does not feel up to the task. Sees himself as the lightweight in this struggle. His stomach gripes, and will not be consoled by the pat of his hand. How he already misses the easy comfort of food, the anonymity. He feels a nervousness, an anxiousness like a missed meal, or the temptation of chocolate before sleep. He sways from foot to foot, rocking in place. A terror steals upon him that he cannot fathom, so that his feet are seized in place and his fat plumbs him to the earth while she stands stark and quiet at his side as if forged of consequences larger than his imagining. He sees she is not the rod but the lightning itself, flinty bits striking off — old loves, grudges, misfortunes, a hundred errors in judgment, and more — quizzing his friable heart. He should run. He should bolt, for he senses this is a struggle deeper than the naive courtship he'd embarked on. Not the territory of novices. Not for the uninitiated. It is a journey of days, years, a chronic case of heartache, the relentless wooing to win and lose, again and again. He almost laughs, for all his assurances to Rose of how safe he is — he sees now that it is *she* who is the danger . . . always has been.

Overhead, the clouds quail beneath the rising moon. He turns his face away. He slows his panic by imagining the imaginable: the march of days, the orderliness of work — nights, cleaning, trips to the grocery store, lawn care, and diets. Conversation that spills over from day to day, and running jokes. He wonders how they will look in a year, two, five. Will she grow generous as he grows slight? He steadies, takes a deep breath. What he wants, he realizes, more than anything, is to imagine a time when fear will carry no weight in his heart. When love will need no proof. He squints into the dark, as if to make out the features of that distant time — the heel of a foot striking the floor as she steps down from her side of his bed, the shape of her face, is it Rose? But he cannot know this. Not now. Not yet. And perhaps for now the question is enough. He quashes the impulse to push back his sleeves. Instead, he leads them arm in arm, their bodies swaying each its own way, beneath the steepled canopy of sycamore where the first flush of moonrise swims the wavering shadows in a school of light.

ELIZABETH GRAVER

The Mourning Door

FROM PLOUGHSHARES

THE FIRST THING she finds is a hand. In the beginning, she thinks it's a tangle of sheet or a wadded sock caught between the mattress cover and the mattress, a bump the size of a walnut but softer, more yielding. She feels it as she's lying, lazing, in bed. Often, lately, her body keeps her beached, though today the sun beckons, the dogwoods blooming white, the peonies' glossy buds specked black with ants. Tom has gone to work already, backing out of the driveway in his pickup truck. She has taken her temperature on the pink thermometer, noted it down on the graph — 98.2, day eighteen, their thirteenth month of trying. She takes it again, to be sure, then settles back in, drifting, though she knows she should get up. The carpenters will be here soon; the air will ring with hammers. The men will find more expensive, unnerving problems with the house. She'll have to creep in her robe to the bathroom, so small and steady, like one of the pests they keep uncovering in this ancient, tilting farmhouse — powder post beetles, termites, carpenter ants.

She feels the bump in the bed the way she might encounter a new mole on her skin, or a scab that had somehow gone unnoticed, her hand traveling vaguely along her body until it stumbles, oh, what's this? With her shin she feels it first, as she turns over, beginning to get up. She sends an arm under the covers, palpates the bump. A pair of bunched panties, maybe, shed during sex and caught beneath the new sheet when she remade the bed? Tom's sock? A wad of tissue? Some unknown object (needle threader, sock darner, butter maker, chaff separater?) left here by the gener-

ations of people who came before? The carpenters keep finding
things in the walls and under the floor: the sole of an old shoe, a
rusted nail, a bent horseshoe. A Depression-era glass bowl, unbro-
ken, the green of key lime pie. Each time they announce another
rotted sill, cracked joist, additional repair, they hand an object
over, her consolation prize. The house looked so charming from
the outside, so fine and perfectly itself. The inspector said, Go
ahead, buy it. But you never know what's lurking underneath.

She gets out of the bed, stretches, yawns. Her gaze drops to
her naked body, so familiar, the thin freckled limbs and flattish
stomach. She has known it forever, lived with it forever. Mostly it
has served her well, but lately it seems a foreign, uncooperative
thing, at once insolent and lethargic, a taunt. Sometimes, though,
she still finds in herself an energy that surprises her, reminding her
of when she was a child and used to run — legs churning, pulse
throbbing — down the long river path that led to her cousin's
house.

Now, in a motion so concentrated it's fierce, she peels off the
sheet and flips back the mattress pad. What she sees doesn't surprise her; she's been waiting so hard these days, looking so hard. A
hand, it is, a small pink dimpled fist, the skin slightly mottled, the
nails the smallest slivers, cut them or they'll scratch. Five fingers.
Five nails. She picks it up; it flexes slightly, then curls back into a
warm fist. Five fine fingers, none missing. She counts them again to
be sure. *You have to begin somewhere,* the books say. *You have to relinquish control and let nature take its course.*

She hears the door open downstairs, the clomp of workboots,
words, a barking laugh. Looking around, she spots, on the bedroom floor, the burlap sack that held the dwarf Liberty apple tree
Tom planted over the weekend. She drops the hand into the bag,
stuffs the bag under the bed. Still the air smells like burlap, thick
and dusty. She pulls on some sweatpants, then thinks better of it
and puts on a more flattering pair of jeans, and a T-shirt that shows
off her breasts. She read somewhere that men are drawn to women
with small waists and flaring hips. Evolution, the article said. A
body built for birth. Her own hips are small and boyish; her waist
does not cinch in. Her pubic hair grows thin and blond, grass in a
drought. She doesn't want these workmen, exactly, but she would
like them, for the briefest moment, to want her. As she goes bare-
foot down the stairs to make a cup of tea and smile at the men, she

stops for a moment, struck by a memory of the perfect little hand; even the thought of it makes her gasp. The men won't find it. They're only working in the basement and the attic, structural repairs to keep the house from falling down.

In her kitchen, the three men: Rick and Tony and Joaquin. Their eyes flicker over her. She touches her hair, feels heavy with her secret, and looks down. More bad news, I'm afraid, Rick tells her. We found it yesterday, after you left — a whole section of the attic. What, she asks. *Charred,* he says dramatically. There must have been a fire; some major support beams are only three quarters their original size. She shakes her head. Really? But the inspector never — I have my doubts, Rick says, about this so-called inspector of yours. Can you fix it? she asks. He looks at her glumly through heavy-lidded eyes. We can try, he answers. I'll draw up an estimate, but we'll need to finish the basement before we get to this. Yes, she says vaguely, already bored. Fine, thanks.

Had she received such news the day before, it would have made her dizzy. A charred, unstable attic, a house whittled down by flames. She would have called Tom at work — You're not going to believe this — and checked how much money they had left in their savings account, and thought about suing the inspector and installing more smoke alarms, one in every room, blinking eyes. Today, though, she can't quite concentrate; her thoughts keep returning, as if of their own accord, to what she discovered in her bed. One apricot-sized hand, after thirteen months, after peeing into cups, tracking her temperature, making Tom lie still as a statue after he comes, no saliva, no new positions, her rump tilted high into the air afterward, an absurd position but she doesn't care.

After thirteen months of watching for the LH surge on the ovulation predictor kit — the deep indigo line of a good egg, the watery turquoise of a bad, and inside her own body, waves cresting and breaking, for she has become an ocean, or is it an oceanographer? *Study us hard enough,* the waves call out to her, *watch us closely enough, and we shall do your will.* She has noted the discharge on her underpants — sticky, tacky, scant. Egg white, like she's a chef making meringues or a chicken trying to lay. *Get to know your body,* chant the books, the Web sites, her baby-bearing friends, and oh she has, she does, though it's beginning to feel like a cheap car she has leased for a while and is getting ready to return.

She still likes making love with Tom, the tremble of it, the slow blue wash, the way they lie cupped together in their new old house as it sits in the greening fields, on the turning earth. It's afterward that she hates. She can never fall asleep without picturing the spastic, thrashing tails, the egg's hard shell, the long, thin tubes stretched like IVs toward a pulsing womb. A speck, she imagines sometimes, the head of a pin, the dot of a period. The End — or maybe, if they're lucky, dot dot dot.

But the hand is so much bigger than that, substantial, real. Her own hands shake with relief as she puts on the tea water. Something is starting — a secret, a discovery, begun not in the narrow recesses of her body but in the mysterious body of her new old house. The house has a door called the Mourning Door — the realtor pointed it out the first time they walked through. It's a door off the front parlor, and though it leads outside, it has no stoop or stairs, just a place for the cart to back up so the coffin can be carried away. Of course babies were born here too, added the realtor, her voice too bright. Probably right in this room! After she and Tom moved in, they decided only to use the door off the kitchen. Friendlier, she said, and after all, they're concentrating, these days, on making life.

When she goes back upstairs, she takes the burlap sack and a flashlight to the warm, musty attic, where Tom almost never goes. With the flashlight's beam, she finds, in one dark corner, the section where the fire left its mark. She touches the wood, and a smudge of ash comes off on her finger. She tastes it: dry powder, ancient fruit, people passing buckets, lives lost, found, lost. She leaves the sack in the other corner of the attic, inside a box marked "Kitchen Stuff." Then she heads downstairs to wash her hands.

Three days later she is doing laundry when she comes across a shoulder, round and smooth. She knows it should be disconcerting to find such a thing separated from its owner, a shoulder disembodied, lying in a nest of dryer lint, tucked close to the wall. But why get upset? After all, the world is full of parts apart from wholes. A few months ago, she and Tom went to the salvage place — old radiator covers, round church windows, faucets and doorknobs, a spiral staircase leading nowhere. Then, they bought two doors and a useless unit of brass mailboxes, numbers fifteen through twenty-five. Now she wipes her hands on her jeans and picks the shoulder up. It is late afternoon, the contractors gone, Tom still at work. She takes the shoulder up to the attic and puts it in the sack with the hand. Then she goes to the bedroom, swallows a vitamin the size of a horse pill, climbs into bed, and falls asleep.

Whereas before she had been agitated, unable to turn her thoughts away, now she is peaceful, assembling something, proud. But tired too — this is not unexpected; every day by four or five o'clock she has to sink into bed for a nap, let in dreams full of floaty shapes, closed fists, and open mouths. Still, most days she gets a little something done. She lines a trunk with old wallpaper, goes for a walk in the woods with a friend, starts to plan a lesson sequence on how leaves change color in the fall. Her children are all away for the summer, shipped off to lakes and rivers and seas. Sometimes she gets a "Dear Teacher" postcard: *I found some mica. We went on a boat. I lost my ring in the lake.* The water in the postcards is always a vivid, chlorinated blue. She gets her hair cut, sees a matinee movie with her friend Hannah, starts to knit again. One night Tom remarks — perhaps with relief, perhaps with the slightest tinge of fear — that she seems back to her old self.

In the basement, the men put in Lally columns, thick and red, to keep the first floor from falling in. They construct a vapor barrier, rewire the electricity. They sister the joists and patch the foundation. In her bedroom, she stuffs cotton in her ears to block the noise. She wears sweatpants or loose shorts now, and Tom's shirts. Each time she catches a glimpse of herself in the mirror, she is struck by how pretty she looks, her eyes so bright, almost feverish, her fingernails a flushed, excited pink.

She finds a second hand with five perfect fingers, and a second shoulder. She finds a leg, an arm. No eyes yet, no face. Everything in time, she tells herself, and at the Center for Reproductive Medicine they inject her womb with blue and she sees her tubes, thin as violin strings, curled and ghostly on the screen. They have her drink water and lie on her back. They swab gel on her belly, and she neglects to tell them that her actual belly is at home, smelling like dust and applewood, snoozing under the eaves. They say, Come in on day three, on day ten. They swab her with more gel and give her a rattle, loose pills in an amber jar. Tom goes to the clinic, and they shut him in a room with girlie magazines and take his fish. At home, while he is at the doctor's, she finds a tiny penis, sweet and curled. Tom comes home discouraged — rare for him. He lies down on the floor and sighs. She says, Don't worry, babe, and leans to kiss him on the arm. She would like to tell him about everything she has found, but she knows she must protect her secret. Things are so fragile, really — the earth settles, the house shifts. You put up a wall in the wrong place and so never find the hidden object in the eaves. You speak too soon and cause — with your hard, your hopeful words — a clot, a cramp. Things are so fragile, but then also not. Look at the ants, she tells herself — how they always find a place to make a nest. Look at the people of the earth, each one with a mother. At the supermarket, she stares at them — their hands, their faces, how neatly it all goes together, a completed puzzle.

She knows her own way is out of the ordinary, but then what is ordinary these days? She is living in a time of freezers and test tubes, of petri dishes and turkey basters, of trade and barter, test and track, mix and match. Women carry the eggs of other women, or have their own eggs injected back into them pumped with potential, four or six at a time. Sperm are washed and coddled, separated and sifted, like gold. Ovaries are inflated until they spill with treasures. The names sound like code words: GIFT, IUI, ZIFT. Though it upsets her to admit it, the other women at the center disgust her a little. They seem so desperate, they look so swollen, but in all the wrong places — their eyes, their chins, their hearts. Not me, she thinks as the nurse calls her name and she rises with a friendly smile.

One day she moves the burlap bag from the attic to the back of her bedroom closet. It's such a big house, and the attic is sweltering now, and soon the men will be working up there on the charred wood. Before, she and Tom lived in a tiny, rented bungalow and looked into each other's eyes a lot. She loves Tom; she really does, though lately he seems quite far away. Outside, here, is a swing set made of old, splintered cedar, not safe enough for use. But that same day she finds an ear in it, tucked like a chestnut under a climbing pole. The tomatoes are ripe now. The sunflowers she planted in May are taller than she is, balancing their heads on swaying stalks. In the herb garden, the chives bear fat purple balls. The ear, oddly, is downed with dark hair, like the ear of a young primate. She holds it to her own ear as if she might hear something inside it — the sea, perhaps, a heartbeat or a yawn. It looks so tender that she wraps it in tissue paper before placing it in the bag.

One night on the evening news, she and Tom see a story about a girl who was in a car accident and went into a coma, and now the girl performs miracles and people think she's a saint. The news shows her lying in Worcester in her parents' garage, hitched to life support while pilgrims come from near and far: people on crutches, children with cancer, barren women, men dying of AIDS. Jesus, says Tom, shuddering. People will believe anything — how sick. But she doesn't think it's so sick, the way the vinyl-sided ranch house is transformed into a wall of flowers, the way people bring gifts — Barbie dolls, barrettes, Hawaiian Punch (the girl's favorite) — and a blind man sees again, and a baby blooms from a tired woman's torso, and the rest of the people, well, the rest sit briefly in the full lap of hope, then get in their cars and go home. The girl is pretty, even though she's almost dead. Her braid is black and shiny, her brow peaceful. Her mother, the reporter says, sponge-bathes her each morning and again at night. Her father is petitioning the Vatican for the girl to be made an official saint.

Days now, while the men work in the attic, she roams. She wanders around the house looking for treasures, and on the days when she does not find them, she gets in her car and drives to town, or out along the country roads. Sometimes she finds barn sales and gets things for the house — a chair for Tom's desk, an old egg candler filled with holes. One day at a yard sale she buys a sewing machine, though she's never used one. I'll give you the instruction book, the woman says. It's easy — you'll see. Also at this yard sale is a playpen, a high chair, a pile of infant clothes. The woman sees her staring at them. I thought you might be expecting, she says, smiling. But I didn't want to presume. As a bonus, she throws in a plump pincushion stabbed with silver pins and needles and a blue-and-white sailor suit. It was my son's, she says, and from behind the house come — as if in proof — the shrieks of kids at play.

That night, with Tom in New York for an overnight meeting, she sets up the sewing machine and sits with the instruction manual in her lap. She slides out the trap door under the needle, examining the bobbin. Slowly, following the instructions, she winds the bobbin full of beige thread, then threads the needle. She gets the bag from the closet. She's not sure she's ready (the books say you're never sure), but at the same time her body is guiding, pushing, *urging* her. Breathe, she commands herself, and draws a deep breath. She has never done this before, never threaded the needle or assembled the pattern or put together the parts, but it doesn't seem to matter; she has a sense of how to approach it — first this, then this, then this. She takes a hand out of the bag and tries to stitch it to an arm, but the machine jams, so she unwinds a length of thread from the bobbin, pulls a needle from the pincushion, and begins again, by hand.

Slowly, awkwardly, she stitches arm to shoulder, stops to catch her breath and wipe the sweat from her brow. She remembers backstitch, cross-stitch; someone (her mother?) must have taught her long ago. She finds the other hand, the other arm. Does she have everything? It's been a long summer, and she's found so much; she might be losing track. If there aren't enough pieces, don't panic, she tells herself. He doesn't need to be perfect; she's not asking for that. He can be missing a part or two, he can need extra care. Her own body, after all, has its flaws, its stubborn limits. What, anyway, is perfect in this world? She'll take what she is given, what she has been able, bit by bit, to make.

She stitches feet to legs, carefully doing the seams on the inside so they won't show. She attaches leg to torso, sews on the little penis. The boy-child begins to stir, to struggle; perhaps he has to pee. Not yet, my love. Hold on. She works long and hard and late into the night, her body tight with effort, the room filled with animal noises that spring from her mouth as if she were someone else. She wishes, with a deep, aching pain, that Tom were here to guide her hands, to help her breathe and watch her work. Finally — it must be near dawn — she reaches into the bag and finds nothing. How tired she is, bone tired, skin tired. She must be finished, for she has used up all the parts.

Slowly, then, as if in sleep, she rises with the child in her arms. She has been working in the dark and so can't quite see him, though she feels his downy head, his foot and hand. He curls toward her for an instant as if to nurse, so she unbuttons her blouse and draws him near. He nuzzles toward her but does not drink, and she passes a hand over his face and realizes that he has no mouth. Carefully, in the dark, she inspects him with both her hands and mind: he has a nose but no mouth, wrists but no elbows. She spreads her palm over his torso, and her fingers tell her that he has kidneys and a liver but only six small ribs and half a heart. Oh, she tells him. Oh, I'm sorry. I tried so hard. I found and saved and stitched and tried so hard and yet —

She feels it first, before he goes: a spasm in her belly, a clot in her brain, a sorrow so thick and familiar that she knows she's felt it before, but not like this, so unyielding, so tangible. Six small ribs and only half a heart. While she holds him, he twitches twice and then is still.

Carrying him, she makes her way downstairs. It's lighter now, the purple-blue of dawn. She walks to the front parlor, past the TV, past the old honey extractor they found in the barn. She walks to the Mourning Door and tries to open it. It doesn't budge, wedged shut, and for a moment she panics — she has to get out now; the weight in her arms keeps getting heavier, a sack of stones. She needs to pass it through this door and set it down, or she will break. Trying to stay calm, she goes to the laundry room and finds a screwdriver, returns to the door, and wedges the tool in along the lock placket, balancing the baby on one arm. Finally the door gives, and she walks through it, forgetting that no steps meet it outside. Falling forward over the high ledge, she lands, stumbles, catches her balance (somehow, she hasn't dropped him) to stand stunned and breathless in the still morning air, her knees weak from landing hard.

Across the road, the sheep in the field have begun their bleating. A truck drives by, catching her briefly in its headlights. She lowers her nose to the baby's head and breathes in the smell of him. He's lighter now, easier now. *Depart,* she thinks, the word an old prayer following her through the door. *Depart in peace.* With her hands, she memorizes the slope of his nose, the open architecture of his skull. She fingers the spirals of one ear. Then she turns and starts walking, out behind the house to the barn, where a shovel hangs beside the hoe and rake. It's lighter now. A mosquito hovers close to her face. The day will be hot. Later, Tom will return. She buries the baby under a hawthorn tree on the backstretch of their land and leaves his grave unmarked. My boy, she says as she turns to go. Thank you, she says — to him or to the air — when she is halfway home. She sleeps all morning and gardens through the afternoon.

That night (day sixteen, except she's stopped charting), she and Tom make love, and afterward she thinks of nothing — no wagging fish, no hovering egg, no pathway, her thoughts as flat and clean as sheets. Tom smells like himself — it is a smell she loves and had nearly forgotten — and after their sex, they talk about his trip, and he runs a hand idly down her back. She is ready for something now — a child inside her or a child outside, come from another bed, another place. Or she is ready, perhaps, for no child at all, a trip with Tom to a different altitude or hemisphere, a rocky, twisting hike. They make love again, and after she comes, she cries, and he asks what, what is it, but it's nothing she can describe, it's where she's been, so far away and without him — in the charred attic, the tipped basement, where red columns try to shore up a house that will stand for as long as it wants to and fall when it wants to fall. Nothing, she says, and inside her something joins, or tries to join, forms or does not, and her dream, when she sleeps, is of the far horizon, a smooth, receding curve.

After Cowboy Chicken Came to Town

FROM TRIQUARTERLY

"I WANT MY MONEY BACK!" the customer said, dropped his plate on the counter, and handed me his receipt. He was a fiftyish man, of stout girth. A large crumb hung on the corner of his oily mouth. He had bought four pieces of chicken just now, but only a drumstick and a wing were left on the plate.

"Where are the breast and the thigh?" I asked.

"You can't take people in like this." The man's bulbous eyes flashed with rage. This time I recognized him; he was a worker in the nearby motor factory.

"How did we take you in?" the tall Baisha asked sharply, brandishing a pair of long tongs. She glared at the man, whose crown barely reached the level of her nose.

He said, "This Cowboy Chicken only sounds good and looks tasty. In fact it's just a name — it's more batter than meat. After two pieces I still don't feel a thing in here." He slapped his flabby side. "I don't want to eat this fluffy stuff anymore. Give me my money back."

"No way," Baisha said, and swung her permed hair, which looked like a magpies' nest. "If you hadn't touched the chicken, we'd refund you the money. But —"

"Excuse me," Peter Jiao said, coming out of the kitchen together with Mr. Shapiro.

We explained to him the customer's demand, which Peter translated for our American boss. Then we all remained silent to see how Peter, our manager, would handle this.

After a brief exchange with Mr. Shapiro in English, Peter said in Chinese to the man, "You've eaten two pieces already, so we can only refund half your money. But don't take this as a precedent. Once you've touched the food, it's yours."

The man looked unhappy but accepted the offer. Still he muttered, "American dogs." He was referring to us, the Chinese employed by Cowboy Chicken.

That angered us. We began arguing with Peter and Mr. Shapiro that we shouldn't have let him take advantage of us this way. Otherwise all kinds of people would come in to sample our food for free. We didn't need a cheap customer like this one and should throw him out. Mr. Shapiro said we ought to follow the American way of doing business — you must try to satisfy your customers. "The customer is always right," he had instructed us when we were hired. But he had no idea who he was dealing with. You let a devil into your house, he'll get into your bed. If Mr. Shapiro continued to play the merciful Buddha, this place would be a mess soon. We had already heard a lot of complaints about our restaurant. People in town would say, "Cowboy Chicken is just for spendthrifts." True, our product was more expensive and far greasier than the local braised chicken, which was cooked so well that you could eat even the bones.

Sponge in hand, I went over to clean the table littered by that man. The scarlet Formica tabletop smelled like castor oil when greased with chicken bones. The odor always nauseated me. As I was about to move to another table, I saw a hole on the seat the size of a soybean burned by a cigarette. It must have been the work of that son of a dog; instead of refunding his money, we should've detained him until he paid for the damage.

I hated Mr. Shapiro's hypocrisy. He always appeared goodhearted and considerate to customers but was cruel to us, his employees. The previous month he had deducted forty yuan from my pay. It hurt like having a rib taken out of my chest. What had happened was that I had given eight chicken breasts to a girl from my brother's electricity station. She came in to buy some chicken. By the company's regulations I was supposed to give her two drumsticks, two thighs, two wings, and two breasts. She said to me, "Be a good man, Hongwen. Give me more meat." Somehow I couldn't resist her charming smile, so I yielded to her request. My boss caught me stuffing the paper box with the meatiest pieces, but he remained silent until the girl was out of earshot. Then he dumped on me all his piss and crap. "If you do that again," he said, "I'll fire you." I was so frightened! Later he fined me, as an example to the seven other Chinese employees.

Mr. Shapiro was an old fox, good at sweet-talking. When we asked him why he had chosen to do business in our Muji City, he said he wanted to help the Chinese people, because in the late thirties his parents had fled Red Russia and lived here for three years before moving on to Australia; they had been treated decently, though they were Jews. With an earnest look on his round, whiskery face, Mr. Shapiro explained, "The Jews and the Chinese had a similar fate, so I feel close to you. We all have dark hair." He chuckled as if he had said something funny. In fact that was capitalist baloney. We don't need to eat Cowboy Chicken here, or appreciate his stout red nose and his balding crown, or wince at the thick black hair on his arms. His company exploited not just us but also thousands of country people. A few villages in Hebei Province grew potatoes for Cowboy Chicken, because the soil and climate there produced potatoes similar to Idaho's. In addition, the company had set up a few chicken farms in Anhui Province to provide meat for its chain in China. It used Chinese produce and labor and made money out of Chinese customers, then shipped its profits back to the U.S. How could Mr. Shapiro have the barefaced gall to claim he had come to help us? We have no need for a savior like him. As for his parents' stay in our city half a century ago, it's true that the citizens here had treated Jews without discrimination. That was because to us a Jew was just another foreigner, no different from any other white devil. We still cannot tell the difference.

We nicknamed Mr. Shapiro "Party Secretary," because just like a party boss anywhere he did little work. The only difference was that he didn't organize political studies or demand we report to him our inner thoughts. Peter Jiao, his manager, ran the business for him. I had known Peter since middle school, when his name was Peihai — an anemic, studious boy with few friends to play with. Boys often made fun of him because he had four tourbillions on his head. His father had served as a platoon commander in the Korean War and had been captured by the American army. Unlike some of the POWs, who chose to go to Canada or Taiwan after the war, Peihai's father, out of his love for our motherland, decided to come back. But when he returned, he was discharged from the army and sent down to a farm in a northern suburb of our city. In reality, all those captives who had come back were classified as suspected traitors. A lot of them were jailed again. Peihai's father worked under surveillance on the farm, but people rarely maltreated him, and he had his own home in a nearby village. He was quiet most of the time; so was his wife, a woman who never knew her dad's name because she had been fathered by some Japanese officer. Their only son, Peihai, had to walk three miles to town for school every weekday. That was why we called him Country Boy.

Unlike us, he always got good grades. In 1977, when colleges reopened, he passed the entrance exams and enrolled at Tianjin Foreign Language Institute to study English. We had all sat for the exams, but only two out of the three hundred seniors from our high school had passed the admission standard. After college, Peihai went to America, studying history at the University of Iowa. Later he changed his field and earned a degree in business from that school. Then he came back, a completely different man, robust and wealthy, with curly hair and a new name. He looked energetic, cheerful, and younger than his age. At work he was always dressed formally, in a western suit and a bright-colored tie. He once joked with us, saying he had over fifty pounds of American flesh. To tell the truth, I liked Peter better than Peihai. I often wondered what in America had made him change so much — in just six years from an awkward boy to a capable, confident man. Was it American water? American milk and beef? The American climate? The American way of life? I don't know for sure. More impressive, Peter spoke English beautifully, much better than those professors and lecturers in the City College who had never gone abroad and had learned their English mainly from textbooks written by the Russians. He had hired me probably because I had never bugged him in our school days and because I had a slightly lame foot. Out of gratitude, I never spoke about his past to my fellow workers.

On the day Cowboy Chicken opened, about forty officials from the city hall came to celebrate. At the opening ceremony, a vice mayor cut the red silk ribbon with a pair of scissors two feet long. He then presented Mr. Shapiro with a brass key the size of a small poker.

What's that for? we wondered. Our city didn't have a gate with a colossal lock for it to open. The attendees at the ceremony sampled our chicken, fries, coleslaw, salad, biscuits. Coca-Cola, ginger ale, and orange soda were poured free like water. People touched the vinyl seats, the Formica tables, the dishwasher, the microwave, the cash register, the linoleum tile on the kitchen floor, and poked their heads into the freezer and the brand-new restrooms. They were impressed by the whole package, shipped directly from the U.S. A white-bearded official said, "We must learn from the Americans. See how they have managed to meet every need of their customers, taking care of not only what goes in but also what comes out. Everything was thought out beforehand." Some of them watched us frying chicken in the stainless-steel troughs, which were safe and clean, nothing like a soot-bottomed caldron or a noisy, unsteady wok. The vice mayor shook hands with every employee and told us to work hard and cooperatively with our American boss. The next day the city's newspaper, the *Muji Herald,* published a lengthy article about Cowboy Chicken, describing its appearance here as a significant breakthrough in the city's campaign to attract foreign investors.

During the first few weeks we had a lot of customers, especially young people, who, eager to taste something American, came in droves. We got so much business that the cooked-meat stands on the streets had to move farther and farther away from our restaurant. Sometimes when we passed those stands, their owners would spit on the ground and curse without looking at us, "Foreign lackeys!"

We'd cry back, "I eat Cowboy Chicken every day and gained lots of weight."

At first Mr. Shapiro worked hard, often staying around until we closed at ten-thirty. But as the business was flourishing, he hung back more and stayed in his office for hours on end, reading newspapers and sometimes chewing a skinny sausage wrapped in cellophane. He rested so well in the daytime and had so much energy to spare that he began to date the girls working for him. There were four of them, two full-timers and two part-timers, all around twenty, healthy and lively, though not dazzlingly pretty. Imagine, once a week, on Thursday night, a man of over fifty went out with a young girl who was happy to go anywhere he took her. This made us, the three men hired by him, feel useless, like a bunch of eunuchs, particularly myself, because I'd never had a girlfriend, though I was almost thirty. Most girls were nice to me, but for them I was merely a good fellow, deserving more pity than affection, as if my crippled foot made me less than a man. For me, Mr. Shapiro was just a dirty old man, but the girls here were no better, always ready to sell something — a smile, a few sweet words, and perhaps their flesh.

The day after Mr. Shapiro had taken Baisha out, I asked her about the date, curious to see what else besides money made this paunchy man so attractive to girls. What's more, I was eager to find out whether he had bedded them in his apartment after dinner. That was illegal. If he had done it, we'd have something on him and could turn him in when it was necessary. I asked Baisha casually, "How many rooms does he have?" My hands were busy pulling plates out of the dishwasher and piling them up on a table.

"How should I know?" she said, and gave me a suspicious stare. I must admit, she was smart and had a mind quick like a lizard.

"Didn't you spend some time with him yesterday evening?"

"Yes, we had dinner. That was all."

"Was it good?" I had heard he had taken the girls to Lucky House, a third-rate restaurant near the marketplace.

"So-so."

"What did you eat?"

"Fried noodles and sautéed beef tripe."

"Well, I wish somebody would give me a treat like that."

"What made you think it was his treat?"

"It wasn't?" I put the last plate on the pile.

"I paid for what I ate. I won't go out with him again. He's such a cheapskate."

"If he didn't mean to spend money, why did he invite you out?"

"He said this was the American way. He gave the waitress a big tip though, a ten, but the girl wouldn't take it."

"So afterward you just went home?"

"Yes. I thought he'd take me to the movies or a karaoke bar. He just picked up his big butt and said he had a good time. Before we parted on the street, he yawned and said he missed his wife and kids."

"That was strange."

Manyou, Jinglin, and I — the three male employees — talked among ourselves about Mr. Shapiro's way of taking the girls out. We couldn't see what he was up to. How could he have a good time just eating a meal with a girl? This puzzled us. We asked Peter whether all American men were so stingy, but he said that like us they would generally pay the bill in such a case. He explained, "Probably Mr. Shapiro wants to make it clear to the girls that this isn't a date but a working dinner."

Who would buy that? Why didn't he have a working dinner with one of us, the male employees? We guessed he might have used the girls, because if he had gone to a fancy place like the Four Seas Garden or North Star Palace, which had special menus for foreigners, he'd have had to pay at least five times more than a Chinese customer. We checked with the girls, and they admitted that Mr. Shapiro had asked them to order everything. So he had indeed paid the Chinese prices. No wonder he had a good time. What an old fox. Still, why wouldn't he take the girls to his apartment? Though none of them was a beauty, just the smell of the youthful flesh should have turned his old head, shouldn't it? Especially the two part-timers, the college students, who had fine figures and educated voices; they worked only twenty hours a week and wouldn't condescend to talk to us very often. Probably Mr. Shapiro was no good in bed, a true eunuch.

Our business didn't boom for long. Several handcarts had appeared on Peace Avenue, selling spiced chicken on the roadside near our restaurant. They each carried a sign that declared, PATRIOTIC CHICKEN — CRISPY, TENDER, DELICIOUS, 30% CHEAPER THAN C.C.! Those were not false claims. Yet whenever we saw their signs, we couldn't help calling the vendors names. Most citizens here, especially old people, were accustomed to the price and taste of Patriotic Chicken, so they preferred it to ours. Some of them had tried our product, but they'd complain afterward, "What a sham! So expensive, this Cowboy thing isn't for a Chinese stomach." And they wouldn't come again. As a result, our steady clientele were mainly fashionable young people.

One day Mr. Shapiro came up with the idea of starting a buffet. We had never heard that word before. "What does it mean?" we asked.

Peter said, "You pay a small amount of money and eat all you can."

Good, a buffet would be great! We were all ears. Our boss suggested nineteen yuan and ninety-five fen as the price for the buffet, which should include every kind of Cowboy Chicken, mashed potatoes, fries, salad, and canned fruit. Why didn't he price it twenty yuan even? we wondered. That would sound more honest and also make it easier for us to handle the change. Peter explained that this was the American way of pricing a product. "You don't add the last straw to collapse the camel," he said. We couldn't understand the logic of a camel or a horse or an ox. Anyway, Mr. Shapiro fell in love with his idea, saying that even if it didn't fetch us enough customers, the buffet would help spread our name.

Peter wasn't enthusiastic about it, but we all said it was a brilliant idea and would definitely make us famous. Of course we knew it wouldn't work. We supported it because we wanted to eat Cowboy Chicken. Mr. Shapiro was such a skinflint that he would never give us a discount when we bought chicken for ourselves. He said the company's policy didn't allow any discount for its employees. On the other hand, our friends, when buying chicken here, often asked us to do them a favor — give them either some choice pieces or a discount — but we dared not break the rules for them. Now came an opportunity, so without delay we put out notices and spread the word about the buffet, which was to start the following week. For a whole weekend we biked around town in our free time to make sure the news would reach our relatives, friends, and whoever might benefit from it.

Two feet of snow fell on Sunday night, and traffic was paralyzed the next morning, but we all arrived at work on time. Mr. Shapiro was worried, fearing that the severe weather would keep people indoors. We assured him that they were not hibernating bears and would definitely show up. Still anxious, he stood outside the front door with the fur earflaps of his hat tied around his jaw, smoking and looking up and down the street at the people shoveling snow. Wisps of smoke and breath hung around his head. We all had on dogskin or quilted trousers in such weather, but he wore only woolen pajamas underneath jeans. It was glitteringly cold outside; the wind tossed the phone lines, which whistled like crazy.

With his protruding mouth pointed at Mr. Shapiro, Manyou said to us, "See how hard it is to be a boss in America. You have to worry about your business all the time."

"Boy, he's scared," I said.

"For once he's working," added Feilan, who, though a plump

girl, had a pleasant apple face with two dimples on it. Unlike us, she hadn't gone to high school, because she had flunked two of the entrance exams.

We set the buffet stand in a corner and fried piles of chicken. Gradually people arrived. When about a dozen customers had sat down to their meals, Mr. Shapiro looked relieved, though he couldn't stop rubbing his cheeks and ears, which must have frozen numb. He retreated into his office for coffee, having no idea that this was just the first skirmish of a mighty battle. As the morning went by, more and more people came in, and we could hardly cook enough chicken and fries for them. The room grew noisy and crowded, undoubtedly reaching its maximum capacity, but still our boss was happy. Encouraged by the bustling scene, he even whistled in his office, where he, through bifocal lenses, was reading the *China Daily.*

My father and uncle were among the first dozen customers. Both could hardly walk when done with eating. After they left, my brother brought over six young men from his electricity station; they all had a soda or a beer in their pockets so that they wouldn't have to buy a drink. Without delay they began to attack the buffet; they ate as though this were their last supper on earth. I kept count of their accomplishment — on average they each finished at least a dozen pieces of chicken. Even when they were done and leaving, every one of them held a leg or a wing in his hand. Baisha's family had come too, including her father, uncles, and aunts. So had the folks of Manyou, Jinglin, and Feilan. The two part-timers had no family in town, but more than ten of their schoolmates turned up. In the back corner a table was occupied by five people, whose cat-like faces showed that they belonged to Peter's clan. Among them was a young woman at least seven months pregnant; she was Peter's sister, and surely her unborn baby needed nutrition.

We all knew the buffet was heading for disaster, but we didn't care very much and just continued deep-frying chicken and refilling the salad and mashed potato bowls. Once in a while we also went over to the buffet stand and picked a piece of chicken for ourselves, because today nobody could keep a record. At last we too could eat our fill. I liked the chicken better with soy sauce and slapped plenty on. The employees shared a bottle of soy sauce, which we kept under the counter.

By midday some people in the marketplace had heard of this

rare bargain, and they came in, all eating like starved wolves. Most of them were from the countryside, in town selling and buying stuff; surely they had never dreamed that any restaurant would offer such an abundant meal.

Peter wasn't around most of the time. He had to be at the Tax Bureau in the morning, and in the afternoon he went to the bank to fetch our wages. When he returned at four o'clock, his face darkened at the amount of food consumed by the buffet. Twenty boxes of chicken and eighteen sacks of fries were gone — which should have lasted three days. He went to inform Mr. Shapiro, who came out of his office and looked disconcerted. Peter suggested we stop the buffet immediately. Our boss's face reddened, his Adam's apple going up and down as though he were guzzling something. He said, "Let's offer it a little while longer. We're not sure if we lost money or not."

We closed twenty minutes early that night in order to count the money. The result didn't surprise us: we lost seven hundred yuan, exclusive of our wages.

In spite of his misshapen face, Mr. Shapiro insisted on trying the buffet for another day. Perhaps he meant to show who was in command, reluctant to admit the buffet was a flop. This suited us fine, since not all of our people had come yet.

The next day Mr. Shapiro sat on a chair outside his office and watched the customers stuffing themselves. He looked like a giant bulldog, vigilant and sulky, now shaking his head, now smiling exaggeratedly. At times his face turned grim, his eyelids trembling a little. A few men from my father's office showed up, and two of them even attempted to chat with me in front of my boss. This scared me. I responded to their greetings and questions cursorily, for fear that Mr. Shapiro might detect my connection with them. Fortunately he didn't understand our language, so he noticed nothing.

After my father's colleagues left, a tall, thirtyish man in a buff corduroy jacket turned up. After paying for the buffet, he left his fur hat on a table, then walked across to the stand and filled a plate with drumsticks and breasts. As he was about to return to his seat, Mr. Shapiro stopped him and asked, "Why did you come again?"

The man happened to know some English and said with a friendly grin, "First-time customer."

"You ate tons of chicken and mashed potatoes just now. How come you're hungry again so soon?"

"What's this about?" The man's face changed.

Peter came over, but he wasn't sure if the man had been here before. He turned to us and asked, "Is this his second time?"

Before we could answer, the man flared up. "This is my hundredth time. So what? I paid."

Manyou laughed and told Peter, "There was a fella here just now in the same kind of jacket, but that was a different man."

"That's true," I piped up. I knew the other man — he was an accountant in my father's bureau. This fellow fuming in front of us was a genuine stranger, with a beeper on his belt. He must be a cabdriver or an entrepreneur.

Peter apologized to the man, told him to go ahead and eat, then he explained the truth to Mr. Shapiro, who had become so edgy that some customers began to look identical to him. "How the hell could I tell the difference?" our boss said. "To me they all look alike — they're all real Chinese, with appetites like alligators." He laughed heartily, like a young boy.

Peter interpreted his words to us, and we all cracked up.

On the second day we lost about six hundred yuan, so that was the end of the buffet. Luckily for us, Mr. Shapiro didn't withhold our wages, which we all received the next day. This was the beauty of working for Cowboy Chicken — it was never late in paying us, unlike many Chinese companies, especially those owned by the state, which simply didn't have enough cash to pay employees their full wages. My mother often got only 60 percent of her salary from her weather station, which could not increase its clientele, or run a night school, or have any power over other companies. She'd sigh and say, "The longer I work, the more I lose."

At the sight of my monthly wages — 468 yuan — my father became heartbroken. He'd had a drop too much that night, full of self-pity, and, waving a half-smoked cigarette, he said to me, "Hongwen, I've joined the Revolution for almost forty years, and I earn only three hundred yuan a month. But you just started working and you draw a larger salary. This makes me feel duped, duped by the Communist party I've served."

My youngest brother butted in. "It's never too late to quit, Dad."

"Shut up!" I snapped. He was such an idiot, he couldn't see the old man was really suffering. I said to my father, "You shouldn't think that way. True, you're not paid a lot, but your job is secure, like a rubber rice bowl that nobody can take away from you or smash — even a tank cannot crush it. Every day you just sit at your desk drinking tea and reading newspapers, or chatting away, and at the end of each month you take home a full salary. But I have to work my ass off for a capitalist who pays me by the hour."

"You make so much and always eat high-protein food. What else do you want?"

I didn't answer. In my heart I said, I want a job that pays a salary. I want to be like some people who go to their offices every morning for an eight-hour rest. My father kept on: "Cowboy Chicken is so delicious. If I could eat it and drink Coke every day, I'd have no need for socialism."

I wouldn't argue with him. He was beside himself that night. Indeed, I did often have some tidbits at the restaurant, mainly fries and biscuits. As a result, I seldom ate dinner when I came home, but mainly it was because I wanted to save food for my family. My father, of course, assumed I was stuffing myself with chicken every day.

After the disastrous buffet, Mr. Shapiro depended more on Peter, who in fact ran the place single-handedly. To be fair, Peter was an able man and had put his heart into the restaurant. He began to make a lot of connections in town and persuaded people to have business lunches at our place. This made a huge difference. Because their companies would foot the bill, the businesspeople would order table loads of food to treat their guests to hearty American meals, and then they'd take the leftovers home for their families. By and by our restaurant gained a reputation in the business world, and we established a stable clientele. So once again Mr. Shapiro could stay in his office in the morning drinking coffee, reading magazines, and even listening to a tape to learn the ABCs of Chinese.

One afternoon the second son of the president of Muji Teachers College phoned Peter, saying he'd like to hold his wedding feast at our restaurant. I knew of this dandy, who had divorced his hard-working wife the year before; his current bride used to be a young widow who had given up her managerial position in a theater four years ago in order to go to Russia. Now they had decided to marry, and he wanted something exotic for their wedding dinner, so he picked Cowboy Chicken.

Uneasy about this request, Mr. Shapiro said to Peter, "We're just a fast-food place. We're not equipped to cater a wedding banquet."

"We must not miss this opportunity," said Peter. "A Chinese man would spend all his savings on his wedding." His owlish eyes glittered.

"Well, we'll have to serve alcoholic beverages, won't we? We have no license."

"Forget that. Nobody has ever heard of such a thing in China. Even a baby can drink alcohol here." Peter grew impatient.

Manyou, who could speak a few words of English, broke in. "Mr. Shapiro, Peter is right. Men of China use all moneys for wedding, big money." He seemed embarrassed by his accent and went back to biting his cuticles.

So our boss yielded. From the next day on, we began to prepare the place for the wedding feast. Mr. Shapiro called Cowboy Chicken's headquarters in Beijing to have some cheesecakes, ice cream, and Californian wines shipped to us by the express mail. Peter hired two temps and had the room decked out with colorful ribbons and strings of tiny light bulbs. Since it was already mid-December, he had a dwarf juniper and candlesticks set up in a corner. We even hung up a pair of large bunny lanterns at the front door, as the Year of Rabbit was almost here. Peter ordered us to wear clean uniforms for the occasion — red sweaters, black pants, and maroon aprons.

The wedding banquet took place on Thursday evening. It went smoothly, since most of the guests were from the college, urbane and sober-minded. The bride, a small woman in her mid-thirties, wore a sky-blue silk dress, her hair was permed, and her lips were rouged scarlet. She smiled without stopping. It was too bad that her parents hadn't given her beautiful eyes; she must have been altered by cosmetic surgery, which had produced her tight, thick double lids. Baisha said the woman owned two gift shops in Moscow. Small wonder she wore six fancy rings and a tiny wristwatch in the shape of a heart. With so many diamonds and so much gold on her fingers, she must be lazy, not doing any housework. From her manners we could tell she had seen the world. By comparison, her tall groom looked like a bumpkin despite his fancy outfit — a dark-blue western suit, a yellow tie studded with tiny magpies, and patent leather boots with brass buckles. He had a hoarse voice, often laughing with a bubbling sound in his throat. When he laughed, you could hardly see anything on his face except his mouth, which reminded me of a crocodile's. His gray-haired parents sat opposite him, quiet and reserved, both of them senior officials.

The man officiating at the banquet spoke briefly about the auspicious union of the couple. Next he praised the simple wedding ceremony, which had taken place two hours ago. After a round of applause, he turned to our boss and said, "We thank our American friend, Mr. Ken Shapiro, for providing us with such a clean, beautiful place and the delicious food. This is a perfect example of adapting foreign things to Chinese needs."

People clapped again. All our boss could say in Chinese was "Thank you." He looked a little shy, his cheeks pink and his hazel eyes gleaming happily.

As people were making the first toast, we began to serve chicken, every kind we had — crispy, spicy, barbecued, Cajun, and Cowboy original. An old woman opened a large paper napkin with a flowered pattern on it and studied it for a long time, as though it were a piece of needlework on lavender silk which she was reluctant to spoil. A bottle of champagne popped and scared the bridesmaid into screaming. Laughter followed.

"Boy, this is hot!" the groom said, chewing a Cajun wing and exhaling noisily.

They all enjoyed the chicken, but except for the champagne, they didn't like the American wines, which were too mild for them. Most women wouldn't drink wine; they wanted beer, Coca-Cola, and other soft drinks. Fortunately Peter had stocked some Green Bamboo Leaves and Tsingtao beer, which we brought out without delay. We had also heated a basin of water, in which we warmed the liquor for them. Mr. Shapiro raved to his manager, "Fabulous job, Peter!" He went on flashing a broad smile at everyone, revealing his white teeth. He even patted some of us on the back.

I liked the red wine, and whenever I could, I'd sip some from a glass I had poured myself. But I dared not drink too much for fear my face might change color. When the guests were done with the chicken, fries, and salad, we began to serve cheesecake and ice cream, which turned out to be a big success. Everybody loved the dessert. An old scholarly-looking man said loudly, "Ah, here's the best American stuff!" His tone of voice suggested he had been to the U.S. He forked a chunk of cheesecake into his mouth and smacked his thin lips. He was among the few who could use a fork skillfully; most of them ate with chopsticks and spoons.

That was the first time we offered cheesecake and ice cream, so all of us — the employees — would take a bite whenever we could. Before that day I had never heard of cheesecake, which I loved so much I ate two wedges. I hid my glass and plate in a cabinet so that our boss couldn't see them. As long as we did the work well, Peter would shut his eyes to our eating and drinking.

For me the best part of this wedding feast was that it was sub-dued, peaceful, and short, lasting only two hours, perhaps because both the bride and the groom had been married before. It differed from a standard wedding banquet, which is always raucous and messy, drags on for seven or eight hours, and often gets out of hand, since quarrels and fights are commonplace once enough alcohol is consumed. None of these educated men and women drank to excess. The only loudmouth was the bridegroom, who looked slightly retarded. I couldn't help wondering how come that wealthy lady would marry such a heartless ass, who had abandoned his two small daughters. Probably because his parents had power, or maybe he was just good at tricking women. He must have wanted to live in Moscow for a while and have another baby, hopefully a boy. Feilan shook her head, saying about him, "Disgusting!"

When the feast was over, both Mr. Shapiro and Peter were ex-cited, their faces flushed. They knew we had just opened a new page in Cowboy Chicken's history; our boss said he was going to re-port our success to the headquarters in Dallas. We were happy too, though sleepy and tired. If business was better, we might get a big-ger raise the next summer, Mr. Shapiro had told us.

That night I didn't sleep well and had to go to the bathroom con-tinually. I figured my stomach wasn't used to American food yet. I had eaten fries and biscuits every day but had never taken in ice cream, cheesecake, red wine, and champagne. Without doubt my stomach couldn't digest so much rich stuff all at once. I was so weakened that I wondered if I should stay home the next morning.

Not wanting to dampen our spirit of success, I hauled myself to the restaurant at nine o'clock, half an hour late. As we were cutting vegetables and coating chicken with spiced flour, I asked my fellow workers whether they had slept well the night before.

"What do you mean?" Baisha's small eyes stared at me like a pair of tiny daggers.

"I had diarrhea."

"That's because you stole too much food, and it serves you right," she said with a straight face, which was slightly swollen with pimples.

"So you didn't have any problem?"

"What makes you think I have the same kind of bowels as you?"

Manyou said he had slept like a corpse, perhaps having drunk too much champagne. To my satisfaction, both Jinglin and Feilan admitted they too had suffered from diarrhea. Feilan said, "I thought I was going to die last night. My mother made me drink two kettles of hot water. Otherwise I'd sure be dehydrated today." She held her sides with both hands as if about to run for the ladies' room.

Jinglin added, "I thought I was going to poop my guts out." Indeed, his chubby face looked smaller than yesterday.

As we were talking, the phone rang. Peter answered it. He sounded nervous, and his face turned bloodless and tiny beads of sweat were oozing out on his stubby nose. The caller was a woman complaining about the previous evening's food. She claimed she had been poisoned. Peter apologized and assured her that we had been very careful about food hygiene, but he would investigate the matter thoroughly.

The instant he put down the phone, another call came in. Then another. From ten o'clock on, every few minutes the phone would ring. People were lodging the same kind of complaint against our restaurant. Mr. Shapiro was shaken, saying, "Jesus, they're going to sue us!"

What did this mean? we asked him, unsure how suing us could do the complainers any good. He said the company might have to pay them a lot of money. "In America that's a way to make a living for some people," he told us. So we worried too.

At noon the college called to officially inform Peter that about a third of the wedding guests had suffered from food poisoning and that more than a dozen faculty members were unable to teach that day. The bridegroom's mother was still in Central Hospital, taking an intravenous drip. The caller suspected the food must have been unclean or past its expiration dates, or perhaps the ice cream had been too cold. Mr. Shapiro paced back and forth like an ant in a heated pan, while Peter remained quiet, his thick eyebrows knitted together.

"I told you we couldn't handle a wedding banquet," our boss said with his nostrils expanding.

Peter muttered, "It must've been the cheesecake and the ice cream that upset their stomachs. I'm positive our food was clean and fresh."

"Maybe I shouldn't have gone the extra mile to get the stuff from Beijing. Now what should we do?"

"Don't worry. I'll explain to them."

From then on, whenever a complainer called, Peter would answer personally. He said that our food had been absolutely fresh and clean but that some Chinese stomachs couldn't tolerate dairy products. That was why more than two thirds of the previous night's diners had not felt anything unusual.

His theory of Chinese stomachs was sheer nonsense. We had all drunk milk before and had never been poisoned like this. Three days later, a twelve-hundred-word article appeared in the *Muji Herald*. Peter was its author. He wrote that there was this substance called lactose, to which many Chinese stomachs were allergic because our traditional diet included very little dairy food. He even quoted from a scientific journal to prove that the Chinese had different stomachs from the westerners'. He urged people to make sure they could endure lactose before they ate our dairy items. From now on, he declared, our restaurant would continue to offer ice cream, but also a variety of nonmilk desserts, like Jell-O, apple pie, pecan pie, and canned fruit.

I was unhappy about the article, because I had thought the company might compensate us for the suffering we'd gone through. Even a couple of yuan would help. Now Peter had blown that possibility. When I expressed my dissatisfaction to my fellow workers, Feilan said to me, "You're small-minded like a housewife, Hongwen. As long as this place does well, we'll make more money."

Bitch! I cursed to myself. But I gave a thought to what she said, and she did have a point. The restaurant had almost become our work unit now; we'd all suffer if it lost money. Besides, to file for compensation, I'd first have to admit I had pilfered the ice cream and cheesecake. That would amount to asking for a fine and ridicule.

Soon Peter had Cowboy Chicken completely in his clutches. This was fine with us. We all agreed he could take care of the restaurant better than Mr. Shapiro. We nicknamed him Number Two Boss. Since the publication of his article, which had quieted all complaints, more and more people ate here, and some came especially for our desserts. Young women were partial to Jell-O and canned fruit, while children loved our ice cream. Again we began to cater for wedding banquets, which gradually became an important source of our profits. From time to time people called and asked whether we'd serve a "white feast" — the dinner after a funeral. We wouldn't, because it was much plainer than a wedding banquet and there wasn't much money to be made. Besides, it might bring bad luck.

When the snow and ice had melted away from the streets and branches began sprouting yellowish buds, Mr. Shapiro stopped going out with the girls as often as before. By now most restaurants in town treated him as a regular customer, charging him the Chinese prices. One day Juju, the younger part-timer, said our boss had gotten fresh with her the previous evening when he was tipsy at Eight Deities Garden. He had grasped her wrist and called her "honey." She declared she wouldn't go out with him anymore. We told the girls that if he did anything like that again, they should report him to the police or sue him.

In late April, Mr. Shapiro went back to Texas for a week to attend his stepdaughter's wedding. After he returned, he stopped dating the girls altogether. Perhaps he was scared. He was wise to stop, because he couldn't possibly contain himself all the time. If he did something indecent to one of the girls again and she reported him to the authorities, he would find himself in trouble, at least be fined. Another reason for the change might be that by now he had befriended an American woman named Susanna, from Raleigh, North Carolina, who was teaching English at Muji Teachers College. This black woman was truly amazing, in her early thirties, five foot ten, with long muscular limbs and a behind like a small caldron. She had bobbed hair, and most of the time wore jeans and earrings the size of bracelets. We often speculated about those gorgeous hoop earrings. Were they made of fourteen-carat gold?

Or eighteen-carat? Or twenty-carat? At any rate, they must have been worth a fortune. Later, in the midsummer, she took part in our city's marathon and almost beat the professional runners. She did, however, win the Friendship Cup, which resembled a small brass bucket. She was also a wonderful singer, with a manly voice. Every week she brought four or five students over to teach them how to eat American food with forks and knives. When they were here, they often sang American songs she had taught them, such as "Pretty Paper," "Winter Wonderland," and "Silent Night, Holy Night." Their singing would attract some pedestrians, which was good for business, so we were pleased to have her here. Mr. Shapiro gave them a 20 percent discount, which outraged us. We wondered why he kept a double standard. We had a company policy against discounts, but it must apply only to Chinese employees. Still, we all agreed Susanna was a good woman. Unlike other customers, she gave us tips; also, she paid for her students' meals.

One afternoon in late May, Susanna and four students were eating here. In came a monkeylike man who had half-gray hair and flat cheeks. With a twitching face he went up to Peter, his fist clutching a ball of paper. He announced in a squeaky voice, "I'm going to sue your company for ten thousand yuan."

This was the first time I ever heard a Chinese say he would sue somebody for money. We gathered around him as he unfolded the paper ball to display a fat greenhead. "I found this fly in the chicken I bought here," he said firmly, his right hand massaging his side.

"When did you buy the chicken?" Peter asked.

"Last week."

"Show me the receipt."

The man took a slip of paper out of his trouser pocket and handed it to Peter.

About twenty people formed a half-circle to watch. As the man and Peter were arguing, Mr. Shapiro and Susanna stepped out of his office. Seeing the two Americans, the man wailed at Peter, "Don't dodge your responsibility. I've hated flies all my life. At the sight of this one I puked, then dropped to the floor and fainted. I thought I'd recover soon. No, the next evening I threw up again and again. That gave me a head-splitting migraine and a stomach disorder. My ears are still ringing inside, and I've lost my appetite completely. Since last Wednesday I haven't gone to work and have suffered from insomnia every night." He turned to the spectators.

"Comrades, I'm a true victim of this capitalist Cowboy Chicken. See how skinny I am."

"Like a starved cock," I said. People laughed.

"Stop blustering," Peter said to him. "Show us your medical records."

"I have them in the hospital. If you don't pay me the damages, I'll come again and again and again until I'm fully compensated."

We were all angry. Feilan pointed at the man's sunken mouth and said, "Shameless! You're not Chinese."

Baisha said, "Ten thousand yuan for a fly? How could you dream of that? Even your life isn't worth that much."

When a student had interpreted the man's accusation to Mr. Shapiro and Susanna, our boss turned pale. He moved closer and managed a smile, saying, "Sir, if you have concrete evidence, we'll be willing to consider your demand."

The student interpreted those words to the man, on whose face a vile smile appeared. We were angry at Mr. Shapiro, who again was acting like a number one Buddha. If you run into an evil man, you have to adopt uncivil measures. Our boss's hypocrisy would only indulge this crook.

"Excuse me," Manyou cried, and arrived with a bowl of warm water. He put it on the counter and said to the man, "I'm going to give your fly a hot bath, to see if it's from our place." He picked up the insect with a pair of chopsticks and dropped it into the bowl. We were all puzzled.

A few seconds later, Manyou announced, "This fly is not from Cowboy Chicken, because, see, there isn't any oil on the water. You all know we sell only fried chicken."

Some spectators booed the man, but he wouldn't give way. He fished out the fly with his hand and wrapped it up, saying, "I'm going to take you to court no matter what. If you don't offer a settlement, there'll be no end of this."

With a false smile Jinglin said to him, "Uncle, we're one family and shouldn't be so mean to each other. Let's find a quiet place to talk this out, all right? We can't negotiate in front of such a crowd."

The man looked puzzled, flapping his round eyes. Jinglin hooked his heavy arm around the man's neck while his eyes signaled at me. Reluctantly the crook moved away with him.

I followed them out the front door. It was slightly chilly outside, and the street was noisy with bicycle bells, vendors' cries, and automobile horns. A few neon lights flickered in the north. After about fifty paces, we turned into a small alley and then stopped. Jinglin smiled again, revealing his rotten teeth, and he took out a small pocketknife and a ten-yuan note. He opened the knife and said to the man, "I can pay you the damages now. You have a choice between these two."

"Don't make fun of me! I asked for ten thousand."

"Then I'll let you taste this knife."

The man wasn't frightened by the two-inch blade. He grinned and asked, "Brothers, why help the foreign devils?"

"Because Cowboy Chicken is our company, and our livelihood depends on it," I answered.

Jinglin said to him, "You're the scum of the Chinese! Come on, choose one."

The man didn't lift his hand. Jinglin said again, "I know what you're thinking. I can't stab you with such a small thing, eh? Tell you what — I know your grandson who goes to the Second Elementary School, and I can catch him and cut off his little pecker with this knife. Then your family line will be gone. I mean it. Now, pick one."

The crook was flabbergasted, looking at me and then at Jinglin, whose fat face became as hard as though made of copper sheet. With a trembling hand he took the money and mumbled, "Foreign dogs." He turned and hurried away. In no time he disappeared in a swarm of pedestrians.

We both laughed and walked back to the restaurant. Across the street, three disheveled Russian beggars were playing the violin and the bandora. Unlike most Chinese beggars, who would cry woefully and accost people, those foreign musicians were reserved, with just a porkpie hat on the ground to collect money, as though they didn't care whether you gave or not.

We didn't tell our boss what we had done; we just said the man was satisfied with a ten-yuan note and wouldn't come again. Susanna and her students applauded when they heard the news. Peter reimbursed Jinglin the money on the spot. Still, Mr. Shapiro looked suspicious and was afraid the man would return.

"He won't trouble us anymore," Peter said, smiling.

"Why are you so sure?" asked our boss.

"I have this." With two fingers Peter pulled the crook's receipt out of his breast pocket.

We all laughed. Actually, even with the receipt in hand, that old bastard wouldn't have dared come again. He wasn't afraid of Jinglin exactly but feared his four brothers, who were all stevedores on the riverbank, good at fighting and never hesitant to use a club or a dagger or a crowbar. That was why Jinglin, unlike the rest of us, could get rid of him without fear of retaliation.

Later we revealed to Peter what we had done in the alley. He smiled and promised he would not breathe a word to Mr. Shapiro.

As our business became stable, Peter grew into a local power of sorts. For months he had been building a house in the countryside. We wondered why he wanted his home to be four miles away from town. It would be costly to ride a motorcycle back and forth every day. One Sunday morning, Baisha, Feilan, Manyou, Jinglin, and I set out to see Peter's new home. We pedaled abreast on the wide embankment along the Songhua River, humming movie songs and cracking jokes. Birds were crying furiously in the willow copses below the embankment, while on a distant jetty a team of men sang a work song as they unloaded timber from a barge. Their voices were faltering but explosive. It hadn't rained for weeks, so the river was rather narrow, displaying a broad whitish beach. A few boys fishing there lay on their backs; around them stood some short bamboo poles planted deep in the sand. When a fish bit, a brass bell on one of the poles would jingle. On the other shore, toward the horizon, four or five windmills were turning, full like sails; above them the gray clouds floated lazily by, like a school of turtles.

We knew Peter had a few American dollars in the bank, but we were unsure how rich he really was. His house, though unfinished, staggered us. It was a three-story building with a garage in its back; it sat in the middle of two acres of sloping land, facing a gentle bend in the river and commanding a panorama that included two islands and the vast landscape on the other shore.

Peter wasn't around. Six or seven workers were busy, rhythmically hammering something inside the house. We asked an older man, who looked like a supervisor, how much the house would cost.

"At least a quarter of a million yuan," he said.

"So expensive?" Manyou gasped, his large lashless eyes blazing.

"You know what? It could be even more than that. We've never seen a home like this before."

"What kind of house is this?" asked Feilan.

"It's called Victorian. Mr. and Mrs. Jiao designed it themselves. It has two marble fireplaces, both imported from Hong Kong."

"Damn! Where did he get so much money?" Baisha said, and kicked a beer bottle with her white leather sandal.

We were all pondering the same question, and it weighed down our hearts like a millstone. But we didn't stay long, fearing that Peter might turn up. On the way back we spoke little to one another, unable to take our minds off Peter's house. Obviously he made much more than we did, or he wouldn't have had the money for such a mansion, which was larger even than the mayor's. Before setting out, we had planned to have brunch together at a beer house, but now none of us had an appetite anymore. We parted company the moment we turned away from the quay.

After that trip, I noticed that my fellow workers often looked suspiciously at Peter, as though he were a hybrid creature. Their eyes showed envy and anger. They began learning English more diligently. Manyou attended the night college, working with a textbook called *English for Today,* while Baisha and Feilan got up early in the morning to listen to the study program on the radio and memorize English words and expressions. Jinglin wanted to learn genuine American English, which he said was more natural, so he was studying *English 900.* I was also learning English, but I was older than the others and didn't have a strong memory, so I made little progress.

At work, they appeared friendlier to Mr. Shapiro and often poured coffee for him. Once Baisha even let him try some scallion pancake from her own lunch.

One morning, when we were not busy, I overheard Baisha talking with Mr. Shapiro in English. "Have you a house in U.S.A.?" she asked.

"Yes, I have a brick ranch, not very big." He had a cold; his voice was nasal and thick.

"How many childs in house?"

"You mean children?"

"Yes."

"I have two, and my wife has three."

"Ah, you have five jildren?"

"You can say that."

Mr. Shapiro turned away to fill out a form with a ballpoint pen, while Baisha's narrow eyes squinted at his heavy cheek and then at the black hair on his wrist. She was such a flirt, but I was impressed. She was brave enough to converse with our boss in English! — whereas I could never open my mouth in front of him.

Because we had seen Peter's mansion, our eyes were all focused on him. We were eager to find fault with him and ready to start a quarrel. But he was a careful man, knowing how to cope with us and how to maintain our boss's trust. He avoided arguing with us. If we didn't listen to him, he'd go into Mr. Shapiro's office and stay in there for a good while. That unnerved us, because we couldn't tell if he was reporting us to the boss. So we dared not be too disobedient. Every night Peter was the last to leave. He'd close the shutters, lock the cash register, wrap up the unsold chicken, tie the package to the back of his Honda motorcycle, and ride away.

Ever since the beginning, the daily leftovers had been a bone of contention between Mr. Shapiro and us. We had asked him many times to let us have the unsold chicken at the end of the day, but he refused, saying the company's policy forbade its employees to have leftovers. We even offered to buy them at half price, but he still wouldn't let us. He assigned Peter alone to take care of the leftovers.

It occurred to us that Peter must have taken the leftovers home for the construction workers. He had to feed them well, or else they might jerry-build his mansion. Damn him, he not only earned more but also got all the perks. The more we thought about this, the more resentful we became. So one night, after he closed up the place and rode away, we came out of the nearby alley and pedaled behind him. Manyou was at the night college, and Jinglin had to look after his younger brother in the hospital, who had just been operated on for a hernia, so they couldn't join us. Only Feilan, Baisha, and I followed Peter. He was going much faster than we were, but we knew where he was headed, so we bicycled without hurry, chatting and laughing now and then.

In the distance Peter's motorcycle was flitting along the embankment like a will-o'-the-wisp. The night was cool, and a few men were chanting folksongs from their boat anchored in the river. We were eager to prove that Peter had shipped the leftovers home, so that we could report him to Mr. Shapiro the next morning.

For a long while the light of Peter's motorcycle disappeared. We stopped, at a loss. Apparently he had turned off the embankment, but where had he gone? Should we continue to ride toward his home, or should we mark time?

As we were discussing what to do, a burst of flames emerged in the north, almost two hundred yards away, at the waterside. We went down the embankment, locked our bicycles in a willow copse, and walked stealthily toward the fire.

When we approached it, we saw Peter stirring something in the fire with a trimmed branch. It was a pile of chicken, about twenty pieces. The air smelled of gasoline and burned meat. Beyond him, the waves were lapping the sand softly. The water was sprinkled with stars, rippling with the fishy breeze. On the other shore everything was buried in darkness except for three or four clusters of lights, almost indistinguishable from the stars in the cloudless sky. Speechlessly we watched. If there had been another man with us, we might have sprung out and beaten Peter up. But I was no fighter, so we couldn't do anything, merely crouch in the tall grass and curse him under our breath.

"If only we had a gun!" Baisha whispered through her teeth.

Peter was in a happy mood. With a ruddy face he began singing a song, which must have been made up by some overseas Chinese:

> I'm not so carefree as you think,
> My feelings never unclear.
> If you can't see through me,
> That's because again you waste
> Your love on a worthless man.
>
> Oh my heart won't wander alone.
> Let me take you along.
> Together we'll reach a quiet place
> Where you can realize
> Your sweetest dream . . .

For some reason I was touched by the song. Never had I known he had such a gorgeous baritone voice, which seemed to come a long way from the other shore. A flock of ducks quacked in the darkness, their wings splashing the water lustily. A loon let out a cry like a wild laugh. Then all the waterfowl turned quiet, and Peter's voice alone was vibrating the tangy air chilled by the night.

Feilan whispered, "What a good time he's having here, that asshole."

"He must miss his American sweetheart," Baisha said.

Feilan shook her chin. "Makes no sense. He's not the romantic type."

"Doesn't he often say American girls are better than Chinese girls?"

"Shh —" I stopped them.

When the fire almost went out, Peter unzipped his fly, pulled out his dick, and peed on the embers, which hissed and sent up a puff of steam. The arc of his urine gleamed for a few seconds, then disappeared. He yawned, and with his feet pushed some sand over the ashes.

"Gross!" said Feilan.

Peter leaped on his motorcycle and dashed away, the exhaust pipe hiccuping explosively. I realized he didn't mind riding four miles to work because he could use some of the gasoline provided by our boss for burning the leftovers with.

"If only I could scratch and bite that bastard!" Feilan said breathlessly.

"Depends on what part of him," I said.

Baisha laughed. Feilan scowled at me, saying, "You have a dirty mind."

The next day we told all the other workers about our discovery. Everyone was infuriated, and even the two part-timers couldn't stop cursing capitalism. There were children begging on the streets, there were homeless people at the train station and the ferry house, there were hungry cats and dogs everywhere — why did Mr. Shapiro want Peter to burn good meat like garbage? Manyou said he had read in a restricted journal several years ago that some American capitalists would dump milk into a river instead of giving it to the poor. But that was in the U.S.; here in China, this kind of wasteful practice had to be condemned. I told my fellow workers that I was going to write an article to expose Ken Shapiro and Peter Jiao.

In the afternoon we confronted Peter. "Why do you burn the leftovers every night?" Manyou asked, looking him right in the eye.

Peter was taken aback, then replied, "It's my job."

"That's despicable," I snapped. "You not only burned them but also peed on them." My stomach suddenly rumbled.

Feilan giggled. Baisha pointed at Peter's nose and said sharply, "Peter Jiao, remember you're a Chinese. There are people here who don't have enough corn flour to eat while you burn chicken every night. You've forgotten your ancestors and who you are."

Peter looked rattled, protesting, "I don't feel comfortable about it either. But somebody has to do it. I'm paid to burn them, just like you're paid to fry them."

"Don't give me that crap!" Jinglin cut in. "You're a capitalist's henchman."

Peter retorted, "So are you. You work for this capitalist company too."

"Hold on," Manyou said. "We just want to reason you out of this shameful thing. Why do you waste chicken that way? Why not give the leftovers to the poor?"

"You think I enjoy burning them? If I gave them away, I'd be fired. This is the American way of doing business."

"But you're a Chinese running a restaurant in a socialist country," said Jinglin.

As we were wrangling, Mr. Shapiro came out of his office with coffee stains around his lips. Peter explained to him what we were quarreling about. Our boss waved his hand to dismiss us, as though this were such a trifle that it didn't deserve his attention. He just said, "It's company policy; we can't do anything about it. If you're really concerned about the waste, don't fry too many pieces, and sell everything you've fried." He walked to the front door to have a smoke outside.

Peter said, "That's true. He can't change a thing. From now on we'd better not fry more than we can sell."

I was still angry and said, "I'm going to write to the *Herald* to expose this policy."

"There's no need to be so emotional, Hongwen," Peter said with a complacent smile, raising his squarish chin a little. "There have been several articles on this subject. For example, the *Beijing Evening News* carried a long piece last week about our company. The author praised our policy on leftovers and believed it would reduce waste eventually. He said we Chinese should adopt the American way of running business. In any case, this policy cannot be exposed anymore. People already know about it."

That silenced us all. Originally we had planned that if Mr. Shapiro continued to have the leftovers burned, we'd go on strike for a few days. Peter's words deflated us all at once.

Still, Jinglin wouldn't let Peter off so easily. When it turned dark, he pressed a thumbtack into the rear tire of the Honda motorcycle parked in the back yard. Peter called home, and his wife came driving a white Toyota truck to carry back the motorcycle and him. This dealt us another blow, because we hadn't expected he owned a brand-new pickup as well. No one else in our city could afford such a vehicle. We asked ourselves, "Heavens, how much money does Peter actually have?"

We were all anxious to find that out. On payday, somehow Mr. Shapiro mixed Peter's wages in with ours. We each received an envelope stuffed with a bundle of cash, but Peter's was always empty. Juju said Peter got only a slip of paper in his envelope, which was called a check. He could exchange that thing for money at the bank, where he had an account as if he were a company himself. In Juju's words, "Every month our boss just writes Peter lots of money." That fascinated us. How much did he get from Mr. Shapiro? This question had remained an enigma ever since we began working here. Now his pay was in our hands, and at last we could find out.

Manyou steamed the envelope over a cup of hot tea and opened it without difficulty. The figure on the check astounded us: $1,683.75. For a good moment nobody said a word, never having imagined that Peter received an American salary, being paid dollars instead of yuan. That's to say, he made twenty times more than each of us! No wonder he worked so hard, taking care of Cowboy Chicken as if it were his home, and tried every trick to please Mr. Shapiro.

That night after work we gathered at Baisha's home for an emergency meeting. Her mother was a doctor, so their apartment was spacious and Baisha had her own room. She took out a packet of spiced pumpkin seeds, and we began chatting while drinking tea.

"God, just think of the money Peter's raking in," Jinglin said, and pulled his brushy hair, sighing continually. He looked wretched, as if ten years older than the day before. His chubby face had lost its luster.

I said, "Peter can afford to eat at the best restaurants every day. There's no way he can spend that amount of money."

Feilan spat the shells of a pumpkin seed into her fist, her eyes turning triangular. She said, "We must protest. This isn't fair."

Baisha agreed with a sigh. "Now I know what exploitation feels like."

"Peter has done a lot for Cowboy Chicken," Manyou said, "but there's no justification for him to make that much." He seemed still in a daze and kept stroking his receding chin.

"We must figure out a countermeasure," said Jinglin.

I suggested, "Perhaps we should talk with our boss."

"You think he'll pay each of us a thousand dollars?" Baisha asked scornfully.

"Of course not," I said.

"Then what's the point of talking with him?"

Manyou put in, "I don't know. What do you think we should do, Baisha?"

I was surprised that he could be at a loss too, because he was known as a man of strategies. Baisha answered, "I think we must unite as one and demand that our boss fire Peter."

Silence fell in the room, in which stood a double bed covered with a pink sheet. A folded floral blanket sat atop a pair of eiderdown pillows stacked together. I wondered why Baisha needed such a large bed for herself. She must have slept with her boyfriends on it quite often. She was such a slut.

"That's a good idea. I say let's get rid of Peter," Manyou said, nodding at her admiringly.

Still perplexed, I asked, "Suppose Mr. Shapiro does fire him, then what?"

"One of us may take Peter's job," said Manyou.

Feilan picked up, "Are you sure he'll fire Peter?"

To our surprise, Baisha said, "Of course he will. It'll save him fifteen hundred dollars a month."

"I don't get it," said Jinglin. "What's the purpose of doing this? Even if he fires Peter, he won't pay us more, will he?"

"Then he'll have to depend on us and may give us each a raise," answered Baisha.

Unconvinced, I said, "What if the new manager gets paid more and just ignores the rest of us?"

Manyou frowned, because he knew that only Baisha and he could be candidates for that position, which required the ability to use English. Feilan, Jinglin, and I couldn't speak a complete sentence yet.

"Let's draw up a contract," Feilan said. "Whoever becomes the new manager must share his wages with the rest of us."

We all supported the idea and signed a brief statement, which said that if the new manager didn't share his earnings with the rest of us, he'd be childless and we could get our revenge in any way we chose. After that, Baisha went about composing a letter addressed to Mr. Shapiro. She didn't know enough English words for the letter, so she fetched a bulky dictionary from her parents' study. She began to write with a felt-tip pen, now and again consulting the dictionary. She was sleepy and yawned incessantly, covering her mouth with her left palm and disclosing her hairy armpit. Meanwhile, we cracked pumpkin seeds and chatted away.

The letter was short, but it seemed to the point. Even Manyou said it was good after he looked it over. It stated:

Our Respected Mr. Kenneth Shapiro:
  We are writing to demand you to fire Peter Jiao immediately. This is our united will. You must respect our will. We do not want a leader like him. That is all.

                                        Sincerely,
                                        Your Employees

We all signed our names and felt that at last we had stood up to that capitalist. Since I'd pass our restaurant on my way home, I took charge of delivering the letter. Before we left, Baisha brought out a bottle of apricot wine, and together we drank to our solidarity.

I dropped the letter into the slot in the front door of Cowboy Chicken. After I got home, for a while I was lightheaded and kept imagining the shock on Mr. Shapiro's pudgy face. I also thought of Peter, who, without his current job, might never be able to complete his outrageous mansion. But soon I began to worry, fearing that Baisha might become the new manager. Compared with Peter, she had a volatile temper and was more selfish. Besides, she couldn't possibly maintain the connections and clientele Peter had carefully built up, not to mention develop the business. Manyou wasn't as capable as Peter either. Sometimes he could be very clever about trivial matters, but he had no depth. He didn't look steady and couldn't inspire trust in customers. To be fair, Peter seemed indispensable to Cowboy Chicken. I wouldn't have minded if Mr. Shapiro had paid him five times more than me.

We all showed up at work at eight-thirty the next morning. To our surprise, neither Mr. Shapiro nor Peter betrayed any anxiety. They acted as if nothing had happened, and treated us the same as the day before. We were baffled, wondering what they had planned for us. Peter seemed to avoid us, but he was polite and quiet. Apparently he had read the letter.

We expected that our boss would talk with us one by one. Even if he wouldn't fire Peter, he might make some concessions. But for a whole morning he stayed in his office, as if he had forgotten us altogether. He was reading a book about the Jews who had lived in China hundreds of years ago. His calm appearance agitated us. If only we could have had an inkling of what he had up his sleeve.

When the day was at last over, we met briefly at a street corner. We were confused, but all agreed to wait and see. Feilan sighed and said, "I feel like we're in a tug-of-war."

"Yes, we're in a mental war, so we must be tough-minded and patient," Manyou told us.

I went home with a stomachache. Again my father was drunk that night, singing revolutionary songs and saying I was lucky to have my fill of American chicken every day. I couldn't get to sleep until the wee hours.

The next day turned out the same. Peter assigned each of us some work, and Mr. Shapiro still wouldn't say an unnecessary word to us. I couldn't help picturing his office as a giant snail shell into which he had shut himself. What should we do? They must have devised a trap or something for us. What was it? We had to do something, not just wait like this, or they would undo us one by one.

That night we gathered at Baisha's home again. After a lengthy discussion, we agreed to go on strike. Baisha wrote a note, which read:

Mr. Shapiro:
   Because you do not consider our demand, we decide to strike at Cowboy Chicken. Begin tomorrow.

We didn't sign our names this time, since he knew who we were and what we were referring to. I was unsure of the phrase "strike at Cowboy Chicken," but I didn't say anything, guessing that probably she just meant we'd leave the place unmanned. Again I delivered the letter. None of us went to work the next morning. We wanted the restaurant to lose some business and our boss to worry a little so that he'd be willing to cooperate with his workers. But we had agreed to meet at one o'clock in front of Everyday Hardware, near Cowboy Chicken; then together we'd go to our workplace and start to negotiate with Mr. Shapiro. In other words, we planned to strike only for half a day.

After lunch we all arrived at the hardware store. To our astonishment, a squad of police was standing in front of Cowboy Chicken as if a fire or a riot had broken out. They wouldn't allow people to enter the restaurant unless they searched them. What was going on? Why had Mr. Shapiro called in the police? We were puzzled. Together we walked over as if we had just returned from a lunch break. The front of the restaurant was cordoned off, and three police were stationed at the door. A tall policeman stretched out his arm to stop us. Baisha asked loudly, "Hey, Big Wan, you don't remember me?" She was all smiles.

"Yes, I saw you," Wan said with a grin.

"We all work here. Let us go in, all right? We have tons of work to do."

"We have to search you before letting you in."

"I've nothing on me. How do you search?" She spread her arms, then lifted her long skirt a little with one hand, to show she didn't even have a pocket.

"Stand still, all of you," said Wan. A policewoman waved a black wand over Baisha, a gadget like a miniature badminton racket without strings.

"Is this a mine detector or something?" Jinglin asked the policewoman.

"A metal detector," she said.

"What's going on here?" Baisha asked Wan.

"Someone threatened to blow this place up."

We were all horrified by that, hoping it had nothing to do with us.

The police let us in. The moment we entered, we saw an old couple standing behind the counter taking care of orders. Damn it, Peter had brought his parents in to work! How come he wasn't afraid a bomb might blow them to pieces? In a corner, Susanna and two student-looking girls were wiping tables and placing silver. They were humming "We Shall Overcome," but stopped at the sight of us. In the kitchen the two part-timers were frying chicken. Dumbfounded, we didn't know how to respond to this scene.

Mr. Shapiro came over. He looked furious, his face almost purple. He said to us, his spit flying about, "You think you can frighten me into obeying you? Let me tell you, you are all terminated!"

I didn't know what his last word meant, though I was sure it had a negative meaning. Manyou seemed to understand, his lips twitching as if he were about to cry. He gulped and couldn't say a word.

Peter said to us, "We can't use you anymore. You're fired."

"You can't do this to us," Baisha said to Mr. Shapiro, and stepped forward. "We are founders of this place."

Mr. Shapiro laughed. "What are you talking about? How much stock do you have in this company?"

What did he mean? We looked at one another, unable to fathom his meaning. He said, "Go home; don't come anymore. You'll receive this month's pay by mail." He turned and walked off to the men's room, shaking his head and muttering, "I don't want any terrorists here."

Peter smiled at us with contempt. "Well, the earth won't stop spinning without the five of you."

I felt the room swaying like a lumbering bus. I never thought I could be fired so easily: Mr. Shapiro just said a word and my job was no more. The previous fall I had quit my position in a coal yard in order to work here. Now I was a total loser, and people would laugh at me.

The five of us were terribly distressed. Before we parted company on the street, I asked Manyou to spell for me the word Mr. Shapiro had used. With his fountain pen he wrote on my forearm, "Terminated!" There was no need for an exclamation mark.

At home I looked up the word in my pocket dictionary; it says "finished." My anger flamed up. That damned capitalist believed he was finished with us, but he was mistaken. We were far from terminated — the struggle was still going on. I would ask my elder brother to cut the restaurant's electricity first thing the next morning. Baisha had said she'd have one of her boyfriends create some problems in Cowboy Chicken's mail delivery. Manyou would visit his friends at the garbage center and ask them not to pick up trash at the restaurant. Jinglin declared, "I'll blow up Peter's Victorian!" Feilan hadn't decided what to do yet.

This was just the beginning.

ANDREA LEE

Brothers and Sisters
Around the World

FROM THE NEW YORKER

"I TOOK THEM AROUND the point toward Dzamandzar," Michel
tells me. "Those two little whores. Just ten minutes. They asked me
for a ride when I was down on the beach bailing out the Zodiac. It
was rough and I went too fast on purpose. You should have seen
their titties bounce!" He tells me this in French, but with a carefree
lewdness that could be Roman. He is in fact half Italian, product of
the officially French no man's land where the Ligurian Alps touch
the Massif Central. In love, like so many of his Mediterranean com-
patriots, with boats, with hot blue seas, with dusky women, with the
steamy belt of tropics that girdles the earth. We live above Cannes,
in Mougins, where it is always sunny, but on vacation we travel the
world to get hotter and wilder. Islands are what Michel prefers: in
Asia, Oceania, Africa, the Caribbean, it doesn't matter. Any place
where the people are the color of different grades of coffee, and
mangoes plop in mushy heaps on the ground, and the reef fish are
brilliant as a box of new crayons. On vacation Michel sheds his
manicured ad-man image and with innocent glee sets about turning himself into a Eurotrash version of Tarzan. Bronzed muscles
well in evidence, shark's tooth on a leather thong, fishing knife
stuck into the waist of a threadbare pareu, and a wispy sun-streaked
ponytail that he tends painstakingly, along with a chin crop of Hollywood stubble.

He loves me for a number of wrong reasons connected with his
dreams of hot islands. It makes no difference to him that I grew up

in Massachusetts, wearing L. L. Bean boots more often than sandals; after eight years of marriage, he doesn't seem to see that what
gives strength to the spine of an American black woman, however
exotic she appears, is a steely Protestant core. A core that in its ab-
solutism is curiously cold and Nordic. The fact is that I'm not crazy
about the tropics, but Michel doesn't want to acknowledge that.
Mysteriously, we continue to get along. In fact, our marriage is surprisingly robust, though at the time of our wedding, my mother,
my sister, and my girlfriends all gave it a year. I sometimes think the
secret is that we don't know each other and never will. Both of
us are lazy by nature, and that makes it convenient to hang on to
the fantasies we conjured up back when we met in Milan: mine
of the French gentleman-adventurer, and his of a pliant black goddess whose feelings accord with his. It's no surprise to me when
Michel tries to share the ribald thoughts that run through the laby-
rinth of his Roman Catholic mind. He doubtless thought that I
would get a kick out of hearing about his boat ride with a pair of African sluts.

Those girls have been sitting around watching us from under the
mango tree since the day we rolled up from the airport to spend
August in the house we borrowed from our friend Jean-Claude.
Michel was driving Jean-Claude's car, a Citroën so rump-sprung
from the unpaved roads that it moves like a tractor. Our four-year-
old son, Lele, can drag his sneakers in red dust through the holes
in the floor. The car smells of failure, like the house, which is built
on an island off the northern coast of Madagascar, on a beach
where a wide scalloped bay spreads like two blue wings, melting
into the sky and the wild archipelago of lemur islands beyond. Behind the garden stretch fields of sugar cane and groves of silvery,
arthritic-looking ylang-ylang trees, whose flowers lend a tang of Africa to French perfume.

The house is low and long around a grandiose veranda, and was
once whitewashed into an emblem of colonial vainglory; now the
walls are the indeterminate color of damp, and the thinning palm
thatch on the roof swarms with mice and geckos. It has a queenly
housekeeper named Hadijah, whose perfect *pommes frites* and
plates of crudités, like the dead bidet and dried-up tubes of Bain
de Soleil in the bathroom, are monuments to Jean-Claude's ex-
wife, who went back to Toulon after seeing a series of projects — a

frozen-fish plant, a perfume company, a small luxury hotel — swallowed up in the calm fireworks of the sunsets. Madagascar is the perfect place for a white fool to lose his money, Michel says. He and I enjoy the scent of dissolution in our borrowed house, fuck inventively in the big mildewed ironwood bed, sit in happiness in the sad, bottomed-out canvas chairs on the veranda after a day of spearfishing, watching our son race in and out of herds of humpbacked zebu cattle on the beach.

The only problem for me has been those girls. They're not really whores, just local girls who dance at Bar Kariboo on Thursday nights and hang around the few French and Italian tourists, hoping to trade sex for a T-shirt, a hair clip. They don't know to want Ray-Bans yet; this is not the Caribbean.

I'm used to the women from the Comoros Islands who crowd onto the beach near the house, dressed up in gold bangles and earrings and their best lace-trimmed blouses. They clap and sing in circles for hours, jumping up to dance in pairs, wagging their backsides in tiny precise jerks, laughing and flashing gold teeth. They wrap themselves up in their good time in a way that intimidates me. And I've come to an understanding with the older women of the village, who come by to bring us our morning ration of zebu milk (we drink it boiled in coffee) or to barter with *rideaux Richelieu,* the beautiful muslin cutwork curtains that they embroider. They are intensely curious about me, *l'américaine,* who looks not unlike one of them but who dresses and speaks and acts like a foreign madame and is clearly married to the white man, not just a casual concubine. They ask me for medicine, and if I weren't careful they would clean out my supply of Advil and Bimaxin. They go crazy over Lele, whom they call *"bébé métis"* — the mixed baby. I want to know all about them, their still eyes, their faces of varying colors that show both African and Indonesian blood, as I want to know everything about this primeval chunk of Africa floating in the Indian Ocean, with its bottle-shaped baobabs and strange tinkling music, the *sega,* which is said to carry traces of tunes from Irish sailors.

But the girls squatting under the mango tree stare hard at me whenever I sit out on the beach or walk down to the water to swim. Then they make loud comments in Malagasy and burst out laughing. It's juvenile behavior, and I can't help sinking right down to their level and getting provoked. They're probably about eighteen years old, both good-looking: one with a flat brown face and the long straight shining hair that makes some Madagascar women resemble Polynesians; the other darker, with the tiny features that belong to the coastal people called Merina and a pile of kinky hair tinted reddish. Both are big-titted, as Michel pointed out, the merchandise spilling out of a pair of Nouvelles Frontières T-shirts that they must have got from a tour-group leader. Some days they have designs painted on their faces in yellow sulfur clay. They stare at me, and guffaw and stretch and give their breasts a competitive shake. Sometimes they hoot softly or whistle when I appear.

My policy has been to ignore them, but today they've taken a step ahead, gotten a rise, however ironic, out of my man. It's a little triumph. I didn't see the Zodiac ride, but through the bathroom window I saw them come back. I was shaving my legs — waxing never lasts long enough in the tropics. Squealing and laughing, they floundered out of the rubber dinghy, patting their hair, settling their T-shirts, retying the cloth around their waists. One of them blew her nose through her fingers into the shallow water. The other said something to Michel, and he laughed and patted her on the backside. Then, arrogantly as two Cleopatras, they strode across the hot sand and took up their crouch under the mango tree. A pair of brown *netsuke*. Waiting for my move.

So, finally, I act. Michel comes sauntering inside to tell me, and after he tells me I make a scene. He's completely taken aback; he's gotten spoiled since we've been married, used to my American cool, which can seem even cooler than French nonchalance. He thought I was going to react the way I used to when I was still modeling and he used to flirt with some of the girls I was working with, some of the bimbos who weren't serious about their careers. That is, that I was going to chuckle, display complicity, even excitement. Instead I yell, say he's damaged my prestige among the locals, say that things are different here. The words seem to be flowing up into my mouth from the ground beneath my feet. He's so surprised that he just stands there with his blue eyes round and his mouth a small O in the midst of that Indiana Jones stubble.

Then I hitch up my Soleiado bikini and march outside to the mango tree. *"Va-t'en!"* I hiss to Red Hair, who seems to be top girl of the duo. "Go away! *Ne parle plus avec mon homme!"*

The two of them scramble to their feet, but they don't seem to be going anywhere, so I slap the one with the straight hair. Except for once, when I was about ten, in a fight with my cousin Brenda, I don't believe I've ever seriously slapped anyone. This, on the scale of slaps, is half-assed, not hard. In that second of contact I feel the strange smoothness of her cheek and an instantaneous awareness that my hand is just as smooth. An electric current seems to connect them. A red light flickers in the depths of the girl's dark eyes, like a computer blinking on, and then, without saying anything to me, both girls scuttle off down the beach, talking loudly to each other and occasionally looking back at me. I make motions as if I'm shooing chickens. *"Allez-vous-en!"* I screech. Far off down the beach, they disappear into the palms.

Then I go and stretch out in the water, which is like stretching out in blue air. I take off my bikini top and let the equatorial sun print my shadow on the white sand below, where small white fish graze. I feel suddenly calm, but at the same time my mind is working very fast. "My dear, who invited you to come halfway across the world and slap somebody?" I ask myself in the ultra-reasonable tones of my mother, the school guidance counselor. Suddenly I remember another summer on yet another island. This was in Indonesia, a few years ago, when we were exploring the back roads of one of the Moluccas. The driver was a local kid who didn't speak any language we spoke and was clearly gay. A great-looking kid with light-brown skin pitted with a few acne scars, and neat dreadlocks that would have looked stylish in Manhattan. A Princess Di T-shirt and peeling red nail polish. When we stopped at a waterfall and Michel the Adventurer went off to climb the lava cliffs, I sat down on a flat rock with the driver, whipped out my beauty case, and painted his nails shocking pink. He jumped when I first grabbed his hand, but when he saw what I was up to he gave me a huge ecstatic grin and then closed his eyes. And there it was: paradise. The waterfall, the jungle, and that beautiful kid with his long fingers lying in my hand. It was Michel who made a fuss that time, jealous of something he couldn't even define. But I had the same feeling I do now, of acting on instinct and on target. The right act. At the right moment.

"Mama, what did you do?" Lele comes running up to me from where he has been squatting naked on the beach, playing with two small boys from the village. His legs and backside and little penis are covered with sand. I see the boys staring after him, one holding a toy they've been squabbling over: a rough wooden model of a truck, without wheels, tied with a piece of string to a stick. "Ismail says you hit a lady."

Word has already spread along the beach, which is like a stage where a different variety show goes on every hour of the day. The set acts are the tides, which determine the movements of fishing boats, pirogues, Zodiacs, and sailboats. There is always action on the sand: women walk up and down with bundles on their heads; bands of ragged children dig clams at low tide or launch themselves into the waves at high tide to surf with a piece of old timber; yellow dogs chase chickens and fight over shrimp shells; palm branches crash down on corrugated iron roofs; girls with lacy dresses and bare sandy shanks parade to mass; the little mosque opens and shuts its creaky doors; boys play soccer, kicking a plastic water bottle; babies howl; sunburned tourist couples argue and reconcile. Gossip flashes up and down with electronic swiftness.

I sit up in the water and grab Lele and kiss him all over while he splashes and struggles to get away. "Yes, that's right," I tell him. It's the firm, didactic voice I use when we've turned off the Teletubbies videos and I am playing the ideal parent. "I did hit a lady," I say. "She needed hitting." I, the mother who instructs her cross-cultural child in tolerance and nonviolence. Lele has a picture book called *Brothers and Sisters Around the World,* full of illustrations of cookie-cutter figures of various colors holding hands across continents. All people belong to one family, it teaches. All oceans are the same ocean.

Michel, who has watched the whole scene, comes and tells me that in all his past visits to the island he's never seen anything like it. He's worried. The women fight among themselves, or they fight with their men for sleeping with the tourists, he says. But no foreign woman has ever got mixed up with them. He talks like an anthropologist about loss of face and vendetta. "We might get run out of here," he says nervously.

I tell him to relax, that absolutely nothing will happen. Where do I get this knowledge? It has sifted into me from the water, the air. So, as we planned, we go off spearfishing over by Nosy Komba, where the coral grows in big pastel poufs like furniture in a Hollywood bedroom of the fifties. We find a den of rock lobster and shoot two, and take them back to Jean-Claude's house for Hadijah to cook. Waiting for the lobster, we eat about fifty small oysters the size of mussels and shine flashlights over the beach in front of the veranda, which is crawling with crabs. Inside, Lele is snoring adenoidally under a mosquito net. The black sky above is alive with falling stars. Michel keeps looking at me and shaking his head.

Hadijah comes out bearing the lobster magnificently broiled with vanilla sauce. To say she has presence is an understatement. She got married when she was thirteen and is now, after eight children, an important personage, the matriarch of a vast and prosperous island clan. She and I have gotten along fine ever since she realized that I wasn't going to horn in on her despotic rule over Jean-Claude's house or say anything about the percentage she skims off the marketing money. She has a closely braided head and is as short and solid as a boulder — on the spectrum of Madagascar skin colors, well toward the darkest. This evening she is showing off her wealth by wearing over her pareu a venerable Guns n' Roses T-shirt. She puts down the lobster, sets her hands on her hips, and looks at me, and my heart suddenly skips a beat. Hers, I realize, is the only opinion I care about. "Oh, madame," she says, flashing me a wide smile and shaking her finger indulgently, as if I'm a child who has been up to mischief. I begin breathing again. "Oh, madame!"

"Madame has a quick temper," Michel says in a placating voice, and Hadijah throws her head back and laughs till the Guns n' Roses logo shimmies.

"She is right!" she exclaims. "*Madame a raison!* She's a good wife!"

Next morning our neighbor PierLuigi pulls up to the house in his dust-covered Renault pickup. PierLuigi is Italian, and back in Italy has a title and a castle. Here he lives in a bamboo hut when he is not away leading a shark-hunting safari to one of the wild islands a day's sail to the north. He is the real version of what Michel pretends to be: a walking, talking character from a boys' adventure tale, with a corrugated scar low down on one side where a hammerhead once snatched a mouthful. The islanders respect him and bring their children to him for a worm cure he's devised from crushed papaya seeds. He can bargain down the tough Indian merchants in the market, and he sleeps with pretty tourists and island girls impartially. Nobody knows how many kids he has fathered on the island.

"I hear your wife is mixing in local politics," he calls from the truck to Michel, while looking me over with those shameless eyes that have gotten so many women in trouble. PierLuigi is sixty years old and has streaks of white in his hair, but he is still six feet four and the best-looking man I have ever seen in my life. "Brava," he says to me. "Good for you, my dear. The local young ladies very often need things put in perspective, but very few of our lovely visitors know how to do it on their own terms."

After he drives off, Michel looks at me with new respect. "I can't say you don't have guts," he says later. Then, "You really must be in love with me."

In the afternoon after our siesta, when I emerge onto the veranda from Jean-Claude's shuttered bedroom, massaging Phyto Plage into my hair, smelling on my skin the pleasant odor of sex, I see — as I somehow expected — that the two girls are back under the mango tree. I walk out onto the burning sand, squinting against the glare that makes every distant object a flat black silhouette, and approach them for the second time. I don't think that we're in for another round, yet I feel my knees take on a wary pugilistic springiness. But as I get close, the straight-haired girl says, "*Bonjour, madame.*"

The formal greeting conveys an odd intimacy. It is clear that we are breathing the same air now, that we have taken each other's measure. Both girls look straight at me, no longer bridling. All three of us know perfectly well that the man — my European husband — was just an excuse, a playing field for our curiosity. The curiosity of sisters separated before birth and flung by the caprice of history half a world away from each other. Now in this troublesome way our connection has been established, and between my guilt and my dawning affection I suspect that I'll never get rid of these two. Already in my mind is forming an exasperating vision of the gifts I know I'll have to give them: lace underpants, Tampax, music cassettes, body lotion — all of them extracted from me with the tender ruthlessness of family members anywhere. And then what? What, after all these years, will there be to say? Well, the first thing to do is answer. "*Bonjour, mesdemoiselles,*" I reply, in my politest voice.

And because I can't think of anything else, I smile and nod at them and walk into the water, which as always in the tropics is as warm as blood. The whole time I swim, the girls are silent, and they don't take their eyes off me.

Boys

FROM ELLE

BOYS ENTER THE HOUSE, boys enter the house. Boys, and with them the ideas of boys (ideas leaden, reductive, inflexible), enter the house. Boys, two of them, wound into hospital packaging, boys with infant-pattern baldness, slung in the arms of parents, boys dreaming of breasts, enter the house. Twin boys, kettles on the boil, boys in hideous vinyl knapsacks that young couples from Edison, N.J., wear on their shirt fronts, knapsacks coated with baby saliva and staphylococcus and milk vomit, enter the house. Two boys, one striking the other with a rubberized hot dog, enter the house. Two boys, one of them striking the other with a willow switch about the head and shoulders, the other crying, enter the house. Boys enter the house speaking nonsense. Boys enter the house calling for mother. On a Sunday, in May, a day one might nearly describe as perfect, an ice cream truck comes slowly down the lane, chimes inducing salivation, and children run after it, not long after which boys dig a hole in the back yard and bury their younger sister's dolls two feet down, so that she will never find these dolls and these dolls will rot in hell, after which boys enter the house. Boys, trailing after their father like he is the Second Goddamned Coming of Christ Goddamned Almighty, enter the house, repair to the basement to watch baseball. Boys enter the house, site of devastation, and repair immediately to the kitchen, where they mix lighter fluid, vanilla pudding, drain-opening lye, balsamic vinegar, blue food coloring, calamine lotion, cottage cheese, ants, a plastic lizard one of them received in his Christmas stocking, tacks, leftover mashed potatoes, Spam, frozen lima beans, and chocolate syrup in a medium-sized saucepan and heat over a low flame until thick, afterward transferring the contents of this saucepan into a Pyrex lasagna dish, baking the Pyrex lasagna dish in the oven for nineteen minutes before attempting to persuade their sister that she should eat the mixture; later they smash three family heirlooms (the last, a glass egg, intentionally) in a two-and-a-half-hour stretch, whereupon they are sent to their bedroom until freed, in each case thirteen minutes after. Boys enter the house, starchy in pressed shirts and flannel pants that itch so bad, fresh from Sunday school instruction, blond and brown locks (respectively) plastered down but even so with a number of cowlicks protruding at odd angles, disconsolate and humbled, uncertain if boyish things — such as shooting at the neighbor's dog with a pump-action BB gun and gagging the fat boy up the street with a bandanna and showing their shriveled boy-penises to their younger sister — are exempted from the commandment to *Love the Lord thy God with all thy heart and with all thy soul and with all thy mind, and thy neighbor as thyself.* Boys enter the house in baseball gear (only one of the boys can hit): in their spikes, in mismatched tube socks that smell like Stilton cheese. Boys enter the house in soccer gear. Boys enter the house carrying skates. Boys enter the house with lacrosse sticks, and soon after, tossing a lacrosse ball lightly in the living room, they destroy a lamp. One boy enters the house sporting basketball clothes, the other wearing jeans and a sweatshirt. One boy enters the house bleeding profusely and is taken out to get stitches, the other watches. Boys enter the house at the end of term carrying report cards, sneak around the house like spies of foreign nationality, looking for a place to hide the report cards for the time being (under a toaster? in a medicine cabinet?). One boy with a black eye enters the house, one boy without. Boys with acne enter the house and squeeze and prod large skin blemishes in front of their sister. Boys with acne-treatment products hidden about their persons enter the house. Boys, standing just up the street, sneak cigarettes behind a willow in the Elys' yard, wave smoke away from their natural fibers, hack terribly, experience nausea, then enter the house. Boys call each other *Retard, Homo, Geek,* and, later, *Neckless Thug, Theater Fag,* and enter the house exchanging further epithets. Boys enter house with nose-hair clippers, chase sister around house threatening to depilate her eyebrows. She cries. Boys attempt to induce girls to whom they would not have spoken only six or eight months prior to enter the house with them. Boys enter the house with girls efflorescent and homely and attempt to induce girls to sneak into their bedroom, as they still share a single bedroom; girls refuse. Boys enter the house, go to separate bedrooms. Boys, with their father (an arm around each of them), enter the house, but of the monologue preceding and succeeding this entrance, not a syllable is preserved. Boys enter the house having masturbated in a variety of locales. Boys enter the house having masturbated in train-station bathrooms, in forests, in beach houses, in football bleachers at night under the stars, in cars (under a blanket), in the shower, backstage, on a plane, the boys masturbate constantly, identically, three times a day in some cases, desire like a madness upon them, at the mere sound of certain words, words that sound like other words, *interrogative* reminding them of *intercourse, beast* reminding them of *breast, sects* reminding them of *sex,* and so forth, the boys are not very smart yet, and as they enter the house they feel, as always, immense shame at the scale of this self-abusive cogitation, seeing a classmate, seeing a billboard, seeing a fire hydrant, seeing things that should not induce thoughts of masturbation (their sister, e.g.) and then thinking of masturbation anyway. Boys enter the house, go to their rooms, remove sexually explicit magazines from hidden stashes, put on loud music, feel despair. Boys enter the house worried; they argue. The boys are ugly, they are failures, they will never be loved, they enter the house. Boys enter the house and kiss their mother, who feels differently now they have outgrown her. Boys enter the house, kiss their mother, she explains the seriousness of their sister's difficulty, her diagnosis. Boys enter the house, having attempted to locate the spot in their yard where the dolls were buried, eight or nine years prior, without success; they go to their sister's room, sit by her bed. Boys enter the house and tell their completely bald sister jokes about baldness. Boys hold either hand of their sister, laying aside differences, having trudged grimly into the house. Boys skip school, enter house, hold vigil. Boys enter the house after their parents have both gone off to work, sit with their sister and with their sister's nurse. Boys enter the house carrying cases of beer. Boys enter the house, very worried now, didn't know more worry was possible. Boys enter the house carrying controlled substances, neither having told the other that he is carrying a controlled substance, though an intoxicated posture seems appropriate under the circumstances. Boys enter the house weeping and hear weeping around them. Boys enter the house embarrassed, silent, anguished, keening, afflicted, angry, woeful, grief-stricken. Boys enter the house on vacation, each clasps the hand of the other with genuine warmth, the one wearing dark colors and having shaved a portion of his head, the other having grown his hair out longish and wearing, uncharacteristically, a tie-dyed shirt. Boys enter the house on vacation and argue bitterly about politics (other subjects are no longer discussed), one boy supporting the Maoist insurgency in a certain Southeast Asian country, one believing that to change the system you need to work inside it; one boy threatens to beat the living shit out of the other, refuses crème brûlée, though it is created by his mother in order to keep the peace. One boy writes home and thereby enters the house only through a mail slot: he argues that the other boy is crypto-fascist, believing that the market can seek its own level on questions of ethics and morals; boys enter the house on vacation and announce future professions; boys enter the house on vacation and change their minds about professions; boys enter the house on vacation, and one boy brings home a sweetheart but throws a tantrum when it is suggested that the sweetheart will have to retire on the folding bed in the basement; the other boy, having no sweetheart, is distant and withdrawn, preferring to talk late into the night about family members gone from this world. Boys enter the house several weeks apart. Boys enter the house on days of heavy rain. Boys enter the house, in different calendar years, and upon entering, the boys seem to do nothing but compose manifestos, for the benefit of parents; they follow their mother around the place, having fashioned these manifestos in celebration of brand-new independence: *Mom, I like to lie in bed late into the morning watching game shows,* or, *I'm never going to date anyone but artists from now on, mad girls, dreamers, practicers of black magic,* or, *A man should eat bologna, sliced meats are important,* or, *An American should bowl at least once a year,* but these manifestos apply only for brief spells, after which they are reversed or discarded. Boys don't enter the house at all, except as ghostly afterimages of younger selves, fleeting images of sneakers dashing up a staircase; soggy towels on the floor of the bathroom; blue jeans coiled like asps in the basin of the washing machine; boys as an absence of boys, blissful at first, you put a thing down on a spot, put this book down, come back later, it's still there; you buy a box of cookies, eat three, later three are missing. Nevertheless, when boys next enter the house, which they ultimately must do, it's a relief, even if it's only in preparation for weddings of acquaintances from boyhood, one boy has a beard, neatly trimmed, the other has rakish sideburns, one boy wears a hat, the other boy thinks hats are ridiculous, one boy wears khakis pleated at the waist, the other wears denim, but each changes into his suit (one suit fits well, one is a little tight), as though suits are the liminary marker of adulthood. Boys enter the house after the wedding and they are slapping each other on the back and yelling at anyone who will listen, *It's a party!* One boy enters the house, carried by friends, having been arrested (after the wedding) for driving while intoxicated, complexion ashen; the other boy tries to keep his mouth shut: the car is on its side in a ditch, the car has the top half of a tree broken over its bonnet, the car has struck another car, which has in turn struck a third, *Everyone will have seen.* One boy misses his brother horribly, misses the past, misses a time worth being nostalgic over, a time that never existed, back when they set their sister's playhouse on fire; the other boy avoids all mention of that time; each of them is once the boy who enters the house alone, missing the other, each is devoted and each callous, and each plays his part on the telephone, over the course of months. Boys enter the house with fishing gear, according to prearranged date and time, arguing about whether to use lures or live bait, in order to meet their father for the fishing adventure, after which boys enter the house again, almost immediately, with live bait, having settled the question; boys boast of having caught fish in the past, though no fish has ever been caught: *Remember when the blues were biting?* Boys enter the house carrying their father, slumped. Happens so fast. Boys rush into the house leading EMTs to the couch in the living room where the body lies, boys enter the house, boys enter the house, boys enter the house. Boys hold open the threshold, awesome threshold that has welcomed them when they haven't even been able to welcome themselves, that threshold which welcomed them when they had to be taken in, here is its tarnished knocker, here is its euphonious bell, here's where the boys had to sand the door down because it never would hang right in the frame, here are the scuff marks from when boys were on the wrong side of the door demanding, here's where there were once milk bottles for the milkman, here's where the newspaper always landed, here's the mail slot, here's the light on the front step, illuminated, here's where the boys are standing, as that beloved man is carried out. Boys, no longer boys, exit.

BARBARA KLEIN MOSS

Rug Weaver

FROM THE GEORGIA REVIEW

HIS DAUGHTER-IN-LAW is always wheedling him to leave his rooms over the garage and join her on the patio, but when Ebrahim Nahavendi hears her knocking on the door, his eyelids drop involuntarily. It is not just the southern California sun that makes him squint — this he attributes to his months in a dark cell as a guest of the Revolution — but the sight of so much unabashed skin, so casually displayed. Years of gazing at shrouded women have permanently dulled his eyes. Like the receiver of tablets before him, he doesn't dare to look upon naked glory.

Today she is wearing a cut-off T-shirt and tiny shorts. The long length of her is damp from her daily run, her yellow hair sticking to her neck and shoulders. "A Persian treat is waiting for you," she says. "I stopped at Trader Joe's after dropping the girls off and raided the place for dried fruits — peaches, apricots, plums, dates, figs. The catch is, you're not allowed to eat them in this smoky *cave*." She brushes by him and moves with mock exasperation through the kitchenette into his bed sitting room, raising blinds, opening windows, extinguishing his cigarette in the ashtray balanced on the arm of the couch.

"As soon as you leave, I'll make it dark again," he says. But she is so soft and diffused in her blondness, so much like light herself as she passes through the room, that he allows himself to be swept into her orbit and led outside.

She insists that he sit in the chaise while she showers, and again he complies, although he dislikes looking at his stretched-out legs in their somber trousers. His feet too are overdressed, a pair of immigrant dandies in silk socks and braided sandals. For her sake he tries to adjust his back to the slump of the chair. He hopes she won't tell him to relax. He has no natural talent for it, and ends up contorting himself in postures of exaggerated ease like the boneless princes in Persian miniatures.

"We *live* out here," she had said, showing him around for the first time. Over the last month, he has seen that this is true. The patio is as lush as the interior of the house is spare, filled with green plants, potted flowers, and menacing cacti that she calls succulents — an oddly sensual word for such bristly growths. Toys and games are scattered on the redwood table; the children's bathing suits dry on the backs of rustic chairs. Against the stucco wall is an imposing gas grill, an altar on which, most nights, his son Yousef burns an offering. His daughter-in-law will eat no meat; it pollutes the system, she says. He has imagined with pleasure the sunny corridor of her insides: peach-colored, moistened with delicate washes of herbal tea.

She reappears in one of Yousef's shirts and an ankle bracelet, carrying a large silver tray heaped with fruits, which she sets on the low table at his side. He takes an apricot from the tray — it is a Seder plate that belonged to Mina, his dead wife, and the apricots have been carefully arranged in the gully meant for the roasted egg — and holds it briefly on his tongue before shifting it to the pouch of his cheek.

"Is it good?" she asks. "Is it like the old country?"

"Dried fruit is dried fruit, here or in Iran." The words, flatter than he intended, measurably dim her luster. When you are that fair, he thinks, the slightest pressure leaves marks. "Very nice," he says repentently, and bites down on the softened apricot, the sour sweetness flooding his mouth at just the moment that he says her foolish, long-limbed, gawky deer of a name. "Very nice . . . Kimberly."

Back in his apartment, he does the usual search for his cigarettes, finding them this time in the empty flour canister. Day after day she performs this infant's trick, apparently believing that if an object is out of sight he'll stop wanting it. Her persistence annoys him, but he senses that for her it is a kind of game. A flirtation, even. If she can't convert him to her creed of eternal health, she'll settle for provoking him.

The window in the dining alcove is the only one that suits his purposes. If he shuts the vertical blinds, then opens them so that slivers of light slant in, he can get the effect of bars in the reflection on the opposite wall. He doesn't really need this; it is only, he tells himself, a device for meditation, something to stare at while he focuses his mind. He lights a cigarette and settles back in his chair, feeling the slight vibration under his feet as the station wagon pulls into the garage beneath him. The high voices of the little girls float up in a brief clamor before the kitchen door slams shut. Sucking in smoke, he begins to weave.

First, strands of light teased until they stretch the length of the wall, the thread skeleton flickering like a home movie, reminding him of how humbly he began. Then color rising like mist, uncertain and quivering, the reds mixing with blues and blacks, and out of this chaos the first suggestion of swirling forms. Always this is the moment he fears to lose it all. The pattern assaults him all at once, the shapes he labored over singly bearing down on him in a tangled mass. Panicking, he fixes on a five-pointed star — or a moss rose or a bird on a branch, whatever surfaces first to his eye — and the pattern slows and stills, the whole design bows in submission. He is still the rug's master.

Its servant too. Without it, how would he have survived those days in the cell, contemplating a death like Mina's father's?

The old man was taken first, dragged by Revolutionary Guards through the swinging doors of the carpet emporium he had modeled on a Paris department store, an ornament of the shah's new Teheran. Three days later, they learned that Moses had been condemned as a Zionist agent and shot, along with the refined young Baha'i who assisted in the showroom.

Almost as an afterthought, it seemed, the Revolution came for Ebrahim. One guard held a machine gun to his head while the other — a wild-haired boy young enough to be his son — tore through the files in his small office and ravaged his shelves, flinging to the floor the books of carpet lore he had collected for years. Moses, having recruited Ebrahim as employee and son-in-law chiefly to reap the benefits of his fluent English and educated eye, had liked to indulge him with rare illustrated volumes. As the guards herded him out, they stomped conscientiously on the splayed pages of priceless rugs.

For the first two days he was locked in a room with many others. Amid the terror and confusion, men were removed in the night in a dreamlike constant shifting and others brought in to replace them. Then, inexplicably, he was transferred to his own small cell. He waited, huddled on the foam rubber slab in his English suit, to be taken for interrogation, or worse. But no one came except the guard who brought him food twice a day.

A solitary man, Ebrahim had always recoiled from enforced intimacy, but now he longed for the desperate camaraderie of the other prisoners. He discovered in himself a horror of dying alone, anonymous against a wall, without the sheltering ceremonies of his faith. He was the son of a Talmudic scholar, and even in the realm of business had retained an otherworldly aura that hinted at a preoccupation with higher things. For this also Moses had wooed him.

When Ebrahim thought of Mina, her fear infiltrated him like a virus. He saw her as he had left her, sedated on a couch, her hands still clutching the handkerchief she had been wringing moments before. Her bumbling brothers would have to organize the mourning for the father who had all but disowned them; his own sons, thank God, were at school in Paris, living with an uncle. Although Ebrahim had never loved Mina, his whole office as a husband was to hold her together. Helplessly, he imagined her emerging from drugged sleep, resting for a moment in the dimness of the curtained room before the awful knowledge descended on her. Moaning, she would run from room to room, tearing at her hair and clothes, the servants chattering after her like crows.

He remembered how she had first looked to him when Moses took him to the house — as solid as Mother Earth, a buxom, deep-eyed young woman who lit the Sabbath candles before dinner and spoke the blessing with a slight lisp. As they ate western-style at a gleaming oval table, she kept her eyes on her plate, but Ebrahim caught her glancing at him from beneath her heavy brows. She was in good health, Moses informed him later, pressing his thick fingertips together as if cradling an egg, but a little nervous owing to the early loss of her mother; she had been a dutiful daughter too long and needed the stability of her own household. Ebrahim knew he was being gulled. She was already twenty-six, the only daughter of a rich man and not yet married. Still, the comfort and opulence of the house seduced him, its brocade drapes and polished silver and massive furniture seeming to embody his dreams of France. Mina

was a little heavy for his taste, though not unattractive. "And she
has business sense," Moses said. "More than my useless sons. A
scholar like you needs a woman who can take care of practical matters."

There, at least, Moses had spoken truly. Mina proved to be a
shrewd bargainer, with Moses' feral instinct for quality. She traf-
ficked with importers to furnish the house Moses gave them as a
wedding gift; then, having feathered her nest in the finest European style, she hid herself within its walls. In Ebrahim's presence
she was soft-spoken and eager to please, but emotion billowed up
in her. Any minor thing might unleash it — a lost key or the blunt
reply of a servant. His own words, at first soothing and then accusa-
tory, had little effect. Yet Ebrahim saw that she would like to oblige
him. With birdlike cries she tried to stand against the gale rising
within her, clutching at her skirt with small, futile gestures as if to
keep it from flying in her face. But always the storm carried her
away.

In spite of these eruptions, the life of the household took on a
shape — if only, Ebrahim thought, because there was such a handsome house to contain it. Mina took a voyeur's pleasure in the domestic arts. However unsettled her week, she appeared each Friday
evening to preside over the Sabbath meal at the baronial dining table that she had ordered from Belgium. She was always beautifully
dressed and coiffed for these occasions. Moses, damp-eyed, murmured about her mother coming to life again. The other relatives
beamed on her and nodded their heads. It was, Ebrahim thought,
as if she struggled for six days to subdue her oozing clay, emerging
on the seventh as a fully formed ceremonial wife.

Their restrained lovemaking — neither of them, he realized,
wanted to risk stirring her feelings — produced two sons. Yousef
was born when they had been married little more than a year, a
large, red-faced infant as hairy and demanding as the biblical Esau,
and Sami two years later, after a precarious pregnancy spent mostly
in bed. Mina never really got up again after the second birth. The
children were tangible reminders of the fragility of the world: the
delicate Sami, in particular, drove her into fits of hysterical anxiety
that left her prostrate. Servants were sent from Moses' house to
raise the boys.

At the end of the working day, having dealt with the crises that awaited his homecoming, Ebrahim would retreat to his study, where he ignored the comforts of his walnut desk and leather club chair to sit cross-legged on the carpet, lost in the words of the sages and mystics. He learned the numerical values of letters of the alphabet and meditated on God's garden, its vanished perfumes, its lost light that allowed Adam to see from one end of the world to the other.

Fragments of the texts Ebrahim had read came back to him as he waited in the solitude of his cell — odd bits of Kabbalah or Midrash that floated to the surface of his mind like black spots sailing across his field of vision. He took to speaking them aloud, finding they had an incantatory power that calmed him. One morning he awoke early, nudged out of sleep by the pinkish light drizzling through the bars in the window, and heard, "Paradise is present in our own time, but concealed." The voice was his father's, which since childhood Ebrahim had identified with the voice of God. He repeated the words in a whisper, lying on his back with the light seeping into his half-opened lids. Immediately he was filled with a sense of well-being.

As the day wore on, the feeling faded. No revelation, it seemed, could survive the tedium of endless empty hours. Even his fear of death was blunted into something close and stale, a tumor whose dull ache he had grown used to bearing. He tried to remember the origin of the phrase that had come to him at dawn. It was probably some mystical reference to the hidden meaning of the Torah; the words seemed both concrete and maddeningly elusive, as, no doubt, their author had intended. When Ebrahim spoke them now, he heard a taunt, a challenge to the uninitiated. "Where should I look, then?" he said to the spectral rabbi who mocked him. "If paradise is a state of mind, it can be found anywhere, even here. Shall I check the corners?"

His eye swept over the tiny cell, settling at last on the single window. They had taken his watch when they arrested him, but he could tell by the angle of the sun slanting in that it must be late afternoon. He was struck by how the light appeared at this hour, solid yet delicate, like a bolt of fine fabric stretched across the room. The sun had gnawed at the thickness of the iron bars, reducing them until they appeared as slender and tensile as ropes. In their rectangular frame, they made him think of the looms set against mud-brick walls in the mountain village he had visited with Moses. Ebrahim had liked the half-finished rugs best: the vertical threads of the warp, shot through with sun, seemed as beautiful to him as the ornate pattern creeping upward. "I wish I were the weaver and not the seller," he had said to his father-in-law, as they sat between two towering looms on the earthen floor of a hut, sharing the midday meal. "You'd be bored," Moses told him. "This is no work for intellectuals. These people have the designs in their fingers, from generation to generation. You think they sit around dreaming up symbols?"

Ebrahim had said nothing at the time, but now he argued back. So, Moses, here is the little scholar you bought all those years ago, locked in his cubicle, ready to spin thoughts into gold. Who is left to interrupt me?

He closed his eyes and, with a voluptuous sinking, traced in his head the motions of the Persian knot, passing like a skywriter under one warp thread and around the other, snaring both strands in one loop. When his eyes opened, the bars of the window were threaded with light.

"Come to the store tomorrow," Yousef says. "I could use some help organizing the Labor Day sale."

The air has cooled so quickly after dinner that they have been forced into the living room. Already the days are getting shorter. Ebrahim sighs and shifts in his soft chair. The rugs are on sale continuously, the store in a perpetual state of liquidation. Banners line the windows, announcing 30 percent off, 40 percent on holidays and during the slow season.

"What do I know about sales?" he says. "In all the years I worked for Moses, we never had one. We sold quality, people paid for it. Those who wanted bargains went to the bazaars."

"I'm telling you, it's a different attitude here. Class has nothing to do with it. You take your big-spending tourists or your wealthy retirees, money can be falling out of their pockets but they have to believe they're getting a deal. They have to be seduced."

Directly above Yousef's head, on the wall over the couch, is a large bronze disk that reminds Ebrahim of a rayless sun. It is the room's only ornament, apart from photographs of Kimberly and the children. Yousef has told him that his eyes ache from looking at patterns all day. When he comes home, he wants the simplicity of neutral walls.

Ebrahim fixes his glance on the disk. "If you need me, I don't mind coming. At least I can make myself useful in the office."

"We'll go to Harry's for breakfast. A little celebration. Nahavendi and Son." Yousef extends his arms along the back of the couch, visibly pleased to have won this small battle. He has been pushing Ebrahim to work at the store part-time. "It's healthier for you to be active. Kim is worried you're not adjusting. You stay in all day thinking about the past, you'll get depressed."

"Why do you assume I live in the past? Maybe I'm thinking about what I read in the newspaper. Maybe I'm thinking about you."

"Come on, Baba," Yousef says, grinning. "Since when did you waste time thinking about me?"

His son, Ebrahim reflects, is like Mina without the nerves, Moses without the sly intelligence. A purely physical being. Whatever he is feeling stands out on him like sweat. Just over forty, he already carries the heft of Mina's side of the family. But he is tolerant of his flesh, makes no attempt to contain it. His shirts are always half open, a dark, curly fleece bursting out. His thighs strain at the flimsy cotton of his shorts. Watching him eat, you know exactly how he makes love — the pagan gusto, the avid tongue and lips. Ebrahim would like not to think of it, but sometimes, on sleepless nights, as he lies on his sofabed listening to muffled noises from the house, he does.

Morgan and Sydney run in, wrapped in Disney towels after their Jacuzzi bath, their wet hair swirled in peaks on top of their heads. Blondes, both of them, although the seven-year-old has Yousef's wavy hair and a duskier skin tone. In one generation the Semitic strain has been all but effaced, laundered out in a kind of New World ethnic cleansing. It is possible — Ebrahim has learned to be unsurprised by such things — that they were conceived in the hot tub, Yousef leaning back with his eyes closed, his manhood submerged in tepid water, while Kimberly, the energetic, efficient American, commanded him to relax.

The children head straight for Yousef, who sweeps them into his lap and begins to nuzzle their hair. They never come to Ebrahim unless ordered to do so. When he first arrived, they'd been shyly curious; he had been advertised as the grandfather, the only one they had, since Kimberly's father was dead. Speaking to them quietly in his formal English, he had presented them with costumed dolls before bending to kiss their soft, averted cheeks. For a few days they stood at a little distance, staring at him solemnly as he ate or read the newspaper. If he reached out his hand, they giggled and ran. Now he has become a part of their landscape, no more noticeable than the monumental couches that crouch like sphinxes in the bare expanse of the living room. He doesn't mind. They are alien to him, with their blue eyes and bird bones and English gentlemen's names. Yet he marvels at the fact of them. He would like to send a photograph of them to Mina in the afterlife, where, he imagines, she still tosses restlessly: Be still, be at peace, all our struggles have come to this.

"Bedtime for mermaids," his daughter-in-law announces, bringing a bowl of cherries. She is wearing a short, sea-colored robe and smells pungently of piney shampoo. "Did you say goodnight to Pop-Pop?"

As always, she is vigilant on Ebrahim's behalf. She reaches for the children, but Yousef grabs her and pulls her to him, encircling all three of them in his meaty arms.

"Look what you're doing!" With one hand she clutches the ends of her robe — suddenly modest, Ebrahim notices, because he is watching — and with the other tries to balance the bowl. Fruit spills over their tangle of tanned limbs.

Yousef laughs. "What do you think, Baba?" he says. "How do you like my bouquet of girls?"

After the first exhilaration, the childish acrobatics of his eye, there was nothing for hours. The window was only a window, a frame for the prison yard's harsh spotlights, which pierced the blackness of his cell. Still, he stared at the bars, alert and unmoving, his exhaustion congealed into a leaden attention. Toward morning the thought occurred to him — appearing prosaically, like an equation scratched on a blackboard — that he should begin as God began, by separating light from dark.

So he made a sun. A simple sun such as a child might draw, a round golden plate surrounded by corkscrew rays. He had underestimated the difficulty of transferring it from his head to the lower left corner of the window; it required an effort of imagination that he felt too weak to make, a spasm that was almost physical, as if the object were lodged literally behind his eyes and he had to tear it loose. When, after hours of focused thought, he could see it before him, he set about refining his sun, buffing the color until a reddish tint surfaced and unifying the rays so that their golden tips pointed in one direction. Once he had the pattern, the labor of dreaming came more easily to him. By the time the guard brought his food, he had made a whole row.

After eating Ebrahim fell into a deep sleep, awakening early the next morning with a sense of anticipation, as if some good news had been revealed to him in the night. Still, he had to compose himself before daring to turn his concentration to the window. He shut his eyes, letting the picture form in his mind, and when he opened them the suns were standing at attention like soldiers. He set to work immediately, weaving above them a border of blue with black arabesques, an intricate darkness like the night sky. By late afternoon he was finishing his first moonface, whose blown-out cheeks and sated smile he had seen in his night dreams.

As his confidence increased, he became more playful. It gave him pleasure to enlarge an herb until its branches twined with those of a fruit tree, or to alternate birds with fish, teasing out the symmetry of wings and fins to make a witty rabbinical commentary on two forms of floating. The herd animals refused to come alive for him until he remembered the fragment of the Pazyryk carpet with mounted horses marching around its borders. With these ancient beasts as a model, his sheep and goats and cattle took on motion, reverberating with incipient rhythm like lines of musical notes.

The rug revealed itself to him gradually. He could not admit that he was replicating the grand design of God; his own arrogance appalled him, as if he had dared to speak the holy name. His father's face came to him, as stern as any mullah's, the brows meeting in a disapproval so pure that it was almost impersonal, and he felt again the awe and fear he had known as a child. To free his mind, he had to turn into a Kabbalist, concealing his deeper purposes from himself. Each morning he labored like the humblest craftsman, sweating over the curve of a ram's horn or the arrangement of scales on a fish, refusing to see further than the task of the day. Not until eve-

ning did he allow himself what any weaver took for granted: a look
at the pattern as it grew on the loom. And when he saw what he had
made — how the images in their orderly rows leaped out at him;
how the colors radiated separately and yet submitted to each other;
how, even at this early stage, the figures made an abstraction that
was greater than their parts — he exulted shamelessly.

"Idiots," Yousef mutters. "A pair of idiots."

Ebrahim isn't sure whether he is referring to the sleek but weathered couple who have wandered in from the pink hotel across the
street or to his nephews, Amir and Faraz, who are showing them a
carpet. Sons of Mina's brother, they have worked at the store for
two years without acquiring any skills. "Good for nothing but eating my money" is Yousef's standard complaint. But Ebrahim has to
admire their flair as they unfurl the rug, a dance of servility and
style that jogs his memory of an apprentice waiter in Paris spoon-
ing sauce over a plateful of fish.

Ebrahim has spent a few hours in the office wrestling with the
computer and allowing Yousef to show off a few treasures and elicit
his opinion on some auction finds. Ebrahim does his best to appear
involved, but the business holds no interest for him now. The rugs
are only commodities, their beauty a whore's finery. They will end
up on their backs in the houses of balding executives like this one,
pierced by the spike heels of lacquered women like his wife, who
is now complaining about the busy pattern on a handsome old
Kerman while her husband waits vacantly until it is time to do battle over the price.

Ebrahim turns away from Yousef's earnest sales pitch and wanders over to the window. He had planned to plead a headache and
take the bus home, a ride he likes for its companionable solitude
and views of the cove. But Kimberly is due any minute to take him
to lunch at Balboa Park. The children are spending the day with
friends, and she has insisted on giving him her free afternoon.
Staring at the strip of street between the giant sales signs, his mind
on nothing but the weight of the morning's pancakes in his stomach, he sees at first only a girl in a white linen shift, her long American stride sanctified by the flash of sun on her gold sandals. Although he has been expecting her, he gets a pleasurable frisson of
surprise when she swings through the door.

"I'd take it on approval," the woman customer is saying. "But if it doesn't work, will you cover the cost of shipping it back from Denver?"

Yousef doesn't answer, because he is staring at his wife with the same dazzled awe he wore when he introduced her to Ebrahim. The woman looks too, a brief, assessing glance that takes in her companion, whose alertness has visibly quickened. Behind them, the nephews offer radiant white-toothed smiles above the backup rug, a Tabriz whose corners they elevate with delicate distraction, like attendants lifting the train of a bridal veil. Ebrahim sees it all in a tableau, as he has trained himself to see.

"You got all dressed up for a walk in the park?" Yousef excuses himself and walks over to Kimberly. "You're as bad as my father, with his suit and tie."

"I didn't want my distinguished escort to be ashamed of me. He's always staring at me like he can't believe the way I go around." Kimberly tosses her hair, as if to shrug off the seriousness of this.

"Not true, not at all true," Ebrahim stumbles. "But you look especially charming today. Very Greek. Like a goddess." Immediately he repents of his banality, but before turning his eyes away, he sees that once again he has left his mark on her. A faint flush this time.

Yousef puts his hand to the heightened color on her cheek and rubs it with his thumb. "You have to watch out for the old man," he says. "You think he's contemplating the meaning of heaven and earth, but all the time he's watching you out of lizard eyes." He looks over his shoulder at the customer, who, ignoring the rug and her husband, is chatting vivaciously with Amir and Faraz. "I'd go with you, but if I leave, no business gets done. Take him to the Hacienda for a nice lunch, maybe a margarita. A *small* margarita for a Jewish monk." He reaches into his pocket. "You have money?"

The park on this bright Wednesday is uncrowded, populated with a scattering of tourists, some aimless-looking locals, and groups of schoolchildren who are being herded in ragged lines between the stucco palaces that house the city's small museums. Along the main thoroughfare where they are walking, mimes, magicians, and street musicians compete for sparse audiences.

"Everyone must be at the zoo," Kimberly says. "We have the place to ourselves."

Ebrahim knows that the Moorish buildings with their elaborate wedding-cake ornamentation are not really old; Yousef has explained that they were constructed for an international exposition in 1915. But the lush greenery kindles his old fascination with France. As a boy he had smuggled French novels into his room, reading them at night when he should have been studying Torah. Gradually there grew in his mind a landscape of broad avenues lined with stately houses and tall, thin trees that bowed in the wind like the consumptive aristocrats he read about. He had stared at one illustration so obsessively that he half believed he could pass through the page and join the promenade past the busy café (*Glacé* lightly sketched on its striped awning), at his side the wasp-waisted woman with red lips whose hat brim cast a slanted shadow across her face. In the streets of his dream Paris — he smiles now, remembering it — horse-drawn carriages coexisted seamlessly with the latest racing cars.

"What are you thinking about?" Kimberly asks. "You have this look on your face like you're in a different world. Are you thinking about Iran?"

Her flat tones jar him, but at least she didn't say "the old country." She seems to have in her mind some orientalized version of the scrubbed hearths of her own Dutch ancestors, toward which she assumes he is always helplessly longing.

"I was thinking of the romantic idea of France that I had when I was young. In my mind, it was the opposite of what I saw around me. The hills around Teheran were bare and parched, so Paris had to be like one big garden, flowers everywhere. This place reminds me of it."

"But you *lived* in Paris, didn't you?"

In her voice he can hear her amazement that he would waste time mooning over an imaginary city when he had experienced the real thing.

"Yes, yes. After my release. For three years. But, you understand, it was not my fantasy. We had lost everything and were living in an Algerian neighborhood. Yousef had left school by that time and was working with me at a furniture store; Sami had just started university. My wife — in a strange place, she became more . . . confused. We did the best we could for her, but in the end, I had to send her away. A private place, of course, an old convent, very refined. In six months she was dead. No one knew why. Her heart just stopped. It will always be on my conscience." He reaches for the pack of cigarettes in his breast pocket, remembers, and drops his hand. "But you must have heard all this."

"Yousef has told me. I can't get over how much you went through." She takes his arm, squeezes it. Looking into his eyes, she smiles as if to reassure him that the old, bad days are over.

He has a perverse desire to cloud her forehead by telling her about his visits to the asylum — about the French nuns, oddly familiar in their dark habits, and the way Mina pleaded with him, each time he came, to save her from the "revolutionaries" and take her home for Shabbat. Instead he says, "We did the usual tourist things, of course. The Louvre. The Tour Eiffel. The Tuileries."

"Oh, those names sound gorgeous coming out of your mouth! Did you know I took French all four years in high school? My best friend and I had this plan that we would be flight attendants and have an apartment in Paris and find fabulous French boyfriends. I was halfway through the training when I met Yousef. And then I got pregnant. So I never got to fly the happy skies and see the world." She laughs. "I guess France was my dream too. I almost forgot I had one."

With a gentle pressure, she leads him into a cloistered walkway that fronts one of the baroque facades. In the sudden shadow, half blinded, he is acutely aware of the weight of her arm on his, of the tanned smoothness and the little golden hairs, the idea of them prickling his skin inside his jacket sleeve.

A carved door opens, not into the room he expected but a sunlit courtyard with a fountain in the center. *"Voilà!"* she says.

His first impression of open space alters: the place is crowded, the tables along the walls filled with guests who have the alert, hectic look of tourists, their faces momentarily eclipsed by enormous glass globes from which they sip reverently.

"This fountain is perhaps the Fountain of Youth?" he says to Kimberly. "These people are taking the waters of life?"

But his wit is lost on her. "Don't worry," she tells him, heading for the maitre d'. "I made a reservation."

An arbor of fat red blossoms overhangs their table. Leafy shadows play over her face as she scans the menu. Watching her, he wonders how long it has been since he sat across from a woman. A

Jewish monk, Yousef called him, but he has had his moments: hurried encounters in Paris, intense for all their brevity, and even in Iran, after his return, hints from the wives of friends (veiled, of course, like the bright, clinging dresses beneath their chadors). His good looks have brought him some privileges. He could have the Malaysian student of linguistics; he could grind his sorrows out in her coolly and quickly and be back in time to make dinner for his sons. What he has not had is this simple being-with, this normalcy, this face-to-face.

Would he take the same pleasure if the face were not so purely oval, the eyelids round as a sculpted angel's? There is, he thinks, a certain restfulness about spending time with her. She has no ideas, no real conversation, no demands except the no-smoking variety. All that is required is to take in the way her hair grazes her cheekbones. The humor does not escape him: he who has spent his life excavating hidden meanings finds out in his dotage that the surface is enough.

"You must try a margarita," she urges. "I promised Yousef. It's the national drink around here." When the waiter sets Ebrahim's down — the same size as hers, he notes — he cradles the globe in both hands and brings the salted rim to his lips. The pale liquid slides into his mouth, silvery, elusive. Even after swallowing, he isn't sure what he has tasted.

Kimberly licks the rime from her upper lip. "Tell me more about Paris. I hate that I've never been anywhere."

"Why not get Yousef to go with you? You could stay with Sami; it's about time you met him. Although who knows how he lives? On air, I think. Air and poetry."

"Are you kidding? Yousef would never leave the business. He's obsessed. I swear it's all he thinks about, apart from us. And his beloved California. Why travel if you're living in paradise? Besides" — she glances briefly at her nails — "I shouldn't tell you this, but he really resents Sami. Thinks he's a leech, the way he sits at his desk all day and depends on your uncle for handouts. He's always felt that Sami is your favorite. The one who looks like you. The writer."

The liquor has hobbled Ebrahim's tongue. A graceful denial is called for, but he has lost the power to give shape to it.

"There is a park," he says, enunciating carefully, "not far from where I worked. By day it's just a nice place to sit. A few statues, beds of flowers, old trees, a pond. But you come there at dusk, at the moment the sun is setting, and the shadows deepen in such a way that you would think you had stepped out of time. As if you had lived all your life in a flat world and suddenly you are in three dimensions." He sighs and looks down at the table, where a bowl of red sauce shimmers, untouched. "Maybe I'll take you myself."

"Do you mean it? That's a great idea!" Her skin suffuses with the thought, the pinkness rising so quickly to the surface that she seems actually to glow. "We could go during spring vacation. April in Paris, right? We could do all the things you missed the first time around." She reaches across the table to grab his hand. "It could still be our dream."

How like her, he thinks, to assume that two weeks in her radiant company will wipe away his past. Once the light fades, the park is drab, he wants to tell her, not a place a girl like you would walk at night. Paris when you live there is just another city, a place to work and sleep and bear your troubles. But he is stirred in spite of himself, shaken by how quickly the enchantment comes back to him, all its colors intact, a page of a book not opened for fifty years. His hand with its raised veins and brown spots lies in hers like a dead leaf. He is grateful for the distraction of the plates arriving.

Kimberly attacks her ethereal salad, spearing lettuce as she spins out plans. The girls will stay with her mother. Yousef's cholesterol level will have to be monitored from afar. If Sami has no room for them, they'll stay at a pension or maybe do a house exchange with one of those well-preserved Frenchwomen, who'll make *bifteck* for Yousef — he'd like that, wouldn't he? Ebrahim listens with one ear, his thoughts racing. Why not? It would be the beginning of an education for her. They might get a few glances, but the French are accepting of such things.

"I'd want to see the real Paris," she says, putting down her fork. "Not just the places tourists go. I'd want Sami to show us around. Maybe you could give me some names of poets to read, and we could practice talking about them so he won't think I'm too ignorant." She takes a miniature corncob from her plate and dabbles it absently in the red sauce. "Yousef's mysterious brother. I've been curious about him forever. Does he really look so much like you? When you were young, I mean."

Kimberly is staring at him expectantly, her blue eyes fixed on his. As the moment extends, a faint line appears between her brows.

He tips his glass and takes a long drink of the margarita. Definitely an elixir, but not from the Tree of Life. The Tree of Knowledge, maybe. That fruit would have a little salt in it.

By the end of his second month in prison, he was ready to attempt the central field. Thoughts of it had been germinating in his mind while he worked on the borders. He wanted a garden, of course, but not the compartmentalized squares of the classic garden rugs, each plant penned in its own little plot. What was needed was more of a meadow, an ordered lushness, at once profuse and disciplined.

The first days were difficult. He had trained himself to repeat one or two figures in a straight line. Now he had to mimic spontaneity, planting narcissus here, china roses there, calculating the texture of the green between them. This was, he saw, a higher form of art, approximating more closely the handiwork of the Maker. As he struggled to reproduce every flower he could remember, and to invent what he could not recall, he began to wonder if God was finally taking revenge on him for his ambitions.

Often he was overcome by exhaustion. He woke each day resolved to make progress, but before long the object of his attention would blur and he would fall into a stupor. Not only had exhilaration left him; he lacked even the will to rouse himself. He would sit with his head in his hands, wanting only to lie down on the bed of green he was making and close his eyes. He could almost feel the buoyant cushion of leaves giving way beneath his weight, the mingled fragrances rising up around him.

While he was in this state, two guards came for him. It was midmorning, but he was as dazed as if he had been roused from a sound sleep. As he stumbled between them, one guard muttered to the other, "An old drunk." Ebrahim realized how he must look to them: bearded, filthy, red-eyed. All these weeks he had lived inside his head, giving no thought to his body. Now his natural fastidiousness reasserted itself, rising along with the terror that he had tamed for so long. How could he maintain his dignity when he had been reduced to this?

He was pushed into a brightly lit room, bare except for a large metal desk covered with papers. The man behind the desk raised a long, sallow expanse of face whose blandness was disrupted by black-rimmed glasses and a patchy beard. He shuffled his papers and, with the slight sigh of a bureaucrat interviewing yet another pensioner, said, "You handled overseas business for the firm of Moses Kashani and Company. You have been, no doubt, a key agent in his espionage operation. You are part of an international network of spies seeking to propagate Zionism." He leaned back in his chair as if he had completed his task.

The rote quality of the speech gave Ebrahim courage. Every day of his working life he saw men who looked like this one: office workers scurrying through the business district in their cheap jackets, darting into a tea shop for a quick glass to get them through the afternoon. "I know nothing of espionage or international networks," he said. "I have no interest in Zionism. I have never even been very political. I am a student of the Jewish sacred texts. My father was the scholar Yaghoub Nahavendi."

The man at the desk nodded as if taking in this information, and a guard stepped forward. Raising his arm in a leisurely manner, he struck Ebrahim across the mouth, sending him staggering across the room.

An hour later, nursing his bruises in his cell, Ebrahim wondered if invoking his father's name had saved him from a worse beating. The guards had roughed him up but had shown a lack of zeal. They'd hardly done more than blacken his skin. Had some secret signal restrained them, or were they holding back, keeping him intact for further interrogation? His father had been a personage in Teheran and beyond, a professor known as much for rectitude as for learning. In the shah's Persia, his spirituality and scorn for the material world had made him a misfit, the model of the Old World Jew. What irony, Ebrahim thought: if his father had lived, he would have been at home with the new austerity.

Ebrahim's body ached and his mouth still tasted of blood, but his mind was clear. The torpor of the last days had lifted, leaving him focused and eerily calm. He had no illusion that he would leave the prison alive. The long stasis was over and the procedure for his elimination had begun. He probed at the fact gently, as his fingers probed his damaged flesh, and found that it held little terror for him. His weeks in the cell had worked a purpose in him that was greater than his fear. He had been allotted space to create a paradise, to draw it out of its hiddenness and into the world. All that remained for him was to finish what he had started. Painfully he dropped to the floor and, crouching with his forehead on the ground like an Arab turned toward Mecca, cried out for time.

He saw where he had gone wrong as soon as he began to work.

The garden, for all its beauty, was never meant to be more than a backdrop. "Always look for the essence," his father had taught him. "Think of the letter of the law as the honeycomb and the meaning beneath it as the honey." He had been guilty of the worst kind of legalism, reproducing flowers like a shortsighted botanist when he should have been orchestrating the primal drama.

As if his understanding had seeded it, a tree began to grow in the center of the field. It seemed to grow on its own, so rapidly and effortlessly that he felt almost like a passive observer, lending his faculties to a process that had already been set in motion. First awkward roots appeared, large-knuckled fingers that clutched the bottom border, contrasting with the orderly parade of animals below. Then came the trunk, scarred and deeply furrowed, born old in the new world. He had completed a third of it when a knot on the trunk began to bulge as if it had a life of its own. He sat back calmly, waiting for the protuberance to reveal itself. Perhaps an hour passed before the diamond pattern came clear, barely decipherable at the tail but bolder as the body thickened. Ebrahim laughed out loud. The serpent, audacious as always, had materialized like a stowaway. There would be no finishing the rug without him.

The snake was red and black with glints of gold, a liberated border twisting round and round the darkness of the trunk. Ebrahim let it climb with him all the way up, but took care to leave it headless while he worked on the foliage and fruit. He made each branch separately, adding clusters of leaves from which golden orbs hung like small suns. Only then did the multicolored mosaic of the serpent's head push through the foliage: more pleasing to the eye, Ebrahim thought, than any fruit, and a fit repository for honeyed words.

The opening of the cell door broke his trance of concentration. He had worked all night, barely aware of the altering light. He stood, trying to gird himself for the bright room with the thought of what he had accomplished, but the guard set down his food as always and left. He wondered if his interrogator had decided he wasn't worth wasting muscle on. Whatever their plans for him, then, he hadn't much time left in the cell. Mechanically, he began to eat the rice, surprised to find himself hungry. His work was almost complete. He needed only to add the final symmetry: the figures of Adam and Eve on either side of the tree.

It had always been his opinion that the human form had no place in the pattern of a rug. "Too much like a painting or a medieval tapestry," he had said, when Moses admired a rare old hunting carpet in a museum. "How can I appreciate the design if I'm watching the hunter stalk the deer?" Together they had jeered at the portrait rugs that had appeared in the bazaars, immortalizing President Kennedy and the shah. But now, as he called up the rug for this final effort, he realized that his reservations went deeper than matters of taste. If, as his faith had taught him, it was a sin to imprison God in a form, how could he think about duplicating the first pair made in His image? Until this moment he had believed that God would forgive him his ambitions. He had imagined the Holy One standing back like a connoisseur, withholding judgment out of respect for a fellow artist.

The rug had never looked so beautiful. Long ago it had grown beyond the window, and now the wall glittered with pulsing colors and intermingled patterns. I could stop here, he thought, and give no offense. But already images of Adam and Eve were passing through his mind, piling up like rejected sketches: a primitive, square-bodied couple whose pendulous parts gave them the look of fertility amulets; two refugees from a Flemish tapestry, pale and languid, the woman all but breastless, with a starveling's swollen belly; a matched set of doe-eyed Persians of whom he was sure Mina would approve, tasteful as table lamps, flanking the tree.

None of them had any life. Archetypes, they were as flat as the dust of the ground before God breathed on it. Ebrahim shook his head and let them blow away. A rug is not a painting, he had told Moses, but he wanted his rug to do what a painting did, and more. He wanted the roundness of flesh, faces that spoke. He wanted the moment of fullness just before the Fall, the new world brimming like wine in a cup, ready to spill.

Ebrahim looked again at the window, where he had begun his work. The day that it framed was gray, streaked with a thin winter rain that was soothing to his eyes. He continued to look out, even as he heard the heavy footsteps of the guards, the door being unlocked behind him.

They marched him up one corridor and down another, passing the door he remembered as the interrogation room. He wondered whether they were taking him to the mock court for his trial or if they had decided to dispense with that formality. In the hours after his father-in-law's death, Ebrahim had forced himself to imagine the details, believing that familiarity would neutralize the horror. But there was so much he didn't know. Had the shooting taken place in some hidden room or outside, against a wall? At the end of this wide hall was a gray door with a window in it, a patch of light that showed him Moses' fate and his own.

He was not aware of feeling afraid, but his legs gave way as if they were disconnected from the rest of his body. The guards, still clutching his arms, looked down at him.

"My wife," he said. "I haven't spoken to my wife."

"Don't worry, old man." The taller of the two hoisted Ebrahim up. "You'll be together with her soon enough."

So she's dead, he thought. Dead for being Moses' daughter.

He kept his eyes on the small window. He would go out looking at framed light. An odd fancy came to him of dropping to his knees and pleading for another week of life, time to finish his work. He almost smiled when he thought of explaining to them what his work was. He would have to use a euphemism, of course, something vague like "getting my affairs in order."

The door opened and the guards, as if at a secret signal, let go of him. He stood stupidly on the threshold until one of them pushed him into the yard. Instead of the wall he expected, there was a chain-link fence patrolled by a languid fellow who looked like a parking lot attendant, and beyond it a line of traffic passing with a serene indifference that he found hard to comprehend. "Maybe he's waiting for an umbrella," he heard the smaller guard say, and he was suddenly aware of the rain pelting down on him, much heavier than it had appeared from his window. All around him space gaped, vast and disorienting. He was possessed by his old illusion of stepping through the page into the picture, but the scene he had blundered into was strange to him.

"Old man!"

He forced himself to look around. The guards were standing in the doorway, laughing. The tall one said, "Go home, already. Go home to your wife that you love so much."

Ebrahim stared at them a moment, turned, and began to walk. So this is how they do it, he thought. In the back. They make a game of it. He tried to walk slowly, in a straight line, so it would be over quickly. But when he came to the fence, the attendant opened the gate.

He stumbled into the traffic, weaving like a sleepwalker in and out of the paths of wildly honking cars and trucks. When he reached the pavement, he turned again and looked back at the prison. The guards still stood in the doorway, rifles slung casually over their shoulders, blocking the entrance to his Eden.

Ebrahim walked for hours, driven by an inner compass pointing north to the suburbs where he lived, making a drunkard's path across the city. The sudden assault of noise and activity sloughed off him. He passed through the heart of Teheran as lightly as a ghost, arriving at his own door well after nightfall.

Within a week he and Mina were on a plane to Paris to join their sons. It had all been arranged — his release too, he suspected — by his father's brother, a well-known rabbi who taught at the Sorbonne. As his sedated wife slept in the seat beside him, Ebrahim reflected that perhaps his mullah of a father had proven to be a benevolent spirit after all, guiding and protecting him each day of his long imprisonment. But he could not conjure him up, not during the journey, nor in Paris as he carved out a refugee's existence in the city of his fantasy, nor even when he returned to Iran three years later to pick up the pieces of his old world. In death, it seemed, Yaghoub Nahavendi preferred to disseminate his wisdom in the solitude of the cell.

What he feels for his daughter-in-law is not sexual, Ebrahim tells himself. Not *precisely* sexual.

He is watching her from his kitchen window as she stretches after returning from her run. She has extended one leg behind her in an exaggerated runner's pose, and she bounces rhythmically over the other, blond ponytail flopping as she massages her calf. He is fascinated, as always, by her rapt expression, her absorption in her body. If he feels a wisp of longing for her as she jogs, damp and panting, up the patio steps, it is kin to what the serpent must have felt for Eve: remote and mixed with a kind of pity for her heedless nakedness, for the innocence of her sweat, for the patch of freckled back she offers to his dry eye as she bends to flick an insect off a plant.

He taps a cigarette out of the pack and sits back in his chair. And if she is Eve, what does that make him? The twisted old knower, watching, always watching, from his leafy bower, contemplating the monotonies of a perfect patch of ground? He will woo her with words, tempt her with stories about the wide world. *Arise, my love, my fair one, and come away* . . .

He hears the slap of the sliding screen door. She has gone in to shower, and soon she'll be at his door, wet-haired and wearing some bright scrap of clothing, to invite him to sit outside on the patio while she cooks. Their afternoon has been extended. Yousef is working late and the girls have been invited to stay overnight, so they'll have dinner, as she puts it, *à deux.* She is making *polo,* and as a special concession to him, adding chicken to the casserole of rice, fruit, and nuts. In exchange, she's informed him, she expects to hear more about France. Does he think they can fit in a side trip to Provence? — she wants to get that book that everyone's reading. He never went anywhere near the south, but realizes that it makes no difference. He can invent what he doesn't know. A new thing will be seen on the earth: the sultan will tell stories to Scheherazade.

Ebrahim remembers how, in prison, he awoke once in the middle of the night, wondering what would happen after the rug was completed. Day by day, lost in the rigors of the work, he had avoided thinking about endings, his own or the carpet's. Subconsciously he must have imagined that both ends would come at once: he would tie the last knots — some infinitesimal refinement to please himself, a deepened shadow at a petal's root or the sheen on a tail feather — and the guards would arrive, and he would be marched off with the rug whole in his head. That night he had broken out in a cold sweat at the thought that he might survive. He imagined a long, lax afterlife in exile, Ebrahim the Carpet Peddler carrying his masterpiece around like a dead weight, its colors fading, its patterns sinking into the weave until it was only an idea of a rug. Perhaps this is why he has never attempted another Adam and Eve. Unfinished, the rug is always in process. He is still the weaver.

And now fate has brought him to this new land where his son, dense man of earth, tends shop and prunes prices, and his luminous daughter-in-law is more naked than she knows. Certainly he has no designs on their lives, no thought of interfering. Sanity has returned to him in the lucid half-light of his room. She will go to France, alone or with Yousef or not at all. He'll stay in his murky den and pique his senses with the old man's aphrodisiac, curiosity. Did God, he wonders, know how the tale He told would end, or did

He keep it hidden from Himself? Did He allow Himself the luxury of suspense as Eve pondered the apple?

Without Ebrahim's noticing, the room has darkened around him. He draws deeply on his cigarette and holds the smoke in, feeling it curl around the cavity of his chest. Not since his months in confinement has he experienced such a sense of the fullness of time. As the smoke plumes out of him, he raises his eyes again to the window and waits for it to come to life.

ALICE MUNRO

Post and Beam

FROM THE NEW YORKER

LIONEL WAS TELLING THEM how his mother had died.

She had asked for her makeup. Lionel held the mirror.

"This will take about an hour," she said.

Foundation cream, face powder, eyebrow pencil, eyeshadow, mascara, lip liner, lipstick, blusher. She was slow and shaky, but it wasn't a bad job.

"That didn't take you an hour," Lionel said.

She said, no, she hadn't meant that. She had meant, to die.

Lionel asked her if she wanted him to call his father. His father, her husband, her minister.

She said, "What for?"

She was only about five minutes off in her prediction.

They were sitting behind the house — Lorna and her husband Brendan's house — on a little terrace that looked across at Burrard Inlet and the lights of Point Grey. Lorna had met Lionel's mother just a few months before. She was a pretty little white-haired woman with a valiant charm. She'd come down to Vancouver from a town in the Rocky Mountains to see the touring Comédie Française with her son. Lionel had invited Lorna to go with them. After the performance, while Lionel was holding open his mother's blue velvet cloak, she had said to Lorna, "I am so happy to meet my son's *belle amie.*"

"Let us not overdo it with the French," said Lionel.

Lorna was not even sure what that meant. Beautiful friend. Mistress?

Lionel had raised his eyebrows at her, over his mother's head. As if to say, Whatever she's come up with, it's no fault of mine.

Lionel had once been Brendan's student at the university. A raw prodigy, sixteen years old. The brightest mathematical mind Brendan had ever seen. Lorna wondered if Brendan was dramatizing this, in hindsight, because of his own unusual, almost unnatural generosity toward gifted students. Also because of the way things had turned out. Brendan had put the whole Irish package behind him — his family and his church and the sentimental songs — but he had a weakness for a tragic tale. And sure enough, after his blazing start Lionel had suffered some sort of breakdown, had to be hospitalized, dropped out of sight. Until Brendan met him in the supermarket and discovered that he was living within a mile of their house, here in North Vancouver. Lionel had given up mathematics entirely and now worked in the publishing office of the Anglican Church.

"Come and see us," Brendan had said. Lionel looked a bit seedy and lonely. "Come and meet my wife."

Later, when Lionel reported this exchange to Lorna, he said that he'd wondered what she might be like.

"I considered you might be awful."

"Oh," said Lorna. "Why?"

"I don't know. Wives."

Lionel used to come see them in the evenings, when the children were in bed. The slight intrusions of domestic life — the cry of the baby reaching them through an open window, the scolding Brendan sometimes gave Lorna about toys left lying on the grass instead of being put back in the sandbox, his voice calling from the kitchen asking if she had remembered to buy limes for the gin and tonic — all seemed to cause a shiver, a tightening of Lionel's tall narrow body and intent, distrustful face. Once he sang, very softly, to the tune of "O Tannenbaum," "O married life, O married life." He smiled slightly, or Lorna thought he did, in the dark. This smile seemed to her like the smile of her four-year-old daughter, Elizabeth, when she whispered some mildly outrageous observation to her mother in a public place. A secret little smile, gratified, somewhat alarmed.

Lionel rode up the hill on his high old-fashioned bicycle — this at a time when hardly anybody but children rode bicycles. He would not have changed out of his workday outfit. Dark trousers, a white shirt that always looked grubby and worn around the cuffs and collar, a nondescript tie. When they went to see the Comédie Française, he added to this a tweed jacket that was too wide across the shoulders and too short in the sleeves. Perhaps he did not own any other clothes.

"I labor for a pittance," he said. "And not even in the vineyards of the Lord. In the diocese of the archbishop."

He talked with his head on one side, his gaze on something beyond Lorna's head. His voice was light and quick, sometimes squeaky with a kind of nervous exhilaration. He said everything in a slightly astonished way. He told her about the office where he worked, a few blocks from the cathedral — the small high Gothic windows and varnished woodwork (to give things a churchy feeling), the hat rack and umbrella stand (which for some reason filled him with deep melancholy), the typist, Janine, and the editor of *Church News*, Mrs. Penfound. The occasionally appearing, spectral, and distracted archbishop. There was an unresolved battle over tea bags between Janine, who favored them, and Mrs. Penfound, who did not. Everybody munched on secret eats and never shared.

"For this is Hell," Lionel said, with his sly, apologetic laugh. "Nor am I out of it."

He mentioned the hospital where he had been a patient for a while and spoke of the ways it resembled the office, in the manner of secret eats. Secrets generally. But the difference was that every once in a while in the hospital they came and bound you up and took you off and plugged you in, as he put it, to the light socket.

"That was pretty interesting. In fact, it was excruciating. But I can't describe it. That is the weird part. I can remember it but not describe it."

Because of those events in the hospital, he said, he was rather short of memories. Short of details.

Lorna told him about her life before she married Brendan. About the two houses exactly alike, standing side by side in the town where she grew up. In front of them was a deep ditch called Dye Creek, because the water that ran in it was colored by the dye from the knitting factory. Behind them was a wild meadow where girls were not supposed to go. One house was where she lived with her father; in the other lived her grandmother, her Aunt Beatrice, and her cousin Polly.

Polly had no father. That was what they said and what Lorna had once truly believed. Polly had no father, in the way that a Manx cat had no tail. Aunt Beatrice had had no social life involving a man since the time of her blotted-out disgrace, and she was so finicky, so desperate about the conduct of life, that it was easier to think of Polly's conception as miraculous. The only thing that Lorna had ever learned from her Aunt Beatrice was that you must always press a seam from the side, not wide open, so that the mark of the iron will not show, and that no sheer blouse should be without its slip to hide your brassiere straps.

"Oh, yes. Yes," said Lionel. He stretched out his legs as if appreciation had reached his very toes. "Now, Polly. Out of this benighted household, what is Polly like? Is she like you?"

"I think she's more . . . competent." She wondered what Lionel meant when he said "like you."

Polly was okay, Lorna said. Full of energy and sociability, kindhearted, confident.

"Ah," said Lionel.

Lorna told him about her only memory of her mother. Lorna was downtown with her mother on a winter day. There was snow between the sidewalk and the street. She had just learned how to tell time, and she looked up at the post office clock and saw that the moment had come for the soap opera she and her mother listened to every day on the radio. She felt a deep concern, because she wondered what would happen to the people in the story with the radio not turned on and them not listening. It was more than concern she felt — it was horror, to think of the way things could be lost, could *not* happen, through some casual absence or chance.

And even in that memory her mother was only a hip and a shoulder in a heavy coat.

Lionel said that he could hardly get more of a sense of his father than that, though he was still alive. A swish of a surplice? Lionel and his mother used to make bets on how long his father could go without speaking to them. He had asked his mother once what made his father so mad, and she had answered that she really didn't know.

"I think perhaps he doesn't like his job," she said.

Lionel said, "Why doesn't he get another job?"

"Perhaps he can't think of one he'd like."

Brendan would sit down with Lorna and Lionel for a while, say-ing, "What are you two gabbling about?" and then, with some re-lief, as if he had paid his dues for the time being, he would get up, saying that he had some work to do, and go into the house. He seemed happy about their friendship, as if he had in a way fore-seen it and brought it about, but their conversation made him restless.

"It's good for him to come up here and be normal for a while instead of sitting in his room," Brendan had said to Lorna. "Of course he lusts after you. Poor bugger."

He liked to say that men lusted after Lorna. Particularly when they'd been to a department party and she had been the youngest wife there. She would have been embarrassed to have anybody hear him say that, lest they think it a wishful and foolish exaggera-tion. But sometimes, especially if she was a little drunk, it roused her as well as Brendan to think that she might be so universally ap-pealing. In Lionel's case, though, she was pretty sure that it was not true, and she hoped very much that Brendan would never hint at such a thing in front of him. She remembered the look that Lionel had given her over his mother's head. The disavowal, the mild warning in it.

She did not tell Brendan about the poems. Once a week or so, a poem arrived, quite properly sealed and posted, in the mail. These were not anonymous — Lionel had signed them. His signature was just a squiggle, quite difficult to make out — but then, so was every word of every poem. Fortunately, there were never many words — sometimes only a dozen or two in all, making a curious path across the page, like uncertain bird tracks. Lorna was not a person un-familiar with poetry, or a person who gave up easily on whatever she did not quickly understand. She read a lot, though she often avoided talking about what she read, for fear of making mistakes in pronunciation.

After the first poem, she agonized about what she should say. Something appreciative but not stupid. All she managed was "Thank you for the poem" — when Brendan was well out of ear-shot. She kept herself from saying, "I enjoyed it." Lionel gave a jerky nod and made a sound that sealed off the conversation. Poems continued to arrive, and were not mentioned again. She began to think that she could regard them as offerings, not as messages. But not love offerings — as Brendan, for instance, would assume. There was nothing in them about Lionel's feelings for her, nothing personal at all. She thought to say that they reminded her of impressions you can sometimes see on the sidewalks in spring — shadows left by wet leaves plastered there from the year before. But that might sound affected.

There was something else, more urgent, that she did not speak about to Brendan. Or to Lionel. Polly, her cousin, was coming from home.

Polly was five years older than Lorna and had worked, ever since she graduated from high school, in a bank. She was on her way across the country, by bus. To Polly it seemed the most natural and appropriate thing to do — to visit her cousin and her cousin's family. To Brendan it would seem almost certainly an intrusion, something nobody had any business doing unless invited. He was not averse to visitors — look at Lionel — but he wanted to do the choosing himself. Every day Lorna thought of how she must tell him. Every day she put it off.

And this was not a thing she could talk about to Lionel. You could not speak to him about anything seen seriously as a problem. To speak of problems meant to search for, to hope for, solutions. And that was not interesting — it did not indicate an interesting attitude toward life. Rather, a shallow and tiresome hopefulness. Ordinary anxieties, uncomplicated emotions, were not what he enjoyed hearing about. He preferred things to be utterly bewildering and past bearing, yet ironically, half merrily borne.

She had told him one thing that might have been chancy — how she had cried on her wedding day and during the actual wedding ceremony. But she was able to make a joke of that, by adding that she had tried to pull her hand out of Brendan's grip to get her handkerchief but he would not let go, so she had to keep on snuffling. In fact she had cried not because she didn't want to be married or didn't love Brendan. She had cried because everything at home suddenly seemed so precious to her — though she had always planned to leave — and the people there seemed closer to her than anyone else could ever be, though she had hidden all her private thoughts from them. She cried because she and Polly had laughed as they cleaned the kitchen shelves and scrubbed the lino-

leum the day before and she had pretended she was in a sentimental play and said, "Goodbye, linoleum. Goodbye, crack in the teapot. Goodbye, place under the table where I used to stick my gum.
Goodbye." Polly had said, "Why don't you just tell him to forget it?"
But of course she didn't mean it. She was proud, and Lorna herself
was proud, eighteen years old and never had a real boyfriend and
here she was marrying a good-looking thirty-year-old man, a professor.

Nevertheless she cried, and cried again when she got letters from
home, in the early days of her marriage. Brendan had caught her at
it, and said, "You love your family, don't you?"

She thought he sounded sympathetic. But then he sighed and
said, "I think you love them more than you love me."

She said that was not true; it was only that she felt sorry for her
family sometimes. They had a hard time, her grandmother teaching fourth grade year after year, though her eyes were so bad that
she could hardly see to write on the board, and Aunt Beatrice with
too many nervous complaints ever to have a job, and her father —
Lorna's father — working in the hardware store that wasn't even
his own.

"A hard time?" said Brendan. "They've been in a concentration
camp, have they?"

Then he said that people needed gumption in this world. And
Lorna lay down on the marriage bed and gave way to one of those
angry weeping fits that she was now ashamed to remember. Brendan came and consoled her after a while, but still believed that she
cried as women always did when they could not win the argument
any other way.

Some things about Polly's looks Lorna had forgotten. How tall she
was and what a long neck and narrow waist she had, and an almost
perfectly flat chest. A bumpy little chin and a wry mouth. Pale skin,
light-brown hair cut short, fine as feathers. She looked both frail
and hardy, like a daisy on a long stalk. She wore a ruffled denim
skirt with embroidery on it.

For forty-eight hours Brendan had known she was coming. She
had phoned, collect, from Calgary, and he had answered the
phone. He had three questions to ask afterward. His tone was distant but calm.

How long is she staying?

Why didn't you tell me?

Why did she phone collect?

"I don't know," said Lorna.

Now, from the kitchen, where she was preparing dinner, Lorna strained to hear what they would say to each other. Brendan had just come home. His greeting she could not hear, but Polly's voice was loud and full of a risky jollity.

"So I really started out on the wrong foot, Brendan, wait till you hear what I said. Lorna and I are walking down the street from the bus stop and I'm saying, 'Oh shoot, this is a pretty classy neighborhood you live in, Lorna' — and then I say, 'But look at that place, what's it doing here? It looks like a barn.'"

She couldn't have started out worse. Brendan was very proud of their house. It was a contemporary house, built in the West Coast style called post-and-beam. Post-and-beam houses were not painted; the idea was to fit in with the original forests. So the effect was plain and functional from the outside, with the roof flat and protruding beyond the walls. Inside, the beams were exposed and none of the wood was covered up. The fireplace in this house was set in a stone chimney that went up to the ceiling, and the windows were long and narrow and uncurtained. The architecture is always preeminent, the builder had told them, and Brendan repeated this, as well as the word "contemporary," when introducing anybody to the house for the first time.

He did not bother to explain this to Polly, or to get out the magazine in which there was an article about the style, with photographs — though not of this particular house.

Polly had brought from home the habit of starting off her sentences with the name of the person she was specifically addressing. "Lorna —" she would say, or "Brendan —" Lorna had forgotten about this way of talking. It seemed to her now rather peremptory and rude. Most of Polly's sentences at the dinner table began with "Lorna —" and were about people known only to her and Polly. Lorna knew that Polly did not intend to be rude, that she was making a strident but brave effort to seem at ease. And she had at first tried to include Brendan. Both she and Lorna had done so — they had launched into explanations of whomever it was they were talking about. But it did not work. Brendan spoke only to call Lorna's attention to something needed on the table or to point out that Daniel had spilled his mashed food on the floor.

Polly went on talking while she and Lorna cleared the table and then as they washed the dishes. Lorna usually bathed the children and put them to bed before she started on the dishes, but tonight she was too rattled — she sensed that Polly was near tears — to attend to things in their proper order. She let Daniel crawl around on the floor while Elizabeth, with her interest in social occasions and new personalities, hung about listening to the conversation. This lasted until Daniel knocked the high chair over — fortunately not on himself, but he howled with fright — and Brendan came in from the living room.

"Bedtime seems to have been postponed," he said as he removed his son from Lorna's arms. "Elizabeth. Go and get ready for your bath."

Polly had moved on from talking about people in town to describing how things were going at home. Not well. The owner of the hardware store — a man whom Lorna's father had always spoken of as more of a friend than an employer — had sold the business without a word of what he was intending until the deed was done. The new man was expanding the store at the same time that business was being lost to Canadian Tire, and there was not a day that he did not stir up some kind of a row with Lorna's father. Lorna's father came home from the shop so discouraged that all he wanted to do was lie on the couch. He was not interested in the paper or the news. He drank bicarbonate of soda but wouldn't discuss the pains in his stomach.

Lorna mentioned a letter from her father in which he made light of these troubles.

"Well, he would, wouldn't he?" said Polly. "To you."

The upkeep of both houses, Polly said, was a continual nightmare. They should all move into one house and sell the other, but now that their grandmother had retired she picked on Aunt Beatrice — Polly's mother — all the time, and Lorna's father, Uncle Art, could not stand the idea of living with the two of them. Polly often wanted to walk out and never come back, but what would they do without her?

"You should live your own life," said Lorna. It felt strange to her to be giving advice to Polly.

"Oh, sure, sure," said Polly. "I should've got out while the going was good, that's what I guess I should have done. But when was that? I don't ever remember the going being so particularly good. I was stuck with having to see you through school first, for one thing."

Lorna had spoken in a regretful, helpful voice, but she refused to stop in her work and give Polly's news its due. She accepted it as if it concerned some people she knew and liked but was not responsible for. She thought of her father lying on the couch in the evenings, dosing himself for pains he wouldn't admit to, and Aunt Beatrice next door, worried about what people were saying about her, crying because she'd gone to church with her slip showing. To think of home caused Lorna pain, but she could not help feeling that Polly was hammering at her, trying to bring her to some capitulation, wrap her up in some intimate misery. And she was determined not to give in.

Just look at you. Look at your life. Your stainless steel sink. Your house where the architecture is preeminent.

"If I ever went away now, I think I'd just feel too guilty," Polly said. "I couldn't stand it. I'd feel too guilty leaving them."

Of course, some people never feel guilty. Some people never feel at all.

"Quite a tale of woe you got," said Brendan when they were lying side by side in the dark.

"It's on her mind," Lorna said.

"Just remember. We are not millionaires."

Lorna was startled. "She doesn't want money."

"Doesn't she?"

"That's not what she's telling me for."

"Don't be too sure."

She lay rigid, not answering. Then she thought of something that might put him in a better mood.

"She's only here for two weeks."

His turn not to answer.

"Don't you think she's nice-looking?"

"No."

She was about to tell him that Polly had made her wedding dress. She had planned to be married in her navy suit, but Polly had said, a few days before the wedding, "This isn't going to do." So she got out her own ice-blue high school formal (Polly had always been more popular than Lorna; she had gone to dances) and she put in gussets of white lace and sewed on white lace sleeves. Because, she said, a bride can't do without sleeves.

But what could he have cared about that?

Lionel had gone away for a few days. His father had retired, and Lionel was helping him move from his town in the Rocky Mountains to Vancouver Island. On the day after Polly's arrival, Lorna got a letter from him. Not a poem — a real letter, though it was very short: "I dreamt that I was giving you a ride on my bicycle. We were going quite fast. You did not seem to be afraid, though perhaps you should have been. We must not feel called upon to interpret this."

Brendan had gone off early. He was teaching summer school and said he would eat breakfast at the cafeteria. Polly came out of her room as soon as he was gone. She wore slacks instead of the flounced skirt, and she smiled all the time, as if at a joke of her own. She kept ducking her head slightly to avoid Lorna's eyes.

"I better get off and see something of Vancouver," she said. "Since it isn't very likely I'll ever get here again."

Lorna marked some things on a map and gave her directions, and said she was sorry she couldn't go along, but it would be more trouble than it was worth, with the children.

"Oh. Oh, no. I wouldn't expect you to. I didn't come out here to be on your hands all the time."

Elizabeth sensed the strain in the atmosphere. She said, "Why are we trouble?"

Lorna gave Daniel an early nap, and when he woke up she got him into the stroller and told Elizabeth they were going to a playground. The playground she had chosen was not the one in a nearby park — it was down the hill, close to the street Lionel lived on. Lorna knew his address, though she had never seen the house.

It did not take her long to get there — though no doubt it would take her longer to get back, pushing the stroller uphill. But she had already passed into the older part of North Vancouver, where the houses were smaller, perched on narrow lots. The house where Lionel rented a room had his name beside one bell, and the name B. Hutchison beside the other. She knew that Mrs. Hutchison was the landlady. She pressed that bell.

"I know Lionel's away and I'm sorry to bother you," she said.

"But I lent him a book — it's a library book, and now it's overdue — and I just wondered if I could run up to his apartment and see if I could find it."

The landlady said, "Well." She was an old woman with a bandanna around her head and large dark spots on her face.

"My husband and I are friends of Lionel's. My husband was his professor at college."

The word "professor" was always useful. Lorna was given the key. She parked the stroller in the shade of the house and told Elizabeth to stay and watch Daniel.

"This isn't a playground," Elizabeth said.

"I just have to run upstairs and back. Just for a minute, okay?"

Lionel's room had an alcove at the end of it for a two-burner gas stove and a cupboard. No refrigerator and no sink, except for the one in the toilet. A Venetian blind stuck halfway down the window and a square of linoleum whose pattern was covered by brown paint. There was a faint smell of the gas stove, mixed with a smell of unaired heavy clothing, perspiration, and some menthol decongestant, which she accepted — hardly thinking of it and not at all disliking it — as the intimate smell of Lionel himself.

Other than that, the place gave out hardly any clues. She had come here not for any library book, of course, but to be for a moment inside the space where he lived, to breathe his air and look out of his window. The view was of other houses, probably like this one, chopped up into small spaces, on the wooded slope of the mountain. The bareness, the anonymity of the room were severely challenging. Bed, bureau, table, chair. Just the furniture that had to be provided so that the room could be advertised as furnished. Even the tan chenille bedspread must have been there when he moved in. No pictures — not even a calendar — and, most surprisingly, no books.

Things must be hidden somewhere. In the bureau drawers? She couldn't look. Not only because there was no time — she could hear Elizabeth calling her from the yard — but because the very absence of whatever might be personal made the sense of Lionel stronger. Not just the sense of his austerity and his secrets but of a watchfulness — almost as if he had set a trap and was waiting to see what she would do.

What she really wanted to do was not to investigate anymore but to sit down on the floor, in the middle of the square of linoleum. To sit for hours, not so much looking at this room as sinking into it. To stay in this room where there was nobody who knew her or wanted a thing from her. To stay here for a long, long time, growing sharper and lighter, light as a needle.

On Saturday morning, Lorna and Brendan and the children were to drive to Penticton. A graduate student had invited them to his wedding. They would stay Saturday night and all day Sunday and Sunday night as well, and leave for home on Monday morning.

"Have you told her?" Brendan said.

"It's all right. She isn't expecting to come."

"But have you told her?"

Thursday was spent at Ambleside Beach. Lorna and Polly and the children rode there on buses, changing twice, encumbered with towels, beach toys, diapers, lunch, and Elizabeth's blow-up dolphin. The physical predicaments they found themselves in, and the irritation and dismay the sight of their party roused in other passengers, brought on a peculiarly feminine reaction — a mood of near hilarity. Getting away from the house where Lorna was installed as wife was helpful too. They reached the beach in triumph and ragtag disarray and set up their encampment, from which they took turns going into the water, minding the children, fetching soft drinks, Popsicles, French fries.

Lorna was lightly tanned, Polly not at all. She stretched a leg out beside Lorna's and said, "Look at that. Raw dough."

With all the work she had to do in the two houses, and with her job in the bank, she said, there was not a quarter-hour when she was free to sit in the sun. But she spoke now matter-of-factly, without the undertone of virtue and complaint. Some sour atmosphere that had surrounded her — like old dishrags — was falling away. She had found her way around Vancouver by herself — the first time she had ever done that in a city. She had talked to strangers at bus stops and asked what sights she should see, and on somebody's advice had taken the chairlift to the top of Grouse Mountain.

As they lay on the sand, Lorna offered an explanation.

"This is a bad time of year for Brendan. Teaching summer school is really nerve-racking — you have to do so much so fast."

Polly said, "Yeah? It's not just me, then?"

"Don't be stupid. Of course it isn't you."

"Well, that's a relief. I thought he kind of hated my guts."

She then spoke of a man at home who wanted to take her out.

"He's too serious. He's looking for a wife. I guess Brendan was too, but I guess you were in love with him."

"Was and am," said Lorna.

"Well, I don't think I am." Polly spoke with her face pressed into her elbow. "I guess it might work, though, if you liked somebody okay and you went out with them and made up your mind to see the good points."

"So what are the good points?" Lorna was sitting up so that she could watch Elizabeth ride the dolphin.

"Give me a couple of minutes," said Polly, giggling. "No. There's lots. I'm just being mean."

As they were rounding up toys and towels, she said, "I really wouldn't mind doing all this over again tomorrow."

"Me neither," said Lorna. "But I have to get ready to go to the Okanagan. We're invited to this wedding." She made it sound like a chore — something she hadn't bothered speaking about till now because it was too disagreeable and boring.

Polly said, "Oh. Well, I might come back by myself, then."

"Sure. You should."

"Where is the Okanagan?"

The next evening, after putting the children to bed, Lorna went into the room where Polly slept. She wanted to get a suitcase out of the closet, expecting the room to be empty — Polly, as she thought, still in the bathroom, soaking the day's sunburn in lukewarm water and soda.

But Polly was in bed, with the sheet pulled up around her like a shroud.

"You're out of the bath," said Lorna, as if she found all this quite normal. "How does your burn feel now?"

"I'm okay," said Polly, in a muffled voice. Lorna knew at once that she had been and probably still was weeping. She stood at the foot of the bed, not able to leave the room. A disappointment had come over her which was like sickness, a wave of disgust.

"What is it?" Lorna said. She feigned surprise, she feigned compassion.

Polly looked out at her now.

"You don't want me."

Her eyes were brimming, not just with tears and the bitter accusation of betrayal but with an outrageous demand to be welcomed, blessed, comforted.

Lorna would sooner have hit her. What gives you the right, she wanted to say. And, do you know how ugly you look? What are you leeching onto me for? What do you think I can do about Brendan? What gives you the right?

Family. Family gives Polly the right. She saved her money and planned her escape, with the idea that Lorna would take her in. That is what she must have dreamed of — staying here and never having to go back. Becoming part of Lorna's good fortune, Lorna's transformed world.

"What do you think I can do?" said Lorna, quite viciously and to her own surprise. "Do you think I have any power? He never even gives me more than a twenty-dollar bill at a time."

She dragged the suitcase out of the room.

It was all so false, putting her own lamentations forth in that way, to match Polly's. What did the twenty dollars at a time have to do with anything? She had a charge account; he never refused her when she asked.

She couldn't go to sleep, berating Polly in her mind.

The heat of the Okanagan made summer seem more authentic than summer on the coast. The hills with their pale grass, the sparse shade of the drylands pine trees, seemed a natural setting for so festive a wedding, with its endless supply of champagne, its dancing and flirtation and overflow of instant friendship and good will. Lorna got rapidly drunk and was amazed at how easy it was, with alcohol, to be loosed from the bondage of her spirits. Forlorn vapors lifted. She went to bed still drunk, and lecherous, to Brendan's benefit. Even her hangover the next day seemed mild, cleansing rather than punishing. Feeling frail but not at all displeased with herself, she lay by the shores of the lake and watched Brendan help Elizabeth build a sandcastle.

"Did you know that your daddy and I met at a wedding?" she said.

"Not much like this one, though," said Brendan. He meant that the other wedding, when a friend of his married the McQuaig girl (the McQuaigs being a top family in Lorna's hometown), had been officially dry. The reception had been at the United Church Hall — Lorna was one of the girls recruited to pass sandwiches — and the drinking had been done in a hurry, in the parking lot. Lorna was not used to smelling whiskey on men and thought that Brendan must have put on too much of some unfamiliar hairdressing. Nevertheless she admired his thick shoulders, his bull neck, his laughing and commanding golden-brown eyes. When she learned that he was a teacher of mathematics, she fell in love with what was inside his head too. She was excited by whatever knowledge a man might have that was utterly strange to her. A knowledge of auto mechanics would have worked just as well.

His answering attraction to her seemed to be in the nature of a miracle. She learned later that he had been on the lookout for a wife: he was old enough, it was time. He wanted a young girl. Not a colleague or a student, perhaps not even the sort of girl whose parents could send her to college. Unspoiled. Intelligent, but unspoiled. A wildflower, he said in the heat of those early days, and sometimes even now.

On the drive back they left this hot golden country behind, somewhere between Keremeos and Princeton. But the sun still shone, and Lorna had only a faint disturbance in her mind, like a hair in her vision that could be flicked away or could float out of sight on its own.

But it kept coming back, it grew more ominous and persistent, till at last it made a spring at her and she knew it for what it was.

She was afraid — she was half certain — that while they were away, Polly would have committed suicide in the kitchen of the house in North Vancouver.

In the kitchen. It was a definite picture Lorna had. She saw exactly the way in which Polly would have done it. She would have hanged herself just inside the back door. When they returned, when they came into the house from the garage, they would find the door locked. They would unlock it and try to push it open but be unable to because of the heavy lump of Polly's body against it. They would hurry around to the front door and come into the kitchen that way and be met by the full sight of Polly dead. She would be wearing the flounced denim skirt and the white drawstring blouse — the brave outfit in which she had first appeared to try their hospitality. Her long pale legs dangling down, her head twisted fatally on its delicate neck. In front of her body would be the kitchen chair she had climbed onto and then stepped or jumped from, to see how misery could finish itself.

Alone in the house of people who did not want her, where the very walls and the windows and the cup she drank her coffee from must seem to despise her.

Lorna remembered a time when she had been left alone with Polly, left in Polly's charge for a day, in their grandmother's house. Perhaps her father was at the shop. But she had an idea that he too had gone away — all three adults were out of town. It must have been an unusual occasion, since they never went on shopping trips, let alone trips for pleasure. A funeral, almost certainly a funeral. The day was a Saturday, there was no school. Lorna was too young to be in school anyway. Her hair had not grown long enough to be put into pigtails. It blew in tender wisps around her head, as Polly's did now.

Polly was going through a stage then in which she loved to make candy, or rich treats of any kind, from her grandmother's cookbook. Chocolate date cake, macaroons, divinity fudge. She was in the middle of mixing something up that day when she found that an ingredient she needed was not in the cupboard. She had to ride uptown on her bicycle to charge it at the store. The weather was windy and cold, the ground bare — the season must have been late fall or early spring. Before she left, Polly pushed in the damper on the woodstove. But she was fearful because of stories she had heard about children who perished in house fires when their mothers had run out on similar quick errands. So she directed Lorna to put on her coat and took her outside, around to the corner between the kitchen and the main part of the house, where the wind was not so strong. The house next door must have been locked, or she would have taken her there. She told her to stay put. Stay there, don't move, don't worry, she said. Then she kissed Lorna's ear and rode off to the store. Lorna obeyed her to the letter. For ten minutes, maybe fifteen, she remained crouched behind the white lilac bush, learning the shapes of the stones, the dark and light ones, in the house's foundation. Until Polly came tearing back and flung the bike down in the yard and came calling her name — "Lorna, Lorna" — throwing down the bag of brown sugar or walnuts and kissing her all over her head. For the thought had occurred to her that Lorna might have been spotted in her corner by lurking kidnappers — the bad men who were the reason that girls were not supposed to go down into the field behind the houses. She had prayed all the way back for this not to have happened. And it hadn't. She bustled Lorna inside to warm her bare knees and hands.

"Oh, the poor little handsies," she said. "Oh, were you scared?" Lorna loved the fussing and bent her head to have it stroked, as if she were a pony.

The pines gave way to the denser evergreen forest, the brown lumps of hills to the rising blue-green mountains. Daniel began to whimper, and Lorna got out his juice bottle. Later she asked Brendan to stop so that she could lay the baby down on the front seat and change his diaper. Brendan walked at a distance while she did this, smoking a cigarette. Diaper ceremonies always affronted him a little.

Lorna also took the opportunity to get out one of Elizabeth's storybooks, and when they were settled again she read to the children. It was a Dr. Seuss book. Elizabeth knew all the rhymes, and even Daniel had some idea of where to chime in with his made-up words.

Polly was no longer that person who had rubbed Lorna's small hands between her own, the person who knew all the things Lorna did not know and who could be trusted to take care of her in the world. Everything had been turned around, and it seemed that in the years since Lorna got married, Polly had stayed still. Lorna had passed her by. And now Lorna had the children in the back seat to take care of and to love, and it was unseemly for a person of Polly's age to come clawing for her share.

It was no use for Lorna to think this. No sooner had she put the argument in place than she felt the body knock against the door as they tried to push it open. The deadweight, the gray body. The body of Polly, who had been given nothing at all. No part in the family she had come to join, and no hope of the change she must have dreamed was coming in her life.

"Now read *Madeline*," said Elizabeth.

"I don't think I brought *Madeline*," said Lorna. "No. I didn't bring it. Never mind, you know it by heart."

She and Elizabeth started off together:

> In an old house in Paris that was covered with vines
> lived twelve little girls in two straight lines.
> In two straight lines they broke their bread
> and brushed their teeth and went to bed.

This is stupidity, this is melodrama, this is guilt. This will not have happened.

But such things do happen. Some people founder, they are not helped in time. They are not helped at all. Some people are pitched into darkness:

> In the middle of one night
> Miss Clavel turned on her light
> and said, "Something is not right!"

"Mommy," said Elizabeth. "Why did you stop?"

Lorna said, "I had to, for a minute. My mouth got dry."

At Hope, they had hamburgers and milkshakes. Then down the Fraser Valley, the children asleep in the back seat. Still some time left. Till they got to Chilliwack, till they got to Abbotsford, till they saw the hills of New Westminster ahead and the other hills crowned with houses, the beginnings of the city. Bridges still to go over, turns they had to take, streets they had to drive along, corners they had to pass. All this in the time before. The next time she saw any of it would be in the time after.

When they entered Stanley Park, it occurred to her to pray. This was shameless — the opportune praying of a nonbeliever. The gibberish of let-it-not-happen, let-it-not-happen. Let it not have happened.

The day was still cloudless. From the Lions Gate Bridge they looked out at the open water.

"Can you see Vancouver Island today?" said Brendan. "You look — I can't."

Lorna craned her neck to look past him.

"Far away," she said. "Gabriola. Then Vancouver Island. Quite faint, but it's there."

And with the sight of those blue, progressively dimmer, finally almost dissolving mounds that seemed to float upon the sea, she thought of one thing there was left to do. Make a bargain. Believe that it was still possible, up to the last minute it was possible to make a bargain.

It had to be serious, a most final and wrenching promise or offer. Take this. I promise this. If it can be made not true, if it can not have happened.

Not the children. She snatched that thought away as if she were grabbing them out of a fire. Not Brendan, for an opposite reason. She did not love him enough. She would say she loved him, and mean it to a certain extent, and she wanted to be loved by him, but there was a little hum of hate running along beside her love, nearly all the time. So it would be reprehensible — also useless — to offer him in any bargain.

Herself? Her looks? Her health?

It occurred to her that she might be on the wrong track. In a case like this, it might not be up to you to choose. Not up to you to set the terms. You would know them when you met them. You must promise to honor them without knowing what they were going to be. Promise.

But nothing to do with the children.

Up Capilano Road, into their own part of the city and their own corner of the world, where their lives took on true weight and their actions took on consequences. There were the uncompromising wooden walls of their house showing through the trees.

"The front door would be easier," Lorna said. "Then we wouldn't have any steps."

But Brendan went the usual way, saying, "What's the problem with a couple of steps?"

"I never got to see the bridge," Elizabeth cried, suddenly wide awake and disappointed. "Why didn't you wake me up to see the bridge?"

Nobody answered her.

"Daniel's arm is all sunburnt," she said, in a tone of incomplete satisfaction.

Lorna heard voices that she thought were coming from the yard of the house next door. She followed Brendan around the corner of the house. Daniel lay against her shoulder, still heavy with sleep. She carried the diaper bag and the storybook bag, and Brendan carried the suitcase.

The people whose voices she had heard were in her own back

yard. Polly and Lionel. They had dragged two lawn chairs around so that they could sit in the shade. They had their backs to the view.

Lionel. She had forgotten all about him.

He jumped up and ran to open the back door.

"The expedition has returned with all members accounted for," he said, in a voice that Lorna did not believe she had ever heard before. An unforced heartiness in it, an easy and appropriate confidence. The voice of the friend of the family. As he held the door open he looked straight into her face — something he had almost never done — and gave her a smile from which all subtlety, secrecy, ironic complicity, and mysterious devotion had been removed. All complications, all private messages had been removed.

She made her voice an echo of his.

"So — when did you get back?"

"Saturday," he said. "I'd forgotten you were going away. I came laboring up here to say hello and you weren't here, but Polly was here, and of course she told me and then I remembered."

"Polly told you what?" said Polly, coming up behind him. This was not really a question, but the half-teasing remark of a woman who knows that almost anything she says will be well received. Polly's sunburn had turned to tan, or at least to a new flush, on her forehead and neck.

"Here," she said to Lorna, relieving her of both the bags carried over her arm and the empty juice bottle in her hand. "I'll take everything but the baby."

Lionel's floppy hair was now more brownish black than black — of course, she was seeing him for the first time in full sunlight — and his skin too was tanned, enough for his forehead to have lost its pale gleam. He wore the usual dark pants, but his shirt was unfamiliar to her. A yellow short-sleeved shirt of some much-ironed, shiny, cheap material, too big across the shoulders, maybe bought at the church thrift sale.

Lorna carried Daniel upstairs. She laid him in his crib and stood beside him, making soft noises and stroking his back.

She thought that Lionel must be punishing her for her mistake in going to his room. The landlady would have told him. Lorna should have expected that, if she had stopped to think. She hadn't stopped to think, probably because she had the idea that it would not matter. She might even have thought that she would tell him herself.

I was going past on my way to the playground and I just thought I would go in and sit in the middle of your floor. I can't explain it. It seemed like that would give me a moment's pure peace, to be in your room and sit in the middle of the floor.

She had thought — after the letter? — that there was a bond between them, not to be made explicit but to be relied on. And she had been wrong, she had scared him. Presumed too much. He had turned around and there was Polly. Because of Lorna's offense, he had taken up with Polly.

Perhaps not, though. Perhaps he had simply changed. She thought of the extraordinary bareness of his room, the light on its walls. Out of that might come such altered versions of himself, created with no effort, in the blink of an eye. In response to something that had gone a little wrong, or to a realization that he could not carry something through. Or to nothing that definite — just the blink of an eye.

When Daniel had fallen into true sleep, she went downstairs. In the bathroom she found that Polly had rinsed the diapers properly and put them in the pail, covered with the blue solution that would disinfect them. She picked up the suitcase that was sitting in the middle of the kitchen floor, carried it upstairs, and laid it on the big bed, opening it to sort out which clothes had to be washed and which could be put away.

The window of this room looked out on the back yard. She heard voices — Elizabeth's raised, almost shrieking with the excitement of homecoming and perhaps the effort of keeping the attention of an enlarged audience, Brendan's authoritative but pleasant, giving an account of their trip.

She went to the window and looked down. She saw Brendan go over to the storage shed, unlock it, and start to drag out the children's wading pool. The door was swinging shut on him, and Polly hurried to hold it open.

Lionel got up and went to uncoil the hose. She would not have thought he even knew where the hose was.

Brendan said something to Polly. Thanking her? You would think they were on the best of terms.

How had that happened?

It could be that Polly was now fit to be taken account of, being Lionel's choice. Lionel's choice and not Lorna's imposition.

Or Brendan might simply be happier because they had been away. He might have dropped for a while the burden of keeping his household in order. He might have seen, quite rightly, that this altered Polly was no threat.

A scene so ordinary and amazing, come about as if by magic. Everybody happy.

Brendan had begun to blow up the rim of the plastic pool. Elizabeth had stripped to her underpants and was dancing around impatiently. Brendan hadn't bothered this time to tell her to run and put on her bathing suit because underpants were not suitable. Lionel had turned the water on, and until it was needed for the pool he stood watering the nasturtiums, like any householder. Polly spoke to Brendan and he pinched shut the hole he had been blowing into and passed the half-inflated heap of plastic over to her.

Lorna recalled that at the beach Polly had been the one to blow up the dolphin. As she said herself, she had good wind. She blew steadily and with no apparent effort. She stood there in her shorts, her bare legs firmly apart, skin gleaming like birch bark. And Lionel watched her. Exactly what I need, he might be thinking. Such a competent and sensible woman, pliant but solid. Someone not vain or dreamy or dissatisfied. That might well be the sort of person he would marry someday. A wife who could take over. Then he would change and change again, maybe fall in love with some other woman, in his way, but the wife would be too busy to take notice.

That might happen. Polly and Lionel. Or it might not. Polly might go home as planned, and if she did there wouldn't be any heartbreak. Or that was what Lorna thought. Polly would marry or not marry, but whichever way it was, the things that happened with men would not be what broke her heart.

In a short time the rim of the wading pool was swollen and smooth. The pool was set on the grass, the hose placed inside it, and Elizabeth was splashing her feet in the water. She looked up at Lorna as if she had known she was there all the time.

"It's cold," she cried in a rapture. "Mommy — it's cold."

Now Brendan looked up at Lorna too.

"What are you doing up there?"

"Unpacking."

"You don't have to do that now. Come on outside."

"I will. In a minute."

Since she had entered the house — in fact, since she had first understood that the voices she heard came from her own back yard and belonged to Polly and Lionel — Lorna had not thought of the vision she'd had, mile after mile, of Polly lashed to the back door. She was surprised by it now as you sometimes are surprised, long after waking, by the recollection of a dream. It had a dream's potency and shamefulness. A dream's uselessness as well.

Not quite at the same time but in a lagging way came the memory of her bargain. Her weak and primitive, neurotic notion of a bargain.

But what was it she had promised?

Nothing to do with the children — she remembered that.

Something to do with herself?

She had promised that she would do whatever she had to do when she recognized what that was.

That was hedging, that was a bargain that was not a bargain, a promise that had no meaning at all.

But she tried out various possibilities. Almost as if she were shaping this story to be told to somebody — not Lionel now, but somebody — as an entertainment.

Give up reading books. Take in foster children from bad homes and poor countries. Labor to cure them of wounds and neglect.

Go to church. Agree to believe in God.

Cut her hair short, stop putting on makeup, never again haul her breasts up into a wired brassiere.

She sat down on the bed, tired out by all this sport, this irrelevance.

What made more sense was that the bargain she was bound to was to go on living as she had been doing. The bargain was already in force. To accept what had happened and be clear about what would happen. Days and years and feelings much the same, except that the children would grow up, and there might be one or two more of them, and they too would grow up, and she and Brendan would grow older and then old.

It was not until now, not until this moment, that she saw so clearly that she had been counting on something happening, something that would change her life. She had accepted her marriage as one big change but not as the last one.

So nothing now but what she or anybody could sensibly foresee. That was to be her happiness, that was what she had bargained for. Nothing secret, or strange.

Pay attention to this, she thought. This is serious. She felt like getting down on her knees. Elizabeth called again, "Mommy! Come here." And then the others — Brendan and Polly and Lionel, one after the other — were calling her, teasing her.

"Mommy!"

"Mommy!"

"Come here."

It was a long time ago that this happened. In North Vancouver, when they lived in the post-and-beam house. When she was twenty-four years old and new to bargaining.

PETER ORNER

The Raft

FROM THE ATLANTIC MONTHLY

MY GRANDFATHER, who lost his short-term memory sometime during the first Eisenhower administration, calls me into his study because he wants to tell me the story he's never told anybody before, again. My grandmother, from her perch at her beauty table, with the oval mirror circled by little bulbs I used to love to unscrew, shouts, "Oh, for God's sake, Seymour. We're meeting the Dewoskins at Twin Orchards at seven-thirty. Must you go back to the South Pacific?"

My grandfather slams the door and motions me to the chair in front of his desk. I'll be thirteen in two weeks. "There's something I want to tell you, son," he says. "Something I've never told anybody. You think you're ready? You think you've got the gumption?"

"I think so."

"Think so?"

"I know so, sir. I know I've got the gumption."

He sits down at his desk and rips open an envelope with a gleaming letter opener in the shape of a miniature gold sword. "So, you want to know?"

"Very much."

"Well then, stand up, sailor."

My grandfather's study is carpeted with white shag, which feels woolly against my bare feet. I twist my toes in it. Many cactuses are also in the room. My grandfather often encourages me to touch their prickers to demonstrate how tough an old boy a plant can be. My grandfather captained a destroyer during World War II.

"It was late," he says. "Someone knocked on my stateroom door.

I leaped up. In those days I slept in uniform — shoes too." My grandfather smiles. His face is so perfectly round that his smile looks like a gash in a basketball. I smile back.

"Don't smile," he says. "Just because I'm smiling, don't assume I couldn't kill you right now. Know that about a man."

"Oh, Seymour, *my God*," my grandmother protests through the door. "Isn't he supposed to be at summer camp, anyway? Call his mother."

He looks straight at me and snarls at her, "Another word out of you, ensign, and I'll have you thrown in the brig, and you won't see Beanie Dewoskin till V-J Day."

"I'll make coffee," my grandmother says.

"It was late," I say. "Someone knocked."

"Two knocks," he says. "And by the time he raised his knuckle for the third, I'd opened the door. 'A message from the watch, sir. A boat, sir, three miles due north. Very small, sir. Could be an enemy boat, sir; then again, it might not be. Hard to tell, sir.' I told the boy to can it. Some messengers don't know when to take a breath and let you think. They think if you aren't saying anything, you want to hear more, which is never true. Remember that. I went up to the bridge. 'Wait,' I told them. 'Wait till we can see it. And ready the torpedoes,' I told them, or something like that. I forget the lingo."

"The torpedoes?" I say.

"Yes," he says. "The torpedoes. I couldn't see it clearly, but the chance that it wasn't a hostile boat was slim. You see what I'm driving at?"

"I do, sir."

"No, you don't, sailor."

"No, I don't," I say. "Don't at all."

"We'd been warned in a communiqué from the admiral to be on high alert for kamikaze flotillas. Do you have any idea what a kamikaze flotilla is?"

"Basically," I say, "it hits the side of your boat, and whango."

"You being smart with me? You think this isn't life and death we're talking about here?"

"Sorry, sir."

"So I waited. It took about a half-hour on auxiliary power for us to get within a quarter mile of the thing — then I could see it with the search."

My grandfather pauses and then opens his right-hand desk

drawer, where he keeps a safety-locked pistol and a stack of tattered pornographic comic books. They are strange books. In the cartoons men with long penises with hats on the ends of them and hair growing up the sides, so that to me they look like pickles, chase women with skirts raised over their heads and tattoos on their asses that say things like "Uncle Sam's my Daddy" and "I never kissed a Kaiser." He whacks the drawer shut and brings his hands together in front of his face, moving his thumbs around as if he's getting ready either to pray or to thumb-wrestle.

"Japs," he says. "Naked Japs on a raft. A raftload of naked Jap sailors. Today the bleedyhearts would probably call them refugees, but back then we didn't call them anything but Japs. Looked like they'd been floating for days. They turned their backs to the light, so all we could see was their backsides, skin and bone fighting it out and the bone winning."

I step back. I want to sit down but I don't. He stands and leans over his desk, examines my face. Then he points at the door and murmurs, "Phyllis doesn't know." On a phone-message pad he scrawls "BLEW IT UP" in capital letters. He whispers, *"I gave the order."* He comes around the desk and motions to his closet. "We can talk in there," he says, and I follow him into his warren of suits. My grandfather has long ago moved all his clothes out of my grandmother's packed-to-the-gills closets. He leaves the light off. In the crack of sun beneath the door I can see my grandfather's shoes and white socks. He's wearing shorts. He was working on his putting in the driveway.

"At ease, sailor," he says, and I kneel down amid the suits and dangling ties and belts. And I see now that it's not how many times you hear a story but where you hear it that matters. I've heard this before, but this is the first time I've been in a closet alone with my grandfather.

"Why?" I say. "Why, if you knew it wasn't —"

"Why?" he says, not as if he's repeating my question but as if he really doesn't know. He sighs. Then, still whispering even though we're in the closet, he says, "Some men would lie to you. They'd say it's war. I won't lie to you. It had zero to do with war and everything to do with the uniform I was wearing. Because my job was to make decisions. Besides, what the hell would I have done with a boatload of naked Japanese? There was a war on."

"But you just said —"

"Listen, my job. Just because men like me made the world safe for men like your father to be cowards doesn't mean you won't ever blow up any civilians. Because you will. I do it once a week at the bank." He places a stumpy, powerful hand on my shoulder. *"Comprende?"*

"Never," I breathe.

"Good," he says, and we are standing in the dark and looking at each other and the story is the same and different — like last time except this time his tears come so fast they're like lather. He blows his nose into his hand. I reach and offer him the sleeve of one of his tweed jackets. "I'll let myself out," he says, and leaves me in the confessional, shutting the door behind him.

I don't imagine anything, not even a hand that feels like a fish yanking my ankle. Another door opens. "Seymour? Seymour?" my grandmother says. "Where's the kid?"

ROY PARVIN

Betty Hutton

FROM FIVE POINTS

HE WAS A BIG MAN who looked like trouble, even with his glasses. A cruel fact of nature that made Gibbs a prisoner of his own body long before he became an actual one, at Pine River or the various and lesser security county facilities before that.

He'd been back in the world for months now and had few things to show for it, chiefly a girlfriend and a parole officer, neither of whom was able to give Gibbs what he really needed or wanted, and truth be told, Gibbs himself hadn't the clearest idea of what that might be either.

"I guess I'm waiting for opportunity to suggest itself to me," he'd explained to his parole bull. "I think it's one of those little-birdy-will-tell-me type situations."

"A birdy," O'Donoghue echoed, a stick of a man with a third-act sort of look to him. "Now I've heard it all. I guess a birdy beats grifting antiques, though."

"I'm not thinking a bird is going to actually speak to me," Gibbs had said. "Unless it's a parakeet or something." He was not stupid, though it often seemed the world was telling him otherwise. All he knew about was old things or how to make a thing look old. During his last bit in the can he'd seen killing, and what struck him about it was how easy it was. Anybody could do it.

From the deck of Jolie's second-story apartment he could glimpse the Atlantic, if he craned his head, perching on tiptoes. It was October of 1975, the year beginning to die more than just a little, the Jersey shoretown of Barnegat Light wearing the season like a down-at-the-heels beauty queen, the summer crowds vacating after Labor Day, neon glaze of the arcades finally switched off, revealing a pitted sweep of beach with all the charm and color of dirty concrete, the slack Atlantic crawling ashore, a pocket watch winding down.

But it was what stood at his back, the ocean of land behind Gibbs, that pulled at him like a tide. He'd never been farther west than the eastern fringe of Pennsylvania, had never been anywhere. He'd heard about Montana, though, a place that sounded like everything hadn't yet been decided, where there still might be some time left. A cellmate had told him of the chinooks, the southerly winds capable of turning winter into spring in a matter of hours, sometimes a ninety-degree temperature swing, and it had seemed to Gibbs lying in their dank cement crib, it seemed if such a thing as the chinooks was possible, anything was.

It was a sandblasted fall morning that he happened on the Chrysler, a rust-scabbed Newport parked along a dead end of bungalows clapped shut for the season, the car blue and about the size of a narwhal, its white vinyl roof gone to peel, a whip antenna for a CB the car no longer owned. It looked like the beginning to a thought that Gibbs couldn't see his way to the end of.

As he stared at the car, two things came to mind. That Jolie had been hiding her squirrel's stash of mad money in a coffee can on a high kitchen shelf. And the practical knowledge gleaned from his time at the wall of how to jack an automobile, which indeed proved easy enough, a matter of popping the door, taking a screwdriver to the steering column, touching off the appropriate wires, and then, like some low-grade miracle, the car rattling awake, exhaling an extravagant tail of blue smoke.

That was how it started: with two wrongs. After a lifetime of wrongs, what were two more? Nothing, Gibbs told himself, nothing. It was just possible he'd finally stumbled on the two wrongs that actually might produce a right.

He didn't take much with him: a leather satchel swollen with a few changes of clothes, his shaving kit, sundry effects; a paper sack of sham works — jades and Roman carnelians and openwork medallions; and, shoved between both on the back seat, an antique pistol, a keepsake handed down in his family, more a piece of history than an actual piece, the only article of legitimate value among the lot. Out the back window, Barnegat Light framed like a diminishing postcard. That was where trouble would come from when it did, from behind. He tugged on the rearview mirror, yanked it free from its mooring, and then there was only the gray road ahead.

A tattered map inside the Chrysler's glove box ran as far as Harrisburg. After that, Gibbs imagined himself, past the banks of the Susquehanna, falling out the other side of the country, running free, into territory unbound by state lines or the iron sway of laws.

He drove clear around the circle of hours, until all the license plates on the road read Wisconsin. Gibbs pulled off to refuel, him running on fumes as much as the car. A gas jockey shaped like a butterball stepped out of the office, and Gibbs stood to stretch his legs, to take measure on the endless table of land fleeing to every point of horizon. At the far corner of the lot, tethered to a pole, was the strangest animal he'd ever seen, looked like he didn't know what, devil eyes set high on its head.

Gibbs said, "What kind of dog is that?"

"It's a goat," the gas jockey told him.

Gibbs nodded heavily. "I didn't think it was a dog."

"Michigan," the jockey said, and it took Gibbs a few beats to catch his meaning and then he remembered swapping plates the evening before at a rest stop outside Franklin, Pennsylvania, with a listing Travelall bearing Michigan tags.

"Yeah, the Lions and Tigers. Motor City."

The jockey asked what he wanted, couldn't have been any more than seventeen, all pimples and baby fat. Over his heart, *Hank* stitched in script. Gibbs glanced around for anybody else and there was no one. Back at Pine River, a whole class of inmates specialized in burgling gas stations, called it *striking oil.*

"What do I want." Gibbs laughed. "Well, Hank, I want it all."

"I meant gas."

"Right. Good man. Fill it with regular. Knock yourself out."

Hank propped the hood. On the pump, the scratchy spinning of the gallon dial. The roll of money that Gibbs had filched from Jolie bulged the pocket of his trousers, the size of a baby's fist. He sized up the goat as it grazed leggy plants in a flower box.

And then a strange thing.

It was as if the person who was Gibbs vanished altogether, and he could see the entire scene like it was in front of him, a big man standing in the filling bay, a teenager under the hood of a car wiping the dipstick with a rag, the numbing horizontal of land on all sides. And he watched to see what the big man would do, waiting for the squeal of the hood's hinges as it dropped, the blackjack crunch of it slamming the jockey on the crown of his head, laying him out on the oil-splotched concrete, peaceful as an afternoon nap.

It was the pump boy's hand reaching over the lip of the hood that brought Gibbs back to the there-and-then, the hood gently closing, Hank leaning on it till the catch held fast. Gibbs stared off at a windbreak of buckeye chestnuts, his heart throttling, the dry rattle of the few leaves still on the branches.

Hank pulled a part from a pocket, massaged it with a rag as if trying to screw it into his palm. "You're missing a rearview mirror, you know."

Gibbs said, "I've seen enough of what's behind me."

Nothing left to do but pay. He was spooked yet. Hank appeared none the wiser, doling out change slowly, making sure to get it right.

Gibbs folded himself into the Chrysler. In a few moments he'd be back on his way. For the time being, though, all he was was afraid. A close call, he told himself. Easing out of the filling bay, he rolled down the window. "It's a funny world, Hank," he said, pointing at the goat. "Things aren't always what they seem. You know the one about wooden nickels, don't you?"

"Yes sir."

"Good man."

Two days later and it was Montana.

Thus far it wasn't entirely what Gibbs had expected. The sky was indeed big and everywhere. But Hokanson, his cellmate from Pine River, had mentioned mountains. He'd told about mining too, the strikes of gold and silver. "An occupation," Hokanson had promised, "where nothing's required other than doggedness and luck." Gibbs had liked the sound of that.

For a distance of miles the road banded the tracks of the Great Northern and he raced a train with a string of cars long enough almost to be considered geography. There were no posted speed limits, so Gibbs could open the Chrysler up.

He drew a high line through the eastern end of the state, through flat prairie grasslands and fields already disked for winter wheat, through one-horse towns so small they hardly rated as towns at all, a grain elevator at the outskirts, then a short business strip, usually a grange hall and a church or two and a crosshatching of streets off the main, the neat rows of side-gabled houses at the edge of the frontier.

It was not until after Devon had spread across the front windshield and out the back, after Ethridge and Cut Bank had come and gone, not until Blackfoot that he saw the mountains. They rose before him, out of the west and yellowed plain like a wave, and Gibbs drove toward them, his anticipation gathering like a wave itself.

He made Glacier as the sun was emptying from the sky. The calendar still said October, though it felt later than that now, the mountaintops webbed in snow, switchbacked roads cut high onto the white shoulders, as if with pinking shears. A different world from the one he'd left behind: wilder and somehow older.

It was late enough in both the day and the season that the guard at the gate to Glacier just waved him through, and Gibbs wheeled the Chrysler down a park road lined with the tall green of Engelmann spruce and Doug fir, pulling up at a lake a couple miles on.

It was lovely — he had no other words to match up with the landscape — only lovely and cold. The lake looked even colder yet and it stretched out before him glassy as a marble, the smudge of twilight already descending, the surround of mountains holding a few clouds within their spires like a cage. A solitary bird flew low over the water, the lake reflecting sky and bird so that it looked like two birds on the wing. Off in the distance, he could see the road following the contours of the shore.

In the foreground: a beach of fine pebbles, a woman and a little kid seated at water's edge. Gibbs couldn't remember his last real conversation that hadn't concerned gas or lodging, and with the day guttering like a candle all he wanted right now was to share the moment with someone, an exchange of pleasantries that he associated with regular life.

He skimmed through what he had to say for himself. So many places and things in the last few days, the mad rush out, but all the hours and miles of driving bled in a dreamy smear now.

The kid didn't look more than a year and change, just a tyke scooping handfuls of stones, flinging them into the shallows with both arms, exclaiming a pleased trill of gibberish with each throw.

"He has all the earmarks of a major leaguer," Gibbs said, coming up from behind.

The woman started as if a gun had been fired over her shoulder.

Gibbs smiled at her as harmlessly as he could, showing his impossible teeth, wideset as old tombstones in a cemetery. "Just look at him," he said softer, indicating the boy, "throwing with either arm, swinging from both sides of the windmill."

The woman regarded Gibbs, a shielding hand over her eyes to block the last light, like an explorer gazing off into a great distance. Her surprise resettled into a pleasant face, her hair not blond or red but falling somewhere in between, the kid's coloring pretty much the same and it suited them both. Gibbs figured she was younger than him, though not by a lot, a bit late for family rearing. That was how it was done these days, sometimes not even a man in the picture, which could have been the case here.

"I never know what to call them at that age," he said. "Babies or toddlers."

"Elliot," the woman said, and smiled herself.

The kid held up another handful of rocks. Gibbs winked and the boy tossed them, pockmarking the skin of water.

"A handsome little man," Gibbs told her. "A crackerjack. I'm sure you get tired of hearing that."

"Oh, I don't think so," the woman said.

"No, I wouldn't think so either," Gibbs said. He liked her smile, how it closed the space between them, held nothing back, no room for anything but it. It made him feel more than who he was.

A diving platform a hundred yards off bobbed and slapped at the water, the far rim of the lake now more an idea than a physical thing.

"They say you can see two hundred miles," the woman said. "On a clear day. That's hard to believe."

"That's something," Gibbs agreed. "Two hundred miles."

"I read it in a brochure."

"Well, then it must be true."

In rapid strokes the day dimmed, clouds blacking out, pinprick of stars here and there. The wind kicked up a chop on the lake, like pulled stitching. Gibbs watched the woman button the kid against the evening chill, the coat ill-fitting, perhaps a hand-me-down or from the church donation bin. The kid squirmed worse than an eel, wanting no part of it, wanting only the rocks. The woman persisted as if nothing were more important than this, than making sure the kid was warm, her face tired yet burnished with devotion, a face that said to Gibbs that things might not have been the easiest but if she got this simple task right, then maybe life might tell a different story for the boy, a hope that attached to her like a shine.

Gibbs felt he was spying on them. He drifted back to the car, sat behind the big circle of steering wheel. In the dark, the woman's face stayed with him. A raven flapped over the windshield, like a hinged W; across the way, twin pearls of headlights throwing cables into the black. Gibbs would have bet down to the green felt of the table that the boy was an accident, all she had to show for bad times and worse memories.

There was still her hope, so much it seemed to extend to Gibbs as well. She could have gathered up the kid back there, turned tail, the daily papers full of accounts of what could happen to a woman and a child alone in the night. A face that held that much trust — Gibbs would have stolen another auto, driven another nineteen hundred miles just to look into another such face.

He reached for the paper sack on the back seat, withdrew a jade piece he could identify by touch alone, stood out from the car, and double-timed back to the lakeshore, fearing the woman and Elliot might have moved on, but they were still there, turning to Gibbs as he approached, as if waiting.

He bent to show what was in his hand, told about the fish, which was green and long and slender, fashioned with incised fins and a squared mouth. "From the Shang dynasty," he said. "It dates back to well over a thousand years before Jesus. Something this ancient — in its own way, it's a lot like seeing two hundred miles, isn't it?" Gibbs was tempted to hand the jade over to the boy but thought better of it because it just might wind up in the drink, and gave it to the woman instead.

She turned it with a careful finger. "It's pretty," she said, and it was. In some circles it wouldn't amount to more than a passable imitation, but it was still pretty; he'd even gone to the trouble of filing an edge off one corner of the tail. By his lights, all that should be worth something.

"For the boy's college fund," Gibbs explained. He'd not see her after tonight, would never see her again, but maybe they'd remember him for that.

The woman switched her gaze from the jade to him.

"How do you like that, bub," Gibbs said, poking the boy in his tight round of belly. The kid ducked behind the woman, peeked out.

"I'm Claire," she said.

"Gibbs," he told her. "My name's Gibbs."

He thought she'd beg it off, a gift from a stranger, but she curled her hand around the jade, shook it like dice. She swept her other arm back behind her to bring the boy forward. "Look at this, Elliot," she said, then studied Gibbs, a face like a question. "Well, we thank you, Mr. Gibbs."

"No, it's just Gibbs," he said. "There's no mister about it."

It was full night when he quit Glacier. The road wound amid close hills, and high above, cold points of stars flashed. He had everywhere and nowhere to go.

He thought the random thoughts of a man behind the wheel of a car. He considered his kid brother, hadn't in the longest time and now he did. Miles was a scientist who researched genes. The last time Gibbs had seen him was the old man's funeral, before Pine River. After the burial, Miles had talked about his work, the fact of DNA carrying the code of a person's makeup, down to the soul practically. Gibbs followed the spiral of explanation the best he could, nodding like a woodpecker, until all the talk of markers sounded only like poker. Miles grew increasingly fidgety, and Gibbs had wondered if maybe there wasn't something else his brother was trying to tell him. In the end Miles had said maybe it wasn't such a good idea for Gibbs to contact him for a while, his forehead crumpling like paper. "It's just that I have a wife now and there's the kids," he said, leaving the thought unfinished, for it to spin in the air between them like flies. "It's okay, Miles," Gibbs had assured him. "If I were related to me, I wouldn't want to know me either. No harm, no foul."

As it turned out, it'd been like mourning two deaths for Gibbs, that of the old man and Miles too. And he was the only one left.

There'd been Hokanson, the sole opportunity for fraternity that custody had afforded. Hokanson was a nasty piece of work, a transfer from a distant facility out west, his crimes so monstrous that he was remanded thousands of miles back to the tidal flats of Jersey for his own safety. None of the other numbers could say exactly what he'd done, only talk, but even the hardest cases swung wide of him.

Hokanson and Gibbs, though, had got on without incident. After lights-out, he'd tell Gibbs stories of Montana, that eerie, raspy voice, almost like metal on metal, the trail of words leading into the nameless hours.

The facility at Pine River was erected on marshy land hard by the steady rustle of the Atlantic. On nights of particular full moons the water table rose, the floor of their matchbox quarters awash in brine, and on those nights Hokanson's words were of unique comfort. As long as he talked, that barred world went away, the murmurings down the cellblock row of dangerous men crying and praying and talking in their sleep, the stories sticking with Gibbs long after Hokanson had gone, tales of a place big enough that there still might be room for someone like him.

He stayed that night outside Glacier in a town called Hungry Horse, in an efficiency unit at a motel, a room with mismatched burners on the gas stove and a stale ammonia odor, like a convalescent home. Gibbs suspected he was the only guest for the evening but later heard a car trunk slam and the scrabble of a key finding the lock, then the door to the next room swinging open on creaky hinges. A woman's throaty voice carried through the shared wall. "You *already* told me more than I want to know," it said, and then a deeper voice answering, unintelligible, little more than a grunt.

Gibbs woke during the middle of the night to a train whistle. A picture came to mind, an old-timey locomotive chug-chugging through the pleats of hill, a plume of smoke mingling with the feathering evergreens, a soothing image.

Sleep seemed like another place he'd left behind. There was a light outside the curtained window, the moon, the same moon shining over the shoretown in Jersey he'd fled, although it didn't feel that way. He mulled over what he knew about motels, how they were largely a charge card business these days, whatever cash on hand probably secured in a strongbox. And he could sense the impulses edging in, as familiar and thick as blood, and he tried to think of something else. He thought about the Claire woman from earlier, from the lake, how her hope seemed to flow as easy as instinct, as easy as breathing, a gift. Gibbs would have given almost anything for such hope. Years before, he'd forsaken drink, and at the time it'd seemed like the hardest thing in the world but he now understood it wasn't.

A dog barked out on the road and down the way another answered it, back and forth, and he could imagine the chorus being picked up in houses farther down the line, the call and response carrying all through Montana, as long as the road stretched, and he suddenly felt far away from anything he'd ever known. Gibbs dropped into sleep, picturing again a locomotive, a mare's tail of smoke over a steel trestle bridge and a bottomless gorge below, the warm sensation that he was arriving at some destination but wasn't quite there yet.

For the next few days, Gibbs was content to stay put, operating without purpose, letting the hours assume their own shape. He had money in his pocket, and he put up in motels and ate as if he'd the key to the king's larder.

He whiled away an afternoon in Kalispell watching planes wing in to the airport. In Whitefish he found a park with a lake that was not as big or majestic as the lake in Glacier, and along the rocky beach, a canoe. Nobody was around and Gibbs paddled out.

An overcast day, gray mountains ringing the horizon and merging with sky, the lakeshore vacation homes perched on stilty legs, dark and empty. From experience he knew one couldn't count on finding anything of value in such places, but you never really knew — sometimes you got lucky. Gibbs considered the steep A-frames as possibilities, then paddled back.

Happy hour: sounds of drinking, lively discussion about if it might snow wafting out of the avenue bars. He walked to the end of town, suppertime in the boxy hall-and-parlor houses. He watched in the dark as he would a TV with the sound off, tried to envision himself inside among them.

He used to taunt his prey, in the prickly moments before hands got thrown, used to ask, "Do you know physics? Do you know what happens when an object comes up against an immovable object?" To a man they'd been more chump than victim, would have done the same to him if they could have — that was what he told himself then, what he repeated now. And he watched the cheery scenes on the other side of the glass, brothers and sisters passing servings around kitchen tables, Gibbs taking it in like something he needed, almost like food.

So far it'd all been fine and good, but Gibbs had no further clue about that place that might have him.

He drove north one morning, the road following the river, which fattened into a reservoir, at one end a dam straddling the shores like a giant ship. He crossed a bridge to the other side, the road snaking in the green of fir and spruce, turning into a hill, a bit of snow skiffed in some places, then more, then everything coated, the evidence of a recent plow, the oil-and-gravel surface still navigable.

Gibbs hadn't encountered another vehicle since gaining the woods. He wondered how close he was to Canada. At the crest of a hill, a pocket alpine lake iced over, and in the middle of it a plywood shanty. Woodsmoke pulled out of a stack on the top and a pair of window squares were glazed in mist; a tiny house on the ice. He'd never seen a house on the ice before.

He wasn't prepared for the chill outside the Chrysler, which struck like a hammer. He rapped on the door, heard a shuffling inside, then the door opening, a blocky, lumpish fellow in gumboots and nylon pants blinking up, a pile of white hair on his head like a tornado funnel. Behind, a lantern glowed. Gibbs could not get over the tidy cubby — wood benches on opposite walls, shelves all around, a little hinged table that dropped down, a kerosene heater, the floor covered in board except for a few circles cut away to expose the ice below.

"Shoot, fella, you gave old Ernest here quite a scare," the man said. "Thought you might be the missus. I'm taking me one of those mental health days."

Gibbs explained himself the best he could.

"Jesus, man. You must be catching the death of it." Ernest stepped back to admit Gibbs into the shanty. "So you never been hard-water fishing is what you're telling me."

Gibbs allowed that he'd not.

"Then you're in for a treat. Gibbs, you said it was? A name you don't hear every day. I suppose that's your business." He looked over Gibbs, then handed him a spoon augur, demonstrating how to bore into the ice. "You're a big enough man to handle it yourself. Good Lord, look at your feet. Must make buying shoes a trial. You know what they say about big feet, don't you. Big feet, big shoes. You can tell me to shut up anytime."

He outfitted Gibbs with a tip-up equipped with a bell that jingled when a fish was on the take. Ernest managed a jig pole, a rod so small it looked like gear for a pygmy. He told Gibbs about himself, blinking rapidly the whole time, about his panel truck, how he hauled trash for a number of the homes dotting these hills. Winters he fit a blade on the front end and did some plowing. "A lazy man who's always had the curse of having to work hard. Married twice. First time was poison, the second the cure. Wife number one accused me of being Ernest in earnest, and vice versa."

Gibbs smiled. "I bet you are."

A whiff of kerosene hung in the interior. Ernest cracked a window, air entering like a knife but still cozy in the ice bob.

Gibbs realized it was his turn. "I guess I'm between things," he said.

"Good for you. Sit one out and think about it."

"I'm currently on a ramble."

Ernest chewed at the corner of his mouth. "I'd say we're about the same vintage. What are you, forty-seven or thereabouts?"

"Forty-three." Gibbs offered an abridged version of his run west, leaving out the parts that a man alone in an ice shanty with an ex-con might not care to know. There wasn't much to say.

"Hold on there, friend," Ernest said. He jiggered the rod, sang out, "Fish on the line!" He reeled in smoothly, eventually pulling a perch up through the gray water and smacking it smartly about the head. "Let's put this in the fridge." Ernest opened the door, dropped the fish on the ice. "Cold enough to turn shit blue out there. You were saying."

"A crony of mine used to tell me stories. I figure I had to see this place for myself before it was all said and done. Just to see if he was jerking my chain or not." Considering what had come of Hokanson, some of the stories were no doubt hogwash and prison fiction. He'd even told one that included the motion picture actress Betty Hutton. But he'd said other things too. Gibbs could get behind the idea of mining gold.

"Ah, the lure of the west," Ernest said. "Not the first man to be se-duced by it, and won't be the last. But it's a true thing, the promise of it all. Else they wouldn't say it."

"I hope so," Gibbs said. "You're throwing a rope to a drowning man."

"Just look at you," Ernest said. "A tall stranger riding into town. Like what you used to hear off the radio serials, the shoot-'em-ups. How did it go? 'His skin is sun-dyed brown, the gun in his holster is gray steel and rainbow mother-of-pearl, its handle un-marked.'"

From deep memory Gibbs recalled the rest, joined in, '"People call them both the Six-Shooter.'"

They laughed, Ernest dabbing his eyes with the heel of his palm. "We are such old farts, we don't even smell anymore."

They discussed what the world was coming to. Ernest talked about growing up in these woods. "That river you seen on your way up here. We used to tie one end of a length of rope around a stout tree, the other end around your waist. The spring melt would be spilling down gangbusters and we'd jump in the water like that, snap to the end of the line like a fish. The ride of your life. And *cold*. I swear you could sneeze ice cubes. When we got a bit older we used to take girls out there, have them climb on our backs. I tell you, a girl on your back in a cold river that's yelling watery death in your ears. It was like . . ." He ran a hand through his hair. "Well, like a young girl on your back in the cold water."

"It sounds like a time," Gibbs agreed. He could remember tun-ing in to the serials with his father, the console about as big as a Stutz Bearcat. He thought again of his brother Miles, the authori-ties having already phoned him, informing him that Gibbs had jumped parole.

The bell on his tip-up rang like a telephone.

"Heigh-ho, friend. Hop to. Fish on the line."

Gibbs fell asleep from the heat of the shanty, and roused to the ice pack expanding like a crack of a gun. He couldn't at first place where he was, the echo from the depths jarring loose memories of the sharpshooter's rifle sounding in the boggy scrublands outside the wall.

He woke to himself idly sizing up the immediate world of the shanty, eyeing the contents of the ice bob, the surprise of finding amid the crowded shelves what appeared to be a small bear, a primitive terra-cotta handwork of pre-Columbian origin, possibly a tomb figure not worth much. From where he sat he couldn't make it out any better than that. It could have just been an odd-shaped rock. But it got Gibbs wondering anyway, if it was a piece Ernest might have encountered along his trash route, a case of someone not knowing what they had. He wondered too what other items of interest the hut might contain. Perhaps Ernest kept a gun for the grizzlies. Even so, Gibbs didn't expect too much fight from the chatterbox. He considered the patchwork of clouds quilting the blue; he himself had the antique sidearm back in the Chrysler.

Ernest crouched over a gas Coleman, a whooshing of its jets. "You got quite the snore, friend, that and the whistling sound from your nose. A bigger commotion than a brass band."

Outside a wind swirled from the empty, wooded hills, shaking the shelter down to its two-by-four blocks, and for a time that's all Gibbs heard, the rushing air. He closed his eyes again, thought of Hokanson's chinooks, the fact that all it took was a favorable wind, the possibility of everything turning in a moment.

He sensed the opportunity for action slipping away and let it, the fading prospect of knocking over Ernest leaving a taste of iron in his mouth, cramping his insides like a vise. He'd heard of cons back at Pine River shitting themselves like babies after losing the nerve and fire for the business, and maybe a bit of that was beginning to happen to him now.

Ernest diced a slab of bacon, cooked it over a low flame, the bacon popping like Chinese firecrackers. He decanted the grease into a jar, added a can of kernel corn to the bacon, a chopped bell pepper, and five eggs, then fired another burner, gilled and boned two of the perch, and broiled them, using the ice skimmer in lieu of a pan.

"It smells like Thanksgiving in here," Gibbs said, voice thick with sleep, not quite sure he could manage food.

"I wouldn't know about that. The last few years my nose has gone deaf on me. At least you can die saying you had some of old Ernest's apache corn."

The two men in the tight confines of the shack — it reminded Gibbs of Pine River.

"Don't be bashful," Ernest said. "A growing boy like you."

Gibbs dug in and it was good, the chow, its heat momentarily jab-bing a nerve in a tooth.

"You were looking a little indisposed back there," Ernest said. "Girl trouble, right?"

Gibbs reddened. "I was thinking about my brother," he lied. "Haven't seen him in a long time. His two kids wouldn't know me from Adam."

"Family problems," Ernest said, setting a coffeepot on a burner. "Biggest tragedy of them all. Shakespeare would have been out of business if it weren't for families."

Gibbs stared into the ice holes, like deep-set eyes. "My brother — a scientist. He used to tell me how the littlest drop of blood could tell you all about a person. A lot of things change in life, but some don't."

Ernest emptied the grounds directly into the boiling water. "What, like a disease?"

"Maybe," Gibbs said.

Ernest screwed up his face. "I don't know anything about that. Unless it's a cat he was talking about. Nothing you can do with a cat. An established fact of nature." The smell of brewing rose in the shack. "It's a big life, though. Full of surprises. Just look at you."

"Just look at me," Gibbs said.

"One day, you never been ice fishing. The next day, you have."

Ernest retrieved two mugs hanging on hooks and poured out the coffee. He opened a cabinet on the wall, withdrew a pint. "How about some sweetener? Guaranteed to wash away the blues."

"My drinking days are over," Gibbs said. "If I have a whiskey, it makes me feel like a new man. The only problem is, pretty soon the new man starts wanting a whiskey too."

"I hear you. Stuff will kill you." Ernest added a splash to his mug. "Ah me, it'll be my funeral." He helped Gibbs with the tip-up, this time rigging a topwater spool, baiting the lure with mousie grubs, and into the afternoon they fished.

A light snow snicked and whisked against the windows, the day darkening, sun dipping behind the hills, only past four in the after-noon but good as night. Ernest suggested taking a sweat in the sauna he'd built. It was snugged in a swale onshore, had rough-hewn boards, a door that looked like the portal to an elf's house.

It was cold enough to freeze the stuff in Gibbs's nose when they

left the fish house. He'd brought only a greasy mac from Jersey and
he balled his hands under his armpits. Out on the road, the Chrysler sat collecting flakes.

The building consisted of two rooms. Gibbs ducked into the
outer room's soupy dark, a slip of a space with hooks on the wall, a
narrow bench, wooden slatwork over a stone foundation. A door
opened onto a second chamber and this was larger, a steel tub containing granite stones situated to one side. Underneath this, a
woodstove, which Ernest mended with splits of piss fir and lodge-
pole pine. Two tiers of wooden benches were fastened against the
wall across from the stove. In the corner of the room, Ernest had
sunk a tub into the floor, an overhead shower above the drain, a
contraption that stored water which could be heated from the fire
for a proper shower.

Gibbs whistled. "You're a busy little booger, aren't you?"

"Idle hands," Ernest said. "One head, a lot of hats."

The two men stripped down in the anteroom. The sauna chamber was hotter than before, smelled of wood. "Engelmann spruce,"
Ernest said, indicating the benches and walls. Gibbs's glasses
misted over and he removed them, the room softening. Ernest
poured a dipper of water seasoned with red cedar onto the hot
granite stones, which sizzled, a greenish scent rising. "The Indian
influence," he explained. "The sweat lodge tradition." He prof-
fered a cigar. "I don't have a peace pipe, but I do have these."

The men smoked and dripped.

Even without his glasses, Gibbs noticed Ernest staring at his arm,
his biceps, his tattoo, an interlocking design from a Grecian urn,
the number thirteen and a half, the handiwork of a con at Pine
River who'd adapted an electric razor and length of guitar string
for the purpose.

"You put the pin to the skin," Ernest said.

"It seemed like a good idea at the time."

"Twelve jurors, one judge, and one half-assed chance. I've done
that too. The house of pain. My hellcat days. Mostly drunk and
disorderlies."

Gibbs said, "I'm basically an antique dealer gone bad. Once
upon a time, I worked the legal end of the trade, but that never
amounted to much more than pin money."

He explained how he liked old things. Put an old thing in his hand and it spoke to him, told a story, had always been this way. Back as a little kid, his old man had somehow come into a handful of pieces of eight, reales from the Potosí mines in Bolivia, the first mint in the new world. Even before Gibbs could read he sensed the magic in the coins, sat for wordless hours studying them. And later, they held his interest in a way school never did, the rogue accounts of Pizarro in the steeps of the Andes, amazing that so much could be bound in those rough, tarnished circles of silver.

"Counterfeits carry a different sort of story," Gibbs said. "Actually two stories." There was the one that got recounted to customers and then the actual truth of the work's pedigree, each intertwined around the other, snakes coiled on a scepter. The trick had been hawking a piece authentic enough, and he'd been cunning in that end of it, ferreting out jewelers on the downside of their careers, individuals with too few scruples and too many bills, who'd not think twice about using their craft to disguise their cast marks on a mold for a phonied-up bronze. But it was the other half of the equation, conjuring a history equally true, that had from time to time tripped him up. Gibbs owned an erratic gift of blarney: it came and went. There was more he could have told, the occasions he'd had to employ his hands rather than his mouth to see a deal through, but he left all that in the shadows.

Ernest said, "Sounds like you put the tits on the monkey."

"The what?"

"You did it up right. I can respect a man who does it up right, even if it's a wrong thing he's doing." Ernest rubbed his jawline. "You're a betting man. That's how I read you. A man who relishes a ticklish situation."

"I do have the danger gene," Gibbs agreed. He pulled on the cigar, exhaled smoke out the side of his mouth, waving a hand to disperse it. "There was this dealer once," he said. "A hundred years ago. In London." He couldn't recall the fellow's name, only the boys he used to send into the Thames: mudboys, they were called — Billy and Charley. The story went that these mudboys would emerge from the river with artifacts of ungodly value. Coats of arms in openwork medallions. Oil lamps from the Roman era. Bronze Medusas.

"Here's the thing," Gibbs said.

Ernest nodded. "There's always a thing."

"The dealer, he made a tidy fortune on the stock, and word spread, and then, wouldn't you know, somebody was always finding something on a piece that didn't quite make sense, shouldn't have been there. Turns out the whole lot is a trove of fantasy pieces. The mudboys just made for a more convincing story."

The fire ticked in the stove.

"It's crazy," Gibbs continued. "The pieces the mudboys excavated — there's actually a market for them now. Called Billy-and-Charleys."

"You're shitting me."

"I shit you not."

Ernest ladled water onto the fire, and the granite stones spat. "I guess if enough time goes by, anything can happen. You should live so long. We both should."

Outside it was dark and only that. The lantern cast a sallow shine, their indistinct shadows on the walls.

"I would like to think that part of my life is over," Gibbs said.

Their sweat hitting the benches: like a light rain.

Ernest stuck the cigar in the corner of his mouth. "You were thinking of taking me down," he said evenly. "Before. Back in the shanty. In the afternoon."

Gibbs took the cigar from his mouth, placed it on the bench, felt the other man's eyes on him. He inspected the back of his hands, his face flushing from shame, from the dry fire of the sauna. "I didn't, though," he said. "That should be worth something."

"It wouldn't have been sporting. Me teaching you fishing."

"No, it wouldn't have been." It was somehow worse without his glasses. He wiped the lenses on the end of a towel, fit them on, found Ernest watching him more than carefully, and removed his glasses again. "I guess I should go," he said.

The men dressed in the anteroom, Ernest like a fever blister in his red union suit. "But you're right, pal," he said. "You didn't do it. You didn't roll me. Far be it from me to hold you accountable for a thing you didn't do."

It was cooler in the dressing room. Gibbs leaned against the back wall, could feel the cold from the outside but remained hot from the sauna.

"The Finnish people," Ernest said, "typically roll in the snow after taking in a sauna." He smiled. "I could always use another hand for my trash-hauling business. A good back. You just might happen on some diamonds in the rough. I could tell you stories."

"You shame me, Ernest."

"You're not such a bad man."

"Sometimes I don't know."

"Take it from Ernest then."

"There's this place I still want to get to," Gibbs said.

Out on the ice, steam ascended from their heads.

"That would be you up there," Ernest said, pointing to the Chrysler. A moon had lifted above the timbered hill, its light thrown across the lake and snowy ground. There were more stars than Gibbs had ever seen, the night stippled with them.

"I jacked the car," Gibbs said. "Back in Jersey."

Ernest blinked. "You didn't kill anybody."

"No."

"There you go. I'd say you're rehabilitated."

They laughed, the sound of it carrying across the frozen water. It was cold, the effects of the sauna wearing off.

"Fish on the line," Gibbs said.

"Right-o," Ernest said, and they shook on it.

On his way back to the Chrysler, Gibbs glanced over his shoulder, Ernest in his union suit a reddish blob against a white field of hills but nothing that might look like a mine.

"Hey!" he yelled. "What is this place?"

"Here?" Ernest puffed on the last of his cigar. "This is officially nowhere."

Gibbs threw a wave, like a man erasing a blackboard, then continued toward the snow-clad vehicle.

Gibbs felt so cheap after the ice fishing he could have been bought all day long for a penny. He'd hoped that he'd put distance between him and his old self, that it was left back there, along the road, like so much other trash, but his afternoon with Ernest had chased more than a little of that optimism.

He thought about Jolie. He'd not suffered a minute's remorse before then for making off with her mad money, sailing out of her life, not so much as a note. These were people — Jolie, and Ernest too — who'd cared for him, taken him in, and look how he'd acted.

He'd known her from the bars where he'd once bent elbows, though it was only after he'd stopped drinking, after his last stint at the facilities, that they hooked up. A little thing: blond hair from one bottle, tan skin from another, a tattoo along the bikini line of her hip that read DO YOU WANT TO DANCE. It'd been hunky-dory for a while, his early days out from the wall, Jolie returning home from the graveyard shift at the bakery, a flecking of maple frosting still on her. Outside, the sun hoisted over a gray ocean and Gibbs licked her like a postage stamp from stem to stern.

His thieving past had excited her. She also liked things on the rough side, and for a while he liked that too. "Isn't that how they did it in the pokey?" she'd tease him. "Isn't this how it was done?" It was new and seemed like kicks, but over time it'd only reminded him of all he cared to forget, didn't feel like any love he'd ever hoped for, only one more wall in his life, one more thing he didn't have use for any longer.

Now Gibbs recalled the thrumming animal rush of his run. Aside from the two wrongs — stealing the car and Jolie's money — he'd not done anything else wrong since. His thoughts were a different story. But as Ernest had said, you couldn't hold a man accountable for ideas that never grew legs.

Gibbs decided he still needed to road-dog until he happened on the right situation. Luck couldn't avoid him all his life.

He fired the Chrysler, drove to the south and west, and Montana remade itself, the bunched, scoliotic spines of mountains spreading out until they were bookends on the sides of far valleys, the habitations in the lee of distant hills. Rails traced the road for a while and then not.

He motored the Bitterroots, then mining country, the towns that got fat a century ago, the avenue buildings constructed of brick, made to last. He lodged in seedier accommodations, a nod to economy, fearing the day when his roll would unpeel to zip. He'd not counted the money — it felt like bad luck to do so — but he'd steadily nibbled away at it like a holiday roast, didn't know what would happen after he reached the bottom of his pocket.

At the edge of town the high plains met the main, the mountains on the western horizon hooded in snow, not unlike the sugar-dusted crullers Jolie sometimes brought back from the bakery.

Gibbs studied them, as if the place he still hankered to get to might blow in from there. The locals hurried about their business, pickups loaded down, townspeople walking the streets bent with purpose, all of it a world unconnected to his own. It was only the wind that blew in from the mountains, and if it spoke of anything, it was winter.

And then one morning Gibbs woke to a crown going off in his head. His teeth were never any good, and ham-fisted prison dentistry hadn't improved matters any. The nerve howled like an alarm, like it was jerked on a string all the way back to Jersey, and he took it as an omen.

He made for the western mountains, a blustery day, a sky like bleach. It must have snowed up high during the night, certainly chill enough, the mountains now entirely covered in an enamel of white, and he drove toward them for the better part of the day. Nearing the foothills, the road began to climb, and off to one side a weather-beaten mining flume girded the shoulder of hill.

A sign along the road indicated the Continental Divide ahead, the falling snow not much at first, spokes of bluestem grass still sticking out of the spotty carpet that had accumulated. And then more, the air a white screen. A few more sheer miles and he was in the chowdery thick of it, the blizzard splitting the season like a frozen maul.

Late afternoon and then twilight. Both Gibbs and the Chrysler running feverish, the infection in his sick tooth, the car missing every now and then. The road rose in a ladder of switchbacks, only the mess of horizontal weather, everything else erased in the swirl. Gibbs stood on the pedal, the engine hammering more than a tinker's workshop.

It was only when he crested the pass that he saw them — the horses. They ran ahead, somewhere beyond the throw of the headlights. A snow mirage, he thought at first. Then he caught them again in the television static of the storm: a kick of hooves, flickers of rumps big as ship sterns. Gibbs was on the western side of the divide now, where the rivers flowed to the opposite end of the continent, to a different ocean, and it seemed possible he could be chasing a gang of wild mustangs through a stone-blind snow.

The roadway tipped down and momentum carried the Chrysler

forward. The scratch of wipers on the windshield. He strained for another glimpse but they were gone, his glasses not of much help anyway, two prescriptions behind what they ought to be. After a few miles of descent, the living world came into view: treeline, aspens plumb as flagpoles, then clumps of red willow, and then an occasional split-wood fence amid the snowfields.

Gibbs more sledded than drove. As he rounded a bend, his beams locked on a lone horse in a paddock, not one of the stampede but a roan so emaciated it could have been a stick-figure drawing. He stopped. No house or barn, only the horse in white up to its knees, its tumbledown pen. The two regarded each other for several minutes. Gibbs debated whether to set it free. It could get hit by a car, not any kinder fate than freezing to death right here.

The Chrysler sounded like it was eating itself. He assumed the glinting lights were a constellation of stars, so far away. But they couldn't have been: Gibbs was above them. Flakes fell out of the coarse night and he stared at the winking bracelet, at the lights in the valley below.

The Chrysler seized up for good in the flats at the outskirts of town, and he plodded the remaining distance on foot. A sign read LADLE and beyond that another, of homemade variety, GO AWAY.

Wind scared up snow ghosts, the town like something out of a Lionel train set, a run of buildings of board-and-batten construction on either side of the street. A string of lights shook, the yaw of a gooseneck lamp on its mooring.

He pitched through the drifts like a man on stilts. It was only when circling back to the other side of the street that he spotted the dry goods store in an alley, the faint luster of a burning bulb behind a fogged shop window. The door opened onto a dusty room, two runs of deep wooden shelves for aisles, burlap sacks of rice and grain along the wall as well as tack and feed. A graying woman behind the counter, a beatific face that said she might have been expecting him for ages. A fire cracked in a potbellied stove. Gibbs tracked snow across the floor scuffed the color of tobacco.

"The first storm of the season," she said, as if the answer to a question he might have asked and maybe he had.

The shelves contained a motley assortment — tins of kippers and jellies, sourdough mix. He'd not thought of his tooth for a long time and now he did, its spiking twinge. He must have looked ridiculous, snow capping his hatless head, epaulets of it across the shoulders of his mac. Gibbs told her of the white-knuckle ride down the divide. The last miles of the descent the heater had surrendered, then the wipers and power steering, and he'd the sensation of going down in a plane, searching for the best place to ditch.

As he talked, he noticed, high on a shelf above the woman's head, a bronze known as *Christ of the Tender Mercy* if he could trust his eyes, a highly prized collectible. He himself had traded in a counterfeit of the piece, coating it with varnish to fake the patina of age.

"Is there a dentist in town?" he asked.

"Brownie might be of help with the car," the woman told him.

"Brownie," Gibbs said, as if a name he should know.

"He's the only one left in Ladle who can figure cars. Brownie would be the one." She glanced at her watch. "He's probably at the Silver Cloud. The roadhouse." She gave directions, through the alley, behind the shuttered-up buildings on the main. "You'll see the red from the beer signs."

The lights dimmed, a brownout, then the electricity catching, the click and whir of refrigeration starting up.

"Thank you," Gibbs said, feet clomping toward the door, which opened with a shiver of bells. He turned, squinted up at the high shelf. "You know, that's a *Christ of the Tender Mercy*," he ventured before leaving, gesturing up at the bronze. He'd have liked to take the stepladder over, to make sure.

The woman smiled, eyes nearly closed. "Yes," she said. "Yes, He certainly is."

On the outside the Silver Cloud appeared normal enough. The inside, however, was fashioned after a maritime passenger ship, the tavern in the front done up like a quarterdeck: a railing on one side of the room, an oceanscape painted beyond it; a row of portholes that looked out onto the snowy world; in one corner, a lifeboat slung to davits, a web of standing rigging held fast in lanyards and deadeyes; over by the billiards table, a ventilator cowl, upthrust like a brass mushroom.

It was in the back room that he found Brownie, playing poker with three others. Gibbs stood in the doorway and watched, the quarters modeled after a stateroom, walls bloodied burgundy, streaky with water stains, a fire blazing away in the hearth. Over-head, a pendant lamp of flash copper, the plaster ceiling in a cou-ple of areas eaten away, the tin roof above as well, and snow fell through the gap, shaking out like rock salt down into cook pots.

Much later it would all seem to Gibbs as if the four could have been playing cards for days, or quite possibly forever, this strange, beached ship in the high mountains, the sea of snow.

The storm raged like an animal that wanted in.

"I'm looking for someone called Brownie," Gibbs said.

A sprite of a man, a beard like deer moss on his chin, said, "That would be me."

"I got some business with a car," Gibbs said.

"Maybe you care to join us. Our little kitchen table game."

The dying nerve in Gibbs's mouth banged away, a nail being driven into his head. There was noplace else for him to go and he could do with extra funds, not down to scared money but close. Gibbs listened to the wolf wind, as if that could decide it for him, but to his eyes, there was only trouble inhabiting this room. He told them thanks but no thanks, told this Brownie he'd wait up front for him.

At the bar in the quarterdeck tavern, he allowed the lady bar-tender to pour a club soda. In the corner by the lifeboat, a jukebox all lit up like the county fair. A small crowd was in from the storm, their talk largely speculation regarding its severity and duration, a few having snowshoed, their gear leaning by the door, cakes of snow melting on the deck flooring, mostly men, canvas coats still on their backs.

Gibbs sat amid the gabble of conversation, a mongrel aroma of smoke, sweat, booze. From behind someone said, "It'll be a bumpy ride." And then from another end of the room, as if answering it, "You got the soul of a fat woman."

A few stools down the line, a couple of smart-alecks getting pleas-antly stinko, arm wrestling for drinks and cigars. Gibbs considered his options and there wasn't much to consider. He thought about the poker, the open seat at the table tempting him like an open bottle.

He was relieved when somebody took the barstool next to him. "It's freezing," he found himself saying.

"A good blow," the fellow agreed, and told Gibbs it was nothing like Alaska, where he once worked, running gravel for the oil concerns. Gibbs had heard about that, the money to be made, and was glad to think about something else besides the pull of the other room.

They carried on. Gibbs recounted seeing some fool in a bear costume waving customers to a diner in Battle Lake, Minnesota, during his run out, and they laughed about how crazy the world was. They reached the bottom of their glasses at roughly the same time and Gibbs offered the next round.

"Oh no you don't," the fellow said. "You don't pull coin in my town."

"Okay, club soda then," Gibbs said.

"The wagon?"

"Afraid so."

"Sobering," the other man said. "Sounds an awful lot like 'so boring,' doesn't it?"

After a while, he left Gibbs at the bar alone. All the forward motion of the run collected within, like a hunger, nowhere else to go. He thought of Hokanson, the lights-out stories, one feeding to another until what bobbed to the surface was the one that concerned Betty Hutton.

It'd occurred during the war. She'd been on some sort of tour to spur the boys in the ore drifts, give them cheer for their end of the effort. If Gibbs remembered it right, there'd been a storm then too. Betty was only supposed to visit an afternoon, a few hours, but wound up weathered in for days, this the first blush of her fame and she glowed brighter than anything the mines would ever excavate, like magic, the days snowbound in town, the world lost behind the storm, only Betty and a hundred lucky souls.

There was the usual that one might expect, Betty giving her heart — and perhaps a bit more — to some of the local men. But what remained glued in Gibbs's mind was not that. "She promised she'd be back," Hokanson had rasped. The presence of Betty in the town had lent the place a quality it'd not owned before, given it hope, made it somehow bigger. On her last night, she'd stood atop the bar in the saloon, blond hair shiny as bullion, and belted "Let's Not Talk About Love," her hit song of the time, stopping shy of the big ending in the final verse, telling the gathered people she'd finish it properly for them upon her return. "One more reason so you don't forget me," Betty had said, winking at the lot of them.

According to Hokanson, though, she never visited again, only word of her motion pictures making their way to town from time to time, her snapshot in magazines. "She said she'd be back," Hokanson had said. "People are still waiting for her."

Listening to the story in the narrow raft of his bunk, Gibbs had thought maybe Betty Hutton was dead and that explained it, but he said nothing. Later, after Hokanson had flown, he ran across a story on her in a *Life* magazine in the prison library, and she was indeed alive. It'd been a tough life, more disappointment than joy perhaps, a bad marriage and a stalled career, a brief comeback in the fifties, a stage show where she fired six-shooters and sang a medley of her movie hits, but it didn't last. And Gibbs could understand why she might have broken the promise. And it seemed sad to him, the saddest thing, what age and life could do, that Betty Hutton wasn't even Betty Hutton anymore, and if she had returned, would anybody have recognized her even so?

Gibbs surveyed the tavern now. He could not recall the name of that town, but it struck him that this could have been it, the beaten, lined expressions on the folks around him, faces that said that they might be waiting out more than just the end of a blizzard. He searched the walls, the flotsam of nautical gewgaws — standing blocks and capstans and running lights — but no evidence of Betty, no autographed, fading glamour shot, and Hokanson had never mentioned a bar that looked like a ship anyway.

It snowed and snowed.

Hours later the game broke for refreshment, the four men walking up from the back room. There was a fat man, perhaps the fattest Gibbs had ever seen, and he took a seat in a corner booth. The two players besides Brownie were mouthy types, one with an ill-advised mustache like a push broom. The other, older and a little worse for wear, limped like he had a sack of nails in his shoe, a *pop-siss* that Gibbs realized must be a prosthetic leg. Both were done up in checked cowboy shirts and looked like idiots.

From up at the bar, Gibbs observed the four with interest. He did not need to be in the game to understand what was going down, had sat in on enough poker to know the story. The idiots were obviously a couple of rammer-jammers who'd blown into town before him, had the good fortune of catching the heater of their life, every card falling their way; they were unbeatable. Perhaps too they were riding more than a hot streak — from their antics at the pool table, Gibbs would have guessed cheap trucker speed.

He could not get a read on the fat man in the corner or Brownie, who'd settled into a nearby booth. Gibbs walked over, sat down without invitation, told the little man about the trials of the Chrysler.

"That's a real unfortunate story," Brownie said when Gibbs was done, his eyes red-rimmed and small as scattershot.

Gibbs did not want to be there. The game would turn, as it always did, and then there'd be hell to pay one way or the other, and he wanted to be miles distant by then.

Brownie said, "There's nothing I can do, seeing as I'm conducting business back there."

The lady bartender asked for food orders and Brownie simply nodded at her and Gibbs ordered a dish called red flannel hash because it sounded like something he could choke down without much chewing. He'd not eaten since his tooth had gone off that morning, since his flyer into the mountains.

The two men watched the flakes spill down on the other side of the porthole, the evening lost in tatters of white.

"What is this place, anyway?" Gibbs asked.

"What is this place," Brownie said, and then told him, and Gibbs leaned forward to hear it, hoping maybe it'd be the Betty Hutton story, but it wasn't.

"Believe it or not, this used to be somewhere," Brownie said. "A company town. Mining. They own everything here down to the nails. This establishment included."

Gibbs tried to imagine it but couldn't. All he could see was a forgotten nest in the mountains.

"They're closing us down," Brownie said. "Once was thirteen thousand of us, during the boom years. Now hardly a handful left. An end to a life." He smoothed the tablecloth. "Welcome to Ladle, mister."

Gibbs thought the little man might cry. A shelf of snow slid off the tin roof: a deep rumble, like continents shifting.

"It's not been a good year," Brownie continued. On top of it all, his dog up and died on him, a Heinz 57. He pulled a photo from his shirt pocket. "One of those supermarket dogs, the kind they have out front. So gentle it wouldn't bite its own fleas." He'd buried and dug it up five times, not wanting to believe, hoping it was just a seizure or something. "Friends — they come and go. But a dog is a dog."

The talk of Brownie's mutt reminded Gibbs of the spectral run of the horses he'd seen after topping the divide, and they galloped through him again. "I saw some horses," he said. "On my way in, before the car died. Wild horses."

Brownie considered him balefully. "I don't know anything about that."

From over at the billiards table, the ruckus of the two jokers in checked cowboy shirts, the rammer-jammers. Brownie and Gibbs glanced over, Brownie lifting an eyebrow.

"You could still buy into the game," he said, and told Gibbs that they'd all agreed to play until the snow stopped.

The bartender conveyed a tray of food down to the fat man in the corner, so many platters it could have fed a small battalion.

"You want to know about Tap," Brownie said. Gibbs did not care to know, only wanted out. Brownie told him anyway, about a terrible mining accident years ago concerning a fraternal twin brother, this Ladle seeming to be somewhere peopled with more desolate stories than actual souls, as far away from that place he'd longed to reach as the moon.

Across the table, the little man, flinty as a prospector or at least what Gibbs thought a prospector should look like. He suspected he'd encountered Brownie's sort before, that they might not have been very different men at all, his wrist bearing a spidery tattoo with all the earmarks of prison scratch: old, but like it might have been still bleeding.

Gibbs held up both hands, as if in surrender. "I'm doing my best here to be a standup citizen. The hardest thing in the world sometimes."

Their food arrived, the red flannel hash the consistency of prison chow, a brick-colored slurry, but tasted better, Brownie's fare a slab of unspecified meat, orange as neon. Gibbs stared at it.

"What," Brownie said, "you never seen elk before?"

"What is that," Gibbs said, "some kind of deer?"

They busied themselves with their food. The men, Gibbs knew, would return soon to the card table, the stateroom drawing on him like a tide or gravity. He sucked on his fouled tooth, the pain offering something else to focus on. From out of the blue, he remembered that Claire woman from Glacier, her kid Elliot, his first day in Montana, the trust she'd extended. It felt like long ago to Gibbs, like an antique he still wished he owned.

After Hokanson had escaped Pine River the entire cellblock was put under lockdown, Gibbs thrown into the hole once the battery of interrogation had run its course. He'd nothing to tell, could have told any of a hundred stories, the scrape of Hokanson's voice covering the scrape of his jerry-built file across the heating vent above his upper bunk, the one-word note left under his pillow, *Smile.*

He thought of this after the four cardplayers resumed the game. It was just possible that the Chrysler was hale again, that all it needed was to cool down after the ordeal of climbing the divide. Cars had their own agenda, and Gibbs never fully understood them.

The world on the other side of the door was unlike any he'd ever witnessed, the midnight sky flinging lightning now in addition to snow, forks walking the shoulders of mountain, illuminating the peaks. With the drifts piled waist-high and higher, it was more like swimming than striding, the cold cracking the left lens of his glasses, numbing his extremities into clubs, boring a hole through the inflamed nerve in his jaw, up into his head.

Somewhere, a bell ringing or maybe just the wind.

It was a fight to keep on, and what Gibbs thought about to hold off the cold was all the various brawls he'd been in. He would have liked to say he didn't like hitting people, although he had certainly done that. A fight had sent him to Pine River, the result of a ruinous transaction of no-good works of figurative jewelry he couldn't move, Gibbs resorting to strong-arm methods to setting things aright. The subsequent fact of fraud, a broken nose, and a shattered cheekbone had made it aggravated circumstances, and as a matter of course he'd graduated to a new level of convict. It was not the first time he'd relied on such tactics in a business dealing. Sometimes it hadn't even been called for, but he'd done so anyway because he felt it'd been expected from a person like him. And, of course, the scuffles in his drinking days. Whiskey used to turn him into someone else. He remembered one time breaking a bottle over a man's head for the crime of telling a joke wrong.

Every freezing step, another fracas. Gibbs had walked clear of Ladle, the buildings on the main appearing over his shoulder in a snap of lightning. Back as kids, he'd beat on Miles for the sport of it, because he could. And Gibbs gasped at it all, the icy intake of air, wind tearing a hole in his face.

The Chrysler was nowhere to be seen. Gibbs spun a tight circle in the drifts. The signs had disappeared, the one that read LADLE and the other, GO AWAY. It occurred to Gibbs then that perhaps he was on top of the car, that it'd snowed that much, and he spotted the last of the whip antenna sticking out of the white like a hank of unruly hair, dug down with bare hands, located the back door, cleared around so it could swing open, the dome light still working but nothing else, like a coffin inside.

Gibbs sat in the back seat. He could remain, allow the blizzard to pile up over the car, a prison of snow. He tried to keep his teeth from chattering but it was no good, a feeling like someone twirling his failing crown by the root. Hokanson's chinook winds blew into mind, except the process seemed to be working the other way, fall turning to winter in a matter of hours, this the other side of the coin, he realized, like some law of physics, that if a life could be redeemed in a moment, it could go south just as fast.

Next to him on the seat, between his satchel of effects and the sack of counterfeit works, the familiar wooden handle of the sidearm, which looked like two handles, the refraction of his cracked lens. He pulled it out, took it in hand, examined the piece like an answer to a question he'd not yet asked, the bluing on the barrel gone to pitch, the curly filigrees above the trigger. The old man used to finger it when they listened to the serials, a few splashes in his glass to chase the hours of operating the elevator, the up and down and never going anywhere, all of it held at bay for a time by whiskey and myth.

Gibbs mulled it over, but there was really no other option. He gathered up the phonied works, tucked the gun into the waistband of his slacks, left the satchel where it was, and stepped out into the riot of flakes. He retraced his footprints, the occasional glint of lightning, boom of thunder. Along the way, he peered in the window of the dry goods store he'd stopped in earlier. No lights burning, no bronze of Christ of the Tender Mercy on the high shelf, only dustcloths shrouding every surface, as if it'd been closed for years.

He sat down to a different game from before. There was the spiral of snow threading through the gap of roof and the four other men at the table, the bench to the upright piano in the corner broken up for firewood.

But it was a different game. Nobody'd bothered to tell the pair in the checked cowboy shirts that the heater they'd caught like a rocket was fast crashing back to earth. They tried to bull the action even so, their chips rapidly traveling across the table, some to Gibbs but mostly to the other two, the fat man, Tap, wagering in the softest voice, oily as tallow, Gibbs recalling the mining accident story that Brownie'd told about the twin brother, a loss that Tap appeared to be grieving yet.

They played cards — Omaha and lowball, stud and draw. Sometime in the little hours, the lights blacked out. "The weight of snow on the lines," Brownie said, lighting a lantern.

The hours swam as in Gibbs's drinking days of old. When they broke for food one last time, he visited the bathroom instead, lit a match to see himself in the mirror, retracted his cheek to inspect the angry red of his gumline, a haggard face staring back at him from the dark, worn as a shoe. He was up in the game but couldn't count on it lasting, and the thought of what lay ahead only made him tired. He retreated to the stall toilet, sat on the can, propped his feet on the metal partition, and dozed.

He woke to the two clowns banging lines on the sink counter, hatching a plan for what would come next.

"We should sack these boys," the one with the push-broom mustache said. "I tell you, they'll never know what hit."

"I don't know," the pegleg answered.

"Then why don't we just hand over all the rest of our money?" Mustache had a voice like a needle.

"What about the stranger?" Pegleg wanted to know.

"The lummox?" Mustache said. "The lummox concerns me."

Gibbs didn't move for a long time after the boys quit the restroom, sat there, felt his legs going back toward the room even before they were under him, as inevitable as river flow.

All the crazy games walked out of the deck once the poker reconvened, the pot limits thrown through the holes in the ceiling, what Brownie and the fat man had been waiting for all along, the rash play of losing men wanting to once more own the universe. The cards circled the table — hands of southern cross, wild widow, butcher boy — the lantern's modest cast on the bloody walls, like the inside of Gibbs's mouth, like the deer meat that Brownie had supped on earlier, elk he'd called it. The two rammer-jammers began fortifying their toot and resolve with grain alcohol, operating on full tilt. Gibbs played like a leather ass, mucking his cards more often than not, no longer concerned with the outcome of hands, waiting only for the pair to do something stupid, then he would do something, the gun barrel of the six-shooter sticking the shank of his hip like an insistent idea.

It didn't happen like that. The burn Mustache had been riding finally consumed him, knocking him out flat, stranding his pal in the game. And then dawn. They didn't notice at first, the storm having blown out, leaving in its wake a white-swept expanse, a sapphire sky through the ceiling, the last flakes sifting in like talc.

It was Gibbs's deal and he heard again Hokanson, the scratchy voice: "She said she'd be back." And it would all come down to this, the two words he'd utter next. "Betty Hutton," Gibbs said. "Some of you might know Kankakee. Betty Hutton is fives and nines wild." They would play the final hand blind, the cards dealt facedown, unseen by the players, a contest of chicken to determine who'd be standing last, Gibbs tired and desperate enough to resign his fate to the disposition of kings and queens.

They wagered after each card, raised in giant steps, beyond reason, until everything was heaped in the middle, four men with nothing else to lose.

Seventh Street, the final card. The fat man pulled a creased deed from a pocket, let it flutter in, the family claim he told them. Brownie tossed in the key to his Willys jeep. Pegleg scoured himself so thoroughly it seemed he might even unhitch his prosthetic leg and offer that too. He ransacked Mustache's pockets instead, once his own were down to lint, went as far as disengaging the massive rodeo belt buckle from his slumped confederate, unlooping it, dropping belt and buckle into the pile like an exotic three-foot snake wearing a gold helmet.

Gibbs unpeeled the last of Jolie's mad money, emptied his sack of fantasy works, the gaudy carnelians and jades. He knew from the old radio serials what a fellow was supposed to do in such a circumstance and reached in his mouth, pulled the offending crown until it broke loose, a jolt as clarifying and sharp as a white flame.

A small lifetime — his years in rooms overcrowded with men. From outside, chiming voices, kids cavorting in the morning's untracked drifts. He thought of Miles, not the scientist but them as boys, riding bikes like a couple of cowboys roving the range, a cocked hand all that was needed to convey a gun. And even with his rotten glasses, Gibbs saw it clearer then, what he'd been driving at all this time, since jacking the car and before, not a place, only a feeling, the understanding of what his body could do and had done, the difference of what ran in his blood and resided in his heart. It was an awful truth, just how much his arms had kept the world at a distance, a lonelier confinement than any prison he'd ever know. And for the briefest moment, the wild horses blew through him again, more like a scavenging wind than the roll of hooves this time, then the hopelessness of the immediate situation returning.

He smiled, a new space among the composition of his teeth, the eyes of the others traveling on a wire between the bloody stub of porcelain and gold on the green felt and Gibbs, each of them with a different variation of the same look, like they might have drunk milk that had turned bad.

It would be so easy. If it came to it, he figured he could squeeze off two shots and maybe that would be enough, the ancient sidearm just as liable to blow up in his face as shoot true, which might've been okay too.

Later that morning, Gibbs thought maybe Brownie was trying to welsh on the jeep, the little man bent on showing him the town after that last hand was on the books. He was glad to see the place anyway, all that he'd missed under the cover of dark and weather the evening before. A morning of sunshine, jeweled glimmer of snow, a sky the color of a pretty girl's eyes.

It was situated in the bottom corner of a canyon, Ladle, and the mine. The Silver Cloud was located where the sheer walls met, behind the run of main. With the crust of white, the squared angles of rock, the land reminded Gibbs of an icebox.

Brownie showed him the tailing carts rusting on narrow-gauge tracks, piles of waste rock and slag from the operation. They ducked through the adit and walked a distance into the drift, the sides closing in on Gibbs, and inside the mine he thought not of Hokanson's pie-in-the-sky stories but of Tap, the accident with his twin, that there were worse things that could be visited on a pair of brothers.

Gibbs was unprepared for what he found at Brownie's house. It was a string of structures actually, the old assay office, pay and samples, boiler shop, and hoist house cabins, the tin roofs rusted to a fine brown stubble, wood beams silvery with age, Brownie evidently an unofficial caretaker for the dead mine. The buildings contained a staggering collection of antiques — mica windows, walls of painted oilcloth, sinks adapted from the lacquered wood of whiskey barrels, like a seashell clasped to his ear, the life Gibbs could hear breathing out. A wall calendar said the right month but the wrong year. The newspaper stuffing the stove in one of the cabins dated 1941. In one of the buildings, toys of First World War vintage; in another, a lunch bucket left on a counter from forty years before.

He'd the sense of strolling through a museum, a place frozen in storage, something even more of a miracle than that last hand of Betty Hutton. A hardbound copy of Zane Grey's *Twin Sombreros* sat on a shelf, and Gibbs again remembered listening to the shoot-'em-ups on the radio with his old man, and it came to him, thumbing the yellowed pages, that perhaps Miles somehow had it wrong, that maybe blood wasn't quite as fixed as he'd said, that what ran in them stepped back through their father, back to the oldest living things, that there was still room for possibility, enough to have produced the both of them.

"I try to keep it how it was," Brownie said.

Gibbs nodded. He stopped cataloguing the items when he reached a turn-of-the-century Marvel cookstove, bygone kitchen utensils hanging from the close rafters, stopped guessing the value and just took it in, the buildings ticking like a heart, a time when the outside world had beat a path to Ladle, when it had been a place; Brownie's life too, his untold days of preserving a thing nobody had use for anymore.

It was real and Gibbs had no words for what he saw. He would be among the last to hear what the town had to say for itself. And he toured the cabins, studied their contents like something he needed to memorize, to fix in mind.

He stood on Brownie's covered porch before taking claim on the Willys and shoving off. From the incline of hill, the town spread out below, the high sides of rockwall, the mountains behind everything like gears of a terrible machine. The air had a nip to it, but not so bad. A gauzy sickle moon had attached itself in the low blue.

"I thought you might have been a mechanic with the cards," Brownie said. "I watched you deal, though, and it wasn't that. All the fives and nines. Just lucky."

Gibbs leaned over the railing. In the front yard, the snow-capped shape of a '55 De Soto which Brownie told him he'd stopped driving ever since the Arabs monkeyed with the gas prices.

"Lucky," Gibbs said. "I wouldn't have said so." He thought about the word, how it matched up with his life, trying it on like some new hat. "Maybe," he said.

Brownie squinted. "The gems and curios you threw in. They real?"

"Does it matter?" Gibbs said. He considered the avalanche chutes on the slopes, ascending back in the direction of the divide. He had gotten someplace, only part of the way to where he had to go, and the remaining distance — he couldn't guess how long that might take. "I suppose it does matter," he said.

From somewhere in the valley, the sound of a radio, a big band tune from the forties, the bell-like tones of a songbird carrying like a breeze, filling up the canyon. The western end of the rockface seemed close enough for Gibbs to reach out and touch, like touching the other side of the earth.

"What are you going to do?" Gibbs asked. "This place."

"We're running out of time," Brownie said. "There's hardly any left."

Gibbs watched the little man, noticed that part of one ear was chewed off, the hangy-down of his lobe, and the idea occurred to him that perhaps Brownie might be dying. "So what happens after?"

"There's talk of a theme park. Tearing all this down to erect a ghost-town theme park," Brownie said.

Gibbs shook his head. "The world is a broke-dick operation." He reached into a pocket, found the slip of paper, pulled out the mining claim. "You can give this back to that Tap fella," he said. "I have no use for blood money. I myself have a brother."

Brownie smiled more hard-won than happy. "The clutch will stick on you, but you won't be unsatisfied."

They looked at the boxed landscape of snow, rock, sky. Gibbs thought of the buried Chrysler, how next spring when the white receded it'd reveal itself again, one door open, a hulk of metal, and the rest mystery.

"I expect you'll be going, though you don't have to," Brownie told him.

"Oh, I might come back," Gibbs said.

Brownie kicked a mantle of snow from the porch. "Okay, but I won't hold you to it."

Late afternoon. Gibbs drove west, following a cleft in the canyon, like a roofless tunnel through the mountains. The Willys ran with a constant shout, a body square as a flivver, its back seat containing the contents of the last round of poker: a sack with more money than he might have ever held and the various other spoils.

He climbed in altitude and the landscape unfolded ahead, a dashing stream on one side, rapids white as shaving soap. He had enough scratch to pay Jolie back and still live fat, though he probably wouldn't. He thought about calling his brother Miles, another thing he'd not do.

On the approaching slope, treeline, the dense network of aspens frosted in new snow, the hills lit in the alpenglow of impending twilight. It was then that he saw them again, the animals. They indeed had the hindquarters of horses, but the forequarters were something else entirely. They looked like deer on steroids, that big and chesty. They ran in a clattering herd ahead of him, and he followed, goosing the accelerator, attempting to close the distance.

And then the word came to him. "Elk," Gibbs said, and laughed, the teeth and gumline around the space in his mouth where his crown was once twanging like a guitar string. *Elk,* like the first word of a new language he was only now beginning to learn.

NANCY REISMAN

Illumination

FROM TIN HOUSE

Buffalo, 1933

LUCIA MAZZANO IS A LOAF OF BREAD. Black hair pinned into a
tight rosette, black lashes, olive neck, olive fingers, tapered, small,
her dress a long flute, yellow of forsythia, yellow of butter.

The young lawyers fawn and loiter at her desk, the older ones
wink, Moshe Schumacher grins: fat Moshe, fat boss, herring breath
and stench of cigars. "Good morning," Lucia says, and returns
to her filing, while Moshe Schumacher lights up and watches her
legs. She's young, at the job a month, Catholic in a firm that hires
Jewish.

From her own desk, Jo watches the men parade, pretends she's
alone in another building, concentrates on typing *in such instance,
the injured party shall be granted no less and no more than one-third the
proceeds,* carbon paper the indigo sky after dusk.

And when Schumacher finally leaves, Lucia crosses the office
from her desk to Jo's and holds out her hands. Bread, Jo thinks.

"Take a look." Lucia holds a pile of buttons, shiny black geomet-
ric hills. Her palms are pink. "For the jacket I'm making. Aren't
they smart?"

Smart? Yet Jo reaches over, takes one, and there's a tightening
low in her belly when she runs her finger over the ridges and polished planes.

"Sophisticated," Jo says.

Lucia's teeth: white against her carmine lipstick.

*

Bread. A hard thing to refuse, if you are Jo, if you picture your life as filament tracking back and forth between your father's house and the lawyer's typewriter, between men obsessed with order: brown suits, black ledgers, tobacco clouds. Weekday hours partitioned by documents: wills, contracts, letters, motions, pleadings, orders of the court filed alphabetically by client, daily and chronologically, so the story unfolds backward as you read from the top. Evening: dinner at the appointed hour, fish and potatoes, eggs and noodles, chicken for Friday night. A pot of tea at eight and the dishes washed, the dining table cleared and rubbed with linseed oil. Then pipe smoke seeps up from the parlor, the evenings her father stays in.

Even her body seems reduced to wire: sealed, unerring, monochrome. So unlike her sisters, the married ones, spawning in the neighborhoods off Hertel. Or unmarried Celia, who can't keep her own thoughts straight, who starts for the department store and ends up at the soup kitchen or the burlesque. *A half-step from vagrancy.* Celia would spawn if she could, *try to keep her from rutting in alleys.* Not the kind of thing you say aloud.

Jo's brother Irving, a bachelor, comes and goes as he pleases and leaves his dirty clothes at the top of the stairs.

Pour the tea at eight, precisely; five minutes past and her father will begin to sniff and glance about, ten minutes and in an irritated tone he'll call her name. Pour tea and then he works in silence on his store ledgers. Celia listens to the radio. Jo reads the newspaper and bathes and retires early, so she can wake before dawn, when the others are asleep: then it's as if the house is hers. Nothing encroaches and she can fill the emptiness as she chooses. Lately she's allowed herself to pretend her family has vanished and the sleep belongs to someone else. A woman, young, with black lashes, her yellow dress hanging over a chair. Lucia Mazzano in the predawn light, asleep in the next room while the tea steeps and Jo considers breakfast. Jo curls into the sofa and drifts and does not rise. The furnace blows and ticks. Wet breeze against the house: the lake ice is almost melted. Late April, and the dampness has its own weight.

The light arrives. Her father stirs. He'll be downstairs soon, waiting for breakfast, and Irving will follow, and then Celia, loud and clinging.

And the house is again an alien thing.

*

In the fifth week of Lucia Mazzano, Jo is called away from the office. It's Tuesday, early afternoon, she hasn't yet taken lunch. Celia again. This time, a coffee shop. It's Minnie Greenglass who calls, Minnie Greenglass from Hadassah, Minnie who even in high school didn't say much to Jo, she was mousy then, her last name Rabinowitz, but now she's married and plump and in the habit of hiring maids. When Jo steps through the doorway of Schroeder's Coffee & Lunch, Minnie's in a lush burgundy suit and new heels and pearls, talking with her hands. Celia really is a lovely woman, Minnie tells the owner, but she has troubles, has some terrible days, and this is one. "We all know about troubles," Minnie says.

Celia is docile, sitting at a counter stool next to Minnie Greenglass and the skeptical owner, neck bent, lipstick reddening the corners of her mouth. The counter in front of her is strewn with broken pie. At a nearby table a man thumbs a paper and glares at Jo. He's blue-eyed, German-handsome, slightly dissolute. Blotches of purple mar the right panel of his shirt.

Schroeder the owner sizes up Jo. His forehead is wide and meaty, his mouth a thin slit. "The lovely woman disturbed my customers," he tells Jo. "And wouldn't pay."

"Please accept our apologies," Jo says. She tries to be small, innocuous, but Schroeder frowns.

"Minnie, thank you," she says. Lays a hand on Celia's shoulder. "How much is the bill?"

"Mrs. Greenglass has taken care of it," Schroeder says.

"Minnie, what do I owe you?"

"It's nothing," Minnie says.

"No, really."

"I'm happy to help," Minnie says. "Celia and I go back a long way."

"That's kind of you," Jo says. Schroeder and Minnie Greenglass lean close together, a unified smugness, and Jo urges Celia by the elbow. "Very kind," Jo says.

"Very kind," Celia repeats, and after a pause. "Sorry. Thank you. Sorry."

The streetcar, the walk over to Delaware and Lancaster, the white frame house rising into pastel green — bursting elm buds, frilly maples. Celia doesn't explain. Won't. And Jo is left to puzzle out the incident using Minnie Greenglass's summary and the raw evidence: pie stains, the averted eyes of the female customers, the raised eyebrows of the men. Celia slumps and in the hazy light seems frailer than usual. Her hands are small and bony and she doesn't know what to do with them, finally tucks them into her coat pockets. At the house, she heads directly to her bedroom, coat on, and lies down on the bed. Jo offers to help her with her shoes, which she allows. "What were you doing?" Jo says.

"Nothing," Celia says. "Goodbye."

When Jo hesitates, Celia starts to hum. And it is safe to leave her now: she'll stay in her room for the rest of the afternoon. It's what she does after being humiliated.

Jo's been away from the office two hours: she'll have to work late. As she returns, she tells Lucia, "My sister is unwell."

"Oh no." Lucia's neck and face flush pink.

"Sorry to leave you alone here."

Lucia shakes her head. "I'll pray to Saint Michael."

And then they are both typing, there is only the sound of typing and breathing, the occasional shuffling of paper, a suggestion of leaves.

It's not the first time Lucia has mentioned saints: the Blessed Virgin Mary, Saint Francis, Saint Luke, Saint Vincent de Paul, Saint Joseph, Saint Agnes, Saint Catherine, Saint Nicholas, Saint Michael, Saint Stephen, Saint Mark, Saint Anthony, Saint Jude. She's studied their lives and deaths, talks of them as if they lived next door. When Lucia describes their torments, Jo sees a chorus of macabre dolls, most of them missing parts.

But no, Lucia tells her, after death they are restored. After death they are beautiful and holy.

"Saint Cecilia," Lucia says, "unsuccessfully beheaded."

That Sunday, Jo wakes early, thinking of Lucia's wrists, the point just below her palm where the veins branch, slim bones, delicate skin, imprint of cologne. Jo's walking up Delaware when the bells begin, stitching Sunday together. Saint Everything, ringing in tandem. If you let yourself into the heart of the city and walk, the calls come from the neighborhoods.

Once, last year, the windows of her father's jewelry store were soaped with *Christ killers* in Polish. Catholics, and not the first with their threats and profanity and soap. But imagine Lucia in her yellow dress, her hands extended, those sweet wrists, while the bells multiply, the chimes hovering over Lucia and her mother and their army of saints, Lucia praying to Saint Michael for Celia's health, Lucia with her eyes closed, mouthing the rosary, mouthing *Hail, Mary, Mother of Grace.* Picture her in the grass, *Mother of Grace,* she says, black hair loose against the green. Her saints descend and rise, miraculous, their eyes restored, their breasts intact, necks swanlike, uncorrupted. They are blessing the onions. They are feeding the birds.

Jo follows the bells. Thick clouds slide over Saint Louis's elaborate spire, the door of the church opens into — what? A dark vestibule, beyond which Jo cannot see, only invent. Outside: pale husbands in tight suits, wives — brunette, earnest, fake flowers pinned to their hats — herding children who are scrubbed miniatures of the parents, all of them approaching the entry with careful steps. The door closes and the sounds of the pipe organ leak out into the street. Once mass has begun, Jo ascends the stone stairs, touches the thick door, and sniffs the air, which smells like evaporating rain and wax and libraries. *Illumination,* Lucia says. *Miracles can happen anywhere.* As the organ bleats and Latin harmonies rise from the choir, Jo closes her eyes and leans into the door.

That night, when Jo is alone again, she conjures the thick wood and old rain and thinks yes, Lucia illuminated, floating in the yellow dress, holding out her hands, offering buttons and transcendence. Wind pulls at the dress, there's a dampness between Jo's legs. In the vision, Jo is wearing a brown fedora. She's near enough to touch Lucia's hem.

In daylight, Jo types pleadings and imagines the texture of Lucia's skin, while Lucia organizes files and takes letters for a jittery, myopic attorney named Feigenbaum. As usual, Feigenbaum leans too close to Lucia; Jo's impulse is to swat him away. She turns instead to the windows, imagines the neckline of Lucia's dress plunging, Jo herself sailing up to the highest branches of the elms. An unaccustomed lightness overtakes her.

Such pleasure feels new, addictive. *The elms,* Jo tells herself, *remember the elms,* and her fantasies multiply, deepen by the day: Lucia beneath the trees in Delaware Park, her dress gauzy and sheer; Lucia in repose, waking in a low-lit bedroom, her breasts exposed, repeating Jo's name in a voice laced with desire. The fantasies multiply despite Lucia's long hemlines and safe necklines and careful office behavior, intensify with the thrill of secrecy, a giddy ache that overcomes Jo at the typewriter. They multiply despite all signs that Lucia — with her talk of gabardine and linen, infant nephews, holiday cooking — is really no different from Minnie Greenglass before marriage, no different from Jo's married sisters, who come around with their babies in prams, who enter the house and sigh, tell Jo to see a dentist, a hairdresser, a tailor, who make Celia wash her face and bribe her with cakes and leave, back to their husbands, their marital beds, their mahjongg games and flower arrangements and charitable works. Jo pretends otherwise, imagines the dark thatch between Lucia's legs. Pretends the saints, in all their eccentricity, hold sway. Pretends that the ordinary is a disguise Lucia will shed in time.

For now, Jo adopts disguises of her own. Clothes are only clothes, but the ones she wears — heavy cotton dresses dulled from wash — will get her nowhere with Lucia. In early June she counts out her savings and shops downtown Main Street, acquires a pale blue suit, a cream-and-plum-striped dress, three blouses in pastel and white, a beige skirt, new leather pumps. Visits a beauty parlor on Hertel, where a plump, efficient woman named May cuts and curls her hair and insists on regular appointments.

"Beautiful," Lucia says, and fingers the sleeve of Jo's silk blouse. Wonders aloud if it's French. Offers Jo a lipstick. And Jo takes the tube, peers into Lucia's compact, and dabs the color on her mouth. Lucia hovers, waiting for the result.

"Pink Bouquet," Lucia says, "that's you."

For the moment, Jo accepts this: she is as much Pink Bouquet as anything else. A small price for Lucia's approval.

On Friday night, when Celia lights the candles, Jo silently prays to the candlesticks and the tin ceiling *Blessed art Thou, O Lord our God, bless and keep Lucia and bring her to me.* But then her father barks the other blessings, his tone of accusation seeping into the food. Irving opens a second bottle of sugary wine, having drained the first: he's sloppy and loud, though harmless. The ceiling does not change, the table does not change, and Jo thinks, fleetingly, of shul — services? should she go? — and then, depressingly, of Minnie Greenglass.

How long will it take? How long before Lucia can see Jo as Jo cannot even see herself? Consecutive Sundays, Jo dresses simply, pins on a small blue hat, sits across from Saint Gregory's, Saint Michael's, Saint Joseph's, and watches the parishioners arrive. On a weekday afternoon she walks into Saint Mary of Sorrows. There is a scattering of women, each alone, in separate church pews. A table of candles beside the Virgin Mary, a city of small flames, leaning and nodding in the slight draft. One of the women crosses herself and kneels to the Virgin, leaves a coin in the box and lights a candle. When she's gone, Jo leaves a coin and lights one of her own, as if she speaks the language of the Virgin. As if Mary might recognize her longing and dispense grace.

At home, her father seems to recognize nothing. He does not mention the blue suit, the lipstick, the stylish sweep of Jo's bangs. Not her new pumps or his missing fedora or the tobacco she has recently pinched from his study. He does not look at her the way he looks at her married sisters — appraising, pleased — despite the white silk. It's too late for that; how long has she deliberately made herself plain? He regards her as if she were a kitchen table. Reminds her to fix the loose porch rail.

Irving follows their father's lead, gives her suit a glance, shrugs. Only Celia remarks: she stands in doorways, holding the cat, sizing up Jo's clothes, assessing her face. *Pretty one*, Celia says. *You are the prettiest one.*

"Jo, take a letter," Moshe Schumacher says, flicking his eyes over the plum-and-cream dress. "Well. You got yourself a beau?" and she smiles at him the way Lucia smiles at him, calm, benign, follows him to his office, sits in the side chair taking shorthand while he paces and gestures with thick hands. Today she feels as if she's inhabiting someone else's skin, a body over her own. Only her fingers are recognizable. Worth it, she tells herself, and begins the second letter, her notes fast and fluid, and words imprinting themselves and drifting: *Dear, it is a pleasure, when we next meet, I remind you, please call, I look forward, most sincerely.*

At her desk, typing, she glances over to Lucia, who is explaining Atty. Levy's handwriting to Atty. Levy. Lucia rolls her eyes at Jo, smiles. In that moment, what else does Jo need? *Most sincerely a pleasure. Most sincerely, please join me. Most sincerely, yes.* In the afternoon Moshe Schumacher leaves for court. The other attorneys are burrowed in their offices, and Lucia stands beside Jo's desk, her dress a field of white dots over peach.

"What Mr. Schumacher asked," Lucia says, "about a beau?"

Drops her voice to a near whisper. Her face is flushed, she's absently stroking a loose strand of hair. Smiles. And for an instant, Jo hovers at the edge of anticipated joy, up in the elms, Lucia floating, they are far from the office and the house on Lancaster, they are falling into the grass, Jo immersed in the green of the lawn, the black of Lucia's hair. There's a two-second delay before Jo registers the name *Anthony*, which Lucia embroiders with sighs. A city clerk, Lucia says, eyes the color of walnuts. On Wednesdays after work Lucia does not go to mass but instead meets this clerk, who buys her cups of coffee and rides the streetcar with her back to her neighborhood.

Jo's throat dries and she's overcome by a choking sensation, like fishbones needling her esophagus. "That's lovely," she says. There's a slight distortion in the sounds from the street, a whining echo, and the light in the room splits into patches, which seem to swim away from each other.

"It's still a secret." There's a low thrill in Lucia's voice. "He hasn't met my father yet."

"You look happy." Jo searches for a handkerchief, then pretends she is backlogged with her work for the day. She squints at her own shorthand, coughs, leaves the room to fill a glass with water. Her slip clings to her thighs as she walks, the dress moving as her body moves, though it seems to be someone else's. In the ladies' room she splashes water on her face. It will not last, she tells herself. She ignores the water glass and drinks from her hands. Surely Lucia will not fall for the polite door-opening, for the cups of coffee and escorts home, transparent rituals that mean nothing. This Anthony will exit from Lucia's life as quickly as he's entered it. Perhaps he will prove himself unworthy. Perhaps he will die. Jo regains control of her throat, slicks on the Pink Bouquet, crosses the hall to the office. "Your dress," she tells Lucia. "Lovely."

For a few hours, a numb calm descends, a state Jo associates with frostbite and emergencies. She stays late at the office, and after Lucia leaves, after the last client and even the attorneys leave, she crosses the room to the desk along the wall and opens Lucia's cabinet of active files. Her hands move over the folders, fingers pick at documents and pull them out, a simple shifting of rectangles. She takes a real estate agreement from the Saltzman file and slides it into the Schwartz file.

On the streetcar home, Jo's exhausted. She stumbles into the house and up to bed. Dusk: the afternoon's seeped away through the trees, which are black against a backdrop of indigo. The streetlight casts a yellow the color of bruises almost healed. New rain, honeysuckle blooming on the side of the house. It makes you yearn the way radio symphony does, the way Lucia's wrists do. And then Celia's in the bedroom doorway calling, "Jo? What about dinner?"

In the morning, while the house is hers, Jo tries on her father's spare fedora, soft brown darkened by rain, slightly misshapen. For a while, her face assembles itself. For a while the desire to break out of her body abates.

In summer, Celia spends whole days in the garden: this seems to keep her out of trouble. But if it rains for too long, Celia's agitated, distraught; she paces, chews her hair. "What is it?" Jo asks her. "What now?" When Jo gets home from work, Celia demands to play gin rummy and checkers, games she quickly abandons. Bad signs, Jo knows, but who can keep track? It's enough to make dinner, brew the eight o'clock tea. Jo smokes her father's tobacco on the back porch, while the rain falls and Celia rants: today the postman ignored her. But evening company is not enough for Celia, not if the rain persists, which it does. In the morning, she follows Jo to work. Not the first time: occasionally, Jo buys her coffee and sends her home. But now the streetcar lurches, the passengers lurch, the scents of lake water, soap, wet leather shoes mix with old smoke while Celia breathes into Jo's ear, "You hate me, don't you?"

"Not this," Jo says. "Why aren't you home?"

"I hate you too," Celia says.

"Don't be stupid," Jo says. "You hate the rain."

"Stupid," Celia says. "That's what you think."

"What is it you want? You want a danish?"

"Hate," Celia says. "The truth is out." She points to a young man hunched over a newspaper. "He doesn't hate me."

It's the sort of maneuver that can escalate in seconds: harassment of strangers, angry conductors, annoyed police. The man wisely stays hunched. "Let's get off," Jo says.

"No. I'm riding. I paid."

What choice does Jo have? She takes the streetcar past her office stop, down to the base of Main Street, and uptown again, rain pum-

meling the packed car, until Celia calms down and Jo can get her
home. But it's a lost day. Jo convinces Celia to change into dry
clothes — "I don't hate you. Try this dress." — brews tea, and, at
Celia's request, rolls out pie dough, washes strawberries, measures
sugar. When the pies are in the oven, Jo chews a finger of horseradish. Her body seems to flatten and gray until its lines are indistinguishable from the walls. It's only the horseradish, the daily tobacco, reminding her that she is separate.

Celia sits on the porch and hums. Water draining from the roof
ticks over garden tools and mud. Once the rain stops, she moves
down to the flower beds. Yellow print cotton dress, thick apron,
bare feet. She's pulling weeds from between wet calla lilies, damp
patches spreading over her dress. The peonies are blooming, the
grass is again thick, seductive. Watching Celia move through the
yard, Jo can almost forget her wildness. She's almost a picture of
holy.

Wine helps. After dinner, even when there is no rain, Jo pours
herself the sugary kosher wine; a glass or two and the day's distur-
bances retreat. Trouble appears as if on the far shore of the river,
tiny, increasingly remote: city clerks waving to Lucia, Celia's petty
thefts. From the near shore you can sift through Lucia's stories, decide what to save, what to erase: the Archangel Gabriel, leading the
Herald Angels; Saint Agnes, the Virgin, accused of witchcraft; Anthony the clerk bringing snapdragons to Lucia's mother. When Lucia speaks, her face seems incandescent. Keep that. Keep Agnes's
death sentence, the white and yellow snaps, the singing angels. Forget Saint Cecilia's damaged neck. Let the rest blur and fall away.

It's July, a Sunday at Old Saint Joseph's: Jo's across the street, beside a sycamore. Parishioners arrive, dark suits in the heat, long
dresses and small hats, automobiles parking with slow deliberation.
Jo no longer watches their faces, only their bodies moving through
the heavy air, the fluttering arms of the women, the solemn gaits of
the men. But her reverie is interrupted by the O of Lucia, today in
deep blue, hair pinned beneath a matching hat with a tiny veil, a
flock of family around her. Lucia does not look at the street or the
sycamore but ahead to the entrance of the church, increasing her
pace. Follow her gaze and there he is, a handsome suit holding a
hat, hair a cap of black, dark eyes and long lashes floating above a

flash of teeth. A body bending toward her, and she toward him; he is bowing to the family at the door, he is taking her arm in their presence. The church entry swallows them and they do not reappear. The door closes. Jo waits for it to reopen, but of course it does not; the service begins and she paces. Her legs move independently, carrying her in circles around the church, up one block and down the next: up over down across, up over down across. The breeze increases, and she is a thin vertical line moving over the horizontal of the sidewalk, the city is a scattering of rays, and the sky fills with its customary banks of clouds, occasional patches of blue among the bloated layers. She breaks into even finer lines — arms, fingers, legs — all in flat continuous motion down one side street, up another, now away from the church and onto broader avenues, until she's in front of a department store on Main Street. Only there does she notice her location and the blank interval that brought her from Old Saint Joseph's. Think. Think. She can imagine the route as if to give directions, but not today's version, not the particulars of open windows and parked cars and broken curbstones. The sky seems half familiar. Did she walk the whole way, or was there at some point a streetcar? She cannot remember a streetcar. This isn't like her, she's never lost time this way; it's Celia who appears at unplanned destinations, forgetting how she got there, panic in her face when you ask what happened.

Supper and collapse, sweat and collapse, bitter insomnia, stifled weeping, open weeping, sharpness in the belly: two days. Two days of moving from the bed only to relieve herself and make her way back, of pretending *Father, I am ill with flu. Best to stay away.* Celia hovers outside the door, disappears, returns with water Jo will not drink, toast she ignores, sugary strawberry pie, cold tea, souring glasses of milk.

By Tuesday night Jo is empty, body slack, worn out. No weeping, no tremors, no waves of nausea, just an awareness of indigo air and the outlines of curtains. Eventually she sleeps. Wednesday morning, when she sits at the edge of the bed, the room appears to have shifted, but how? The bureau, framed pictures, and rocking chair remain themselves. The glass cover of a bookshelf is open — as she left it? Clock tick, faucet drip, barking dog, footsteps on the street, insect fizz. Ordinary, expected sounds. Where was she? Already a blank. She closes her eyes and sees blotches of light shaped like pits and fruit. Where? A vague, untouchable *there,* and didn't *there* include a woman? A line of color, white or perhaps blue? Pale blue or something deeper?

There is one person who loves her, and it is Celia.

When Jo arrives back at work, the office appears unchanged; she approaches her desk the way she has for years, before Lucia Mazzano, barely glancing to the desk along the far wall, acknowledging nothing but the need for more light, the necessary adjustments to the blinds. "How are you, Jo?" Lucia says. She's on her feet, listing in the direction of Jo's desk: Jo glances up long enough to register a blurred, slim figure, green topped with black. She can't focus any longer than that, even if she wills herself to, not in that direction. She nods and bows her head over her desk of files. "Better, then," Lucia says, her voice filtered through air as dense as glass.

Jo remains silent. Isn't that all she has — insulating silence, the silence of retreat? She rolls paper into the typewriter and imagines the monotone percussives filling out into a chant. For an hour, two hours, she types beautifully, unthinkingly. Nods hello to Moshe Schumacher. Nods to Attorneys Feigenbaum and Levy. Takes her lunch in silence, the noise of downtown passing around her, the afternoon light glossy and peculiar. She waits until the end of the day, unaware that she is waiting. The office emptied, she returns to Lucia's files, which she has not touched since the first day of Anthony. This time, Jo rearranges the papers in the Markson file, ruining the chronology. Closes the cabinet. Closes the office. Cooks fish and noodles for dinner, pours her father's tea, sleeps the night without interruption.

By the end of the week, Jo's wearing the cream-and-plum dress to work, bringing Lucia breakfast rolls and coffee, regularly riffling Lucia's files. Lucia smiles her carmine-and-white smile. There's talk of Anthony, Lucia's family warming to him, the invitations to dinner, of the lingering goodbyes and ecstatic hellos, kisses in the theater. Outside the office, a light rain has begun to fall, occasional plinks against the glass. Kisses in the theater, imagine, and his hands, where were his hands? "Delicious coffee," Lucia says, and the theater evaporates. "Thank you."

"Of course," Jo says. Nods. Sets her fingers on the keyboard.

She sticks to the easy misfiles, chooses the busiest and most distracted days. The attorneys appear at Lucia's desk, at first inquiring mildly, then demanding: *The cover letter for the Cohen agreement? Have you seen it? Brodsky case, Motion to Amend — don't you have it? Find it. Now.*

"It's in the file," Lucia repeats, checking her desk, the basket of documents to be filed, the floor, the wastebasket, the desktop again. "I'll have it for you in a few minutes," she says, and the attorneys wait, impatient. She's flushed, miserable-looking. "I'm sure I filed them," Lucia tells Jo. "I know I did."

The deadline on Brodsky arrives. Jo nods in the direction of the attorneys' offices. "One of them probably has it. I'll help you look." Together they search the files, trying different dates, searching out other Brodsky matters, checking under the client's first name, Jacob. Try the files on either side: Blumenthal. Broadman. Bryson.

It's in Broadman. The attorneys nod and retreat.

"Such stupid mistakes," Lucia says.

"Don't give it a second thought," Jo says. "These things happen."

Twice, Jo stays late retyping Lucia's work, this time with errors.

Two weeks of misfiles and Lucia does not smile at the attorneys, does not speak of Anthony, does not mention the saints. There is no talk of lipstick: there is almost no talk. As if she's absorbed Jo's silence. She stops objecting when the attorneys point out errors, turns beseechingly to Jo. *Let me help,* Jo says. *I can proofread. I'll take the Lipsky pleadings. Why don't I file that last group of letters?* Once, Jo asks Moshe Schumacher to wait while she helps Lucia correct an error.

He stares at Lucia, his mouth a flat pout. "Miss Mazzano will have to do that herself," he says.

"I understand." Jo says, and then, more quietly, "Give her time."

To which he makes no answer.

Jo can't remember her dreams, but that is familiar, the old way. She does not consider the grass, observing instead the space between trees, the neighboring yards. Continues to smoke tobacco in the evenings behind the house, while Celia watches without comment, the orange cat rumbling, its eyes pressed shut. There is no pleasure in smoking, no pleasure in anything. But also no tremors, no bitter cramps or ragged breathing.

It's a Monday morning in early August when Lucia is called to

Moshe Schumacher's office. She leaves her desk for no more than five minutes, returning tight-lipped. Pale blue dress, hair pulled back tightly, head bent, her gestures jagged and fast. From her desk drawer she grabs up a compact, a handkerchief, a palm-sized print of the Virgin.

"What happened?" Jo says.

Lucia's lashes are wet spikes against her face. She forgets herself and bites at her knuckle.

"What is it?" And Jo crosses to Lucia's desk, shocked: in that instant she does not remember the sabotage. She touches Lucia's shoulder. "What can I do?" Jo is sincere, she could even save Lucia, earn her gratitude. It's a chance, isn't it? To prove, finally, that though Lucia has been foolish, she can still be forgiven, that with Jo she can be redeemed.

"He's got another girl lined up," Lucia says. She steps away and organizes her desktop into rectangles and squares — files, stationery, message slips — and beyond it the parquet floor extends to the sharp lines of the windows. Lucia herself is blue curves. She hands Jo a lipstick. "It's a new one," she says. "Why don't you keep it?" she says. And then she's at the door.

Jo mumbles Oh, and thank you and Oh, but already Lucia is fleeing, an echo of footsteps in the hall.

At her desk, Jo completes a letter in the matter of *Brodsky* v. *Ludwig*.

Celia weeds and waters and the zinnias bloom. Delphiniums, snapdragons, honeysuckle, common daisies, roses in yellow and red and white. Some of these Celia cuts and brings into the house; others she won't dare touch. Peas blossom and mature, green tomatoes fatten. It's best to think only of the colors, to be empty except for yellow against green against red. The back porch is the only place Jo can breathe, at least for a while; she can't cook dinner unless the porch door is open, and she won't sit at the dining room table, despite her father's complaints.

At summer's end, Moshe Schumacher's cousin Gert, a terse, stout woman in her forties, takes up Lucia Mazzano's desk. Daily, Jo falls into the percussive hum of the typewriter, works precisely and without thought. She walks instead of taking the streetcar, and her body seems as light as a lifted fever. Still, the cooling nights are marred by poor sleep, which seems connected to no one but Celia: Jo imagines Celia humming through wounds in her throat; imagines the roses in the yard blooming over Celia's body until she falls beneath their weight, until she is buried in roses. Their malignant proliferation speeds on, obliterating the house. Even when Jo is awake, the humming persists, mixed with patternless ticking and faint sporadic bells.

JESS ROW

The Secrets of Bats

FROM PLOUGHSHARES

ALICE LEUNG HAS DISCOVERED the secrets of bats: how they see without seeing, how they own darkness, as we own light. She walks the halls with a black headband across her eyes, keening a high C — *cheat cheat cheat cheat cheat cheat* — never once veering off course, as if drawn by an invisible thread. Echolocation, she tells me, it's not as difficult as you might think. Now she sees a light around objects when she looks at them, like halos on her retinas from staring at the sun. In her journal she writes, *I had a dream that was all in blackness. Tell me how to describe.*

It is January: my fifth month in Hong Kong.

In the margin I write, *I wish I knew.*

After six, when the custodians leave, the school becomes a perfect acoustic chamber; she wanders from the basement laboratories to the basketball courts like a trapped bird looking for a window. She finds my door completely blind, she says, not counting flights or paces. Twisting her head from side to side like Stevie Wonder, she announces her progress: another room mapped, a door, a desk, a globe, detected and identified by its aura.

You'll hurt yourself, I tell her. I've had nightmares: her foot missing the edge of a step, the dry crack of a leg breaking. Try it without the blindfold, I say. That way you can check yourself.

Her mouth wrinkles. This not important, she says. This only practice.

Practice for what, I want to ask. All the more reason you have to be careful.

You keep saying, she says, grabbing a piece of chalk. E-x-p-e-r-i-m-e-n-t, she writes on the blackboard, digging it in until it squeals.

That's right. Sometimes experiments fail.

Sometimes, she repeats. She eyes me suspiciously, as if I invented the word.

Go home, I tell her. She turns her pager off and leaves it in her locker; sometimes police appear at the school gate, shouting her name. Somebody, it seems, wants her back.

In the doorway she whirls, flipping her hair out of her eyes. Ten days more, she says. You listen. Maybe then you see why.

The name of the school is Po Sing Uk: a five-story concrete block, cracked and eroded by dirty rain, shoulder-to-shoulder with the tenements and garment factories of Cheung Sha Wan. No air conditioning and no heat; in September I shouted to be heard over a giant fan, and now, in January, I teach in a winter jacket. When it rains, mildew spiderwebs across the ceiling of my classroom. Schoolgirls in white jumpers crowd into the room forty at a time, falling asleep over their textbooks, making furtive calls on mobile phones, scribbling notes to each other on pink Hello Kitty paper. If I call on one who hasn't raised her hand, she folds her arms across her chest and stares at the floor, and the room falls silent, as if by a secret signal. There is nothing more terrifying, I've found, than the echo of your own voice: *Who are you?* it answers. *What are you doing here?*

I've come to see my life as a radiating circle of improbabilities that grow from each other, like ripples in water around a dropped stone. That I became a high school English teacher, that I work in another country, that I live in Hong Kong. That a city can be a mirage, hovering above the ground: skyscrapers built on mountainsides, islands swallowed in fog for days. That a language can have no tenses or articles, with seven different ways of saying the same syllable. That my best student stares at the blackboard only when I erase it.

She stayed behind on the first day of class: a tall girl with a narrow face, pinched around the mouth, her cheeks pitted with acne scars. Like most of my sixteen-year-olds, she looked twelve, in a baggy uniform that hung to her knees like a sack. The others streamed past her without looking up, as if she were a boulder in the current; she stared down at my desk with a fierce vacancy, as if looking itself was an act of will.

How do you think about bats?

Bats?

She joined her hands at the wrist and fluttered them at me.

People are afraid of them, I said. I think they're very interesting.

Why? she said. Why very interesting?

Because they live in the dark, I said. We think of them as being blind, but they aren't blind. They have a way of seeing, with sound waves — just like we see with light.

Yes, she said. I know this. Her body swayed slightly, in an imaginary breeze.

Are you interested in bats?

I am interest, she said. I want to know how — she made a face I'd already come to recognize: *I know how to say it in Chinese* — when one bat sees the other. The feeling.

You mean how one bat recognizes another?

Yes — recognize.

That's a good idea, I said. You can keep a journal about what you find. Write something in it every day.

She nodded vehemently, as if she'd already thought of that.

There are books on bat behavior that will tell you —

Not in books. She covered her eyes with one hand and walked forward until her hip brushed the side of my desk, then turned away, at a right angle. Like this, she said. There is a sound, she said. I want to find the sound.

18 September

First hit tuning fork. Sing one octave higher: A B C. This is best way. Drink water or lips get dry.

I must have eyes totally closed. No light!!! So some kind of black — like cloth — is good.

Start singing. First to the closest wall — sing and listen. Practice ten times, twenty times. IMPORTANT: can not move until I HEAR the wall. Take step back, one time, two time. Listen again. I have to hear DIFFERENCE first, then move.

Then take turn, ninety degrees left.

Then turn, one hundred eighty degrees left. Feel position with feet. Feet very important — they are wings!!!

I don't know what this is, I told her the next day, opening the journal and pushing it across the desk. Can you help me?

I tell you already, she said. She hunched her shoulders so that her head seemed to rest on them, spreading her elbows to either side. It is like a test.

A test?

In the courtyard rain crackled against the asphalt; a warm wind lifted scraps of paper from the desk, somersaulting them through the air.

The sound, she said impatiently. I told you this.

I covered my mouth to hide a smile.

Alice, I said, humans can't do that. It isn't a learned behavior. It's something you study.

She pushed up the cover of the composition book and let it fall.

I think I can help you, I said. Can you tell me why you want to write this?

Why I want? She stared at me wide-eyed.

Why do you want to do this? What is the test for?

Her eyes lifted from my face to the blackboard behind me, moved to the right, then the left, as if measuring the dimensions of the room.

Why you want come to Hong Kong?

Many reasons, I said. After college I wanted to go to another country, and there was a special fellowship available here. And maybe someday I will be a teacher.

You are teacher.

I'm just learning, I said. I am trying to be one.

Then why you have to leave America?

I don't, I said. The two things — I took off my glasses and rubbed my eyes. All at once I was exhausted; the effort seemed useless, a pointless evasion. When I looked up she was nodding, slowly, as if I'd just said something profound.

I think I will find the reason for being here only after some time, I said. Do you know what I mean? There could be a purpose I don't know about.

So you don't know for good. Not sure.

You could say that.

Hai yat yeung, she said. This same. Maybe if you read you can tell me why.

This is what's so strange about her, I thought, studying her red-rimmed eyes, the tiny veins standing out like wires on a circuit board. She doesn't look down. I am fascinated by her, I thought. Is that fair?

You're different from the others, I said. You're not afraid of me. Why is that?

Maybe I have other things be afraid of.

At first the fifth-floor bathroom was her echo chamber; she sat in one corner, on a stool taken from the physics room, and placed an object directly opposite her: a basketball, a glass, a feather. Sound waves triangulate, she told me, corners are best. Passing by at the end of the day, I stopped, closing my eyes, and listened for the difference. She sang without stopping for five minutes, hardly taking a breath: almost a mechanical sound, as if someone had forgotten their mobile phone. Other teachers walked by in groups, talking loudly. If they noticed me, or the sound, I was never aware of it, but always, instinctively, I looked at my watch and followed them down the stairs. As if I too had to rush home to cook for hungry children or boil medicine for my mother-in-law. I never stayed long enough to see if anything changed.

Document everything, I told her, and she did; now I have two binders of entries, forty-one in all. *Hallway. Chair. Notebook.* As if we were scientists writing a grant proposal, as if there were something actual to show at the end of it.

I don't keep a journal or take photographs, and my letters home are factual and sparse. No one in Larchmont would believe me — not even my parents — if I told them the truth. *It sounds like quite an experience you're having! Don't get run over by a rickshaw.* And yet if I died tomorrow — why should I ever think this way? — these binders would be the record of my days. Those and Alice herself, who looks out of her window and with her eyes closed sees ships passing in the harbor, men walking silently in the streets.

26 January
Sound of light bulb — low like bees hum. So hard to listen!

A week ago I dreamed of bodies breaking apart, arms and legs and torsos, fragments of bone, bits of tissue. I woke up flailing in the sheets, and remembered her immediately; there was too long a moment before I believed I was awake. *It has to stop,* I thought, *you have to say something.* Though I know that I can't.

Perhaps there was a time when I might have told her, *This is ridiculous,* or, *You're sixteen, find some friends. What will people think?* But this is Hong Kong, of course, and I have no friends, no basis to judge. I leave the door open, always, and no one ever comes to check; we walk out of the gates together, late in the afternoon, past the watchman sleeping in his chair. For me she has a kind of professional courtesy, ignoring my whiteness politely, as if I had horns growing from my head. And she returns, at the end of each day, as a bat flies back to its cave at daybreak. All I have is time; who am I to pack my briefcase and turn away?

There was only once when I slipped up.

Pretend I've forgotten, I told her, one Monday in early October. The journal was open in front of us, the pages covered in red; she squinted down at it, as if instead of corrections I'd written hieroglyphics. I'm an English teacher, I thought, this is what I'm here for. We should start again at the beginning, I said. Tell me what it is that you want to do here. You don't have to tell me about the project — just about the writing. Whom are you writing these for? Whom do you want to read them?

She stretched, catlike, curling her fingers like claws.

Because I don't think I understand, I said. I think you might want to find another teacher to help you. There could be something you have in mind in Chinese that doesn't come across.

Not in Chinese, she said, as if I should have known that already. In Chinese cannot say like this.

But it isn't really English, either.

I know this. It is like both.

I can't teach that way, I said. You have to learn the rules before you can —

You are not teaching me.

Then what's the point?

She strode across the room to the window and leaned out, placing her hands on the sill and bending at the waist. Come here, she said, look. I stood up and walked over to her.

She ducked her head down, like a gymnast on a bar, and tilted forward, her feet lifting off the floor.

Alice!

I grabbed her shoulder and jerked her upright. She stumbled, falling back; I caught her wrist, and she pulled it away, steadying herself. We stood there a moment staring at each other, breathing in short huffs that echoed in the hallway.

Maybe I hear something and forget, she said. You catch me then. Okay?

28 January

It is like photo negative, all the colors are the opposite. Black sky, white trees, this way. But they are still shapes — I can see them.

I read standing at the window, in a last sliver of sunlight. Alice stands on my desk, already well in shadow, turning around slowly as if trying to dizzy herself for a party game. Her winter uniform cardigan is three sizes too large; unopened, it falls behind her like a cape.

This is beautiful.

Quiet, she hisses, eyebrows bunched together above her headband. One second. There — there.

What is it?

A man on the stairs.

I go out into the hallway and stand at the top of the stairwell, listening. Five floors below, very faintly, I hear sandals skidding on the concrete, keys jangling on the janitor's ring.

You heard him open the gate, I say. That's cheating.

She shakes her head. I hear heartbeat.

The next Monday, Principal Ho comes to see me during the lunch hour. He stands at the opposite end of the classroom, as always: a tall, slightly chubby man in a tailored shirt, gold-rimmed glasses, and Italian shoes, who blinks as he reads the ESL posters I've tacked up on the wall. When he asks how my classes are and I tell him that the girls are unmotivated, disengaged, he nods quickly, as if to save me the embarrassment. How lucky he was, he tells me, to go to boarding school in Australia, and then pronounces it with a flattened *a*, *Austrahlia*, so I have to laugh.

Principal Ho, I ask, do you know Alice Leung?

He turns his head toward me and blinks more rapidly. Leung Ka Yee, he says. Of course. You have problem with her?

No sir. I need something to hold; my hands dart across the desk behind me and find my red marking pen.

How does she perform?

She's very gifted. One of the best students in the class. Very creative.

He nods, scratches his nose, and turns away.

She likes to work alone, I say. The other girls don't pay much attention to her. I don't think she has many friends.

It is very difficult for her, he says slowly, measuring every word. Her mother is — her mother was a suicide.

In the courtyard, five stories down, someone drops a basketball and lets it bounce against the pavement, little *pings* that trill and fade into the infinite.

In Yau Ma Tei, Ho says. He makes a little gliding motion with his hand. Nowadays this is not so uncommon in Hong Kong. But still there are superstitions.

What kind of superstitions?

He frowns and shakes his head. Difficult to say in English. Maybe just that she is unlucky girl. Chinese people, you understand — some are still afraid of ghosts.

She isn't a ghost.

He gives a high-pitched, nervous laugh. No, no, he says. Not her. He puts his hands into his pockets, searching for something. Difficult to explain. I'm sorry.

Is there someone she can talk to?

He raises his eyebrows. *A counselor*, I am about to say, and explain what it means, when my hand relaxes, and I realize I have been crushing the pen in my palm. For a moment I am water-skiing again at Lake Patchogue: releasing the handle, settling against the surface, enfolded in water. When I look up, Ho glances at his watch.

If you have any problem, you can talk to me.

It's nothing, I say. Just curious, that's all.

*

She wears the headband all the time now, I've noticed: pulling it over her eyes whenever possible, in the halls between classes, in the courtyard at lunchtime, sitting by herself. No one shoves her or calls her names; she passes through the crowds unseen. If possible, I think, she's grown thinner, her skin translucent, blue veins showing at the wrists. Occasionally I notice the other teachers shadowing her, frowning, their arms crossed, but if our eyes meet they stare through me, disinterested, and look away.

I have to talk to you about something.

She is sitting in a desk at the far end of the room, reading her chemistry textbook, drinking from a can of soymilk with a straw. When the straw gurgles she bangs the can down, and we sit silently, the sound reverberating in the hallway.

I give you another journal soon. Two more days.

Not about that.

She doesn't move: fixed, alert, waiting. I stand up and move down the aisle toward her, sitting two desks away, and as I move her eyes grow slightly rounder and her cheeks puff out slightly, as if she's holding her breath.

Alice, I say, can you tell me about your mother?

Her hands fall down on the desk, and the can clatters to the floor, white drops spinning in the air.

Mother? Who tell you I have mother?

It's all right —

I reach over to touch one hand, and she snatches it back.

Who tell you?

It doesn't matter. You don't have to be angry.

You big mistake, she says, wild-eyed, taking long swallows of air and spitting them out. Why you have to come here and mess everything?

I don't understand, I say. Alice, what did I do?

I trust you, she says, and pushes the heel of one palm against her cheek. I write and you read. I *trust* you.

What did you expect? I ask, my jaw trembling. Did you think I would never know?

Believe me. She looks at me pleadingly. Believe *me*.

Two days later she leaves her notebook on my desk, with a note stuck to the top. *You keep.*

1 February
Now I am finished
It is out there I hear it

I call out to her after class, and she hesitates in the doorway for a moment before turning, pushing her back against the wall.

Tell me what it was like, I say. Was it a voice? Did you hear someone speaking?

Of course no voice. Not so close to me. It was a feeling.

How did it feel?

She reaches up and slides the headband over her eyes.

It is all finish, she says. You not worry about me anymore.

Too late, I say. I stand up from my chair and take a tentative step toward her: weak-kneed, as if it were a staircase in the dark. You chose me, I say. Remember?

Go back to America. Then you forget all about this crazy girl.

This is my life too. Did you forget about that?

She raises her head and listens, and I know what she hears: a stranger's voice, as surely as if someone else had entered the room. She nods. *Whom do you see?* I wonder. *What will he do next?* I reach out, blindly, and my hand misses the door; on the second try I close it.

I choose this, I say. I'm waiting. Tell me.

Her body sinks into a crouch; she hugs her knees and tilts her head back.

Warm. It was warm. It was — it was a body.

But not close to you?

Not close. Only little feeling, then no more.

Did it know you were there?

No.

How can you be sure?

When I look up to repeat the question, shiny tracks of tears have run out from under the blindfold.

I am sorry, she says. She reaches into her backpack and splits open a packet of tissues without looking down, her fingers nimble, almost autonomous. You are my good friend, she says, and takes off the blindfold, turning her face to the side and dabbing her eyes. Thank you for help me.

It isn't over, I say. How can it be over?

Like you say. Sometimes experiment fails.

No, I say, too loudly, startling us both. It isn't that easy. You have to prove it to me.

Prove it you?

Show me how it works. I take a deep breath. I believe you. Will you catch me?

Her eyes widen, and she does not look away; the world swims around her irises. Tonight, she says, and writes something on a slip of paper, not looking down. I see you then.

In a week it will be the New Year: all along the streets the shop fronts are hung with firecrackers, red-and-gold character scrolls, pictures of grinning cats, and the twin cherubs of good luck. Mothers lead little boys dressed in red silk pajamas, girls with New Year's pigtails. The old woman sitting next to me on the bus is busily stuffing twenty-dollar bills into red *lai see* packets: lucky money for the year to come. When I turn my head from the window, she holds one out to me, and I take it with both hands, automatically, bowing my head. This will make you rich, she says to me in Cantonese. And lots of children.

Thank you, I say. The same to you.

She laughs. Already happened. Jade bangles clink together as she holds up her fingers. Thirteen grandchildren! she says. Six boys. All fat and good-looking. You should say Live long life to me.

I'm sorry. My Chinese is terrible.

No, it's very good, she says. You were born in Hong Kong?

Outside, night is just falling, and Nathan Road has become a canyon of light: blazing neon signs, brilliant shop windows, decorations blinking across the fronts of half-finished tower blocks. I stare at myself a moment in the reflection, three red characters passing across my forehead, and look away. No, I say. In America. I've lived here only since August.

Ah. Then what is America like?

Forgive me, aunt, I say. I forget.

Prosperous Garden no. 4. Tung Kun Street. Yau Ma Tei.

A scribble of Chinese characters.

Show this to doorman he let you in.

The building is on the far edge of Kowloon, next to the reclamation; a low concrete barrier separates it from an elevated highway that thunders continuously as cars pass. Four identical towers around a courtyard, long poles draped with laundry jutting from every window, like spears hung with old rotted flags.

Gong hei fat choi, I say to the doorman through the gate, and he smiles with crooked teeth, but when I pass the note to him all expression leaves his face; he presses the buzzer and turns away quickly. Twenty-three A-ah, he calls out to the opposite wall. You understand?

Thank you.

When I step out into the hallway I breathe in boiled chicken, oyster sauce, frying oil, the acrid steam of medicine, dried fish, Dettol. Two young boys are crouched at the far end, sending a radio-controlled car zipping past me; someone is arguing loudly over the telephone; a stereo plays loud Canto-pop from a balcony somewhere below. All the apartment doors are open, I notice, walking by, and only the heavy sliding gates in front of them are closed. Like a honeycomb, I can't help thinking, or an ant farm. But when I reach 23A the door behind the gate is shut, and no sound comes from behind it. The bell rings several times before the locks begin to snap open.

You are early, Alice says, rubbing her eyes, as if she's been sleeping. Behind her the apartment is dark; there is only a faint blue glow, as if from a TV screen.

I'm sorry. You didn't say when to come. I look at my watch: eight-thirty. I can come back, I say, another time, maybe another night —

She shakes her head and opens the gate.

When she turns on the light I draw a deep breath, involuntarily, and hide it with a cough. The walls are covered with stacks of yellowed paper, file boxes, brown envelopes, and ragged books; on opposite sides of the room are two desks, each holding a computer with a flickering screen. I peer at the one closest to the door. At the top of the screen there is a rotating globe and, below it, a ribbon of letters and numbers, always changing. The other, I see, is just the same: a head staring at its twin.

Come, Alice says. She has disappeared for a moment and re-emerged dressed in a long dress, silver running shoes, a hooded sweatshirt.

Are these yours?

No. My father's.

Why does he need two? They're just the same.

Nysee, she says impatiently, pointing. Footsie. New York Stock Exchange. London Stock Exchange.

Sau Yee, a hoarse voice calls from another room. Who is it?

It's my English teacher, she says loudly. Giving me a homework assignment.

Gwailo a?

Yes, she says. The white one.

Then call a taxi for him. He appears in the kitchen doorway: a stooped old man, perhaps five feet tall, in a dirty white T-shirt, shorts, and sandals. His face is covered with liver spots, his eyes shrunken into their sockets. I sorry-ah, he says to me. No speakee English.

It's all right, I say. There is a numbness growing behind my eyes: I want to speak to him, but the words are all jumbled, and Alice's eyes burning on my neck. Goodbye, I say, take care.

See later-ah.

Alice pulls the hood over her head and opens the door.

She leads me to the top of a dark stairwell, in front of a rusting door with light pouring through its cracks. *Tin paang,* she says, reading the characters stenciled on it in white. Roof. She hands me a black headband, identical to her own.

Hold on, I say, gripping the railing with both hands. The numbness behind my eyes is still there, and I feel my knees growing weak, as if there were no building below me, only a framework of girders and air. Can you answer me a question?

Maybe one.

Has he always been like that?

What like?

With the computers, I say. Does he do that all the time?

Always. Never turn them off.

In the darkness I can barely see her face: only the eyes, shining, daring me to speak. *If I were in your place,* I say to myself, and the phrase dissolves, weightless.

Listen, I say. I'm not sure I'm ready.

She laughs. When you be sure?

Her fingers fall across my face, and I feel the elastic brushing over my hair, and then the world is black: I open my eyes and close them, no difference.

We just go for a little walk, she says. You don't worry. Only listen.

I never realized, before, the weight of the air: at every step I feel the great mass of it pressing against my face, saddled on my shoulders. I am breathing huge quantities, as if my lungs were a giant recirculation machine, and sweat is running down from my forehead and soaking the edge of the headband. Alice takes normal-sized steps and grips my hand fiercely, so I can't let go. Don't be afraid, she shouts. We still in the middle. Not near the edge.

What am I supposed to do?

Nothing, she says. Only wait. Maybe you see something.

I stare fiercely into blackness, into my own eyelids. There is the afterglow of the hallway light, and the computer screens, very faint; or am I imagining it? What is there on a roof? I wonder, and try to picture it: television antennas, heating ducts, clotheslines. Are there guardrails? I've never seen any on a Hong Kong building. She turns, and I brush something metal with my hand. Do you know where you're going? I shout.

Here, she says, and stops. I stumble into her, and she catches my shoulder. Careful, she says. We wait here.

Wait for what?

Just listen, she says. I tell to you. Look to left side: there's a big building there. Very tall white building, higher than us. Small windows.

All right. I can see that.

Right side is highway. Very bright. Many cars and trucks passing.

If I strain to listen I can hear a steady whooshing sound, and then the high whine of a motorcycle, like a mosquito passing my ear. Okay, I say. Got that.

In the middle is very dark. Small buildings. Only few lights on.

Not enough, I say.

One window close to us, she says. Two little children there. You see them?

No.

Lift your arm, she says, and I do. Put your hand up. See? They wave to you.

My God, I say. How do you do that?

She squeezes my hand.

You promise me something.

Of course. What is it?

You don't take it off, she says. No matter nothing. You promise me?

I do. I promise.

She lets go of my hand, and I hear running steps, soles skidding
on concrete.

Alice! I shout, rooted to the spot; I crouch down, and balance
myself with my hands. Alice! You don't —

Mama, she screams, ten feet away, and the sound carries, echoes;
I can see it slanting with the wind, bright as daylight, as if a roman
candle had exploded in my face. *Mama mama mama mama mama
mama mama,* she sings, and I am crawling toward her on hands and
knees, feeling in front of me for the edge.

She is there, Alice shouts. You see? She is in the air.

I see her. Stay where you are.

You watch, she says. I follow her.

She doesn't want you, I shout. She doesn't want you there. Let
her go.

There is a long silence, and I stay where I am, the damp concrete
soaking through to my knees. My ears are ringing, and the numbness has blossomed through my head; I feel faintly seasick.

Alice?

You can stand up, she says in a small voice, and I do.

You are shaking, she says. She puts her arms around me from behind and clasps my chest, pressing her head against my back. I
thank you, she says.

She unties the headband.

6 February
Man waves white hands at black sky
He says arent you happy be alive
arent you
He kneels and kisses floor

ANNETTE SANFORD

Nobody Listens When I Talk

FROM DESCANT

LOCATE ME IN A SWING. Metal, porch type, upholstered in orange-striped canvas by my mother. I am spending the summer. My sixteenth, but the first I have spent in a swing. I could say I'm here because I have a broken leg (it's true I do have pain) or ear trouble or a very strict father. I could say I like to be alone, that I'm cultivating my mind, that I'm meditating on the state of the universe. I could say a lot of things, but nobody listens when I talk, so I don't. Talk. Not often, anyway. And it worries people.

My mother, for instance. She hovers. She lights in a wicker chair by the banister and stares at me periodically. She wears a blue-checked housedress or a green one under the apron I gave her for Christmas with purple rickrack on the hem. She clutches a dust-cloth or a broom handle or the woman's section of the *Windsor Chronicle*.

"Marilyn," she says, "a girl your age should be up and doing things."

Doing things to her is sweeping out the garage or mending all my underwear. Doing things to me is swimming, hanging on the back of a motorcycle, water-skiing. To her, a girl my age is an apprentice woman in training for three meals a day served on time and shiny kitchen linoleum, but she would be happy to see me dancing the funky chicken if it would get me on my feet.

I stay prone. I don't want to do her kind of thing, and I can't do mine. The fact is, I don't fit anywhere right now. Except in a swing. So here I am, reading.

My father arrives in the evening. He has worked all day in an office where the air conditioner is broken, or with a client who decides at five minutes to five to invest with another company. He flops in the wicker chair and communes with my mother's ghost.

"Marilyn," he says, "a pretty girl like you ought to realize how lucky she is."

Lucky to him is being sixteen with nothing to worry about. My father grew up in Utopia, where everyone between two and twenty dwelt in perpetual joy. If he were sixteen now he would have a motorcycle and a beautiful girl riding behind him. But it wouldn't be me. If he were sixteen and not my father, he wouldn't look at me twice.

From time to time my friend comes. I give her half the swing and she sits like a guru and pops her gum. She can do that and still look great. When she blinks, boys fall dead.

"Marilyn," she says, "a girl like you needs a lot of experience with different men."

She will get me a date with her cousin. With her sister-in-law's brother. With the preacher's nephew from Syracuse. She will fix me up in the back seat of a car with someone like myself, and we will eat popcorn and watch the drive-in movie and wish it were time to go home.

I could say, *I'm not that kind of girl at all.* I could say, *Someone should be kissing me madly, buying me violets, throwing himself in front of Amtrak for want of my careless glance.*

Who would listen?

So I say, "No." I say, "Maybe next week." Then I lie in the swing and watch the stars come out and wonder why I didn't go.

When you lie in a swing all day, you remember a lot. You close your eyes and listen to the locusts humming in the elm trees and you think of who you are.

You think of you at six, crying into a blue corduroy bedspread because your uncle has laughed at your elephant, which has no tusks. You have drawn it as a gift for him. You have never heard of tusks before.

You think of lying in the big iron bed at Grandpa's house, listening to the cistern water tapping on the stones outside the window, knowing you are safe because you are the baby and everybody loves you. You think of the dancing class grand ball when you are twelve in a pink dress with ribbons in your hair and a head taller than the boy who brought you. His mother has made a corsage for you, and when you dance it rubs against his nose. You pretend he pulls away because of this, but when you are sixteen lying in a swing, you know it was the scent of your own self-doubt mingling with the rose and lavender that sent you to the chairs waiting by the wall.

When you lie in a swing all day, you live in the world you read about. You drag a bare foot back and forth across the floor and hear the song the chains sing, but you aren't really you.

You are a woman standing by a table, reading a letter from a box of other letters. A dead man wrote them. His face, as young as yours, he has given to the baby sleeping by the window where the boats pass. He has dreamed his own death and written a passage from the Psalms: *His days are as grass, in the morning they flourish, in the evening they wither and are cut down.*

You are a father counting cracks in the sidewalk passing under your feet. You have waited a long time in a railroad station for a train carrying the child who walks beside you, who says, *My mother made me come even though I hate you.*

You are a girl, pregnant, alone in a car you have parked on a country lane. You are kin to the brown cow chewing across the fence. *You are wet and sticky and blind, curled in the cow's stomach waiting for your birth.* You are sick in the ditch.

You are a boy in a room with bars on the window, an old woman on white sheets looking at the Good Shepherd trapped in a frame, a child with a scar on his face.

When you aren't really you, then the who that you are is different somehow: strong, and part of everything . . . sure of a harvest for every season . . . glad to be sad. You are a riddle with hundreds of answers, a song with a thousand tunes.

When you lie in a swing all summer, fall comes before you notice. Suddenly elm leaves pave the street, and you have been seventeen for three days.

It is time to get up.

In the kitchen my mother is still in her apron, frying the supper steaks. I sit at the table and eat a grape. I could say, *Don't worry about the underwear. When the time comes, I can mend it. I can cook and clean a house and love a lonely daughter. I was watching all summer.*

Instead, I yawn, and she looks at me. "A whole summer," she says, and shakes her head.

In the den the weatherman is promising rain. I kiss the top of my father's head where the hair doesn't grow anymore and lay my cheek on his whiskers. I could say, *I really am, like you said, beautiful.*

"Try something light for a change," he says, and hands me the funnies. I curl on the couch and call my girlfriend. She tells me she has kissed a trumpet player. He has an incredible lip. She tells me bikinis are on sale, blond men get bald first, mud is good for the skin.

I could tell her, *Summer's over.* I could say, *Men are born and die and are born again. The rest is only details.* I could say,

> Roses are red,
> violets are blue.
> I grew up,
> *but nothing happened to you.*

I don't, though. It hurts too much. And besides, nobody listens when I talk.

Sometimes not even me.

KATHERINE SHONK

My Mother's Garden

FROM TIN HOUSE

SPRING HAD COME to my hometown. When I got off the bus at
the entrance to the contamination zone, Oles was standing at the
guard station in a lightweight uniform instead of his padded military jacket, his gun swung loosely over his back. The thaw seemed
to have improved his usually sullen mood; he nodded his appreciation of the flowered fabric I'd brought for his wife and let me pass
through the gate without even looking at my documents.

I strayed from the silent, wide street that led into the abandoned
town, turning instead into the forest. I prefer to take the long route
to my mother's house in the village, averting my eyes from the
town's yawning high-rise apartment buildings, the rusting yellow
Ferris wheel, and, in the far distance, the plant itself. Here the trees
grew dense and undisturbed, and the familiar scent of spring filled
the air. The fresh, heady smell hadn't yet reached our new home —
funny that after twelve years I still think of it as "new" — less than
fifty kilometers away on the barren, flat steppe.

I emerged from the woods into the broad field where I used to
play as a child. During my last visit, just a month ago, it had been a
smooth blanket of snow, but now feathery grass reached my knees.
Across the field, the village looked almost as it did just before the
evacuation, the little pastel houses rising in two neat rows, shaded
by budding trees. White clouds meandered across a sky the color of
periwinkles. A breeze blew up from the river, rustling the grass and
swaying the sign that leaned in the middle of the field, its red warning chipped and peeling.

"Yuuuulia!" Mama cried, brandishing her ax in greeting. She

and her friend Ganna, their aprons filled with pine branches, met me in the field. They smiled, wide and gap-toothed, squinting in the cool sunlight, their soft fat faces framed with kerchiefs. They were waiting for me to touch them, a kiss or a pat, but I hesitated, and the moment passed.

"Ganna, take some of these logs I've brought Mama," I said. But they had begun to divvy up their branches, each scolding the other for not taking her fair share.

Inside the house, I stacked the logs I'd brought by the stove. "I've got a perfectly good forest in my back yard, and you bring me firewood," Mama complained.

She made me a cup of tea and examined my loot, grunting her approval at the sausage links, the bag of sugar, the box of tea. "Enough for a dress," I said, unfolding a length of flowered fabric. The white material shone like a beam of light in the rundown house, where the teacups were stained brown, the wallpaper roses buried beneath a layer of grit.

Mama showed me a bucketful of green onions she'd grown in her garden. "Delicious," she said, chomping on one. "Here, you try."

"Mama, you know I won't eat that," I said.

"Summer is coming," she said. "Ganna's Oksana is bringing her little girls here in a few weeks."

"They should be arrested for bringing children here." Each time I visit, my mother hints that she'd like me to bring my thirteen-year-old daughter, Halynka, to see her. She doesn't seem to understand that it is something I will never do.

"Look at this beautiful onion." She sliced the tip off a stalk and held it beneath my nose. It smelled sweet. Juice coated the tender white rings like syrup on a cut pine. "They come up earlier than before, and they taste better too."

"How many times do I have to tell you, Mama? Just because it looks healthy doesn't mean it is." With the possible exception of God, my mother only believes what she sees.

"I had a visitor the other day," she said in a singsong voice that told me she was planning to win the argument with a sneak attack. "I heard something rustling outside, and I thought it was a deer or a rabbit. I looked out the window and nearly jumped out of my skin. There was a man poking around my garden with one of those counters, wearing white clothes and a mask. He looked like a cosmonaut."

"We should all dress like that around here."

"'What are you doing in my garden?' I shouted. He came to the door and started speaking to me in Russian."

"Who was he?"

"He told me that he was an American and he didn't speak Ukrainian."

"An American? What did he want?"

"Some of my onions. He told me he was a scientist and he wanted to do a test on them."

"Did you give him some?"

"I did, but only to teach him a lesson in hospitality. This American, he was trespassing on my property, wearing a mask, like the very air he's stealing isn't good enough for him."

"Maybe he'll come back and put some fear into you."

"There's nothing to be afraid of here." Her fingers fluttered over the fabric daisies and carnations. On the bus, I had pictured myself draping the material around her waist, taking measurements, then cutting and stitching. Mama's fingers were so stiff and callused that I doubted she could thread a needle anymore. But now I was ready to leave.

She filled one of my plastic bags with onions. "Here. These'll make Mykola strong."

"Thank you, Mama." There was no sense in refusing.

"Soon the grandchildren will be here," she said.

"You just told me that, Mama."

"Healthy, playful kids, they are. Not a one of them sick."

"For now, maybe."

"They'll eat our berries. Drink water from the well."

"Halynka's not coming here, Mama." I gave her a swift kiss, my lips glancing her cheek, my hand grazing her sweater. It never ceases to shame me, this fear I have of touching my mother, of carrying the poison in her skin and clothes to my daughter. And I could tell by her rigid posture, her refusal to yield to my touch, that Mother was ashamed of me too, and that she had been ashamed outside when I stood stiffly in front of her and Ganna.

"Mama, would you do something for me?"

"Eh?"

"If the American comes back, see if he can stop by here next Saturday, say at two o'clock."

"I know what I'll say if he tells me he didn't like my onions: 'Go back home and eat American onions, then!' We'll see what he has to say to that."

"Just ask him, all right, Mama? I'll come back again next week."

"Don't trouble yourself. I do just fine on my own."

I walked out the front way, down the dirt road, past the tottering, deserted houses of former neighbors. I was born in this village and lived here until I was twenty-three, when I moved into my husband's apartment in the nearby town. The windows of the cottages are still framed with hand-carved woodwork, but the paint is bleached and flaking, and many of the panes are broken. I usually avert my eyes as I walk past, out of respect for those who left their homes so quickly, in such disarray. But this time as I passed the Teslenkos', I turned, just for a second. An old loom was set up in the front room, strung with gray yarn, or perhaps just cobwebs, and something pink hung out of an opened bureau drawer. Their daughter, my daughter's best friend, died six months ago. I tossed the bag of onions down the side of the road and watched it disappear into the weeds.

At home, my husband was standing in the scruffy yard of our sinking apartment building in his tracksuit and house slippers, talking to the old women seated on the bench. He was gesturing wildly, knees bent and feet apart in an anchoring stance, as if he expected the world to take off at any moment. Mykola was once considered a handsome man — certain people were surprised he chose someone as plain as me to marry — but the neighbors do not notice his wavy hair and solid build anymore. I am grateful that we settled here with our own people after the accident, rather than among strangers in Kiev. Mykola can wobble about the yard shouting nonsense, and no one will talk about him behind his back. Here, people make allowances.

"The pistons need to be kept clean," he was saying. "It's the most important thing. The most important!" The women were nodding; like me, they have learned to pretend they understand his discourses on automobile repair. Mykola was one of the first men to participate in the cleanup at the reactor, and shortly afterward he began to suffer from dizzy spells. He was fired from his job as a mechanic five years ago, after he lost control of a car and crashed into a tree. That day marked the beginning of his confused thoughts and odd behavior.

"Be careful, I'm dirty," I said, backing away when Mykola reeled toward me.

"How's Mama?" one of the women asked about their old friend.

"As stubborn as ever." I sighed.

"We should all be as stubborn as her," said Evhenia Vlodimirovna. "She's living in her own home, happy as can be."

"She wants me to bring Halynka to visit her."

"Why shouldn't you?"

"Sure, why not?" echoed Maria Sergeyevna. "Not for long, of course."

Mykola picked up a candy wrapper and disappeared inside the building. I heard him shuffle up the stairs, then the whine of the garbage chute.

"I'm not taking her there," I said. "It's bad enough that I go."

"Listen to me, Yulia." Evhenia wagged her finger at me. "You know why they don't want us to move back?"

"Why?" I asked.

"It would cost too much to start up the town again after all these years. They'd have to redo the electricity and telephone lines and such. That's the only reason why. I saw it on television."

"An American scientist came by my mother's house," I said. "He's going to do a test on her onions."

"See?" Evhenia said. "He'll tell you there's nothing to worry about, and you can let your mother have a nice visit from her granddaughter before she dies."

"We'll see," I said.

Upstairs, I undressed in the bathroom, dumping everything in the bathtub, even my muddy boots. Then I turned on the shower, hot, and scrubbed my skin until it was red and raw. I lathered my hair with shampoo, stomped my clothes underfoot, and rinsed the boots, inside and out, until finally I felt clean again. Then I fetched Halynka from the Teslenkos' place, where she was watching television with Danylo, their son. Halynka left the apartment without saying goodbye, as if she were just going off to the bathroom.

"Grandmama says hello," I told her on the stairs, but she had nothing to say to that. She hasn't seen her grandmother since

Mama disappeared two years ago, leaving only a note that read: "I've gone home. Come and visit me." Halynka cried for days after that. Her grandmother practically raised her; I've worked as a bookkeeper for the grocery store since we moved here twelve years ago. Halynka didn't understand when I explained that she couldn't visit her grandmother because the village would make her sick. After a while, Halynka simply stopped asking about her. I suspect she feels abandoned by her grandmother, though she has never said this to me directly.

Halynka does not like to reveal herself to me. I began to notice this fact a year ago, when the Teslenkos' daughter was diagnosed with thyroid cancer. During the next six months, Halynka often slept on the floor next to Viktoria's bed, and even traveled with the family to the hospital in Kiev. Lilia, Viktoria's mother, told me that Halynka would rub her friend's back for hours to help ease the terrible pain. In the months since Viktoria's death, Halynka has spent most of her time outside of school with the Teslenkos, returning home only to sleep and eat. She has developed an attachment to Lilia that I envy, and a closeness to sixteen-year-old Danylo that worries me.

We cooked supper in silence, cutlets and fried potatoes. When the food was almost done, Halynka went to the balcony to call in her father, but he wasn't outside.

I found Mykola in the bedroom, lying in the dark. "Please," he whispered.

One of his migraines had descended, so I placed a damp towel on his forehead and shut the door. I would sleep on the couch, so as not to disturb him with my snoring. I knew that the next evening I would find the apartment in perfect order, the dishes put away, my clothes ironed, the rugs vacuumed. He has grown increasingly tidy since the car crash, taking over responsibilities I assumed in the early years of our marriage. But I try not to compare our present life to the past. We are two different people now; it is the only explanation that makes sense.

Coming home from work a few days later, I found Lilia Teslenko waiting for me in the yard. She was trim in her housedress, her short, dark hair neatly curled, and she smiled at me as I approached, her hand shading her eyes. Ignoring Mykola, who was talking with his lady friends, she asked me up for tea. She had sent Danylo and Halynka off on an errand, she told me, so that we could have a nice, quiet chat.

I sat at the kitchen table, dreading whatever it was she had to say.

"I haven't taken the opportunity, Yulia, to express how grateful I am that my Viktoria had such a wonderful friend as Halynka," she said as we sipped our tea.

"Viktoria was a precious gift to Halynka," I said. "She misses her terribly."

'Yes, I know." Lilia looked into her cup. "She often talks to me, and to Danylo, about her feelings, her grief. It has been difficult for all of us."

I was silent, steeling myself.

"Yulia, I'm worried about Halynka." She met my eyes. "I feel she depends on me and Danylo too much. It's as if she expects us to be her family. As if she hopes to take over Viktoria's place in our hearts."

"I'm sure she would never expect that," I said. But in truth, I wasn't sure of this at all.

"Perhaps I'm overstating it. But I am worried about her, and I just don't have the energy . . ." Her hands were laced tightly on the table. "To be frank, I don't want another daughter. And Danylo doesn't want a sister, or a girlfriend — do you understand what I'm saying?"

I stood up. "I understand. I'm sorry Halynka has been such a burden."

"Oh, not a burden. Please, don't think that. But . . . I think she needs to spend more time with her family — with you, at least."

I felt a surge of protectiveness for my husband. Why were his eccentricities more shameful than Viktoria's illness, when they both flowed from the same source?

"I'll make sure she doesn't bother you anymore," I said. "You've had a difficult enough time. I should have intervened earlier."

Halynka came home an hour later and went straight to her room. Finding her lying on the bed, I sat down and squeezed her shoulder. The narrow angel wings of her back rose up in defense, and I moved my hand away.

"I had a talk with Lilia Teslenko today," I said.

"I know," she said. Her voice was small and weary.

"I told Lilia that I wanted you to visit them less often. Your father and I hardly see you."

"I want to go stay with Grandmama for the summer," she said.

"Darling, you know I won't let you go there."

"There are some little kids who spend the whole summer with their grandparents," she said.

"Their parents are making a mistake. Those children will get sick, like Viktoria."

"I don't care if I get sick."

"Halynka, don't say that." I longed to cradle her thin body in my arms, but I thought of my own need to protect myself from my mother — an urge perhaps less warranted than my daughter's need to wall herself off from me — and I restrained myself.

"Papa wouldn't care if I went to Grandmama's," she said. "He doesn't even notice me."

"Halynka, that's not true." But in a way it was. As he slowly lost his mind, Mykola had become more and more perplexed by Halynka, avoiding her until they were like neighbors in a communal apartment. "We would both miss you very much."

"I've never even seen the place where I was born," she said. Her voice was high and slow; she was drifting off to sleep.

"It was just like any other Soviet town. There was nothing special about it." This was true, except, of course, that it had been our home. But I didn't want her to get any romantic notions about the town. I wanted her to look ahead to the future, to go to college, to move away, to Kiev or even to Europe. I wanted her to forget that she had been born in a place so elusive and unnatural that its entire population had disappeared overnight.

"Drink, drink," I heard my mother say as I approached her house the next Saturday.

A man was sitting at the kitchen table, his body covered in brilliant white, from his jumpsuit to a cloth mask that revealed only his eyes — brown, crinkled at the edges — to a stiff white cap. Mama was wafting a cup of tea under his nose. Between them lay several onion stalks, a notebook and pen, and a tape recorder, its spools turning.

"Please turn that off," I said.

"I was hoping to interview you and your mother," the man said.

His Russian was purer than my own. "My name is George. George Hayes. I'm an environmental toxicologist." He rose, and I saw that he was wearing rubber gloves.

"This is Yulia, my daughter," Mama said.

I had no intention of talking to a stranger about my life, and I felt protective of my mother's privacy as well. "Please," I said. "We don't want to be recorded."

He turned off the machine and we both sat down.

"Go on, tell her," Mama said. "Tell her what you told me about my onions."

"I ran a Geiger counter over them, and there's no question they're highly contaminated. She shouldn't be eating anything from that garden. She shouldn't drink the well water or burn wood from the forest. She shouldn't be living here at all."

"I've told her all of this a thousand times," I said.

"Tell her the rest," Mama said.

"I did some tests on these onions," the American said. "Despite the radiation, or maybe even because of it, they're quite robust. You can tell just by the size and color, but the cell structure and nutritional value are both strong as well."

"It's like I told you, they're even better than before," Mama said.

"What difference does it make, if they're going to make her sick?" I said.

"Well, yes, exactly. There's no doubt they're inedible," he said.

"He says it's healthy," Mama said.

"Not healthy, exactly . . . let me explain. I've been testing mice in the area, and I've found that they're actually becoming bigger and stronger with each generation." He spoke quickly, with increasing fervor. "All over the zone I'm finding these amazing examples of nature's ability to preserve itself, and even to advance genetically. But the acceleration we see in these onions — and that I've noticed in my mice — is abnormal. It may lead to mutations as the years go by."

"I'll give you some tomatoes when they're ready, and potatoes in the fall," Mama said. "Real beauties. I'll make you some soup."

I scraped back my chair. "May I speak to you outside?"

"Of course," the scientist said.

We stood by the garden fence. "I want you to stay away from my mother," I said.

"Stay away?"

"You're confusing her, and I'm the one who has to cope with her."

"I'm sure I can make her understand —"

"She's trying to talk me into bringing my thirteen-year-old daughter here for a visit."

"Oh, you shouldn't do that."

"Of course not. But she points to her onions, her berries, her clear water, and she tells me there can't possibly be anything wrong with them, because they look healthy and they taste good."

"But doesn't she know . . ."

"She ran away from our new home seven times in the first ten years after we moved, until she finally convinced the guard to let her back in. She's determined to die here. No, she doesn't understand. She doesn't believe that something she can't see can hurt her."

He shook his head. "I guess it would be hard to argue with that point of view."

"Her friends' grandchildren visit them every summer. The parents let their kids drink the dirty water and breathe the dirty air, and she thinks I'm unreasonable for not letting my daughter join them." I frowned at him. "The wind goes right through that mask of yours. I can see it."

He looked away. "It's better than nothing. Would you like me to bring you some gear?"

I shook my head. "I don't worry about myself."

"For your daughter's sake, you should."

I turned back toward the house.

"I won't confuse your mother anymore, I promise," he called after me. "In fact I'll try to talk some sense into her."

"Good luck," I said over my shoulder. "I've been trying to do that for the past twelve years."

I thought I would wait another month before returning to the village. My visits seemed only to agitate my mother and myself, and I knew there was nothing I brought that she truly needed or even wanted. Her little community of elderly squatters — there are about ten of them — gathers on Sundays at the village prayer house, and there is a delivery of bread twice a week. Sometimes the old men share the fish they catch in the polluted river with Mama and the other women. A doctor comes by to check on their health and distribute their pensions, and some teenage boys bring them provisions for a fee. It is a pleasant life for my mother, and perhaps a more peaceful end than might have been predicted for a child who was born in the aftermath of the famine and grew up during the German occupation.

There was another reason I stayed away: the children would be arriving soon. I did not want to see the wistful expression on my mother's face as she fed them bread with jam made from contaminated cranberries. I did not want to see them playing in the sun, their little bodies soaking up the poison that was resting in my own daughter's body, waiting to attack.

In the next two weeks, I felt hopeful that life was getting back to normal. Halynka began to come home straight from school and study with her bedroom door ajar, music playing softly. She told me shyly one day that she was going to be presented with an award for her high marks. I watched her walk across the school stage, fresh and pretty in her pale blue dress, a matching ribbon trailing in her shiny brown hair. There was a moment of silence for the three students who had died in the past year, Viktoria and two others. Lilia Teslenko approached us afterward, her eyes brimming with tears, Danylo at her side. I'm ashamed to say that I felt a certain satisfaction when Halynka pulled away from the woman's embrace.

On the first day of summer vacation, Halynka was gone when I returned from work. When she still hadn't come home by the time supper was ready, I called down to Mykola and the old women from the balcony. "I saw her walk off this morning, and I haven't seen her since," Evhenia Vlodimirovna yelled. Mykola only gazed at me blankly. I went to the Teslenkos', and Lilia woke Danylo from a nap, but he said he hadn't seen Halynka all day.

Mykola was agitated during supper, giving me a long lecture on carburetors and crankshafts. While I cleaned up the kitchen, he pulled the chairs away from the table and ran his homemade vacuum over the rug again and again. I looked up from the dishes and was startled to see a man standing in the hallway, dressed in tan pants and a blue pullover shirt. As I moved toward Mykola to snap off the machine, I realized it was the American scientist, stripped of his protective clothing.

"I'm sorry — I knocked but there was no answer," he said. He was balding, and his face was round, childlike, though he was at least forty.

"Pleased to make your acquaintance," Mykola said when I introduced them. Sometimes strangers provoke him to emerge momentarily from his little world.

"I was just at the entrance of the zone," the American said. "Your daughter's there."

"What?" I cried. "Where is she now?"

"Oles is holding her there. She said she wanted to see her grandmother, but he wouldn't let her in. Did you tell her that she could go there?"

"No, no, of course not."

"Have you come from Moscow?" Mykola asked. "Have you come for the cleanup?"

"The cleanup?"

"George is American, Mykola," I said. "He's a scientist."

"Your daughter wouldn't let me drive her home. Can I take you there?"

"I would be so grateful if you would," I said, grabbing my purse. "Mykola, I'll be home soon with Halynka."

The American drove an old Lada that stalled frequently as we drove along the wide dark road toward the town. George told me that he was a professor back in Boston but had studied in Moscow when he was young and returned there often to work with Russian scientists. He had been living here in Ukraine for a couple of months, renting an apartment in New Martinovichi and going into the zone every day to collect samples for his experiments.

"Your family back in America must miss you," I said.

"Well, I'm divorced, and I don't have any children. But I suppose my parents miss me."

"I'm sure they're proud of the work you do."

"They don't understand what I do." He smiled at me. "Just like your mother. I've been talking to her, by the way. I've been trying to convince her that it would be dangerous for your daughter to visit her."

"I appreciate that, but I think you're wasting your time. She's a stubborn old woman. Unfortunately, as you've found out, my daughter takes after her."

The border crossing was a circle of light surrounded on all sides by darkness, the tall abandoned buildings of the town rising like black monoliths in the distance. Halynka was sitting inside the little guard station with Oles, drinking tea.

"Halynka," I said. "Your father and I were worried sick about you."

"I was going to visit Grandmama." I noticed a duffel bag by her chair, packed full.

"I told her she couldn't go anywhere without her parents' permission," Oles said.

"Thank you, Oles. Halynka knew she was forbidden to come here." I tugged her roughly by the arm. "Hurry up. We've taken enough of Mr. Hayes's time already."

We rode back in silence, save for the rattling of the car and its tendency to putter to a stop every few kilometers. Halynka sat in the back seat and stared out the window. For a moment I imagined that we were an American family on vacation, driving through Colorado or California, looking for a hotel where we could spend the night. It was a silly fantasy, and not one that I wished would come true. Americans had their own problems, after all. George had had a wife and had somehow failed to keep her. My husband and I loved each other, in our peculiar way, and our precious daughter was healthy and safe.

Back at home, I thanked George for his help and followed Halynka up to her bedroom.

"Young lady, I want you to explain why you ran away," I said.

"I wanted to see Grandmama." She was pulling clothes out of her bag, not looking at me.

"You know, your grandmother could have stayed here, but she didn't. She decided to leave us."

Halynka looked at me with tears in her eyes. "Does she know about Vika?"

"Yes, darling, I told her. But she doesn't understand what made Viktoria sick."

"Maybe she's right. Maybe it wasn't the town. Maybe Vika got sick for no reason."

"It's possible, sweetheart, but you know what the doctors said."

"I was going to talk to Grandmama about her."

"You could write a letter and I could take it to her. Would you like that?"

"I don't want to write her a letter. I want to talk to her."

"I wish I could let you, darling. Would you like to talk to me instead?"

She shook her head.

I left her room and went out on the balcony. Down below, Mykola was bent over the American's car, his hands darting like a pianist's under the hood. George shone a flashlight and handed tools to Mykola. The old women watched from their bench. The windows of the other buildings in the settlement were lit up, gold and flickering blue boxes. Children were playing ball off on the horizon, barely visible against the black sky and black earth, their cries punctuating the still air. Other men gathered at the car, shaking George's hand, and Mykola began to narrate his gestures for the benefit of the crowd. A man lit a cigarette for George. Slender plumes of smoke drifted in the dim light, disappearing into the blackness.

Two little blond girls in summer dresses were playing in the sunlit field when I emerged from the pine forest the following Saturday. One dropped, disappearing into the tall grass, and then the other stumbled about with her eyes closed until she tripped over her friend. When I approached, they stared at me, still as statues, waiting until I had crossed the field before continuing their game.

My mother met me at the door. She had made a dress from the fabric I'd brought; the carnations and daisies widened across her broad belly. "What do you have?" she asked, grabbing my bags.

"Aren't you even going to say hello?" I asked.

She pushed past me. "Tara, Olya, come here!" The little girls ran up to her from the field. "Girls, take these things to Grandmama, and tell her this is what you're to eat. All right?" The girls looked into the bags at the flour and salt, the sticks of wood, and nodded solemnly. "Go on home, now."

"What was that all about?" I asked.

"Ganna doesn't feed them right," Mama said, settling heavily into her chair.

"Oh?"

"That American's been coming around, talking to us, taking pictures."

"Has he?" I wondered if he had told Mama about Halynka's attempt to visit her, and decided he was probably more discreet than that.

"Here, I want you to see this." She picked up a photograph from the table. Her face was in the center of the picture, unsmiling, determined. "He gave this to me yesterday." The photo was printed on thick paper in tones of green, and the image was strewn with faint white dots. "See the snow?" she said. "The American said it's radiation. He said he has a special camera that can see it."

I stared in fascination at the photograph. It did look as if snow were falling inside the house, swirling around my mother, speckling her face.

"Yulia, do you think the American is an honest man?" Mama asked as she fiddled with a handkerchief.

I put the photograph aside. "Yes, Mama. I do think he's an honest man."

She stood up. "I don't want you to come here anymore."

"Why not, Mama?"

"I should never have told you to visit." Her voice quavered, and she brushed her eyes with the back of her hand.

"Mama." I reached for her, but she pushed me away.

"The American and I showed the picture to Ganna, but she just laughed. Stupid old fool. That's what we all are — stupid old fools."

"The girls will be all right," I said. "They'll go home soon."

Mama cupped her face in her hands. "Halynka was outside the entire day after the accident."

"Shh, shh, Mama." I held her shoulders, trying to draw her near, but she shrugged me away. "Halynka's all right," I said. "She's healthy."

"She used to have such a terrible cough, it would keep her awake at night."

"She hasn't had it for a long time."

"Her little friend died, the blond girl. They were the same age." She crumpled against me, sobbing.

I held her tight, wanting to both shake her and kiss her. After twelve long years, she finally understood. She had only needed to see it with her own eyes.

I took the picture home. "Come with me," I said to Mykola, and he followed me up to the apartment. Halynka watched in surprise as I turned off the television and placed the photograph on the coffee table. "You wanted to see your grandmother," I said. "I brought you a picture of her. Don't touch it — it's dirty. But I want you to look at it, closely." Then I went into the bathroom to cleanse myself.

When I came out in my robe, Mykola and Halynka were facing each other on the couch. "They gave us two counters to keep track of the levels, one in your boot, the other in your pocket," Mykola said, slapping his chest. He jumped to his feet. "Into the uniform. Heavy aprons, lined with lead. Gloves. A big mask." He pantomimed pulling on the uniform. "Then up to the roof of the reactor. Five minutes at a time, that's all we had." He pushed an imaginary shovel against the carpet. "Quick, quick, push through the rubble, look for the rods. Watch your step. Helicopters loud overhead." He whirled around, staring at the ground. "Here's some." He made a scooping motion. "Collect as much as you can. Dark rods. Find the trash bin. Careful — it'll burn through your boots. Hard to see. Time's running out, hurry up." He dashed around the living room, staring intently at the ground. "Ah, here's one. And here's some more. They're calling now, time's up." He tossed the shovel aside. "They grab the counters, no chance to read them." He collapsed into a chair, panting. "Time for a smoke."

I stood at the edge of the room, watching as Halynka helped Mykola light a cigarette. "Good job, Papa," she said softly, and retreated to the couch.

Mykola wiped sweat from his forehead as he puffed smoke into the room. "Just enough time for a smoke. Then up to the roof. Up to the roof again."

When I came home from work on Monday, Halynka was lying on the couch reading, and there was a stack of library books on the floor beside her. For a moment I was hopeful that she would spend the summer absorbed in literature, but when I flipped through some of the books, I saw that she was reading about the accident. The writing was dense and technical, illustrated with complicated graphs. When I asked if she found the books interesting, she only shrugged.

The next evening after supper we took the bus to New Martinovichi. The American answered his door wearing his casual clothes. "Yulia," he said. "And Halynka. Hello. Please come in."

"I'm sorry to stop by unannounced," I said. "I got your address from Oles."

"I'm glad you're here. Would you like some tea?" The apartment was terribly messy. Papers were strewn about the tables and floor, and there were half-filled cups of coffee everywhere.

"I'll get the tea," I said. "Halynka has some questions she'd like to ask you."

"Of course." He cleared a space on the kitchen table and they sat down.

I moved about the apartment, gathering the dirty dishes, and washed them slowly. I heard my daughter's shy voice gaining confidence as she asked the American about safety procedures at the reactor and the odds of a meltdown happening again. George answered her questions directly and thoroughly, using simple terms. I could tell he was being careful not to frighten her, yet expressing concern about the damage caused by the accident and the possibility that someday it could happen again, here or in another part of the world.

I served them tea and sat quietly at the other end of the table.

"Were you alive when it happened, Halynka?" George asked when she had run out of questions.

Halynka looked at me. "I had just had my first birthday. Right, Mama?"

"Yes. We had a party the day after the accident. Before we knew anything was wrong."

"No one had any idea, did they?" George asked.

I shook my head. "They waited two days to evacuate us." I felt my throat tightening.

"Were you scared?" Halynka asked.

"Not scared . . . it's hard to describe." They both looked at me, waiting. "We should be going," I said, standing up.

George insisted on driving us home. The car ran smoothly, and he praised my husband's repair job. In front of our building, Mykola ran up and opened Halynka's door, then mine. He greeted the American and trotted off. "Wait, Papa," Halynka called after him.

"Thank you for talking to her," I said to George.

"I can only tell her the facts. She'll have to find out the rest from you."

His tape recorder was lying on the seat between us. "Could I borrow this?" I asked.

"Sure. I won't need it anymore." He showed me how to use the machine, testing it on his own voice. Before I got out of the car, George told me that he was returning to America in a few days but that he hoped to see me next summer. As I climbed the stairs behind my husband and daughter, I imagined George walking into his empty, quiet apartment in Boston. Entering my own home, I smiled, for it occurred to me that he too was probably feeling sorry for me as he drove away.

"Halynka?" my mother shouted. "This is Grandmama."

"You don't need to talk so loud, Mama," I whispered. We were sitting at her kitchen table and I was holding the tape recorder up to her mouth.

"Halynka, this is Grandmama talking to you on the machine," she shouted. "Your mama said you'll be able to hear me. I want to say hello to you. I hope you're doing well. Everything's fine here. My tomatoes are growing. The flowers are blooming." She paused and looked out the window, breathing loudly through her nose. "I heard about Viktoria. I'm so sorry, my dear." She looked at me.

"You can stop if you like."

She turned back to the machine and cleared her throat. "I told your mama that she wasn't allowed to visit me anymore, but she came anyway. She said you can talk back to me on the machine if you want. I would like that very much. I miss you terribly, my darling."

When we had finished, I walked down the road in front of the house. Reaching the main street, I turned toward the town rather than heading back toward the border. I held the tape recorder to my mouth and began to speak.

"Halynka, I'm walking into your hometown. Since I won't let you come here, I thought I would describe it for you. I myself haven't been here since we left. I was afraid to come here, to see our old home looking so empty and desolate.

"The reactor is off in the distance, towering over the town. There are two great smokestacks, striped, and huge buildings shaped like a mountain. From here it all looks normal. This was a young city, built for workers in the plant. So many of us were just starting our families, and there were lots of children here. I'm passing some apartment buildings now. It almost seems as if they're not empty at all. There are curtains on the windows, and I can see furniture inside.

"Here's a store where I used to shop. I brought you with me, of course." I looked through the window. "There are still a few cans of food on the shelves — I recognize the old paper labels. I remember the day you first walked into the store by yourself, holding my finger. The women behind the counters clapped, and I was so proud.

"I'm turning onto the street where we used to live." I heard some birds chirping, but that was all. "I can see the Ferris wheel between some buildings. It was brought in especially for May Day. Your papa and I had planned to take you to the carnival. But of course we all left just a few days before.

"Here it is, our building." My voice caught, and I lowered the recorder from my mouth. I stared up at the window, waiting until my breathing was even. "It's just six stories high, and we were on the top floor. It looks like the pink curtains I sewed have faded. We left the apartment neat as a pin. Your father used to tease me about the way I tidied up before we went anywhere. I swept and did the dishes that day, even though we only had a few hours to get ready."

I peered through a scratched plastic window. "The entryway is dark and dingy, paper and garbage everywhere. We stood there waiting for the buses — by that time we knew better than to stand outside. It was hot and crowded, and you cried."

I had planned to go upstairs, look for the spare key under the doormat, enter our home, and describe it for Halynka. But now that I was here, I was frightened. The apartment might have been looted; at the very least it would be dusty and terribly quiet. I turned back to the road, knowing that I had come as close as I could.

"The accident happened in the middle of the night, as George told you. In the morning there was a steady dark line of smoke coming out of the reactor. Your papa told me he had heard an explosion. I had slept through it. We turned on the radio, but nothing was said about it on the news.

"Of course we didn't have time to think about the reactor. It was an important day: your first birthday party. I put on my nicest dress, and your papa wore a suit and tie. I had sewn you a yellow dress edged with lace.

"We walked over to the park around noon. I'm heading there now. It was a warm spring day and everyone was outside. Women were shopping at the market, and children were playing. There was no sign that anything was wrong. Here, here is the park. Back then the grass was worn away, but now it's overgrown with weeds.

"Your Uncle Ivanko butchered a pig the week before, and my friends and I prepared sausages, dumplings, and meat pies. Your grandmama made pancakes, and Lilia Teslenko baked a four-layer frosted torte. We had gone to little Viktoria's birthday celebration just a month before at their home in the village. Lilia was a great beauty, and when we were growing up, I used to be jealous of her. But after we both had baby girls, we became friendly. You and Viktoria took to each other immediately. Even when you were just a few months old, you seemed to have your own private language, cooing and laughing together.

"All of our friends were at the party. Most of them worked at the reactor, like your papa. There was talk of the explosion, and we watched the dark smoke rising into the sky. Someone said that foamy water had been gushing onto their street and that children were playing in it. But no one was really worried. You have to understand, we never imagined that anything bad would happen to us, and we were sure we would be notified if there was any reason to be concerned. But I still feel guilty for taking you outside that day. Sometimes I wonder if I would have been more sensible if I hadn't been distracted by the party. Maybe we would have all stayed inside with our windows closed. Sometimes I wonder if Lilia blames me for this.

"In the late afternoon we woke you up for the ceremony — your first haircut. Your papa stood you on a chair at the head of the table, and everyone gathered around. Your grandmother took up the scissors and snipped off a lock from your forehead. She did the same at the back of your head, and then on each side, so that she had cut from north, south, east, and west, the four directions of the world. Then she passed the scissors to your Uncle Ivanko, and it was his turn. Then Lilia and Yuri Teslenko cut your hair.

"You were always a good baby, rarely fussing, but on that day you were especially quiet and still, as if you realized something important was happening — almost, I thought later, as if you knew that everything was about to change. To me, your haircut was a reminder that you would grow up and leave me, just as I had left my own mother. I got a little teary, and your papa hugged me, and everyone laughed, understanding why I was sad."

I began to walk back toward the border. I was ready to see the look on Halynka's face when she heard her grandmother's voice. And, I confess, I was eager for my daughter to hear my own story for the first time.

"The evacuation began the next day. They told us that we would be able to come home in three days. The envelope with your locks of hair was the only memento I packed when we left. I suppose part of me realized that we might never return, though I don't remember thinking this at the time. I threw the envelope away later, crying as I did. I threw away everything we had brought with us from the town. Of course you didn't understand when I tried to explain that I had thrown out your favorite doll because it was dirty. How cruel I seemed to you. Do you understand now, Halynka? I didn't feel I had a choice. I had to get rid of everything from the past."

I turned off the recorder. The bus was pulling up to the gates, and Oles waved and shouted at me to hurry. I began to jog, laughing at the spectacle I was making, a middle-aged woman running to catch a bus, as if in my rush to leave the town I had forgotten myself, just for a moment, and thought that I was still a young girl.

MARISA SILVER

What I Saw from Where I Stood

FROM THE NEW YORKER

DULCIE IS AFRAID OF FREEWAYS. She doesn't like not being
able to get off whenever she wants, and sometimes I catch her holding her breath between exits, as if she's driving through a graveyard. So even though the party we went to last week was miles
from our apartment in Silver Lake, we drove home on the surface
streets.

I was drunk, and Dulcie was driving my car. She'd taken one look
at me as we left the party, then dug her fingers into my front pocket
and pulled out my keys. I liked the feel of her hand rubbing against
me through my jeans; she hadn't been touching me much lately.

I cranked open the window to clear my head as we drove
through Santa Monica. Nice houses. Pretty flowers. Volvos. Dulcie
and I always say we'd never want to live out here in suburbia, but
the truth is, we can't afford to, not on our salaries. Dulcie's a sec-
ond-grade teacher in Glendale, and I'm a repairman for the telephone company.

When we reached Hollywood, things got livelier. There were
skinny guitar punks patrolling the clubs on the strip with their
pudgy girlfriends in midriff tops and thigh-high black skirts. A lot
of big hair, big breasts, boredom. Further east, there were boys
strutting the boulevard, waiting to slip into someone's silver Mer-
cedes and make a buck. One leaned against a fire hydrant and
picked at his sallow face, looking cold in a muscle T-shirt.

We hit a red light at Vermont, right next to the hospital where
Dulcie lost the baby, a year ago. She'd started cramping badly one
night. She was only six months pregnant. I called the emergency

room, and the attendant said to come right over. By the time we got there, the doctors couldn't pick up a heartbeat. They gave Dulcie drugs to induce labor, and the baby was born. He was blue. He was no bigger than a football.

Dulcie looked up at the hospital and then back at the road. She's a small girl, and she sank behind the wheel, getting even smaller. I didn't say anything. The light turned green. She drove across Vermont and I nodded off.

I woke up when a car plowed into us from behind. My body flew toward the windshield, then ricocheted back against my seat. Dulcie gripped the wheel, staring straight ahead out the window.

"Something happened," she said.

"Yeah," I heard myself answer, although my voice sounded hollow. "We had an accident."

We got out to check the damage and met at the back of the car. "It's nothing," Dulcie said as we studied the medium-sized dent on the fender. It was nothing to us, anyway; the car was too old and beat-up for us to feel protective of it.

Behind me, I heard the door of a van slide open. I hadn't thought about the people who'd hit us, hadn't even noticed if they'd bothered to stop. I started to wave them off. They didn't need to get out, apologize, dig around for the insurance information they probably didn't have. But when I turned, there were four or five men in front of me. They were standing very close. They were young. I was beginning to think that Dulcie and I should just get back into our car and drive away, when the van's engine cut out and a tall guy wearing a hooded sweatshirt called back toward it, "Yo, Darren! Turn it on, you motherfucker!"

His cursing seemed to make his friends nervous. Two of them looked at their feet. One hopped up and down like a fighter getting ready for a bout. Someone was saying, "Shit, shit, shit," over and over again. Then I heard "Do it, do it!" and a short, wide kid with a shaved head and glow-in-the-dark stripes on his sneakers pulled out a gun and pointed it at my face. It didn't look like the guns in movies. Dulcie screamed.

"Don't shoot. Please don't shoot us!" Her voice was so high it sounded painful, as if it were scraping her throat.

"Your keys!" the tall one shouted. "Give us your motherfucking keys!"

Dulcie threw the keys on the ground at their feet. "Please! I don't have any money!"

"I'll get it," I heard myself say, as if I were picking up the tab at a bar. I was calm. I felt like I was underwater. Everything seemed slow, and all I could hear was my own breathing. I reached into my back pocket and pulled out my wallet. I took out the bills and handed them over. The tall guy grabbed the money and ran back to the van, which made me feel better until I noticed that the kid with the shaved head was still pointing the gun at me.

That's when I got scared. As though someone had thrown a switch, all the sound returned, loud and close. I heard the cars roaring past on Sunset. I heard Dulcie screaming, "No! No! No!" I heard an argument erupt between two of the guys. "Get in their car! Get in their fucking car or I'll do you too!" I grabbed Dulcie's hand, and I pulled her around the front of our car, crouching low, so I could feel the heat of the engine under the hood. The van revved up. I stood, bringing Dulcie up with me, and there, on the driver's side, no more than three feet from me, was the kid with the shaved head. He had the gun in one hand and Dulcie's keys in the other. I could see sweat glistening over the pimples on his face.

"Hey!" he said, looking confused. "What the fuck?"

Then it was as if I skipped a few minutes of my life, because the next thing I knew, Dulcie and I were racing down a side street toward the porch lights of some bungalows. We didn't look back to see if we were being followed. Sometimes Dulcie held my hand, sometimes we were separated by the row of parked cars. We had no idea where we were going.

After the police and their questions, and their heartfelt assurance that there was nothing at all they could do for us, we took a cab back to our apartment in Silver Lake. Dulcie was worried because the crackheads — that's what the police called them — had our keys, and our address was on the car registration. But the police had told us that the carjackers wouldn't come after us — that kind of thing almost never happened.

Still, Dulcie couldn't sleep, so we sat up all night while she went over what had happened — she'd seen the van on the street earlier, but hadn't it been in front of us, not behind? Why had they chosen our car, our sorry, broken-down mutt of a car? How close had we come to being shot?

"We saw them," she said. "We know what they look like."

"They weren't killers. They were thieves. There's a difference, I guess," I said.

"No," she said, twisting her straight brown hair around her finger so tightly the tip turned white. "It doesn't make sense."

"It doesn't. But it happened."

Dulcie needs things to be exact. You have to explain yourself clearly when you're around her, so she's probably a good teacher. For a minute I wondered whether she wished we had been shot, just for the sake of logic.

She'd done this after losing the baby too, going over and over what she might have done to kill it. Had she exercised too much? Not enough? Had she eaten something bad? She wanted an answer, and she needed to blame someone; if that person turned out to be her, that would still be better than having no one to blame at all. A few days after the delivery, a hospital social worker called to check on her. She reassured Dulcie that what had happened hadn't been her fault. It was a fluke thing, the woman said. She used the word "flukish."

"I should have noticed them tailing me," Dulcie said now. "How could I not notice a car that close?"

"Don't do that," I told her. "Don't think about what could have happened."

"I have to think about it," she said. "How can you not think about it? We were this close," she said, holding her fingers out like a gun and aiming at my chest.

I drove Dulcie's car to work the next day. When I got home that night, Dulcie had moved the mattress from our bed into the living room, where it lay in the middle of the floor, the sheets spilling over onto the carpet. She'd taken a personal day to recover from the holdup. Her eyes were red, and she looked as though she'd been crying all afternoon.

"It's the rat," she said. "He's back."

A month earlier, a rat had burrowed and nested in the wall behind our bed. Every night it scratched a weird, personal jazz into our ears. We told the landlord, and he said he would get on it right away, which meant *You'll be living with that rat forever, and if you don't like it there're ten other people in line for your apartment.* I checked around the house to make sure the rat couldn't find a way inside. I

patched up a hole underneath the sink with plywood and barri-
caded the space between the dishwasher and the wall with old towels. After Dulcie was sure that there would be no midnight visitor
eating our bananas, she was okay with the rat. We even named him
— Mingus.

She wasn't okay with it anymore.

"He's getting louder. Closer. Like he's going to get in this time,"
she said.

"He can't get in. There's no way."

"Well, I can't sleep in that room."

"It's a small apartment, Dulcie." The living room was smaller
than the bedroom, and the mattress nearly filled it.

"I can't do it, Charles. I can't."

"All right. We can sleep anywhere you want," I said.

"I want to sleep in the living room. And I want you to change the
message on the answering machine," she said. "It has my voice on
it. It should have a man's voice."

"You're worried about the rat hearing your voice on the machine?"

"Don't make fun of me, okay? Those guys know where we live."

Later that night, I discovered that she wanted to sleep with all
the lights on.

"I want people to know we're home," she said. "People don't
break in if they think you're there."

We were lying on the floor on our mattress. She felt tiny, so delicate that I would crush her if I squeezed too hard or rolled the
wrong way.

"You don't mind, do you?" she said. "About the light. Is it too
bright?"

She'd let me throw one of my shirts, an orange one, over the
fixture hanging from the ceiling. It gave the room a muffled, glowy
feel.

"No," I said. I kissed her forehead. She didn't turn to me. Since
the baby, we've had a hard time getting together.

Dulcie sat up again. "Maybe it's a bad idea," she said. "Maybe a
thief will see the light on at 4 A.M. and think that we're actually out
of town. I mean, who leaves their light on all night when they're
home?"

"No one."

"You know," she said, "I saw in a catalogue once that you could buy an inflatable man to put in a chair by your window. Or in your car. You could put him in the passenger seat if you were driving alone."

She looked at me, but I didn't know what to say. To me, driving with a plastic blow-up doll in the seat next to you seemed very peculiar.

"Lie down," I said, stroking her back beneath her T-shirt. Her skin was smooth and warm.

She lay down next to me. I turned over on my stomach and laid my hand across her chest. I liked the feel of the small rises of her breasts, the give of them.

Dulcie's milk had come in two days after the delivery. The doctor had warned her that this would happen and had prescribed Valium in advance. I came home from work and found Dulcie, stoned, staring at her engorged breasts in the bathroom mirror. I'd never seen anything like it. Her breasts were like boulders, and her veins spread out across them like waterways on a map. Dulcie squeezed one nipple, and a little pearl of yellowish milk appeared. She tasted it.

"It's sweet," she said. "What a waste."

For the next two days, she lay on the couch holding packs of frozen vegetables against each breast. Sometimes we laughed about it, and she posed for a few sexpot pictures, with packs of peas pressed against her chest like pasties. Other times she just stared at the living room wall, adjusting a pack when it slipped. I asked her if her breasts hurt, and she said yes, but not in the way you'd think.

I slid my hand off Dulcie's chest, turned back over, and stared at the T-shirt on the light fixture.

"Did you know," she said, "that when you're at a red light the person next to you probably has a gun in his glove compartment?"

"Defensive driving," I said, trying for a joke.

"Statistically speaking, it's true. Until yesterday, I never thought about how many people have guns," Dulcie said. "Guns in their cars, guns in their pocketbooks when they're going to the market, guns . . ."

A fly was caught between the light and my T-shirt. I could see its shadow darting frantically back and forth until, suddenly, it was gone.

*

The next evening, as I was driving home from work, someone threw an egg at my car. I thought it was another holdup. I sucked in so much air that I started to choke and almost lost control. Two kids then ran by my window. One was wearing a Dracula mask and a cape. The other one had on a rubber monster head and green tights. I'd forgotten it was Halloween.

Dulcie takes holidays pretty seriously, and when I got home I expected to see a cardboard skeleton on the door, and maybe a carved pumpkin or two. Usually she greets the trick-or-treaters wearing a tall black witch hat that she keeps stashed in a closet the rest of the year. When she opens the door, she makes this funny cackling laugh, which is kind of embarrassing but also sweet. She's so waifish, there's not much about her that could scare anybody. But when I got home and climbed the outside stairs to our second-floor apartment, there was nothing on our door and the apartment was dark.

"What are you doing with all the lights off?" I asked when I got inside. She was sitting at the kitchen table, her hands folded in front of her as if she were praying.

"Shut the door," she said. "A whole pack of them just came. They must have rung the bell five times."

"They want their candy."

"We don't have any."

"Really? You didn't buy any?"

"Charles, we don't know who any of these people are," she said slowly, as if I were six years old. "I'm not going to open my door to perfect strangers."

"They're kids."

"What about the ones who come really late?" she asked. "All those teenagers. They're looking for trouble."

I sat down and reached across the table for her hands. "It's Halloween, Dulce. It's just kids having fun."

"Plenty of people aren't home on Halloween. This is just going to be one of those places where nobody's home."

The doorbell rang.

"Dulcie —"

"Sh-h-h!" She hissed at me like a cat.

"This is ridiculous." I got up.

"Please!" she called out after me.

The bell rang again. I grabbed a box of cookies from the shelf and went to the door. A little kid was walking away, but he turned back when he heard the door open. He was six, eight years old. An old man I recognized from the neighborhood, maybe his grandfather, stood a few steps behind him.

The boy wore a cowboy outfit — a fringed orange vest over a T-shirt with a picture of Darth Vader on it, jeans mashed down into plastic cowboy boots, and a holster sliding down over his narrow hips. He took a gun out of the holster and waved it around in the air.

"Bang," he said, without enthusiasm.

"You got me," I answered, putting my hands to my chest and pretending to die.

"It's a fake gun," the boy said. "No real bullets."

"You mean I'm not dead?" I tried to sound amazed, and I got a smile out of the kid.

The grandfather said something impatiently in another language, Russian or maybe Armenian.

"Trick or treat," the boy said quietly. He held out a plastic grocery sack with his free hand.

I looked into the bag. There were only a few pieces of candy inside. Suddenly the whole thing made me sad. I offered my box of mint cookies.

The boy looked back at his grandfather, who shook his head. "I'm only allowed to have it if it's wrapped," the boy said to me.

I felt like a criminal. "We didn't have a chance to get to the store," I said, as the boy holstered his gun and moved off with his grandfather.

When I went back inside, Dulcie was standing in the middle of the dark living room, staring at me. Three months after the baby died, I came home from work and found her standing in that same place. Her belly underneath her T-shirt was huge, much bigger than when she'd actually been pregnant. For one crazy second, I thought that the whole thing had been a mistake and that she was still pregnant. I felt a kind of relief I had never felt before. Then she lifted her shirt and took out a watermelon from underneath it.

A group of kids yelled "Trick or treat!" below us. They giggled. Someone said "Boo!" then there was a chorus of dutiful thank you's. I heard small feet pound up the rickety wooden stairway to the second-floor apartments. I walked over to Dulcie and put my arms around her.

"We can't live like this," I said.

"I can," she said.

Dulcie went back to work three days after the carjacking. I dropped her off at school in my car, and she arranged for one of her teacher friends to give her a lift home. I took it as a good sign, her returning to work. She complains about the public school system, all the idiotic bureaucracy she has to deal with, but she loves the kids. She's always coming home with stories about cute things they did, or about how quickly they picked up something she didn't think they'd understand the first time. She was named Teacher of the Year last spring, and a couple of parents got together and gave her this little gold necklace. Her school's in a rough part of Glendale. The necklace was a big deal.

She was home when I got off work, sitting on the couch. She waved a piece of pink paper in the air.

"What's that?" I said.

"We're not allowed to touch the children anymore," she said.

"What are you talking about?"

She told me that a parent had accused a teacher of touching his daughter in the wrong way. Social Services came in, the works. When they finally got around to questioning the girl, she told them the teacher had just patted her on the back because she answered a question right.

"Now the district's in a panic — they don't want a lawsuit every time some kid exaggerates. So no touching the students."

"That's nuts," I said. "Those kids need to be hugged every once in a while. They probably don't get enough affection at home."

"That's a racist generalization, Charles," she said. "Most of the parents try hard. They love their kids just as much as you and I would."

Neither of us said anything. Dulcie hadn't brought up the idea of our having kids since we'd lost the baby. She had just stepped on a grenade, and I was waiting through those awful seconds before it explodes.

"This is a fucked-up town," she said finally.

I wasn't sure what had made her say this. The school thing? The carjacking? "Maybe if we turn on the TV we'll catch a freeway chase," I said.

"Or a riot."

"Or a celebrity bio."

She started laughing. "That's the real tragedy," she said. "The celebrity bio."

We laughed some more. When we stopped, neither of us knew what to say.

"I'm not racist," I said at last.

"I know. I didn't mean that."

"I may be prejudiced against celebrities, though."

She squeezed out a smile. It was worth the stupid joke.

The next Saturday, Dulcie called an exterminator. She'd decided that we should pay for one out of our own pocket, because she'd read that some rats carry airborne viruses.

"People died in New Mexico," she said. "Children too."

It turns out that the exterminator you call to get rid of bugs is not the kind you call to get rid of a rat. There's a subspecialty — Rodent Removal. Our rodent remover was named Rod. Rod the Rodent Remover. I was scared of him already.

When he came to the door, he was wearing a clean, pressed uniform with his name on it. "Rod," I said. "Thanks for coming."

"It's really Ricardo, but I get more jobs as Rod. Ricardo is too hard for most people to remember. You have a problem with rats?" he said helpfully.

"Yeah. In here," I opened the door wider and led him into the apartment. "It's not really *in* the apartment, but we hear it from in here."

If Ricardo thought it was strange that the mattress was on the living room floor, he didn't say anything. Dulcie was waiting for us in the bedroom.

"It's there," Dulcie said, pointing to a gray smudge where the head of our bedframe met the wall. "He's in there."

Ricardo went over and tapped the wall with his knuckle. Dulcie held her breath. There was no sound from the rat.

"They usually leave the house during the day," Ricardo said.

"How does he get in?" Dulcie says.

Ricardo raised his finger toward the ceiling. "Spanish tile roof. Very pretty, but bad for the rat problem," he said. "They come in through the holes between the tiles."

"So there's nothing we can do?" Dulcie asked, alarmed.

"We can set a trap in the wall through the heating vent there,"

Ricardo said, pointing to the one vent in our entire apartment, which was, unhelpfully, in the hallway outside our bedroom.

"Then he'll die in the wall?"

"It's a bad smell for a few days, but then it goes away," Ricardo said.

I could see that none of this was making Dulcie feel any better.

"Or I can put a trap on the roof," Ricardo said.

"Do that," Dulcie said quickly.

"Okay," he said. "Now we have a plan."

He reached into his pockets and took out two yellow surgical gloves. Dulcie was horrified, the gloves confirming her suspicions about disease. But Ricardo smiled pleasantly. This was a guy who dealt with rats every day of his life, and it didn't seem to faze him.

"Why do they come inside?" Dulcie said as we followed Ricardo toward the door. "The rats. Why do they live in the walls? There's no food there."

"To keep warm," Ricardo said. "Sometimes to have their babies."

He smiled and gave us a courtly nod as I let him out. When I turned back, Dulcie was still staring at the closed door, her hand over her mouth.

"It's just a rat," I said. I touched her shoulder. She was shaking.

A month after the baby died, the mailman delivered a package that I had to sign for. We don't get a lot of packages, so it was an event. The box was from a company called La Tierra. The name sounded familiar, but I couldn't place it; I was about to call back into the apartment for Dulcie when I remembered. La Tierra was the name of the company that cremated the baby.

"What is it?" Dulcie said from behind me. "Who was at the door?"

I turned around. This will kill her, I thought.

"What is it?" she said again, holding out her hand.

I had no choice but to hand it to her. She looked at it. Her face crumpled. "It's so light," she said finally.

I went to put my arms around her, but she stepped back. Then she started laughing. Her laughter became the kind of giggling you can't turn off. She bit her lips and clenched her teeth, but the giggles kept coming back, as if they were tickling her insides in order to get out.

"You probably thought it was something from your mom," she said through her laughter. "Or some freebie from a computer com-

pany. Oh, my God," she said. "Can you believe this is our life?" I
smiled, but it was that weird, embarrassed smile you offer when you
feel left out of a joke.

We decided to take the ashes to the beach and scatter them on
the water. We drove out to the Ventura County line, to a beach
called El Pescador. You have to climb down a steep hillside to get
to it, and there's usually no one there, especially in the off season.
We parked and scrambled unsteadily down the trail. We were so
busy concentrating on not falling that we didn't see the ocean until we were at its level. We both got quiet for a moment. The water
was slate gray, pocked by the few white gulls that every so often
swooped down to the surface and then rose up again. There were
no boats in the ocean, only a couple of prehistoric oil derricks in
the distance.

"I think we should do it now," Dulcie said.

We opened the box. Inside was some Styrofoam with a hole
gouged out. Nestled inside that hole, like a tiny bird, was a plastic
bag filled with brown dust. There could not have been more than a
tablespoonful. I took the bag and handed the box to Dulcie. Then I
kicked off my shoes, rolled up my jeans, and walked out into the
water. When I was calf deep, I opened up the bag. I waited for
something to happen, for some gust of wind to kick up and take
the ashes out to sea. But the day was calm, so I finally dumped the
ashes into the water at my feet. A tiny wave moved them toward the
shore. I worried that the ashes would end up in the sand, where
somebody could step all over them, but then I felt the undertow
dragging the water back toward the sea.

"I think that's the bravest thing I've ever seen a person do,"
Dulcie said as I came out of the water.

As we headed back to the trail, she picked up a smooth stone and
slipped it into her pocket. Halfway up the path, she took the stone
out and let it drop to the ground.

A week after the holdup, the police called. They had found our stolen car. Once the kids run out of gas, the officer explained, they
usually abandon the car rather than pay for more. He gave us the
address of the car lot, somewhere in South Central.

"Go early in the morning," the officer warned. "Before they get
up."

"'They'?" I asked.

"You a white guy?" the policeman asked.

"Yeah."

"You want to be down there before wake-up time. Trust me."

Dulcie said it was a self-fulfilling prophecy. Everybody expected things to be bad, so people made them bad. She saw it at her school. The kids who were expected to fail, well, they blew it every time out, even if they knew the work cold.

Still, we took the officer's advice and went down to the lot at seven in the morning. I admit I was nervous, driving through those streets. You like to think you're more open-minded than that, but I guess I'm not. I kept thinking about drive-by shootings and gangs and riots and all the things you read about, thinking, Those things don't happen near where I live, so I'm okay.

We found our car. It was a mess. It had been stripped of everything; even the steering wheel was gone. There was every kind of fast-food wrapper scattered on the back seat, and French fries and old hamburger buns on the floor. You get hungry when you're high. It wasn't worth the price of towing, so we signed it over to the pound and left it there.

As I drove Dulcie to work, I told her the police had asked us to come identify the suspects in a lineup.

"But they'll know it was us who identified them," she said. "They know where we live."

"They were busy getting high. I don't think they were memorizing our address."

"I don't even remember what they looked like. It was dark."

"Once you see some faces, it might come back."

"Charles, don't make me do this. Don't make me!" she cried.

"I'm not going to make you do anything. Jesus. What do you think I am?"

She didn't answer me. I dropped her off at the school. She got out and walked toward the front door, then turned to wave at me, as if it were any regular day, as if we weren't living like some rat trapped in our own wall.

I took the day off. I'd already used up my sick days, and I knew we couldn't throw away the money, but I thought I'd go crazy if I had to be nice to a customer or listen to some technician talk about his bodacious girlfriend or his kid's troubles in school.

I didn't have a plan. I picked up a paper and got some breakfast at a hipster coffee shop on Silver Lake Boulevard. There were a lot of tattooed and pierced people eating eggs and bacon; they looked as though they were ending a night, not beginning a day. I tried to concentrate on my paper, but nothing sank in. Then I got back into my car. I ended up driving along Vermont into Griffith Park, past the roads where guys stop to cruise, all the way up to the Observatory. I parked in the empty lot and got out.

The Observatory was closed; it was still early. I was trying to think of something to do with myself when I saw a trail heading up into the hills. The path was well worn; on the weekends, it was usually packed with tourists and families making a cheap day of it. But that morning I had it to myself. I passed outcroppings where people could stand to look at the view. I wanted to walk. I walked for hours. I felt the sun rise up, and I saw the darkness that covered the canyons lift, as if someone were sliding a blanket off the ground.

By the time I stopped, others were on the trail — runners, or people walking their dogs, some kids who were probably playing hooky. I looked out over the canyon and thought about how I could go either way: I could stay with Dulcie and be as far away from life as a person could be, or I could leave.

I had been looking forward to the baby. I didn't mind talking to Dulcie about whether or not the kid should sleep in bed with us, or use a pacifier, or how long she would nurse him, or any of the things she could think about happily for days. I got excited about it too. But I had no idea what it meant, really. What was real to me was watching Dulcie's body grow bigger and bigger, watching that stripe appear on her belly, watching as her breasts got fuller and that part around her nipples got as wide and dark as pancakes. When the doctors took the baby out of her, they handed him to me without bothering to clean him up; I guess there was no point to it. Every inch of him was perfectly formed. For a second, I thought he would open his eyes and be a baby. It didn't look like anything was wrong with him, like there was any reason for him not to be breathing and crying and getting on with the business of being in the world. I kept saying to myself, This is my baby, this is my baby. But I had no idea what I was saying. The only thing I truly felt was that I would die if something happened to Dulcie.

A runner came toward me on the trail. His face was red, and sweat had made his T-shirt transparent. He gave me a pained smile as he ran past. He kicked a small rock with his shoe, and it flew over the side of the canyon. For some reason, I looked over the edge for the rock. What I saw from where I stood was amazing to me. I saw all kinds of strange cactus plants — tall ones like baseball bats, others like spiky fans. There were dry green eucalyptus trees and a hundred different kinds of bushes I couldn't name. I heard the rustle of animals, skunks or coyotes, maybe even deer. There was garbage on the ground and in the bushes — soda cans, fast-food drink cups, napkins with restaurant logos on them. I saw a condom hanging off a branch, like a burst balloon. For some reason, the garbage didn't bother me. For all I knew, this was one of those mountains that was made of trash, and it was nature that didn't belong. Maybe the trash, the dirt, the plants, bugs, condoms — maybe they were all just fighting for a little space.

I got home before Dulcie. I dragged the mattress back into the bedroom. I took my shirt off the light fixture in the living room and put it in the dresser. When Dulcie came back, she saw what I had done, but she didn't say anything. We ate dinner early. I watched a soccer game while she corrected some papers. Then I turned off the lights in the living room, and we went into the bedroom. She knew my mind was made up, and she climbed into bed like a soldier following orders. When I snapped off the bedside lamp, she gave a little gasp.

We lay quietly for a while, getting used to the dark. We listened for the rat, but he wasn't there.

"You think the traps worked?" she said.

"Maybe."

I reached for her. At first it was awkward, as though we were two people who had never had sex with each other. Truthfully, I was half ready for her to push me away. But she didn't, and after a while things became familiar again. When I rolled on top of her, though, I felt her tense up underneath me. She started to speak. "I should go and get —"

I put my fingers on her mouth to stop her. "It's okay," I said.

She looked up at me with her big, watery eyes. She was terrified. She started again to say something about her diaphragm. I stopped her once more.

"It's okay," I repeated.

I could feel her heart beating on my skin. I could feel my own heart beating even harder. We were scared, but we kept going.

TREVANIAN

The Apple Tree

FROM THE ANTIOCH REVIEW

THE WIDOW ETCHEVERRIGARAY took great pride in the splendid apple tree that grew on the boundary of her property, just beyond the plot of leeks that every year were the best in all the village; and her neighbor and lifelong rival, Madame Utuburu, drew no less gratification from the magnificent apple tree near the patch of *piments* that made her the envy of all growers of that sharp little green pepper. Unfortunately for the tranquility of our village, we are not speaking of two trees here but of one: a tree that grew exactly on the boundary between the two old women's land and was, by both law and tradition, their shared property. It was inevitable that the apples from this tree should lead to dispute, for such has been the melancholy role of that disruptive fruit since the Garden of Eden.

As all the world knows, neither pettiness nor greed has any place in the Basque character, so one must look elsewhere for the cause of the famed Battle of the Apple Tree that became part of our village's folklore. The explanation lies in the bitter rivalry the two women cultivated and nourished for most of their lives. When young, one of them had been accounted the most beautiful girl in our village, while the other was considered the most graceful and charming — although in later years no one could remember which had been which, and, sadly, no evidence of these qualities remained to prompt the memory. As mischievous Fate would have it, both the young women fancied that handsome rogue Zabala, who was not yet called Zabala One-Leg, for he was still to commit the unknown (but doubtless carnal) offense for which the righteous

God the Father punished him by taking one of his legs in the Great War, while His benevolent Son, Jesus, revealed His mercy by leaving him the other to hobble along on. All the village knew that the young women admired Zabala, because neither of them would deign to dance with him at fêtes, and both would turn their faces away and sniff when the cheeky rascal addressed a word to them, or a wink. If further proof of their attraction were needed, both village belles were heard to vow upon their chastity that they would not marry that flirting, two-faced scamp of a Zabala if he were the last man in Xiberoa. They would become nuns first. They would become prostitutes first! They would become Protestants first! (Of course, nobody believed they would go so far as *that.*)

Now, being every bit as crafty as He is good, God knows how to punish us, not only by withholding our wishes but by granting them too. In this case, He chose to cut with the back of His blade. He willed that neither of the young women would have Zabala, for he went from the village to punish Kaiser William, who was at that time raping nuns and spitting Belgian babies on his bayonet, the enlistment posters informed us. Zabala returned three years later, without one leg but with such worldly sophistication that he could no longer remember the Basque word for many things and used the French instead. He bragged about the wonderful places he had seen and the many sinful and delicious things he had done, but he was astonished to learn that in his absence both the women had married simple shepherds far beneath their expectations, that both their weddings had occurred within two months of the exciting and heady fête that marks the harvest of the hillside fern, and that both women had given birth to babies after only seven months of gestation. Short first pregnancies do not occasion criticism in our valley, for it is widely known that the good Lord often makes first pregnancies mercifully brief as His reward to the girl for having preserved her chastity until marriage. Subsequent pregnancies, however, usually run their full terms, which only makes sense, as the very fact that they are not first pregnancies means that the mother was not chaste at the moment of conception. Is it not marvelous how one finds justice and balance in everything? Yet further proof of God's hand in our daily lives.

Over the years, the shepherd Etcheverrigaray slowly increased his flock until he was able to buy a small house on the edge of the village with an overgrown garden that his wife tamed and tended until it was the pride of the village and, it goes without saying, also the envy. But the husband fell into the habit of spending time he ought to have given to the care of his sheep in the café/bar of our mayor, squandering his money on so many small glasses of wine that, after he died suddenly of no disease other than God's will, his widow would have had a hard time making ends meet, had it not been for the productive garden she had enriched over the years with her sweat and her loving care.

As for Madame Utuburu's husband, he was plagued by something worse than drink: he was unlucky. And there is an old Basque saying that teaches us: Unlucky indeed is he who is burdened with bad luck. If there was a thunderstorm in the mountains, you could bet that some of Utuburu's sheep would be struck by lightning. If, upon rare occasions, his ewes had a fruitful season, the price of wool was sure to drop. Nor was the village very sympathetic about his misfortunes, for it is well known that bad luck is the lash with which the Lord chastises those who have sinned, however cleverly and clandestinely. And there was another thing: when the price of wool fell for Utuburu, it fell for everybody — even for us, the lucky and the innocent.

You can imagine how surprised we all were when we learned that Utuburu the Unlucky was to receive an unexpected inheritance from a distant uncle. But the Lord's subtle ways were revealed when, staggering home after celebrating the only bit of good fortune in his life, Utuburu fell into the river and drowned.

With what was left of the inheritance after grasping lawyers had gorged on it, Madame Utuburu bought the small house next to the Widow Etcheverrigaray's, and there she eked out a modest annuity by toiling morning and evening in her garden, which became either the best or the second-best garden in the village, depending on whether one measured a garden by the quality of its leeks or that of its *piments.*

Thus it was that ironic Fate brought the two rivals to live and grow old side by side on the edge of the village, each with no husband, and each with only one son to absorb her love and color her expectations.

The Widow Etcheverrigaray's son soon revealed himself to be a clever and hardworking scholar, first at the village infant school, then in middle school at Mauléon, later at the lycée at Bayonne, and finally at university in Paris. With every advance in his education, he moved farther and farther from his village, so in proportion as his mother had ever greater reason to be proud of him, she had ever fewer opportunities to show him off to her less fortunate neighbor. At first he wrote short letters that the village priest read to Widow Etcheverrigaray over and over until she had them by heart; then she would share them with the women beating their washing clean at the village *lavoire*, her eyes scanning the paper back and forth as she recited from memory. And once her son sent a thick book full of tiny print with his name on the cover, which the priest told us was proof that he had written it: every word, from one end to the other. The book said such clever things about tropical agriculture that not even our priest could read it for long without nodding off. Eventually the son gained a very important position in some Brazil or other, and the village never saw him again.

As for Madame Utuburu's boy, the best that can be said of his educational performance is that the damage he did to school property during his brief stay was not nearly so great as some have claimed. His native gifts lay in another direction: he developed into the most powerful and crafty player of jai alai our village ever produced — and this is saying something, for it was our village that gave the world the fabled Andoni Elissalde, he who crushed all comers from 1873 to 1881, when a blow of the ball to his head made him an Innocent: one so beloved of God that he was no longer tormented by doubts or led astray by curiosity. After young Utuburu made his reputation with our communal team, he went on to play for Bayonne, where he was selected for the team that toured Spain and South America, humbling all before them and making every cheek in Xiberoa glow with pride. Thus, as the lad became more and more famous in that noblest of sports, he played ever farther and farther away from our village and from his proud mother, who nevertheless saved newspapers with pictures of him and words of praise. She saved the whole page lest she cut out the wrong part, because, like her neighbor, she was not exposed to the threats to simple faith that an ability to read entails. While touring South America, the son was offered vast fortunes to play in some Argentina or other. Twice he sent photographs of himself in action, and once he sent a magnificent cushion of multicolored silk with a beautiful (if rather immodest) woman painted on it and the words *Greetings from Buenos Aires*. On the back, in a rainbow of embroidery, was the word *Madre*, which the priest said referred either to Madame Utuburu or to the Virgin Mary, in either case a good thought. After this gesture of prodigal generosity, the son was heard of no more.

In the normal course of things, the two widows would have lived out their years lavishing on their gardens the care and affection their husbands no longer needed and their children no longer wanted, going frequently to early morning mass in their black shawls, certain that their piety would not go unrewarded, and little by little slipping from the notice of the village, as old women should. But such was not the destiny of Widow Etcheverrigaray and Madame Utuburu, for the ever-increasing rivalry between them kept them much in the eye and on the tongues of the women of our village. At first this rivalry was manifested in looking over the stone wall at the other woman's garden and murmuring little words of condolence and of encouragement for next year. Over the years, these drops of sweetened acid matured into expressions of praise or sympathy that each woman would express in the course of her morning marketing rounds. Madame Utuburu constantly lauded her neighbor as a saint for having put up with that slovenly drunk of a husband. But of course, if the old sot hadn't been drunk when first they met, he would never have — Ah, but why bring that up now, after all these years?

And Widow Etcheverrigaray often let escape heartfelt sighs over her neighbor's misfortune in having a husband cursed with bad luck. The poor man had been unlucky in everything, most of all in having to live with a woman who — But enough! He was dead now, and suffering yet greater punishment!

. . . If that is possible.

If there was anything that made Madame Utuburu's mouth pucker with contempt, it was the way some people took a stupid old book along with them to the *lavoire* every Tuesday, and looked at it and fondled it and sighed over it until others were forced to ask about it out of politeness, only to be drowned in a flood of nonsense about the brains and brilliance of some four-eyed weakling who couldn't catch a *pelote* in a *chistera* to save his life, and who never even had the decency to send his poor mother a little something for New Year's! She who had stayed awake nights trying to save the scrawny runt's life when he was sick.

. . . Which was pretty often.

And if there was one thing in this world that made Widow Etcheverrigaray's eyes roll with exasperation, it was the way some people forever lugged about a dusty old cushion, shoving it under your nose until you were forced to ask what on earth it was. Then they would dump a cartload of drivel on you about the strength and speed of some ignorant brute of a wood-for-brains who lacked even the common politeness to send his mother a little gift on her saint's day. She who had carried the oversized beast under her heart for nine months!

. . . Well, seven.

Seasons flowed into years. A paved road penetrated our valley, and soon the wireless was inflicting Paris voices on our ears and planting Paris values and desires in the hearts of our young people. There is a sage old Basque saying that goes: As youth fades away, one grows older. And thus it was with the two women. Stealthily at first, then with a frightening rush, what had seemed to be an inexhaustible pile of tomorrows became a vague little tangle of yesterdays. But still they toiled in their gardens to produce the finest (or second-finest) vegetables in our village, and still they honed and refined their rivalry, urged on in no small part by their neighbors, who were amused by the endless sniping until our peace was shattered by the Battle of the Apple Tree. The tree in question was very old and gnarled, but it never failed to produce an abundant crop of that crisp, succulent fruit with specks of red in the meat that used to be called Blood-of-Christ apples. One never sees a Blood-of-Christ apple anymore, but they are still remembered with pleasure by old men who never tire of telling the young that everything modern is inferior to how things were back in their day: the village fêtes, the weather, the behavior of children.

. . . Even the apples, for the love of God!

Because the tree stood exactly on the boundary between their gardens (indeed, the wall separating them touched the tree on both sides and was buckled by its growth), they had always shared the apples, each picking only from branches that overhung her property. To avoid appearing so petty as pointedly to ignore the presence of the other, they picked on different days, although it could be a tooth-grinding nuisance to have planned for weeks to harvest on a certain morning, only to look out one's window and see that hog of a neighbor picking on that very day! Not to mention the fact that young Zabala would surely have asked one to marry him if someone else had not always been throwing herself at him in the most scandalous way!

The fate of the apples on the disputable branches running along the boundary wall was a source of tension each year. Neither woman would run the risk of picking apples that did not indisputably overhang her own property lest she give the other a chance to brand her a thief at the *lavoire,* so they were obliged to wait until God, disguised as the Force of Gravity, settled the matter at the end of the season, causing the apples to drop on one side or the other of the dividing wall. There were years when the Devil, disguised as a Strong Wind, stirred up strife by causing most of the debatable apples to fall into one garden. And every year a heartrending number of apples fell onto the wall itself, only to rot away slowly on that rocky no man's land under the mournful gaze of the women, both of whom muttered bitterly over the shameful waste caused by that backbiting, gossiping old — May God forgive her.

. . . Even if mankind cannot!

Now, the baker from Licq who drove his van from village to village, sounding his horn to bring out the customers, had a sharp eye for profit, like all those coin-biting Licquois. He knew that everyone liked the rare Blood-of-Christ apples and would be willing to buy some . . . at a just price, of course. Aware of the competition between the two widows, the baker was careful to offer each of them a chance to make a little extra money. After much hard and narrow negotiating, he arranged to buy five baskets of apples from each.

Early the next morning, Widow Etcheverrigaray went out to her tree carrying five baskets that she intended to fill before — what's this?! Madame Utuburu was on the other side of the stone wall, filling *her* baskets with the fine, plump fruit. Under normal circumstances, the widow would never pick at the same time as her greedy neighbor, but as the baker was coming that afternoon to collect his apples, without a word she set grimly to her task. It was not long before she realized that she was unlikely to fill all five baskets, for this year the apples, while especially large and beautiful, were less abundant than usual (thus does God, in His eternal justice, give with one hand while taking with the other). Indeed, when she had picked all the apples from the branches indisputably overhanging her garden, Widow Etcheverrigaray found that she had filled only four baskets. And even this had required a most liberal definition of the term "full" as applied to baskets of apples. A covert glance over the wall revealed that Madame Utuburu was in precisely the same state: her branches stripped and still an empty basket left. And her idea of a "full" basket was obviously one that was not totally empty! At this moment, Widow Etcheverrigaray was shocked to see her neighbor lean over the wall and squint down it, estimating whether some of the branches along the no man's land between them might, upon reconsideration, be judged to be on her side of the wall. The widow's eyes grew round with indignant disbelief! This covetous old greedy-gut of an Utuburu was actually contemplating breaking the unspoken truce that had permitted them to share the apple tree! She stepped forward to forestall her neighbor's iniquity by picking the apples that might just as well be judged to be on her side of the disputable branch. "So!" hissed Madame Utuburu to herself. "This grasping hussy of an Etcheverrigaray wants to play *that* way, does she? We'll see about that!" And she vigorously set herself to harvesting the apples that were erstwhile dubious but had now become clearly her own by right of self-defense — to say nothing of revenge.

They were furiously picking on opposite sides of the same branch when Madame Utuburu happened to tug it toward her just as her rival was reaching for an apple! "What?" muttered Widow Etcheverrigaray between her teeth. "Well, *two* can play at that game! And one even better than the other!" And she boldly grasped the branch and steadied it while she picked frantically with her free hand. "God be my witness!" snarled Madame Utuburu. "Is this shameless strumpet prepared to rip the branches off the tree to satisfy her greed?" And she jerked the branch back to her side, dragging the unprepared widow halfway over the stone wall. "Ai-i-i!" screamed the widow. "So the brazen harlot wants to play rough, does she?" And she was reaching out to wrench the branch back to her side when Madame Utuburu, having picked the last apple, released it, and it sprang back, striking the ample bosom of the astonished Widow, who staggered and ended up sitting with a squish in the middle of her prized leeks. There was no time to allow her fury to seethe and ripen, or to communicate her indignation to the villagers who had begun to gather along the road to watch the fun, for her neighbor was already picking at the moot branch on the far side of the tree. Grunting to her feet and slapping the mud from the back of her skirt, Widow Etcheverrigaray returned to the fray determined to punish this outrage. Crying out every vilification that years of rivalry had stored up in their fertile imaginations, they clawed at apples and ripped them from the branch, all the while decorating one another's reputations with those biologically explicit calumnies for which the Basque language might have been specifically designed, were it not universally known that it was invented in heaven for use by the angels. There was a moment when, as each of them reached for the same apple, their hands touched, and each cried out and recoiled as though defiled by the contact. Still fuming over the way Madame Utuburu had underhandedly released the branch, Widow Etcheverrigaray decided to repay the insult in kind. She set all her weight against the branch, bending it back to her side so that when Madame Utuburu reached out for the fruit, she could let it go, and it would snap back and give —

— the branch broke, and the Widow found herself sitting once again in her leek bed, the hoots and jeers of the spectators flushing her cheeks with rage and embarrassment. She sat there snarling descriptions of Madame Utuburu's character, ancestry, practices, and aspirations, while that thoroughly slandered woman, finding her last basket still not filled and the branch bearing the remaining apples broken off and lying out of reach in her neighbor's garden, lifted her palms to heaven and called upon God to witness this plunder! This larceny! This piracy! And she hastily crossed herself and begged Mother Mary to put her hands over the ears of the baby Jesus, that He might not be offended by the obscenities gushing from the foul mouth of this scurrilous, vulgar, lowborn Etcheverrigaray!

Which description impelled the Widow to make a gesture.

Which gesture obliged Madame Utuburu to throw a lump of mud.

Which assault forced half a dozen villagers to rush up from the road to prevent bodily damage from spoiling the innocent pleasure of their entertainment.

In the final accounting of the Battle of the Apple Tree, it was the

Widow Etcheverrigaray who was able — just — to fill her baskets from the last of the apples, while Madame Utuburu had to bargain long and hard before the tightfisted Licquois baker accepted her scantier baskets with much sighing and many martyred groans and predictions that his children would die in the poorhouse. But many villagers judged Madame Utuburu the victor, for after all, it wasn't *she* who had twice had her broad bottom dumped into her leeks.

For the next few weeks, every time the women in the market-place asked about the battle (which they did with wide-eyed inno-cence and cooing tones of compassion), Madame Utuburu threat-ened to bring legal action against the vicious vandal who had damaged her tree! And Widow Etcheverrigaray made public her suspicions concerning what her neighbor had offered the baker to make up for her missing apples; although, in the Widow's opinion, that commodity had been worth little enough when it was young and fresh and would now be accepted by the baker only if he were attempting to shorten his time in Purgatory by mortifying his flesh.

During the next year, they fought out their rivalry on the bat-tlefield of their gardens, each working from dawn to dark to pro-duce vegetables that were the pride of the village and the despair of other gardeners. The work in the open air kept their bodies strong and flexible, and the praise of passersby kept their spirits alive, par-ticularly if this praise could be interpreted as a slighting compari-son to the other woman's crop.

Then, one cold, wet autumn day, Zabala One-Leg died. Not of anything in particular; he simply ran out of life, as all of us eventu-ally must. Zabala had no family, but he was of the village, so we all went to his burial and stood in the rain while the priest took the op-portunity to promise us that death was the inevitable portion of each and every one of us, so we had all better start preparing for it, and particularly certain people he could name, but he wouldn't mar this solemn occasion with accusations, however just! Every-body left the cemetery, the women to home and work, the men to the café/bar of our mayor to have a little glass in memory of Zabala.

. . . Perhaps two.

Only Madame Utuburu and Widow Etcheverrigaray remained in the churchyard, standing in the rain on opposite sides of the scar of fresh earth, their eyes lowered to the rosaries they held between work-gnarled fingers. For an hour they stood there . . . Two hours . . . Although their shawls became sodden with rain and they had to clench their teeth to keep them from chattering, neither was willing to be the first to leave, for to do so would be to relinquish the role of chief mourner and admit that the other had the most reason for grief.

Their thick black skirts became too heavy with damp to stir in the wind that began to drive the rain diagonally across the grave, but still neither would leave the field in the possession of one for whom that handsome rogue of a Zabala had never cared a snap of his fingers. To do so would be an insult to his memory.

. . . To say nothing of his taste.

In the end, the priest came trotting out from his house beside the church, sleepy-eyed and grumbling about being torn from his meditation by a couple of stubborn old women. He stood at the head of the grave, the wind tugging at his big black umbrella, and angrily ordered them to come away with him. At once! As it is rash to disobey the messenger of God, especially when one is standing so conveniently in a graveyard, they allowed him to shepherd them home, but only after each had made a brief attempt to lag slightly behind. They walked home, one on each side of the priest, each with one shoulder protected by the umbrella while the other shoulder was drenched by rain running from its rim. Without a word, they left the priest at the bottom of their gardens and trudged up their paths, each to her own house.

The next morning dawned with that cold, brittle sunlight that signals the end of autumn, and Madame Utuburu knew it would soon be time to harvest the apples, which had been plentiful this year, but small and not as sweet as usual. (Is not God's evenhanded justice everywhere revealed?) As she worked putting up jars of *piperade*, she glanced from time to time out her kitchen window to see if that greedy Etcheverrigaray was already stripping the tree. But the Widow did not leave her house all day, and Madame Utuburu wondered what sort of game the old hag was playing. Oh-h, wait a minute! Was she pretending to be too stricken with grief to attend to garden chores? Was this her sly way of implying that she had the greatest reason to mourn young Zabala, who had never cared a fig for her? What an underhanded trick!

After mass the next morning, the priest asked Madame Utuburu why her neighbor had not attended service, and she replied that she was sure she didn't know. Perhaps she had given up going to mass, realizing that although God's mercy is infinite, it might not be infinite enough to save certain people who are forever parading their pretended grief! The same kind of people who always go about carrying thick books written by spindly-legged sons who are so feeble they couldn't throw a *pelote* against a *fronton!* No, not if the child Jesus Himself begged him for a game! The priest shook his head and sighed, sorry he had asked.

That afternoon Madame Utuburu looked up from mulching her garden against the coming winter to see the priest plodding duti-fully up the Widow's path. He was inside no more than two minutes before he came out, a leaden frown on his brow. When Madame Utuburu called over the wall, asking what old Etcheverrigaray was playing at, the priest picked his way across to her, holding his skirts up so as not to muddy them. "Your neighbor has been summoned to judgment," he said in that ripe tremolo one associates with calls for funds to reroof the church.

Madame Utuburu could not believe it! That healthy old horse of an Etcheverrigaray? She who was strong enough to rip a branch off another person's apple tree? It couldn't be!

"No doubt her bone marrow caught a fever from standing in the rain at poor Zabala's burial," the priest said. "I found her sitting in her kitchen, her feet in a bucket of water that had gone cold."

The priest went off to make the usual arrangements, and soon four women of the village came down the road wearing hastily-put-on black dresses, their heads bowed, their palms pressed together before them, their tread slow, but each radiating a tremor of re-strained excitement at being part of the great events of Life and Death. They turned into the Widow Etcheverrigaray's to wash, dress, and lay out the body, first opening the bedroom window to let her soul fly up to heaven. Then the First Mourner — who mer-ited this privileged title because, as the oldest of the watchers, she was probably "next in line," though this was never mentioned aloud — went out back to announce the death to the chickens, so they wouldn't stop laying. In other parts of the Basque country, the custom is to go to the Departed One's beehives and whisper that their keeper has died, so that sudden grief will not cause the bees to swarm and abandon their hives. No one in our village keeps bees, so we tell the chickens instead, and it must work, because none of them have ever swarmed and abandoned their roosts.

Back in Widow Etcheverrigaray's kitchen, the mourners sat gossiping in felted voices, thrilling one another with pious reminders that any one of them might be called unexpectedly to God, so they had better be ready with clean souls.

. . . And clean underwear.

The First Mourner suggested that they invite Madame Utuburu to watch with them. After all, the two women had been neighbors for more years than boys have naughty thoughts. But the Second Mourner wondered if it might not offend the Departed One to allow her lifelong rival to nose about in a kitchen she hadn't had time to clean. After some deliberation, it was decided that they would tidy up carefully, *then* invite Madame Utuburu to join the wake.

Stiff and very, very proper, Madame Utuburu sat in her neighbor's kitchen for the first time in her life. Awkward silences were followed by spurts of forced conversation that collapsed into broken phrases, then faded into feeble nods and hums of accord. None of the mourners wanted to praise the Widow in the presence of her rival, and no one dared to gossip about her in the presence of her spirit, so what was there to talk about? Finally, to everyone's relief, Madame Utuburu rose to go, but the First Mourner urged her to follow the ancient tradition and take some little trifle from the house as a memento of the Departed One. At first she declined, but finally — more to get away without further embarrassment than anything else — she allowed herself to be prevailed upon. After she left there was a long moment of silence, then a gush of repressed talk burst from all the watchers' lips at once. Why on earth had she chosen *that* as a memento?

The whole village went to see the Widow off to her reward. Only after standing beside the grave for a respectable amount of time, shivering in a wind that carried the smell of mountain snow on it, did we begin to drift away, the women to their kitchens, the men to the mayor's café/bar to take a little glass as they discussed the priest's warning that every hour of life wounds and the last kills.

. . . All right, maybe two glasses.

Madame Utuburu had not intended to linger beside the grave; it was simply that she didn't notice the departure of the others. Fully an hour passed before she lifted her eyes and, with a slight gasp of surprise, realized that she was alone. Alone. With nothing to mark the passage of her days. No one to prompt her to greater efforts at gardening and to greater praise from the village. No little victories to warm her throat with flushes of pride, no little defeats to sting her ears with flushes of shame. Nothing left to talk about but her expensive, beautiful, hand-embroidered silk cushion from Buenos Aires.

Winter descended from the mountains, and when its task of purifying the earth with cold was accomplished, retreated slowly back up the slopes, allowing spring to soften the ground and melt-water to fill the rushing Uhaitz-handia with waves that danced beneath the earth-colored foam. This was the season when Madame Utuburu usually set out her *piments* under cloches to get a month's head start on the rest of the village, but somehow she did not feel up to it. What was the point? She had no husband to feed, no son to praise her spicy *piperade,* and now no neighbor to vex with her superior crop. Maybe she wouldn't bother with the *piments* this year. Indeed, the task of planting a garden at all seemed terribly heavy and unrewarding.

She began to — I must not say "to understand," for she never submitted the matter to the processes of reasoning. She began to sense that her rival had been, not exactly something to live for, but maybe something to live *against:* a daily grievance, an object of envy, a reason to get up each morning, if only to see what villainy she had been up to.

Down at the *lavoire,* a woman brushed a lock of hair from her forehead with the back of her soapy hand and commented that three washdays had passed without Madame Utuburu showing up. Her neighbor at the next scrubbing stone set aside the paddle with which she had beaten her laundry clean and said that perhaps a couple of them should go down to the edge of the village and see if anything untoward had befallen. After all, she's no longer young and — But look! Here she comes!

And indeed, she was approaching the *lavoire* with a stately tread, her few scraps of dirty laundry tied into a bundle in one hand, while in the other she carried her famous cushion from Buenos Aires, and there was something balanced on top of it.

Oh no, it can't be!

But it was. The Book. And the women were obliged to listen while Madame Utuburu divided her praises between her own son's remarkable strength and the Etcheverrigaray boy's phenomenal brilliance.

And in this way Madame Utuburu kept the Widow Etcheverrigaray alive for several years longer. And herself too.

JOHN UPDIKE

Personal Archeology

FROM THE NEW YORKER

IN HIS INCREASING ISOLATION — elderly golfing buddies
dead or dying, his old business contacts fraying, no office to go to,
his wife always off at her bridge or committees, his children as busy
and preoccupied as he had been in middle age — Fritz Martin
took an interest in the traces left by prior owners of his land. In the
prime of his life, when he worked ten or twelve hours every weekday and socialized all weekend, he had pretty much ignored his
land. Years had passed without his setting foot on some corners of
it. The ten acres were there to cushion his house from the en-
croachments of close neighbors and as an investment against the
day when they would be sold, most likely to a developer, the profit
going to Fritz's widow, Grace, who was six years younger than he.

The place, as he understood it, had been a wooded hill at the
back of an estate until around 1900. A wealthy bachelor, marrying
tardily, built a spacious summer house for his bride and himself on
what had been a boulder-framed picnic spot, with enough trees
felled for a glimpse of the distant Atlantic. There were old roads on
the property, built up on shoulders of big fieldstones, too steep and
with turns too sharp for any combustion-driven car; horses must
have pulled vehicles up these hairpin turns, through these enduring tunnels of green. Even after decades, trees are shy of taking
root on soil once packed tight by wheels. Standing on the edge of
one of the several granite cliffs he owned, Fritz imagined farm wag-
ons or pony carts creaking and twinkling toward him, the narrow
spoked wheels laboring up swales, now choked with greenbrier,
that he imagined to be roadways, bringing young people in sum-

mer muslin and beribboned bonnets and white ducks and straw boaters up past him to a picnic.

But a century ago Massachusetts land was mostly cleared, bare to the wind and sun, cropped by sheep and goats. Perhaps he was picturing it all wrong. The winding roadway ran head on into a spiky wall of monoliths; how had it climbed the rest of the hill? Near the house, granite outcroppings bore enigmatic testimony. There were holes drilled here and there, as if to anchor iron gates or heavy awnings. A veranda with a sea view had long ago rotted away, and Fritz himself had replaced a dilapidated pillared porch on the front of the house, facing the circular asphalt driveway that had once been a gravel carriage turn.

The woods held vine-covered mounds of jagged rock that he took to be left over from the blasting of the house foundations. In the early years of the recently departed twentieth century, crews of masons fresh from Italy roamed this neighborhood, building giant walls that now were gradually, stone by stone, collapsing. One night, a section of retaining wall holding up his wife's most ambitious flower garden collapsed, spilling not just earth and flowers but ashes, of the clinkerish sort produced by a coal furnace, and a litter of old cans and glass jars. The garden's subsoil had been an ash and trash dump. When had the garden been created, then? Later than he thought, perhaps — the same era when the concrete wells for the cold frames were poured, now useless pits roofed by frames of punky wood, crumbled putty, and shattering glass.

In Fritz's mind, the property had had four eras before his own. First, there was the era of creation and perfect maintenance, when the enthusiastic, newly married rich man was still alive, and servants bustled from the stone sinks in the basement out to the bricked drying yard with baskets of steaming laundry, and the oiled cedar gutters poured rainwater down gurgling downspouts into fully functional underground drains. Then this happy man died, and the widow, preferring the society of Boston to her lonely house on the hill, imposed a largely absentee reign, in which one dining room wall with its hand-printed pictorial French wallpaper was ruined by a winter leak and the dainty porches, pillared and balustered appendages exposed to the weather, slowly succumbed to blizzards and nor'easters. There came an era when she too was dead and the house stood empty; perhaps most of the neglect and damage should be assigned to this interregnum, which ended just before the Second World War, when a young and growing family took on the place as a year-round residence. Central heating was installed, and a pine-paneled study was carved from the broad front hall, and the brick chimneys were repointed and the tattered roof shingles replaced. Improvements were halted by the war. The husband and father enlisted to sail the ocean, visible from the windows, which were covered with blackout paper. He returned as a rear admiral, and lived on the place until he was seventy-two and all six of his children had moved on.

From this long and busy era Fritz dated most of the oddments he found in the woods — Mason jars, flowerpots, shotgun shells, rubber tires half sunk in the leaf mold and holding a yellow oblong of scummy water, pieces of buried pipe, rusted strands of wire testifying to some bygone fencing project. Tree houses had been built and abandoned amid the rocky woods; porcelain insulators and insulated copper strands carried the ghost of electricity; parts of a motorcycle engine, filmed with blackened grease, remembered a time when the steep old roads served a young man's racing game.

These acres had absorbed much labor: stacks of wood cut to fireplace length moldered between two still-living trees, and Fritz's shoes scuffed into view beneath the leaves a sparkling layer of carbon, the charcoal residue of old fires. On the lower reaches of the land, where a broad track across pine needles wound downward toward a causeway that led illegally, through several private yards, to a beach, there had been a virtual snowfall of pale plastic litter — container tops, flexible straws, milk containers. Fritz was rewarded, in his occasional harvests with a garbage bag, by finding hidden in the greenbrier and marsh grass tinted bottles of a nostalgic thickness.

By trespassers or owners, the land had been trodden, craggy as it was. Trodden and scarred. In an incident that had been described to him by an ancient friend of the previous owner, a certain dinner guest had slid, one icy, boozy night, into the wall of great stones on a curve of the driveway and knocked out, like a single tooth, a molar-shaped boulder that now sat some thirty feet into the woods — a permanent monument to a moment's mishap, too massive, in this weakling latter age, to be moved back into position. When Fritz inquired about bringing the equipment in to move it back, he was told that the weight of the machinery might break the driveway down.

In a seldom visited declivity beyond this great granite cube, Fritz, picking up deadwood, found a charred work glove, stiff as a dead squirrel, with the word "Sarge" written on the back in the sort of felt-tip marker that didn't come into use until the nineteen-sixties. Who was Sarge? Part of a work crew, Fritz speculated, who had carelessly dropped his glove on the edge of a spreading grass fire. Or a woodsman who, while feeding brush into a blaze, had seen his hand flame up and flung the glove from him in horror and pain. Nearer the house, raking up organic oddments in a spring cleaning, Fritz spied beneath an overgrown forsythia a gleaming curve of white ceramic and, digging with his fingers, found it to be the handle of a teacup. He dug up six or so fragments; the delicate porcelain cup, gilt-rimmed, had been dropped or broken, perhaps by a child, who in his or her fright had buried the evidence in a shrub border. The quality of the china suggested one of the early eras, perhaps the idyllic first. The earth, freezing and thawing in its annual cycle, can at last push up to the surface what the culprit thought had been safely buried and forever hidden.

Fritz's dreams, those that disturbed him enough to be remembered when he awoke, tended to return to a rather brief stretch of his life, when he was embroiled in a domestic double-entendre. There was his first wife, who in these dreams had a certain retreating smoothness, like a ceramic saint seen from below, and his wife-to-be, who was more vigorously plaintive, her discomfort seeming to occupy several corners of the dream's screen while he scrambled to hold on to every human piece of the puzzle. Curiously, in his dreams he invariably lost her — saw her flee and recede — so it was with a soft shock that he awakened and realized that she, and not his first wife, lay beside him in bed, as she had done for twenty years now. His confusion gradually cleared into relief, and he fell back to sleep like a living bandage sealing over a wound. His children figured in the dream dramas indistinctly, shape-shifting participants in a kind of many-bodied party halfway up the stairs; the party's main ingredient, however, was not jollity but pain, a pain glutinously mixed of indecision, stretched communications, unexpressed apologies, and unbearable suspense. Fritz would wake to find that the party was long over, that he was an old man living out his days harmlessly on ten acres covered by a vague mulch of previous generations.

The parties had been vehicles for flirtation and exploration, a train of linked weekends carrying them all along in a giddy din. He and his friends were in the prime of their lives and expected that, amusing and wonderful as things were, things even more wonderful were bound to happen. There were, in fact, two simultaneous parties, two layers of party: the overt layer, where they discussed, as adults, local politics, national issues, their automobiles and schools for their children, zoning boards and home renovations; and the covert layer, where men and women communicated with eye-glance and whisper, hand-squeeze and excessive hilarity. The underlayer sometimes undermined the upper, and with it the seemingly solid structure of the interwoven bourgeois families. Cocktail parties were lethal melees, wherein lovers with a murmur made or canceled assignations. In an upstairs hall, outside a bathroom, Fritz remembered a younger woman, smooth of face and arm, wearing gray-blue silk, daring him to give her a kiss and, as he backed off, saying gently, "Chicken." She was enough younger than he that he had taken her, for an instant in the shadowy hall, as one of their host's adolescent daughters.

But for every moment he consciously remembered from that remote era, there were hundreds he had forgotten and that fought back into his awareness in the tangle of these recurrent party dreams. His sensation in the dreams was the same: stagefright, a feeling that what he was enacting was too big for him, too eternal in its significance. He woke with relief, the turmoil slipping from him, his wife absent from the bed and already padding around downstairs. Sometimes he awoke in a separate bed, because in his old age he helplessly, repulsively snored, and slept in the guest room. When he awoke there, his eyes found, on the opposite wall, a painting that had hung in his childhood home — in the several homes his wandering family had occupied. The painting, a pathetic and precious token of culture which his mother had bought for (if he remembered correctly) thirty-five dollars in a Pennsylvania framer's shop, depicted a Massachusetts scene, some high dunes in Provincetown, with a shallow triangle of water, a glimpse of the sea, framed between the two most distant slopes of sand. Was it this painting which had led him from that commonwealth to this one, to this hilltop house with its glimpse of the sea?

Various other remnants of his boyhood world had washed up in the house: his grandfather's Fraktur-inscribed shaving mug, a dented copper ashtray little Fritz had often watched his father crush out cigarettes in, a pair of brass candlesticks, like erect twists of rope, that his mother would place on the dining room table when they fed relatives from New Jersey. These objects had been with him in the abyss of lost time, and survived less altered than he. What did they mean? They had to mean something, fraught and weighty as they were with the mystery of his own transient existence.

"I'd give anything not to have married you," Grace would say, out of the blue, when angry or soulful. She carried into daylight, he felt, a grudge against him for snoring, though he was as helpless to control it as he was his dreams. "If only I'd listened to my conscience."

"Conscience?" *Chicken,* he remembered. "I don't know about you, but I'm very happy in this marriage. You've been wonderful. Amazing."

"Thank you, dear. But it was so *wrong*. That time upstairs at the Rosses', the way you loped toward me in the hall, you were scary — like a big wolf out of the shadows. Your teeth *gleamed*."

"Gleamed?" He couldn't picture it. He had dull, tea-stained teeth. But he recognized that the gleam was something true and precious unearthed from deep within her, giving her past a lodestar.

At the time he kept dreaming of, strange to recall, he had not had stagefright. He had felt calm, masterful, amid scandal and protest and grief. There had been a psychiatrist encouraging him. His mother, initially indignant, became philosophical, employing postmodern irony and a talk-show tolerance. His children consoled themselves by thinking they would someday grow up and never be so helpless again. In abandoning his family, a man frees up a soothing amount of time. Fritz found himself projected into novel situations — dawn risings from a strange bed, visits to lawyers' offices, hotel trysts hundreds of miles from home — and he behaved like an actor who had rehearsed his lines, who had zealously prepared for his dramatic part and played it creditably, no matter what the reviewers said. So why the stagefright now, in his sleep? It had been there all along and was rising up into him, like his death.

He had recently visited an old friend, a corpulent golfing buddy, in the hospital after a heart attack. Al lay with tubes up his nose and in his mouth, breathing for him. His chest moved up and down with a mechanical regularity recorded by hopping green lines on a monitor on the wall: a TV show, *Al's Last Hours*. It was engrossing, though the plot was thin, those lines hopping on and on in a beautiful luminous green. Al's eyelashes, pale and furry, fluttered when Fritz spoke, in too loud a voice, as if calling from the edge of a cliff. "Thanks for all the laughs, Al. You just do what the nurses and doctors tell you, and you'll be fine." Al's hand, as puffy as an inflated rubber glove, wiggled at his side, on the bright white sheet. Fritz took it in his, trying not to dislocate the IV tubes shunted into the wrist. The hand was warm, and silky as a woman's, not having swung a golf club for years, but didn't seem animate, even when it returned the pressure. Our bodies, Fritz thought, are a heavy residue.

One of his childhood homes had been rural, with some acres attached, and while exploring those little woods alone one lonely afternoon he had come upon an old family dump — a mound, nearly grassed over, of glass bottles with raised lettering, as self-important and indelible as the lettering on tombstones. Many of the bottles were broken, though the glass by modern standards was amazingly thick, like rock candy, the jagged edge making a third surface between the inside and the outside. Malt brown, sea blue, beryl, amber, a foggy white, they bore in relief the names of local bottling works, defunct. The beverages and medicines they had held were gone, drunk, for all the good or ill they had done — not so much as a scummy puddle inside an old tire left. The pile had frightened little Fritz, as a pile of bones would have, yet in his isolation had kept him a kind of obliviously cheerful company. He returned to it often, this trace of vanished life, as if to a playmate, glittering and ideally silent.

On his own acres, wandering, garbage bag in hand, in the lowland beyond the stray rock and the burned glove, he found a number of half-buried golf balls, their lower sides stained by immersion in the acid earth, the cut-proof covers beginning to rot. He remembered how, when first moving to this place and still hopeful for his game, he would stand on the edge of the lawn and hit a few old balls — never more, thriftily, than three at a time — into the woods down below. They seemed to soar forever before disappearing into the trees. He had never expected to find them. They marked, he supposed, the beginning of his era.

DOROTHY WEST

My Baby . . .

FROM CONNECTICUT REVIEW

ONE DAY DURING MY TENTH YEAR, a long time ago in Boston, I came home from school, let myself in the back yard, stopped a moment to scowl at the tall sunflowers which sprang up yearly despite my dislike of them, and to smile at the tender pansies and marigolds and morning glories that Father set out in little plots every spring, and went on into the kitchen.

The back gate and back door were always left open for us children, and the last one in was supposed to lock them. But since the last dawdler home from school had no way of knowing she was the last until she was inside, it was always Mother who locked them at first dark, and she would stand and look up at the evening stars. She seemed to like this moment of being alone, away from the noise in the house.

We were a big house. Besides the ten rooms and the big white-walled attic, there were we three little girls and the big people, as we used to call them.

Father, our mothers, Grampa, and the unmarried aunts. Presently, as I shall tell you, there were two more little ones. Grampa used to say that if we lived in the Boston Museum, which was the biggest building Grampa had ever seen, we'd still need one more room. That was a standing joke in our house. For besides this permanent collection, there were always visiting relatives and friends, for we had a nice house, and we were a hospitable family.

My room was the big third-floor front bedroom. Mostly I shared it with Mother. I remember everything in that room, the big brass bed that had been Father's wedding present to Mother, the wicker settee and the wicker rocker and the wicker armchair, which had once seen service in the parlor until superseded by mahogany and now creaked dolefully on damp nights, making me think of ghosts. There was a built-in marble washstand in the room, and I think Mother was very proud of this fixture. There were taps for running hot and cold water, and on Saturdays and Sundays and holidays the hot tap was really hot. The New England winters were cold then, and although our old-fashioned house had a furnace that sent up some semblance of heat through the registers, there were coal stoves in nearly all the rooms. In my room was a little potbellied stove, and I knew how to tend it myself.

At night I would sift the ashes and bank the fire, and in the mornings I would scoot out of bed onto the freezing carpet, run to the stove, bang the door shut, open the drafts, race back to bed, and lie on my belly doing my algebra until the room had warmed enough for me to dress. My room, for some reason, became the hub of the house. I think it was because that little potbellied stove was one of the only two on the top floor. And whereas I left my window for Mother to open, so I wouldn't cool off the house before it was bedded down for the night, my cousin, in whose room was an ancient, evil, ugly stove, let her fire go out, flung open her window, and shut her door against intruders. At night everyone came into my room to warm himself before going to bed, and an aunt stopping in to toast for a moment before my banked fire and finding another aunt present would fall into conversation, and by and by all the other members of the family, except Father and Grampa, who couldn't come in their nightshirts, would drift in and settle in the wicker furniture, and the rocking chair would sing back and forth, and someone would ask: *Is that child asleep?* And someone would answer: *If she isn't, she'd better be.*

They would sit there until the banked fire gave out no more heat. Then they would sigh and heave themselves up, and their heavy bodies would pad out of the room. Mother would crack the window and let in the stars and turn out the flickering gaslight. Sometimes she slipped in beside me, sometimes not. I would lie and listen to the creaks and groans of the many bedsteads, and it seemed to me a fine and safe thing to have a big family.

That day in my tenth year when I came home from school, my mother was not in the kitchen. This seemed odd, for the children in our Irish neighborhood were often bellicose, and Mother stood ready at all times to rush out and rescue us. I could not fight when I was a child. I shook too much and was too ashamed. But my mother and the cousin who was eleven months older than I were great battlers. It was wonderful to hear my mother tearing into an Irish termagant with a sailor's tongue and to see my girl cousin triumphantly straddling a thirteen-year-old bully.

My mother and my cousin were so much alike that sometimes I had the mean thought that I was not really my mother's child. And oddly enough, my mother's sister was shy and soft and dark like myself. My cousin and I used to wonder quite seriously if our mothers, for some reason, had switched us.

When I could not find my mother in the kitchen, I went softly down the hall to the parlor. I did not call her in the fear that if there were company, I would be summoned. The parlor door stood open, but my cautious peeking revealed no one inside. Suddenly I heard movement in the upstairs sitting room. I went back down the hall and up the back stairs, and sitting down on the top step, I had a clear view of the front room.

Now, looking back, I do not remember the room's furnishings. I can only recall that almost center in the room was a big table-desk that had once been in Father's office, and beside this desk sat a strange white woman with a little brown girl in her arms. I could not see my mother, but I was aware of her presence in that room. Grampa was probably in the grandfather chair, chewing tobacco, spitting into a tin can when it was summer and into the stove when it was winter, not listening to the conversation of the women. My father and my widowed aunts were at work.

My mother and the woman spoke in low voices, and I did not hear anything they said. I wished I could see the baby more clearly, for I loved babies.

She was good, hardly stirring and never uttering a sound. Presently the woman rose. I scrambled down the back stairs as quietly as I could.

That night at supper my mother asked us how we would like a baby boy and girl to play with. We were wildly excited, for we were beginning to think we were too big to play with dolls, and it was hard not to have something to fondle. *Well, we'll see,* said my mother, and sent us out front to play, with Grandfather at the parlor window to watch us so that the roving bands of Irish boys from Mission Hill way would not bother us. We knew that the big people were going to talk about the white lady and wanted us out of earshot.

The day the babies came is as clear in my mind as if it were yesterday. It was a Saturday. We had come home from dancing school, held in the spacious home of a Negro woman who had known a better day, where we were taught parlor dancing by a young and lovely Irish girl, whose mother accompanied her to class because some of the seniors were boys of eighteen and our teacher was only twenty-one. She was engaged and was not interested in the boys at all except as one boy danced better than another. Nor were the boys interested in her, since they were all in school and there were several prettier girls in the class. Now it seems strange that we had a white dancing teacher, but in those days it was the fashion. If you went to a Negro teacher, it was an admission that you could not afford to pay a white one.

When we rang the front bell, Mother came to the door. She smiled and said that the babies had come, and that they were to sleep with me because my bedroom was the biggest. My cousins raced upstairs to see the newcomers. I stayed behind to ask questions. Actually I could not bear the exquisite moment when I would hold two real babies in my arms. I asked my mother how long they would stay. She said they would stay indefinitely, for their mother had gone to work to support them. She was, in fact, going to work as nursemaid for a friend of my unmarried aunt's employer. I asked my mother where their father was. She hesitated for a moment, then said that their father had not been very good to them, and that was why they were here, and I must love them a lot so they would not miss their mother too much.

With my heart bursting with love for these babies, I went slowly upstairs. Finally I reached my room, and I heard my cousins crowing delightedly. At the foot of my bed sat a little boy in pajamas. He looked about three. His hair was very blond and curly, his skin very pink and white. He looked like a cherub as he bounced about outside the covers and chattered in utmost friendliness to my cousins. I started toward him, for I wanted nothing so much as to hug him tight. My cousins began telling me excitedly what a darling he was.

I was almost upon them when suddenly I stopped. I did not do it willfully. Some force outside me jerked me to a halt. The smile left my face, and involuntarily I turned and looked toward the head of the bed.

There was that baby girl, staring solemnly at me. I went slowly toward her. I had forgotten the boy was on earth. I stood above her. She was no more than two. Her hair was as curly as the boy's but softer and longer and brown. Her wide, serious eyes were brown too. She was copper-colored. In all of my life I have never seen a lovelier child. I do not know how long we stared at each other unthinkingly. As clearly as if I had spoken aloud, I heard a voice inside myself say to the inward ear of that child, *I am going to love you best of all.* Then I turned away without touching her and in a minute had joined my cousins, who had already decided the boy would be the most fun.

The months passed, and the girl and I became inseparable. When I came home at half-past two, there was her little face pressed to the windowpane, and no one had told her the time. From the moment I entered the house, I was her mother and she was my child.

Their own mother came to see the children on the one day a week that she was free. But she was so young, only twenty-one, and she had been caring for babies all week, and so after a few minutes with them, Mother sent her out to see her young friends. My mother treated her like a child, which seemed odd to me then. I learned that my mother was her aunt by marriage, and that she remembered the day she was born. I was told she had played with us when we were babies just as we played with her children now. I knew then that she was not white.

The hard winter had set in when Father had to shovel a path from the house to the sidewalk before we children could leave for school. The snow was banked as high as our shoulders. There are no such winters now. We were little girls, and we wore boys' storm boots that laced to our knees, as did all the other little girls. We wore flannel shirts and drawers that made us itch like mad and red flannel petticoats. Some bitter mornings the bells sounded over the city, which meant it was snowing too hard for school.

The babies scarcely left the house that winter, for Mother said they were packed with cold. I think the house was warmer than it ever had been, and sometimes Father grumbled about the cost of coal. Grampa gave the babies a mixture of white Vaseline, lemon juice, and sugar. Mother borrowed my allowance money regularly for patent medicines. They worked on those children all winter. When it was spring, it seemed that Grampa and my mother had succeeded, for the children had gained and grown taller.

The girl was as much a part of me now as my arm. She had grown even closer to me after the long, uncertain winter. I had forgotten the years when she had not been with me. I could not imagine a life without her. As young as she was, and as young as I was, there was an understanding between us of amazing depth. The family remarked our oneness. Her own mother knew without jealousy that the baby loved me best.

Death came on her quietly, and on what mild spring breeze it could have blown we never knew. There was a day when she whimpered and sucked on her thumb, a habit we had broken. I do not remember if the doctor came; I only remember that it seemed to me I could not bear to see her lying there, not whimpering now, but still sucking on her thumb with nobody telling her not to, and her eyes enormous and with a look of suffering.

Then one day — it may have been the next day, it may have been the next year, for the pain I suffered with her — my mother wrapped her up and took her to the hospital.

When Mother had gone, I slipped out of the house and trailed her like a little dog. It was a short walk from our house to the Children's Hospital. Mother went inside, and I stood on the sidewalk opposite and stared up at the hospital windows.

I guess the waiting room was on the second floor, for suddenly I saw my mother in line at a second-floor window. She did not see me, and I cannot say if the baby saw me or not. She lay listlessly in Mother's arms, pulling on her thumb. I stared at her with my hands pressed tight in prayer until they had passed out of sight. Then I ran home and crawled under the bed and lay there quivering, unable to cry, until I heard Mother's weary step in the hall.

We children ran to her, and when we saw she had returned without the baby, we could not bear to ask her what the doctor had said. She would not tell us. She only said the doctor would take good care of her and that she would soon be well.

*

It is so long now that I cannot remember how long it was. Perhaps a week passed, perhaps a month. One night in my sleep I heard the front doorbell or the telephone ring. The next thing I remembered was the soft sound of my mother's sobs. I sat up and stared at her. The boy's blond head lay on the pillow, his face sweet in sleep. My mother looked at me. I do not know why she had come into my room unless to reassure herself that there was life in death. She came to me and hugged me tight, and said in a choked whisper that the baby was dead. Then she straightened almost sternly and told me to go back to sleep. I did not cry. I just felt surprised for a minute and then went to sleep almost instantly.

I was ten, and I was smart for my age. I had been told that the baby was dead, and I had seen the grownups' strained faces, but did not know what death was. The last time I had seen the baby she had been alive. It was not until I looked down at her little white coffin that I knew that she was not. Had she died without pain, she might have looked otherwise. But the sudden swift disease had ravaged her. A bandage covered her eyes, and the agony had left its mark on her mouth. She did not look like a sleeping child. Perhaps the undertaker had not yet perfected his art. This was death unbeautiful and unmistakable. The only mourners were my family.

The mother came home with us that night. I remember her white, frightened, little-girl's face, and my mother's tenderness. She did not go back to work.

There was a week of family conferences, for we children practically spent the whole week outdoors.

Then one day we came home from school, and the boy and his mother had gone. My mother said they had gone far away to another city. She talked to us very seriously, and her eyes were filled with sadness and something that looked like shame. Her words came out slowly, as if reluctantly. Sometimes she could not look at us.

She said the boy and his mother would never come back. They had gone away to begin a new life. If anyone asked us about them, we must say we had never known them. We knew by her face that we must not ask any questions. We went away from her, and we could not play, nor could we look at each other.

So summer came again, and an aunt from the South came to visit us, bringing her two little boys. My cousins had a child apiece and were wildly happy.

Mother and the aunts were happy too, for they had not seen their sister in years.

One day a strange dark man came to our house and talked in an angry voice to my mother. She talked back to him the same way she talked to the Irish termagants. I heard her tell that man that his baby had died because he had neglected it. She told him that his wife and son had gone away, and thrust him out of the house.

Sometime after that a letter came for my mother. I saw her hands tremble when she opened it. She did not say anything to us, but that night she read it aloud to her assembled sisters. My cousins were in the attic playing with the two little boys, and my mother thought I was with them. Actually I was lying underneath my bed, crying for that dead baby. There was not a night for a good six months that I did not cry for her. When I heard my mother and my aunts, I crammed my fist into my mouth. How could I tell them I was crying for a child I was supposed never to have heard of?

My mother and the aunts settled in the wicker furniture. Somebody carefully shut the door. Then Mother read the letter. I do not remember everything it said. All that I remember is something about a marriage, and something about a new life, and something about a husband's being white. Mother opened my little potbellied stove, thrust the letter in, and struck a match to it. Suddenly the sisters silently converged and watched the letter burn. When the letter was ashes, Mother shut the stove door. I heard my unmarried aunt murmur, *God help her to be happy.* Then they filed out, and one of them called upstairs sharply for the children not to make so much noise. They went back downstairs.

I took my fist out of my mouth, and I cried even harder, for now there was much more to cry about.

8 December 1938

Contributors' Notes

*100 Other Distinguished
Stories of 2000*

Editorial Addresses

Contributors' Notes

ANDREA BARRETT is the author of five novels, most recently *The Voyage of the Narwhal*, and a collection of short fiction, *Ship Fever*, which received the 1996 National Book Award. Her new collection, *Servants of the Map*, will be published in 2002. She and her husband live in Rochester, New York.

▪ For some years I've been fascinated by the British botanist Joseph Dalton Hooker and the American botanist Asa Gray — both contemporaries of Charles Darwin and both, in their different ways, great defenders of his controversial theories. I've also long been interested in high mountains, glaciers, and the people who climb and explore them. Somewhere in the intersection of these interests with my own limited experiences camping and hiking in the mountains in winter, and tentatively crossing glaciers, I found the character of Max. Hooker's account of his travels in Sikkim and Nepal led me to the journals of other botanists and travelers across the range in the western Himalayas. Gray's *Lessons in Botany and Vegetable Physiology* taught me what Max was learning. The rest came slowly, through many drafts, as the implications of communicating with one's beloved solely by letters, over a long stretch of time, became clearer to me.

RICK BASS is the author of sixteen books of fiction and nonfiction, including a novel, *Where the Sea Used to Be*. "The Fireman" will appear in a collection, *The Hermit's Story*, to be published in the spring of 2002. Bass lives in northwest Montana with his wife and daughters.

▪ I'm surprised, again and again, by how tactile short stories are for me. Novels seem like entire landscapes, replete with birdsong, the trickling sounds of ice thawing in spring, breezes, odors, lives and deaths, the whole shitaree. And novellas seem to be about color — like one scene, usually a bright one, from a given landscape, or a series of big scenes, the kind which, if painted, might take up a good portion of a wall in a house, and be taller than a person.

Right now I'm staring out my cabin window at a wintry March grayscape, across to the far side of the frozen, snowy marsh, with a wall of dark trees beyond. At the edge of that dark forest of spruce and fir is a little patch of willows, their branches like candelabra, possessing almost the only color, much less illumination, within that beautiful yet wearying March view. In a way I can't articulate, that grove of willows, with the sap stirring in their branches before any others, and that amazing, isolated color, seem somehow like a novella to me, as surely as if the novella is hiding within those leafless gold branches — the novella as much a visual image as the short story is a tactile one.

Short stories seem to me, then, to be about shape and texture, a thing the reader can hold in one hand, or in both hands — differing, in that regard, from the unwieldy painting of a novella, and certainly from the landscape or ecosystem of a novel, which one inhabits, rather than being inhabited by.

I remember only two things about the genesis of "The Fireman," one tactile and the other both auditory and tactile. The first thing is the detail of the threads in the hose telling a lost or blinded firefighter which direction to go; and the second thing is the umbrella-like mist of water, described to me by a fireman I once interviewed, that is emitted when a pressurized fire hose is punctured, whether intentionally or accidentally. The notion of a tiny refuge or brief harbor from duress, either physical or mental, or both, is a concept that I'm deeply interested in, and once I had begun to consider further that one elemental and primal force, fire, I was drawn, in what I think is typically contradictory fashion, to that element's opposite, water. From those two elements, other specificities seemed to arrange themselves as I wrote, and I tried to be conscious of movement, of narrative, moving toward an understanding by the characters of where their puny lives fit between these larger and more elemental forces.

I had spent a few days hanging out with some volunteer firefighters while working on a nonfiction article, and the firefighters had allowed me to go up to alarming heights on the hook-and-ladder, and to suit up in bunker gear and mess around with a few fires. I was impressed by the way their passion for fighting fire assumed its own rhythm in their lives, the passion like its own living thing. And then I worked to make a story in which two such passions existed simultaneously — sometimes in parallel fashion, and other times in opposition — and sought to discover in those passions, as well as in the seams and spaces between those passions, further delineations of refuge.

I'm grateful to *The Kenyon Review* for publishing the story.

PETER HO DAVIES is the author of the story collections *The Ugliest House in the World* and *Equal Love*. His fiction has appeared in *Harper's Magazine, The Atlantic Monthly, Granta, The Paris Review, Ploughshares, Story,* and *Prize Stories: The O. Henry Awards.* This is his third selection for *The Best American Short Stories.* Born in Britain, Davies now makes his home in the United States, where he is a member of the MFA program faculty at the University of Michigan.

▪ "Think of England" is one of those pieces that I've been working at — off and on — for several years, and I'm by no means certain that I'm done with it (or it with me) yet. Having started out as a contemporary story, it became, some time later, part of a historical novel I'm working on. Its current form is a response to my feeling that the novel might need a new approach. I bribed myself to cut material that I loved by reconfiguring some of it into this story. I'd like to thank Gish Jen and Don Lee for taking it for *Ploughshares* and the National Endowment for the Arts for support during the writing of it.

CLAIRE DAVIS lives in Lewiston, Idaho, where she teaches creative writing at Lewis-Clark State College. Her first novel, *Winter Range,* received both the PNBA and MPBA awards for fiction. She is the recipient of a Pushcart Prize, and her short stories have appeared in a number of literary magazines, including *The Gettysburg Review, The Southern Review,* and *Shenandoah.*

▪ "Labors of the Heart" started with Pinky. I had it in my head to write about a man in his middle years who had not yet risked love. For a number of months I lived with him in my head, and he just kept growing, gaining weight, getting more rotund and in need of change on many levels. I began to think about the isolation of so much flesh and what an investment it becomes in terms of lifestyle. Curiously, he also gained an equal portion of tenderness. I found myself quite smitten with Pinky. So of course when I set him loose in the first pages, he had to meet Rose, a stick-thin, full-blown cynic. The resulting courtship was a delight and a terror to write. My friend Kim Barnes calls me a persistent but disillusioned romantic, and certainly I think that played a part in the creation of this story: the part of me who insists that love is a thing we can and must risk, pitted against the cynic who's been there, done that.

ELIZABETH GRAVER is the author of a story collection, *Have You Seen Me?,* and two novels, *Unravelling* and *The Honey Thief.* Her work has appeared previously in *The Best American Short Stories,* as well as in *The Best American Essays* and in *Prize Stories: The O. Henry Awards.* She teaches at Boston College.

▪ I was making the bed one day and passed my hand over a bump that felt like a small fist. The story grew from there. I was trying to get pregnant at the time, and while we ended up not having to enter the maze of reproductive technology, I had friends who were deep inside that maze. The story came, I suppose, from watching them navigate a world that seemed as surreal as my story, as well as from my own anticipatory anxiety. I'm used, as a writer, to being able to make things, to spin them out of thin air — with enough hard work, enough deep attention. Trying to have a baby demands a kind of surrender to the body that I found at once difficult and moving. Our daughter, Chloe, was born right before "The Mourning Door" appeared in *Ploughshares.*

HA JIN has published several books of poetry and fiction. His most recent book is a volume of poems, *Wreckage.* His fiction has received a number of awards, including the PEN/Hemingway Award (for *Ocean of Words,* 1996), the National Book Award (for *Waiting,* 1999), and the PEN/Faulkner Award (for *Waiting,* 2000). His work has been translated into more than twenty languages.

• About ten years ago, I read in a Chinese newspaper that an American fast-food franchise in Beijing would burn its daily leftovers. The author of the article praised the American way of doing business and argued that eventually this practice would reduce waste. I was bothered by the article and later came to know that many Chinese companies adopted the American way. My uneasiness prompted me to write "After Cowboy Chicken Came to Town." I meant to make a bulky story that didn't have to have a plot but should give the feeling of a chunk of life, so I added a couple of episodes.

ANDREA LEE was born in Philadelphia, attended the Baldwin School, and earned A.B. and A.M. degrees from Harvard University. Her fiction and nonfiction writing have appeared in *The New Yorker* and the *New York Times.* Her books include *Russian Journal* and the novel *Sarah Phillips.* "Brothers and Sisters Around the World" is part of a collection of short stories titled *Interesting Women,* which will be published next year. Lee lives with her husband and two children in Torino, Italy.

• Madagascar, the setting of "Brothers and Sisters," is a country I know and love: we have a house on the northwestern coast and visit frequently. This story took off from a chance remark I heard from a tourist on the beach, a remark that amazed me, so that I built a whole fantasy around it and made it the first line of the story. The story explores two of my favorite themes: the uneasy relationship between Africans and African Americans, and the peculiar ways in which links can be forged between strangers — sometimes a slap or a bottle of pink nail polish will do. And the nameless heroine of "Brothers" is typical of the characters in the story collection I'm finishing now: women who are far from their own culture, but not out of their depth.

RICK MOODY was born in New York City. He attended Brown and Columbia University. His first novel, *Garden State,* was the winner of the 1991 Editor's Choice Award from the Pushcart Press and was published in 1992. *The Ice Storm,* published in the United States in 1994, has also been published in the United Kingdom, Taiwan, Germany, Brazil, France, Italy, and Poland. (A film version, directed by Ang Lee, was released in 1997.) A collection of short fiction, *The Ring of Brightest Angels Around Heaven,* was published in 1995. The title story was the winner of the 1994 Aga Khan Award from *The Paris Review.* Moody's third novel, *Purple America,* was published in 1997; editions are forthcoming in Portugal, Brazil, France, Germany, Hungary, the Czech Republic, Spain, Italy, and the United Kingdom. With Darcey Steinke, Moody edited an anthology, *Joyful Noise: The New Testament Revisited* (1997). A new collection of stories, *Demonology,* was published in January 2001. Moody's short work has appeared in *The New Yorker,* the *New York Times, Harper's Magazine, Esquire, Elle, The Atlantic Monthly,* and elsewhere. In 1998, he received the Addison Metcalf Award from the American Academy of Arts and Letters. He has taught at the State University of New York at Purchase, the Bennington Writing Workshops, and the Fine Arts Work Center in Provincetown. He lives on Fishers Island, New York.

▪ I got the idea for "Boys" after hearing a reading by the great southern writer Max Steele. This was in Vermont, where I teach. Max read a long, lyrical, realistic story that had in it the words "Then the boys entered the house." It was really just a connective image in his story, getting those boys from one sequence to another, but for some reason I became preoccupied with this ligament of his story, deciding that it was perhaps the most essential gesture in a boy's life. Entering the house. I started playing around with the sentence, just a little bit at a time, over the course of several weeks, and "Boys" was the result. I have thanked Max several times for lending me the beginning of my story, but maybe this is a good place to thank him again.

BARBARA KLEIN MOSS received her MFA from the Program for Writers at Warren Wilson College. She has published fiction in *New England Review* and *The Georgia Review* and has received a special mention citation in the Pushcart Prize 2001 anthology, a MacDowell Colony fellowship, and an Individual Artist Award from the Maryland State Arts Council. She lives in Annapolis, Maryland, with her husband and daughter and is currently working on a collection of stories and a novel.

▪ The old man sat across the aisle from me on a bus in San Diego. His skin was olive and he was dressed with unusual formality, in a coat and tie; I have a vague memory of pastel linen and a silk pocket handkerchief. He seemed, even in this multicultural city, inexpressibly foreign, but what struck me about him was his air of contained sadness. He appeared to be entirely drawn into himself.

A couple of years later he surfaced again in my notes for a possible story, newly incarnated as an Iranian Jewish rug dealer. I had settled back east with my family by then and had begun to process my experience of southern California in my fiction; I am the kind of writer who needs to be distanced from my subject matter. Certainly some of the cultural astonishment that I had felt as a longtime New Englander transplanted to the other coast was infused into Ebrahim. In time I would see all sorts of useful antitheses: dark versus light, a repressed culture versus an open one, the old world versus the new, the inner life versus the outer. But when I began, I only saw an old man sitting on a patio, watching through half-closed eyes as his golden daughter-in-law jogs up the street.

I had no idea what would become of him. I rarely do when I start writing. Eventually a hairy Esau of a son materialized, inspired by the many Persian rug dealers competing to sell carpets in San Diego, and then a past with an unstable wife. My husband, who traveled in Iran before the revolution, was able to supply some physical details, and I began to collect news articles about the country and books about rugs. One day I scrawled across the top of a page, "Does the old man weave a rug in his mind? In prison?" In the slant of the letters, I can still see the charge of that moment, when the story revealed itself to me. From that point on, the motion was all forward. I had the structure of the story, Ebrahim's past interweaving with his present, and I had the momentum of the dream-weaving of the rug, as Ebrahim struggles to finish it before his own life is cut short. In my earliest notes, I am undecided whether the pattern of the rug will be based on the Song of Solomon or the Garden of Eden. Eden prevailed, as it does in many of my stories, although not so literally as in this one.

Ebrahim makes peace with his past in the end, not by emerging into the California sun but by weaving the new paradise into the pattern of the old. He has discovered the truths that keep writers chained to their desks: the primacy of the inner life and the sheer exhilaration of creating a world from scratch.

A native of Ontario, ALICE MUNRO has twice received the Governor General's Award and is the author of nine collections of short stories, including *Who Do You Think You Are?*, *The Moons of Jupiter*, *Open Secrets*, *Friend of My Youth*, *The Progress of Love*, and, most recently, *The Selected Stories of Alice Munro* and *The Love of a Good Woman*, which won the National Book Critics Circle Award in 1998. Since her first appearance in *The Best American Short Stories*, in 1979, she has been included in these volumes twelve times. Her story "Meneseteung" was selected by John Updike for inclusion in *The Best American Short Stories of the Century*. Her new collection, *Hateship, Friendship, Courtship, Loveship, Marriage*, will be published this year.

- "Post and Beam" came to be written because, in the first place (isn't this always the case?), I knew of a similar situation, and (more important) I was interested in the idea of the bargain. Doesn't everybody at some time make a secret, shaming — because so primitive and anti-rational — bargain? This young wife chooses to honor the deal she made — the marriage — as her bargain. Why? Youthful notion of self-sacrifice? Absolute submission? Bringing some dramatic power to her life? Just to have that belief in obligation, in probity? Little does she know. Will she live her whole life in this faith? Do you hope so?

PETER ORNER was born in Chicago in 1968. He is the author of *Esther Stories*, to be published in November 2001. His work has appeared in *The Atlantic Monthly*, *The Southern Review*, and *The North American Review*. A graduate of the University of Iowa Writers' Workshop, he has taught at Charles University in Prague and Miami University in Oxford, Ohio. He currently lives in San Francisco.

- I wish I could say that this story grew from a desire to explore the notion of guilt, how it haunts, how it gnaws. The truth is more mundane. I am one of those people who repeat stories. One of those people you are always too polite to shout at: "My God, not the purple corduroys story again!" It's possible that this story was an attempt to figure out what makes certain people, like myself, so prone to bore. Are we trying finally to tell it right?

My late grandfather was also a repeater of stories, particularly war stories. Yet unlike the grandfather in "The Raft," my grandfather was the captain not of a destroyer but of what is called a landing ship tank (LST), a sluggish supply boat. My grandfather said that commanding an LST was like yanking a wheelbarrow through muck. No slower boat in the navy. And those loony Poles on their horses were less sitting ducks than we were. In my grandfather's honor, I'll tell his favorite story, a true one. At the beginning of World War II, he was too old to go to war, so he volunteered for the coast guard. He was assigned to the Calumet River in Chicago. Up and down the river he went, trolling for German U-boats. He did such a good job — so the story goes — protecting Chicago from Hitler that the navy promoted him to the real war, the one where people got killed. My grandfather always laughed when he talked about Nazi helmets bobbing in the Calumet River, but he never laughed when he talked about his time in the Pacific. It occurs to me now that he never once told me that he was afraid on LST 504. Maybe it is this simple. Maybe this is why he kept retelling and why he never laughed when he told the last part, so that today I might sit at my kitchen table and wonder about his fear.

ROY PARVIN is the author of two books of short fiction, *The Loneliest Road in America* and *In the Snow Forest*. His work has been awarded the Katherine Anne Porter Prize in Fiction. He lives with his wife and two Border collies in the woods of northern California.

▪ The germ for this story came from paging through a *Hoyle's Encyclopedia of Modern Card Games*, where I found an obscure variety of stud poker actually named after Betty Hutton. For some reason that tickled me. Perhaps I was already vaguely framing a cockeyed western in my head — a modern recasting of a tall stranger blowing into town — and it could be that seeing the name Betty Hutton was the hinge that swung the door open.

My first attempts to get it on paper failed. Parts of the story interested me, but it ultimately resisted evolving into something whole, and I eventually abandoned it. Three years later I remembered Gibbs. I'd just finished a long story, and I suspected that maybe my initial difficulty with "Betty" was that it wanted to cover more ground and pages than I'd originally intended. Fairly late in the game I also realized I had to weave the real Betty Hutton into the plot, a minor role that would amount to far less than a cameo appearance for the actress. Yet somehow that small revelation was like an X-ray that allowed me to see the bones of the story and find my way to its end.

Throughout the countless drafts, Gibbs proved to be good company. I still worry about him, for his well-being and if he'll ever reach that nameless place he's looking for. I believe I might like to visit with him again, somewhere down the road.

NANCY REISMAN's short story collection, *House Fires,* won the 1999 Iowa Short Fiction Award. Her fiction has appeared in *Tin House, Five Points, New England Review, The Kenyon Review, Glimmer Train,* and other journals. She grew up outside of Buffalo, New York, and has taught creative writing in New England, Wisconsin, and Florida. This fall she joined the creative writing faculty at the University of Michigan.

▪ For years I've heard fragments of stories about characters and families — mostly Jewish — in the Buffalo of the 1920s, 1930s, and 1940s. I come from one such family, and I often wonder about that now-vanished world — in particular about the women and men who found the prevailing cultural norms chafing, contradictory, or impossible. Jo is based on an elderly woman I met when I was a child, someone whose eccentricity and bitterness frightened me. One impulse behind "Illumination" was the desire to invent a Jo I could understand; it's an attempt to explore the strange tensions in her life as well as that particular moment in the Jewish community and in Buffalo, a city of great ethnicities and difficult divisions. I started with this image: a silhouette in the doorway of an old house on Lancaster Avenue.

JESS ROW was born in 1974 in Washington, D.C., and is a graduate of Yale and the University of Michigan, where he received his MFA in 2001. From 1997 to 1999 he was a Yale-China teaching fellow at the Chinese University of Hong Kong. "The Secrets of Bats" comes from a collection of stories set in Hong Kong, tentatively titled "Revolutions," which he hopes to finish this year. He has done graduate work in Chinese literature and is a long-time student in the Kwan Um school of Zen. He lives in Ann Arbor with his wife, Sonya Posmentier.

▪ "The Secrets of Bats" is an enigma to me, and has been since shortly after I finished it. I'm not sure how it does what it does, and I'm not sure I could ever do it again. But where it comes from is not mysterious to me at all. My Hong Kong students had been brought up to view English as a tool for communicating with foreigners, teachers, and officials, not a language with its own inner logic and beauty. They resisted my woeful attempts to show them otherwise, and when we really wanted to talk to one another we often had to resort to a puzzle game of Cantonese-Chinglish-English. I knew that they had complex and wonderful lives going on inside their heads that I could not reach and only rarely saw, with a sideways glance. At the same time, in the first year that I lived and taught in Hong Kong, my own life was disintegrating, or so I thought: I had no idea why I'd left America, why I'd arrived in this strange city, or why I could no longer write the kind of fiction I'd been working on for years. What most expatriates call culture shock was for me a kind of ontological crisis; to paraphrase Beckett, I didn't so much forget who I was as that I was. The Buddhist term for this is "form is emptiness, emptiness is form." Although I never knew anyone like Alice Leung, my students did serve as a constant and much-needed reality check, forcing me to step out of my shell every time I entered the classroom. When I did recover my bearings enough to begin writing again, I found that the broken language we shared was the truest form of English I knew. So "The Secrets of Bats" is a tribute to my students, for the gift of language they shared with me.

For help in revising this story, I'd like to thank Charles Baxter, my teacher and friend. I'd also like to thank Don Lee and Gish Jen, for seeing it into print, and all the people who read the story in *Ploughshares* and responded so warmly. Doh jeh daih ga! Thank you all.

ANNETTE SANFORD is the author of more than thirty published stories, some of which are included in her collections, *Lasting Attachments* and *Crossing Shattuck Bridge*. She has held two Creative Writing Fellowships from the National Endowment for the Arts, and her work has appeared in a number of anthologies, among them *The Best American Short Stories* and *New Stories from the South*. She is a former high school English teacher and lives in Ganado, Texas.

▪ "Nobody Listens When I Talk" is a fictional conglomeration of the truth. I did spend a good many summers in the swing while my friends were swimming, which I was forbidden to do because of an ear problem. I did read constantly. I was always waiting in the hot car for the town librarian to open up at one o'clock and let me in. My mother did wish I would sew or cook occasionally, and to this day I am made nostalgic by the drumming of locusts in the trees, but the true heart of the story came out of my need to identify the girl in the swing: to put together who she was from what other people thought of her and what she thought of herself — and ultimately to understand that like any other human being, she was all of those things. And more.

KATHERINE SHONK's stories have appeared in *Tin House, CutBank,* and *American Short Fiction*. She attended the University of Illinois and received an M.A. in fiction writing from the University of Texas. She lives in Evanston, Illinois, where she works as an editor and studies writing with Fred Shafer of Northwestern University. She has completed a collection of stories set in Russia and Ukraine.

▪ In 1996, when my grandmother was dying in Chicago, I was living in Moscow. I made it home in time for the final week of her life, then lingered after the funeral, reluctant to leave my family again. A few months later, when my aunt Wynne visited me in Russia, we spoke often of her mother and of how pleased she would have been to see us having so much fun together, so far from home. In St. Petersburg, we stayed in an opulent hotel — cable, heated tile floors, metal detectors at the front entrance — and in between sightseeing and sleep, I watched too much English-language TV. I happened to catch a CNN retrospective on the 1986 Chernobyl nuclear disaster. Ten years after the meltdown, I learned, elderly villagers were living out their final years in the contamination zone.

For the next two years, I often thought of the old woman who, while feeding the geese in her snowy yard, scoffed at the notion that something invisible would keep her from her home. Research led me to the story, which only began to fall into place once I recognized that the lines the characters would not cross were more important than the ones they would. My mom, Marguerite Delacoma, helped immeasurably in the story's later stages, offering three single-spaced pages of detailed, perceptive comments and suggestions, almost all of which I had the sense to follow.

It does not surprise me that a strong-willed grandmother became the axis on which the story revolved. "My Mother's Garden" is most certainly rooted in Pearl Delacoma's fierce attachment to home and family. It is dedicated to her memory.

MARISA SILVER's first collection of stories, *Babe in Paradise,* was published this year. Her fiction has appeared in *The New Yorker, The Georgetown Review, The Beloit Fiction Journal,* and *Hampton Shorts.* She received her MFA in creative writing from the Warren Wilson Program for Writers. She has also directed four feature films. Born in Ohio and raised in New York City, Silver lives in Los Angeles.

- "What I Saw from Where I Stood" went through several incarnations over the course of a few years. At one time or another it was told from alternating points of view, from the wife's point of view, and in the past tense. A few versions ago, the central event of the story — the loss of the baby — happened to a couple wholly tangential to the story of Dulcie and Charles (and who did not make it to the final version). Through all these experiments, two ideas have never changed. The first is that the story is and has always been an exploration of the manifestations of fear, in this case how fear transforms a couple. The other idea that I dragged through every rewrite was . . . well, rats. The real ones in the wall and the metaphorical ones, the daily anxieties that lurk beneath the surface of life and often threaten to overwhelm it. Once I made the discovery that perhaps I should not give the most emotionally dense event to subsidiary characters, the story came together. I took the loss of the child as well the rats, real and imagined, placed them in the way of this couple, and then explored how they coped, separately and together.

Some stories come to me declaring their point of view. In the case of this story, I circled it for a while, looking in on it from various angles while trying to find the vantage point that would reveal the story in the most interesting and unexpected way. The meaning of a story — that troubling, elusive thing — changes depending on who's telling it. In this case, I wrote from the point of view of the character for whom the meaning of events was the most obscure, so that by the end of the story, both he and I were surprised. I owe a huge debt of thanks to Bill Buford and Meghan O'Rourke, who weighed every word with utmost grace and gave the story its final polish.

After being a drifter, an agricultural laborer, a sailor, a carnival huckster, a factory hand, a waiter, a pearl diver, a door-to-door encyclopedia salesman, an office drudge, a stevedore on a loading dock, an actor, a theater director, and a university professor, TREVANIAN turned to writing in his middle years. Just as his worldview was shaped by his Depression childhood in the slums of a northeastern city, so his criteria for artistic worthiness were formed in Japan immediately after the Hiroshima bombing. The first theater he ever saw was Kabuki; the first film he watched being shot was a real-istic street film by Kurosawa; and the first writer he read for style rather than story was Kawabata Yasunari. Trevanian's academic scholarship was in content analysis, which discipline, combined with his experience as actor and director, made it possible for him to create freestanding writing perso-nae to "write" for him throughout a career of enrobing the material of the classical novel in the structure of a popular genre, a different voice and style for each genre he chose to work in. Critics have been kinder to him than the mass public. For instance, a Dutch critic described his *roman policier, The Main,* as "how Simenon would have written if he had been Balzac." His other novels, each in a different genre, style, and voice, in-clude *Shibumi, The Summer of Katya,* and *Incident at Twenty-Mile.* Now at the end of a stormy renegade career moving from publisher to publisher in a futile search, Trevanian is working on his last book, an experimental blend of the novel and the autobiography. His daughter, also a writer, will finish this book if he cannot.

"The Apple Tree" is featured in the collection *Hot Night in the City,* pub-lished in 2000.

▪ Over the years I have lived in the Basque country I have come to ap-preciate the blend of humor and cynical bitterness that marks their world-view and their storytelling — a blend of honey and vinegar that one finds only one other place in literature: shtetl tales by such writers as Sholem Rabinovitch. To share this special voice with a wider audience, I created the persona of Beñat LeCagot, a tetchy, slightly pompous old man living in a composite village in Soule in the first third of the twentieth century, be-fore roads and radio inflicted the dominating French language and cul-ture upon these mountain people. After writing a bouquet of short stories and placing a few with such vehicles as the *Yale Literary Magazine, Harper's Magazine,* and, most recently, *The Antioch Review,* I considered doing a book of Basque tales, a cycle that would take the reader through the seasons of the year and the seasons of life. But the publisher I was then associated with assured me that American readers were not interested in what hap-pened in a foreign mountain village fifty years ago. My argument that we were dealing here with the universals of life failed to persuade them, so I gave up on the project. For this reason, I am all the more grateful to Houghton Mifflin for helping me disseminate this sample of a lost voice in world letters.

JOHN UPDIKE was born in 1932 in Shillington, Pennsylvania, and gradu-ated from Harvard College in 1954. After a year at an English art school and a two-year stint as a "Talk of the Town" reporter for *The New Yorker,* he moved to Massachusetts in 1957, and has lived there ever since. His most recent work of fiction is *Licks of Love,* twelve short stories and a novella.

Updike made his first appearance in *The Best American Short Stories* in 1959; "Personal Archeology" is his twelfth contribution to these pages.

▪ My hero's inexplicably Germanic name, Fritz, holds the *F* that some time ago, in a lazy code, I began to foist upon short story heroes who were conspicuously alter-egoistic. The device created a sort of brother, not a twin but close in age and outlook to me and, though freed from any obligation to plead my case, able to shoulder, with brotherly good humor, some of my circumstances. A certain Frankness, we could say, was thus attained. I do in fact live on New England land that holds buried clues to its past owners, a class of predecessor to whom Americans, ever since the Puritans took title from the Indians, have been determinedly unsentimental. We move, we buy, we move again. Only retirement offers the leisure to consider where, exactly, we are and who was here before us. The motorcycle parts and white plastic litter are real; I made up the teacup.

From such buried physical treasure it is not a long leap to Freud and those other archeologists of the mind who attempt to explicate and order the results of those hectic nightly digs, our dreams. A life is composed of strata; dreams and waking guilt pangs unearth a scattered, dirty wealth of clues — to what? To the mystery, the evolving majesty even, of each existence. Proust speaks of deciphering underwater hieroglyphs as the writer's essential task. He also speaks of changing perspectives as time's railroad journey rounds a curve. An aging writer cannot but notice how the events he keeps remembering change over time, generating new stories, for which he is grateful.

Dorothy West, 1907–1998, was born in Boston and may have been among the most widely read writers of the Harlem Renaissance era, although this credit eluded her during her long life. In addition to her two novels, *The Living Is Easy* and *The Wedding,* she wrote scores of short stories and edited one collection of her own work, *The Richer, the Poorer.* She published a literary magazine called *Challenge,* later renamed *New Challenge,* in the 1930s, which she coedited with Richard Wright. She wrote columns and fiction for newspapers throughout her life. During a twenty-year stint between 1940 and the 1960s, she may have written as many as forty short stories for the *New York Daily News,* the largest daily-circulation newspaper in the world.

Shortly before she died, West told the *New York Times Book Review* that she was the last leaf on a famous tree of authors from Harlem. She was talking about being the youngest member of an elite cadre of black intellectuals who gathered in New York City in the mid-1920s and participated in the celebrated era of creativity known as the Harlem Renaissance. West went to New York to collect a literary prize for her short story "The Typewriter."

When West died, she was hailed as the last of her kind, and as a writer whose creative flame had flickered briefly in the 1920s. This was a popular, slightly tragic, and romantic story about the premature end of a promising but short literary career. Unfortunately, it does not accurately depict the long writing life that West carved out and lived for most of the twentieth century. A decline in her critical success seemed to coincide with her decision to leave New York in the 1940s. Moving to Martha's Vineyard, she slipped into obscurity. For the next sixty years, her work and name surfaced only periodically. "I didn't stop writing," she told an interviewer. In fact, she wrote and published steadily for most of her life, and her fiction was widely read — by millions of newspaper readers, not literary critics.

Critics rediscovered West in 1995, when Doubleday published a second novel, *The Wedding*, edited by Jacqueline Kennedy Onassis. Reviewers reported that West had been coaxed out of a long retirement by the former first lady. This claim, while partially true, casts a long shadow over scores of unindexed stories, essays, and other writings by Dorothy West.

Much of West's fiction and journalism appeared in the *New York Daily News* and the *Vineyard Gazette*, where her byline appeared on and off for more than half a century. The *Gazette* reprinted this column after she died:

> When I was little, I asked my mother if I could go to my room.
> "Yes," my mother said, "but why do you want to go to your room?"
> "To think," I told her.
> I went to my mother again later. This time I asked if I could go to my room and lock the door.
> "Yes," my mother said, "but why do you want to lock the door?"
> "Because I want to write," I told her.

In the ensuing decades, that room was sometimes in a fashionable section of Boston, on an island in the Atlantic, or in a tenement on 110th Street in Harlem. "My Baby . . ." was written in Harlem in the winter of 1938, while West was a member of the Works Progress Administration's New York Writers' Project. It was first published seventy-two years later, in the fall of 2000, in the *Connecticut Review*, a university literary magazine. Dorothy West may not always have been heard during those years, but she was never silent, not while she lived.

100 Other Distinguished Stories of 2000

COMPILED BY KATRINA KENISON

Editorial Addresses of American and Canadian Magazines Publishing Short Stories

African American Review
Department of English
Indiana State University
Terre Haute, IN 47809
web.indstate.edu/artsci/AAR
$30, Joe Weixlmann

Agni Review
Creative Writing Department
Boston University
236 Bay State Road
Boston, MA 02115
$18, Askold Melnyczuk

Alabama Literary Review
272 Smith Hall
Troy State University
Troy, AL 36082
$10, Donald Noble

Alaska Quarterly Review
University of Alaska, Anchorage
3211 Providence Drive
Anchorage, AK 99508
ayaqr@uaa.alaska.edu
$8, Ronald Spatz

Alfred Hitchcock Mystery Magazine
1540 Broadway
New York, NY 10036
$34.97, Cathleen Jordan

Alligator Juniper
Prescott College
220 Grove Avenue
Prescott, AZ 86301
$7.50, Allyson Stack

American Letters and Commentary
850 Park Avenue, Suite 5b
New York, NY 10021
$5, Anna Rabinowitz

American Literary Review
University of North Texas
P.O. Box 13615
Denton, TX 76203
$15, Lee Martin

American Voice
332 West Broadway
Louisville, KY 40202
$15, Sallie Bingham, Frederick Smock

American Way
4333 Amon Carter Boulevard
MD 5598
Fort Worth, TX 76155
Nancy Stevens

Antietam Review
41 South Potomac Street
Hagerstown, MD 21740-3764
$5, Susanne Kass

Antioch Review
Antioch University
150 East South College Street
Yellow Springs, OH 45387
$35, Robert S. Fogarty

Apalachee Quarterly
P.O. Box 20106
Tallahassee, FL 32316
$15, Barbara Hamby et al.

Appalachian Heritage
Berea College
Berea, KY 40404
$18, James Gage

Ararat
Armenian General Benevolent Union
55 East 59th Street
New York, NY 10022-1112
$24, Leo Hamalian

Arkansas Review
Department of English and
Philosophy
P.O. Box 1890
Arkansas State University
State University, AR 72467
$20, William Clements

Ascent
English Department
Concordia College
901 Eighth Street
Moorhead, MN 56562
$12, W. Scott Olsen

Atlantic Monthly
77 North Washington Street
Boston, MA 02114
www.theatlantic.com
$12.95, C. Michael Curtis

Baffler
P.O. Box 378293
Chicago, IL 60637
$24, Thomas Frank,

Baltimore Review
P.O. Box 410

Riderwood, MD 21139
Barbara Westwood Diehl

Bananafish
P.O. Box 381332
Cambridge, MA 02238-1332
$12.50, Robin Lippincott

Baybury Review
40 High Street
Highwood, IL 60040
$7.25, Janet St. John

Bellingham Review
MS-9053
Western Washington University
Bellingham, WA 98225
$10, Robin Hemley

Bellowing Ark
P.O. Box 55564
Shoreline, WA 98155
$15, Robert Ward

Beloit Fiction Journal
Beloit College
P.O. Box 11
700 College Street
Beloit, WI 53511
$14, Clint McCown

Big Sky Journal
P.O. Box 1069
Bozeman, MT 59771-1069
$22, Allen Jones, Brian Baise

Black Warrior Review
P.O. Box 862936
Tuscaloosa, AL 35486-0027
$14, Christopher Manlove

Bomb
New Art Publications
594 Broadway, 10th floor
New York, NY 10012
www.bombsite.com
$18, Betsy Sussler

Border Crossings
Y300-393 Portage Avenue
Winnipeg, Manitoba

Canada R3B 3H6
$27, Meeka Walsh

Boston Book Review
30 Brattle Street
Cambridge, MA 02138
$24, Theoharis Constantine Theoharis

Boston Review
Building E 53, Room 407 MIT
Cambridge, MA 02139
www.bostonreview.mit.edu
$17, editorial board

Bottomfish
DeAnza College
21250 Stevens Creek Boulevard
Cupertino, CA 95014
$5, David Denny

Boulevard
4579 Laclede Avenue, #332
St. Louis, MO 63108
$15, Richard Burgin

Brain, Child: The Magazine for
Thinking Mothers
P.O. Box 1161
Harrisonburg, VA 22801
www.brainchildmag.com
*$18, Jennifer Niesslein, Stephanie
Wilkinson*

Briar Cliff Review
3303 Rebecca Street
P.O. Box 2100
Sioux City, IA 51104-2100
$8, Phil Hey

Bridges
P.O. Box 24839
Eugene, OR 97402
$15, Clare Kinberg

Callaloo
Department of English
322 Bryan Hall
University of Virginia
Charlottesvile, VA 22903
$35.50, Charles H. Rowell

Calyx
P.O. Box B
Corvallis, OR 97339
calyx@proaxis.com
$19.50, Margarita Donnelly

Canadian Fiction Magazine
Box 946, Station F
Toronto, Ontario M4Y 2N9
$34.24, Geoffrey Hancock, Rob Payne

Capilano Review
Capilano College
2055 Purcell Way
North Vancouver
British Columbia V7J 3H5
$25, Ryan Knighton

Carolina Quarterly
Greenlaw Hall 066A
University of North Carolina
Chapel Hill, NC 27514
$12, George Hovis

Century
P.O. Box 150510
Brooklyn, NY 11215-0510
$20, Robert K. J. Killheffer

Chariton Review
Truman State University
Kirksville, MO 63501
$9, Jim Barnes

Chattahoochee Review
Georgia Perimeter College
2101 Womack Road
Dunwoody, GA 30338-4497
$16, Lawrence Hetrick

Chelsea
P.O. Box 773
Cooper Station
New York, NY 10276
$13, Richard Foerster

Chicago Quarterly Review
517 Sherman Avenue
Evanston, IL 60202
*$10, S. Afzal Haider, Jane Lawrence,
Brian Skinner*

Chicago Review
5801 South Kenwood
University of Chicago
Chicago, IL 60637
www.humanities.uchicago.edu/review
$18, Eirik Steinhoff

Cimarron Review
205 Morrill Hall
Oklahoma State University
Stillwater, OK 74078-0135
www.cimmaronreview.okstate.edu
$16, E. P. Walkiewicz

Clackamas Literary Review
19600 South Molalla Avenue
Oregon City, OR 97045-7998
www.clackamas.cc.or.us/dr
$10, Jeff Knorr, Tim Schell

Colorado Review
Department of English
Colorado State University
Fort Collins, CO 80523
creview@vines.colostate.edu
$24, David Milofsky

Columbia
404 Dodge Hall
Columbia University
New York, NY 10027
$15, Ellen Umansky, Neil Azevedo

Confrontation
English Department
C. W. Post College of Long Island
University
Greenvale, NY 11548
$8, Martin Tucker

Conjunctions
21 East 10th Street, #3E
New York, NY 10003
$18, Bradford Morrow

Connecticut Review
English Department
Southern Connecticut State University
501 Crescent Street

New Haven, CT 06515
Vivian Shipley

Cottonwood
Box J, 400 Kansas Union
University of Kansas
Lawrence, KS 66045
$15, Tom Lorenz

Crab Creek Review
P.O. Box 840
Vashon Island, WA 98070
*$10, Kimberly Allison, Harris Levinson,
Laura Sinai, Terri Stone*

Crab Orchard Review
Department of English
Southern Illinois University at
Carbondale
Carbondale, IL 62901
www.siu.edu/~crborchd
$10, Richard Peterson

CrossConnect
P.O. Box 2317
Philadelphia, PA 19103
ww.ccat.sas.upenn.edu/xconnect
David Deifer

Crucible
Barton College
College Station
Wilson, NC 27893
Terrence L. Grimes

CutBank
Department of English
University of Montana
Missoula, MT 59812
cutbank@selway.umt.edu
*$12, Traver Kauffman, Penelope
Whitney*

Denver Quarterly
University of Denver
Denver, CO 80208
$20, Bin Ramke

Descant
P.O. Box 314
Station P

Toronto, Ontario M5S 2S8
www.descant.on.ca
$25, Karen Mulhallen

Descant
Department of English
Box 32872
Texas Christian University
Fort Worth, TX 76129
$12, Neil Easterbrook, David Kuhne

Distillery
Division of Liberal Arts
Motlow State Community College
P.O. Box 88100
Tullahoma, TN 37388-8100
$15, Niles Reddick

DoubleTake
55 Davis Square
Somerville, MA 02144
www.doubletakemagazine.org
$32, R. J. McGill

Elle
1633 Broadway
New York, NY 10019
$24, Ben Dickinson

Ellery Queen's Mystery Magazine
475 Park Avenue South
New York, NY 10016
$33.97, Janet Hutchings

Epoch
251 Goldwin Smith Hall
Cornell University
Ithaca, NY 14853-3201
$11, Michael Koch

Esquire
250 West 55th Street
New York, NY 10019
$17.94, Rust Hills, Adrienne Miller

Eureka Literary Magazine
Eureka College
300 East College Avenue
Eureka, IL 61530-1500
$15, Loren Logsdon

Event
Douglas College
P.O. Box 2503
New Westminster
British Columbia V3L 5B2
$20, Calvin Wharton

Fantasy & Science Fiction
P.O. Box 3447
Hoboken, NJ 07030
$38.97, Gordon Van Gelder

Fence
14 Fifth Avenue, #1A
New York, NY 10011
$14, Rebecca Wolff

Fiction
Fiction, Inc.
Department of English
City College of New York
New York, NY 10031
www.ccny.cuny.edu/Fiction/
fiction.htm
$7, Mark Mirsky

Fiction International
Department of English and
Comparative Literature
San Diego State University
San Diego, CA 92182
$14, Harold Jaffe, Larry McCaffery

Fiddlehead
UNB P.O. Box 4400
Frederiction
New Brunswick E3B 5A3
$20, Mark Anthony Jarman

Fish Stories Literary Annual
5412 North Clark, South Suite
Chicago, IL 60640
$10.95, Amy G. Davis

Five Points
Georgia State University
Department of English
University Plaza
Atlanta, GA 30303-3083
$15, Pam Durban, David Bottoms

Florida Review
Department of English, Box 25000
University of Central Florida
Orlando, FL 32816
$10, Pat Rushin

Flyway
206 Ross Hall
Department of English
Iowa State University
Ames, IA 50011
$18, Sam Pritchard

Free Press
P.O. Box 581
Bronx, NY 10463
$25, J. Rudolph Abate

Gargoyle
Paycock Press
c/o Atticus Books & Music
1508 U Street NW
Washington, DC 20009
$20, Richard Peabody, Lucinda Ebersole

Georgia Review
University of Georgia
Athens, GA 30602
www.uga.edu/garev
$24, Stephen Corey

Gettysburg Review
Gettysburg College
Gettysburg, PA 17325
$24, Peter Stitt

Glimmer Train Stories
710 SW Madison Street
Suite 504
Portland, OR 97205
$29, Susan Burmeister, Linda Davies

Good Housekeeping
959 Eighth Avenue
New York, NY 10019
$19.97, Arleen L. Quarfoot

GQ
4 Times Square, 9th floor
New York, NY 10036
$19.97, Walter Kirn

Grain
Box 1154
Regina, Saskatchewan S4P 3B4
www.grain.mag@sk.sympatico.ca
$26.95, Elizabeth Philips

Granta
1755 Broadway, 5th floor
New York, NY 10019-3780
$32, Ian Jack

Great River Review
Anderson Center for Interdisciplinary
Studies
P.O. Box 406
Red Wing, MN 55066
$12, Richard Broderick, Robert Hedin

Green Hills Literary Lantern
North Central Missouri College
Box 375
Trenton, MO 64683
$7, Sara King

Green Mountains Review
Box A58
Johnson State College
Johnson, VT 05656
$14, Tony Whedon

Greensboro Review
Department of English
University of North Carolina
Greensboro, NC 27412
$10, Jim Clark

Gulf Coast
Department of English
University of Houston
4800 Calhoun Road
Houston, TX 77204-3012
$22, Marsha Recknagel, Merrill Greene

Gulf Stream
English Department
Florida International University
North Miami Campus
3000 NE 151st Street
North Miami, FL 33181
$9, Lynne Barrett

G. W. Review
Box 20, Marvin Center
800 21st Street NW
Washington, DC 20052
$9, Greg Lantier

Habersham Review
Piedmont College
Demorest, GA 30535-0010
$12, Frank Gannon

Harper's Magazine
666 Broadway
New York, NY 10012
$21, Lewis Lapham

Harvard Review
Poetry Room
Harvard College Library
Cambridge, MA 02138
$16, Stratis Haviaras

Hawaii Pacific Review
1060 Bishop Street
Honolulu, HI 96813
Catherine Sustana

Hawaii Review
University of Hawaii
Department of English
1733 Donaghho Road
Honolulu, HI 96822
$20, Kyle Koza

Hayden's Ferry Review
Box 871502
Arizona State University
Tempe, AZ 85287-1502
www.statepress.com/hfr
$10, Tom Bonfiglio, Tim Hohmann

Hemispheres
1301 Carolina Street
Greensboro, NC 27401
selby@hemispheresmagazine.com
Free, Selby Bateman

High Plains Literary Review
180 Adams Street, Suite 250
Denver, CO 80206
$20, Robert O. Greer, Jr.

Hudson Review
684 Park Avenue
New York, NY 10021
$24, Paula Deitz, Frederick Morgan

Idaho Review
Boise State University
Department of English
1910 University Drive
Boise, ID 83725
$9.95, Mitch Wieland

Image
323 South Broad Street
P.O. Box 674
Kennett Square, PA 19348
www.imagejournal.org
$30, Gregory Wolfe

India Currents
P.O. Box 21285
San Jose, CA 95151
$19.95, Arviund Kumar

Iowa Review
Department of English
University of Iowa
308 EPB
Iowa City, IA 52242
www.uiowa.edu/~iareview
$18, David Hamilton, Mary Hussmann

Iris
Women's Center
Box 323 HSC
University of Virginia
Charlottesville, VA 22908
$9, Eileen Boris

Italian Americana
University of Rhode Island
Providence Campus
80 Washington Street
Providence, RI 02903
$20, Carol Bonomo Albright

Jewish Currents
22 East 17th Street
New York, NY 10003
$20, editorial board

The Journal
Department of English
Ohio State University
164 West 17th Avenue
Columbus, OH 43210
$12, Kathy Fagan, Michelle Herman

Journal of African Travel Writing
P.O. Box 346
Chapel Hill, NC 27514
$10, Amber Vogel

Kairos
P.O. Box 33553
Hamilton, Ontario L8P 4X4
kairos_anthology@hotmail.com
$12.95, R. W. Megens

Kalliope
Florida Community College
3939 Roosevelt Boulevard
Jacksonville, FL 32205
$12.50, Mary Sue Koeppel

Kenyon Review
Kenyon College
Gambier, OH 43022
www.kenyonreview.org
$25, David H. Lynn

Larcom Review
The Larcom Press
P.O. Box 161
Prides Crossing, MA 01965
$20, Ann Perrott, Susan Oleksiw

Laurel Review
Department of English
Northwest Missouri State University
Maryville, MO 64468
$8, Craig Goad, David Slater, William Trowbridge

Lililth
250 West 57th Street
New York, NY 10107
lilithmag@aol.com
$18, Susan Weidman Schneider

Literal Latte
61 East 8th Street, Suite 240

New York, NY 10003
litlatte@aol.com
$11, Jenine Gordon Bockman

Literary Review
Fairleigh Dickinson University
285 Madison Avenue
Madison, NJ 07940
webdelsol.com/tir/
$18, Walter Cummins

Louisiana Literature
Box 792
Southeastern Louisiana University
Hammond, LA 70402
$12, Jack B. Bedell

Lynx Eye
1880 Hill Drive
Los Angeles, CA 90041
$25, Pam McCully, Kathryn Morrison

The MacGuffin
Schoolcraft College
18600 Haggerty Road
Livonia, MI 48152
alinden@schoolcraft.cc.mi.us
$15, Arthur J. Lindenberg

Madison Review
University of Wisconsin
Department of English
H. C. White Hall
600 North Park Street
Madison, WI 53706
$15, Jessica Agneessens

Malahat Review
University of Victoria
P.O. Box 1700
Victoria, British Columbia V8W 2Y2
malahat@uvic.ca
$40, Marlene Cookshaw

Manoa
English Department
University of Hawaii
Honolulu, HI 96822
$22, Frank Stewart

Massachusetts Review
South College
Box 37140
University of Massachusetts
Amherst, MA 01003
www.massreview.com
$22, Jules Chametsky, Mary Heath, Paul Jenkins

Matrix
1455 de Maisonneuve Boulevard West
Suite LB-514-8
Montreal, Quebec H3G IM8
matrix@alcor.concordia.ca
$18, R.E.N. Allen

McSweeney's
394A Ninth Street
Brooklyn, NY 11215
submissions@mcsweeneys.net
$36, Dave Eggers

Meridian
Department of English
University of Virginia
Charlottesville, VA 22903
$10, Ted Genoways

Michigan Quarterly Review
3032 Rackham Building
915 East Washington Street
University of Michigan
Ann Arbor, MI 48109
$18, Laurence Goldstein

Mid-American Review
Department of English
Bowling Green State University
Bowling Green, OH 48109
www.bgsu.edu/midamericanreview
$12, Michael Czyzniejewski

Minnesota Review
Department of English
East Carolina University
Greenville, NC 27858
$20, Jeffrey Williams

Mississippi Review
University of Southern Mississippi
Southern Station, Box 5144
Hattiesburg, MS 39406-5144
www.sushi.st.usm.edu/mrw
$15, Frederick Barthelme

Missouri Review
1507 Hillcrest Hall
University of Missouri
Columbia, MO 65211
www.missourireview.org
$19, Speer Morgan

Ms.
20 Exchange Place
New York, NY 10005
www.msmagazine.com
$35, Marcia Ann Gillespie

Nassau Review
English Department
Nassau Community College
One Education Drive
Garden City, NY 11530-6793
Paul A. Doyle

Natural Bridge
Department of English
University of Missouri, St. Louis
8001 Natural Bridge Road
St. Louis, MO 63121-4499
www.umsl.edu/~natural/index.htm
$15, Steven Schreiner

Nebraska Review
Writers Workshop
WFAB 212
University of Nebraska at Omaha
Omaha, NE 68182-0324
$15, James Reed

New England Review
Middlebury College
Middlebury, VT 05753
NEReview@middlebury.edu
$23, Stephen Donadio

New Letters
University of Missouri

5100 Rockhill Road
Kansas City, MO 64110
$17, James McKinley

New Orleans Review
P.O. Box 195
Loyola University
New Orleans, LA 70118
$15, Christopher Chambers

New Orphic Review
706 Mill Street
Nelson, British Columbia V1L 4S5
$25, Ernest Hekkanen

New Renaissance
26 Heath Road, #11
Arlington, MA 02474
wmichaud@gwi.net
$11.50, Louise T. Reynolds

New Yorker
4 Times Square
New York, NY 10036
$44.95, David Remnick, Bill Buford

New York Stories
English Department
La Guardia Community College
31-10 Thomson Avenue
Long Island City, NY 11101
$13.40, Daniel Lynch

Night Rally
P.O. Box 1707
Philadelphia, PA 19105
www.nightrally.org/interlo.htm
$21, Amber Dorko Stopper

Nimrod
Arts and Humanities Council of Tulsa
600 South College Avenue
Tulsa, OK 74104
nimrod@utulsa.edu
$17.50, Francine Ringold

Noon
1369 Madison Avenue
PMB 298
New York, NY 10128

noonannual@yahoo.com
$9, Diane Williams

North American Review
University of Northern Iowa
1222 West 27th Street
Cedar Falls, IA 50614
$22, Vince Gotera

North Dakota Quarterly
University of North Dakota
P.O. Box 8237
Grand Forks, ND 58202
ndq@sage.und.nodak.edu
$25, Robert Lewis

Northeast Corridor
English Department
Beaver College
450 South Easton Road
Glenside, PA 19038-3295
$10, Susan Balee

Northwest Review
369 PLC
University of Oregon
Eugene, OR 97403
$20, John Witte

Notre Dame Review
Department of English
356 O'Shag
University of Notre Dame
Notre Dame, IN 46556-5639
www.nd.edu/~ndr/review.htm
$15, John Matthias, William O'Rourke

Oasis
P.O. Box 626
Largo, FL 34649-0626
$22, Neal Storrs

Obsidian III: Literature in the African
Diaspora
North Carolina State University
Department of English
Box 8105
Raleigh, NC 27695-8105
obsidian@social.chass.ncsu.edu
$20, Afaa M. Weaver

Ohio Review
344 Scott Quad
Ohio University
Athens, OH 45701-2979
www.ohiou.edu/TheOhioReview/
$16, Wayne Dodd

Oklahoma Today
15 North Robinson, Suite 100
P.O. Box 53384
Oklahoma City, OK 73102
$16.95, Louisa McCune

Ontario Review
9 Honey Brook Drive
Princeton, NJ 08540
www.ontarioreviewpress.com
$14, Raymond J. Smith

Open City
225 Lafayette Street
Suite 1114
New York, NY 10012
editors@opencity.org
$32, Thomas Beller, Daniel Pinchbeck

Other Voices
University of Illinois at Chicago
Department of English, M/C 162
601 South Morgan Street
Chicago, IL 60607-7120
www.othervoicesmagazine.org
$24, Lois Hauselman

Oxford American
P.O. Box 1156
404 South 11th Street
Oxford, MS 38655
www.oxfordamericanmag.com
$16, Marc Smirnoff

Oxygen
535 Geary Street, #1010
San Francisco, CA 94102
oxygen@slip.net
$14, Richard Hack

Oyster Boy Review
P.O. Box 77842
San Francisco, CA 94107

www.oysterboyreview.com
$20, Chad Driscoll, Damon Sauve

Paris Review
541 East 72nd Street
New York, NY 10021
$34, George Plimpton

Parting Gifts
3413 Wilshire Drive
Greensboro, NC 27408-2923
rbixby@aol.com
Robert Bixby

Partisan Review
236 Bay State Road
Boston, MA 02215
www.partisanreview.org
$22, William Phillips

Passages North
English Department
Northern Michigan University
1401 Presque Isle Avenue
Marquette, MI 49007-5363
$10, Anne Ohman Youngs

Pearl
3030 East 2nd Street
Long Beach, CA 90803
*$15, Joan Jobe Smith, Marilyn Johnson,
Barbara Hauk*

Penny Dreadful: Tales & Poems
P.O. Box 719
Radio City Station
New York, NY 10101-0719
mpendragon@aol.com
$12

Permafrost
P.O. Box 75720
University of Alaska, Fairbanks
Fairbanks, AK 99775
$8, Sydney Glasoe, David Houston Wood

Playboy
Playboy Building
919 North Michigan Avenue
Chicago, IL 60611
$29.97, Alice K. Turner

Pleiades
Department of English and
Philosophy, 5069
Central Missouri State University
P.O. Box 800
Warrensburg, MO 64093
$12, R. M. Kinder, Kevin Prufer

Ploughshares
Emerson College
120 Boylston Street
Boston, MA 02116
www.emerson.edu/ploughshares
$21, Don Lee

Porcupine
P.O. Box 259
Cedarburg, WI 53012
ppine259@aol.com
$15.95, group

Post Road
c/o Aboutface
853 Broadway, Suite 1516
New York, NY 10003
www.aboutface.org/postroad
$16, David Ryan, Jaime Clarke, Sean Burke

Potpourri
P.O. Box 8278
Prairie Village, KS 66208
potpourripub@aol.com
$16, Polly W. Swafford

Pottersfield Portfolio
P.O. Box 40, Station A
Sydney, Nova Scotia B1P 6G9
www.pportfolio.com
$17, Douglas Arthur Brown

Prairie Fire
423-100 Arthur Street
Winnipeg, Manitoba R3B 1H3
prfire@escape.ca
$25, Andris Taskans

Prairie Schooner
201 Andrews Hall
University of Nebraska

Lincoln, NE 68588-0334
www.unl.edu/schooner/psmain.htm
$22, Hilda Raz

Prism International
Department of Creative Writing
University of British Columbia
Vancouver, British Columbia V6T 1W5
prism@interchange.ubc.ca
$18, Chris Labonte, Andrea MacPherson

Provincetown Arts
650 Commercial Street
Provincetown, MA 02657
$10, Ivy Meeropol

Puerto del Sol
Department of English
Box 3E
New Mexico State University
Las Cruces, NM 88003
$10, Kevin McIlvoy

Quarry Magazine
P.O. Box 74
Kingston, Ontario K7L 4V6
$15, Andrew Griffin

Quarterly West
312 Olpin Union
University of Utah
Salt Lake City, UT 84112
$12, Margot Schilpp

Queen Street Quarterly
Box 311, Station P
704 Spadina Avenue
Toronto, Ontario M5S 2S8
theqsq@hotmail.com
$25, Suzanne Zelaso

REAL
School of Liberal Arts
Stephen F. Austin State University
Nacogdoches, TX 75962
$15, Dale Hearell

Red Rock Review
English Department, J2A
Community College of Southern
Nevada

3200 East Cheyenne Avenue
North Las Vegas, NV 89030
$9.50, Richard Logsdon

Red Wheelbarrow
De Anza College
21250 Stevens Creek Boulevard
Cupertino, CA 95014-5702
www.deanza.fhda.edu/redwheelbarrow
$5, Randolph Splitter

River City
Department of English
University of Memphis
Memphis, TN 38152
$12, Scott McWaters

River Styx
Big River Association
634 N. Grand Boulevard, 12th floor
St. Louis, MO 63103-1002
$20, Richard Newman

Room of One's Own
P.O. Box 46160
Station D
Vancouver, British Columbia V6J 5G5
www.islandnet.com/Room/enter
$25, Madeleine Thien

Salmagundi
Skidmore College
Saratoga Springs, NY 12866
$18, Robert Boyers

Salt Hill
English Department
Syracuse University
Syracuse, NY 13244
salthill@cas.syr.edu
$15, Caryn Koplik

Santa Monica Review
1900 Pico Boulevard
Santa Monica, CA 90405
$12, Andrew Tonkovich

Seattle Review
Padelford Hall, GN-30
University of Washington

Seattle, WA 98195
$9, Colleen McElroy

Seventeen
850 Third Avenue
New York, NY 10022
$14.95, Patrice G. Adcroft

Sewanee Review
University of the South
Sewanee, TN 37375-4009
$18, George Core

Shenandoah
Troubador Theater, 2nd floor
Washington and Lee University
Lexington, VA 24450-0303
www.wlu.edu/~shenando
$15, R. T. Smith

So to Speak: A Feminist Journal of
Language and Art
4400 University Drive
George Mason University
Fairfax, VA 22030
$10, Katherine Perry

Songs of Innocence
Pendragon Publications
P.O. Box 719
Radio City Station
New York, NY 10101-0719
mpendragon@aol.com
$12, Michael M. Pendragon

Sonora Review
Department of English
University of Arizona
Tucson, AZ 85721
$12, Hannah Haas

South Carolina Review
Department of English
Clemson University
Strode Tower, Box 340523
Clemson, SC 29634-1503
*$10, Wayne Chapman, Donna Haisty
Winchell*

Southern Exposure
P.O. Box 531

Durham, NC 27702
southern_exposure@i4south.org
$24, Jordan Green

Southern Humanities Review
9088 Haley Center
Auburn University
Auburn, AL 36849
$15, Dan R. Latimer, Virginia M. Kouidis

Southern Review
43 Allen Hall
Louisiana State University
Baton Rouge, LA 70803
$25, James Olney, Dave Smith

Southwest Review
Southern Methodist University
P.O. Box 4374
Dallas, TX 75275
$24, Willard Spiegelman

Spindrift
1507 East 53rd Street, #649
Chicago, IL 60615
$10, Mark Anderson-Wilk, Sarah Anderson-Wilk, Amy Jorean

Story Quarterly
431 Sheridan Road
Kenilworth, IL 60043-1220
storyquarterly@hotmail.com
$12, M.M.M. Hayes

Sun
107 North Roberson Street
Chapel Hill, NC 27516
$34, Sy Safransky

Sundog: The Southeast Review
406 Williams Building
Florida State University
Tallahassee, FL 32306-1036
sundog@english.fsu.edu
$10, C. V. Davis, Tony R. Morris

Sycamore Review
Department of English
Heavilon Hall

Purdue University
West Lafayette, IN 47907
www.sla.purdue.edu/academic/engl/
sycamore/
$12, Bekka Rauve

Talking River Review
Division of Literature and Languages
Lewis-Clark State College
500 Eighth Avenue
Lewiston, ID 83501
$14, Sandra Lantz

Teacup
P.O. Box 8665
Hellgate Station
Missoula, MT 59807
$9, group

Thin Air
P.O. Box 23549
Flagstaff, AZ 86002
www.nau.edu/english/thinair
$9, A. Vaughn Wagner

Third Coast
Department of English
Western Michigan University
Kalamazoo, MI 49008-5092
$11, Heidi Bell, Kellie Wells

Threepenny Review
P.O. Box 9131
Berkeley, CA 94709
$16, Wendy Lesser

Timber Creek Review
3283 UNCG Station
Greensboro, NC 27413
timber_creek_review@hoopsmail.com
$15, John Freiermuth

Tin House
P.O. Box 10500
Portland, OR 97296-0500
$39.80, Rob Spillman

Transition
69 Dunster Street
Harvard University
Cambridge, MA 02138

transition@fas.harvard.edu
$27, Kwame Anthony Appiah, Henry Louis Gates, Jr.

TriQuarterly
2020 Ridge Avenue
Northwestern University
Evanston, IL 60208
$24, Susan Firestone Hahn

Virginia Quarterly Review
One West Range
Charlottesville, VA 22903
$18, Staige D. Blackford

War, Literature, and the Arts
Department of English and Fine Arts
2354 Fairchild Drive, Suite 6D45
USAF Academy, CO 80840-6242
donald.anderson@usafa.af.mil
Donald Anderson

Wascana Review
English Department
University of Regina
Regina, Canada
$10, Jeanne Shami

Water Stone
Graduate Liberal Studies Program
Hamline University
1536 Hewitt Avenue
St. Paul, MN 55104-1284
water-stone@gw.hamline.edu
$8, Mary Francois Rockcastle

Weber Studies
Weber State University
Ogden, UT 84408
$20, Sherwin Howard

Wellspring
4080 83rd Avenue North, Suite A
Brooklyn Park, MN 55443
$8, Meg Miller

West Branch
Department of English
Bucknell University
Lewisburg, PA 17837
$7, Robert Love Taylor, Karl Patten

Western Humanities Review
University of Utah
255 South Central Campus Drive
Room 3500
Salt Lake City, UT 84112
$14, Barry Weller

Whetstone
Barrington Area Arts Council
P.O. Box 1266
Barrington, IL 60011
$8.50, Sandra Berris, Marsha Portnoy, Jean Tolle

Willow Springs
Eastern Washington University
705 West 1st Avenue
Spokane, WA 99201
$11.50, Christopher Howell

Wind
Wind Publications
P.O. Box 24548
Lexington, KY 40524
$10, Charlie Hughes, Leatha Kendrick

Witness
Oakland Community College
Orchard Ridge Campus
27055 Orchard Lake Road
Farmington Hills, MI 48334
www.witnessmagazine.com
$15, Peter Stine

WordVirtual.com
1119 North and South Road
St. Louis, MO 63103
bcochran@bridge.com
Brian Cochran

Xavier Review
Xavier University
Box 110C
New Orleans, LA 70125
$10, Thomas Bonner, Jr.

Yale Review
P.O. Box 208243
New Haven, CT 06520-8243
$27, J. D. McClatchy

Yankee
Yankee Publishing, Inc.
Dublin, NH 03444
www.newengland.com
$22, Judson D. Hale

Zoetrope
AZX Publications
126 Fifth Avenue, Suite 300

New York, NY 10011
www.zoetrope-stories.com
$20, Adrienne Brodeur

ZYZZYVA
41 Sutter Street, Suite 1400
San Francisco, CA 94104
editor@zyzzyva.org
$28, Howard Junker

THE B·E·S·T AMERICAN SERIES ™

THE BEST AMERICAN SHORT STORIES 2001
Barbara Kingsolver, guest editor · Katrina Kenison, series editor

0-395-92689-0 CL $27.50 / 0-395-92688-2 PA $13.00
0-618-07404-X CASS $25.00 / 0-618-15564-3 CD $35.00

THE BEST AMERICAN TRAVEL WRITING 2001
Paul Theroux, guest editor · Jason Wilson, series editor

0-618-11877-2 CL $27.50 / 0-618-11878-0 PA $13.00
0-618-15567-8 CASS $25.00 / 0-618-15568-6 CD $35.00

THE BEST AMERICAN MYSTERY STORIES 2001
Lawrence Block, guest editor · Otto Penzler, series editor

0-618-12492-6 CL $27.50 / 0-618-12491-8 PA $13.00
0-618-15565-1 CASS $25.00 / 0-618-15566-X CD $35.00

THE BEST AMERICAN ESSAYS 2001
Kathleen Norris, guest editor · Robert Atwan, series editor

0-618-15358-6 CL $27.50 / 0-618-04931-2 PA $13.00

THE BEST AMERICAN SPORTS WRITING 2001
Bud Collins, guest editor · Glenn Stout, series editor

0-618-08625-0 CL $27.50 / 0-618-08626-9 PA $13.00

THE BEST AMERICAN SCIENCE AND NATURE WRITING 2001
Edward O. Wilson, guest editor · Burkhard Bilger, series editor

0-618-08296-4 CL $27.50 / 0-618-15359-4 PA $13.00

THE BEST AMERICAN RECIPES 2001–2002
Fran McCullough, series editor · Foreword by Marcus Samuelsson

0-618-12810-7 CL $26.00

HOUGHTON MIFFLIN COMPANY / www.houghtonmifflinbooks.com